PENGUIN BOOKS

Before the Dawn

Jake Woodhouse has worked as a musician, wine maker and entrepreneur. He now lives in London with his wife and their young gundog. *Before the Dawn* is the third thriller in his Amsterdam Quartet series, following *After the Silence* and *Into the Night*.

Before the Dawn

JAKE WOODHOUSE

PENGUIN BOOKS

PENGUIN BOOKS

UK | USA | Canada | Ireland | Australia
India | New Zealand | South Africa

Penguin Books is part of the Penguin Random House group of companies
whose addresses can be found at global.penguinrandomhouse.com.

First published 2017

001

Text copyright © Jake Woodhouse, 2017

The moral right of the author has been asserted

Set in 12.5/14.75 Garamond MT Std
Typeset by Jouve (UK), Milton Keynes
Printed in Great Britain by Clays Ltd, St Ives plc

A CIP catalogue record for this book is available from the British Library

ISBN: 978–1–405–92265–4

For Zara

Even on a fast day
this world's hell
is hell

Issa

I can't breathe I   can't breathe what's this this thing in my mouth
                        he's   behind me I can't   breathe my head's

expanding everything's moving I   can't breathe I can't breathe
                        sand against

                        skin why am I here all I   I   can feel the
sand and I can't

                        breathe I can't breathe I can't—

Day One

I

Inspector Jaap Rykel breathes in.

'How can you have *lost* him?' he says, watching a coot scan for food in the canal below. The bird's beak flashes white as it dives, leaving ever-expanding circles on the water's surface.

'Nah, we've got him again,' says the voice on the phone. 'Just a temporary blip at changeover.'

Jaap waits for the bird to reappear, marvelling at how long it can stay under, how long it can hold its breath. He turns and crosses the road, narrowly missing a determined woman on a bike. A small bug-eyed dog glares at him from the handlebar basket as it sails past.

'How temporary?'

'Couple of hours, but like I said, we're on him now. No harm done.'

He hopes that's true. Because the man under surveillance drugged and then murdered two people, and it's taken him three stress-fuelled months of painstaking, and often frustrating, work to get to this stage.

He does *not* want a fuck-up.

'Right, stay on him, and from now on keep me updated on every move,' he says before pocketing his phone, wondering how a surveillance team, whose one job is to keep tabs on someone, messes up like that.

He reaches the station and punches in his code, waiting

5

for the click telling him he can enter. He's anticipating the usual cool blast of air against his face, but as he steps through the door he finds it's even hotter inside than out.

'Bit cold,' he says as he walks past the desk sergeant, 'maybe we could turn the heating up?'

'AC crapped out about an hour ago,' the desk sergeant says, wiping away tiny beads of sweat dappling his face. 'Someone's on their way to fix it. Believe it when I see it, though.'

Jaap takes two flights up, heat increasing with each step. The office itself, open plan and usually glacial, is no better. He walks over to his desk, nestled amongst several others at the far end of the oblong space, and avoids catching anyone's eye, his mind on what's to come.

Three months he's been working this case, and late yesterday evening he'd finally, after laying it all out to Station Chief Henk Smit and getting the official OK, put in the warrant request. In the normal scheme of things, and given the severity of the two crimes involved, he'd get a quick response.

But here he is, the next afternoon, and still nothing.

He checks his phone again, just in case, and then his email. Aside from an Exciting Investment Opportunity and a warning that his Paypal account will be suspended unless he clicks this link right now, there's nothing. No warrant. And no communication explaining why that might be.

Smit's busy when he tries to reach him on the phone, his PA telling him he's in a meeting for at least another hour, so he decides to go back over what he'd submitted, checking he hadn't made some mistake which could be holding everything up.

On 3 May he'd taken a call leading to the first victim, Dafne Koster, a twenty-seven-year-old classroom assistant from Alkmaar. She'd been found in a field, hands tied behind her back, her head wrapped tight in cling film. Even though she'd tried to rub her face against the ground, the many layers of plastic had held tight. Worse, from footprints round the body it looked like someone had stood and watched as she writhed, her desperate attempts to get air into her lungs, trying to cling onto a life rapidly receding.

The investigation had been tough, all the usual avenues pulling blanks, and Jaap was starting to fear it was destined to be every inspector's nightmare, an unsolvable case.

But that was before the second body turned up a month and a half later. Nadine Adelaars, twenty-two, a trainee printmaker from Zwolle. Her body was found on a stretch of land just south of the city, hands tied behind her back, duct tape wrapped round her nose and mouth. In and of itself that wasn't enough to definitively link the two crimes, but a surprising detail emerged which went a long way to proving the killer of both women was the same.

Jaap leans back in his chair, his body full of that pre-arrest anxiety which he always gets, a density in his stomach which will only grow and grow until it's over.

His phone rings – months ago on a long stake-out he'd set it as the *Mission Impossible* theme, a kind of meta-joke which no one seems to get – and his hand shoots out, knocking it off the table in his haste.

'Yeah?' he says once he's retrieved it from the floor.

'Just heard, warrant's going to be issued,' Henk Smit says. 'Might as well head over there so we can move the second it does.'

As he puts the phone down Jaap wonders about the *we* not *you,* a small puzzle which is solved as he's signing out an unmarked from the underground car pool and sees the door swing open to reveal his boss.

Turns out Smit's junked his meeting and is coming along for the ride, the scent of a high-profile arrest too tantalizing to pass up.

Great, Jaap thinks. Just great.

The house, midway down a tree-lined street, is innocent.

It's no different from any of the others – nothing, as far as Jaap can see, hinting that the four suburban walls house a man who in the recent past murdered two young women, stood over them as their lungs fought for air which wasn't to come.

His leg's got that going-to-sleep tingle, and he shifts, trying to stretch it out as much as the footwell allows. Beside him Smit digs at something under his thumb nail. If it was anyone other than Smit, Jaap might think they were nervous.

Unseen, a bunch of sparrows irritate the world with their incessant chirping. A kid freewheels loosely past on a bike way too small for him, white earbuds snaking down his cheeks, his oversize cap on sideways.

'I thought you said it was due any minute?' Jaap says, following the kid till he turns off the road at the far end, disappearing behind a parked SUV with blacked-out windows and a bad scuff on the passenger door.

Smit shrugs. Because he doesn't have to answer to someone he manages.

Leaves flicker shadows onto the pavement. Jaap watches them, suddenly convinced there's a message to their flighty movement, if only he can decipher what it is.

Then he wonders why he always assumes there's a mystery to solve, why he can't just let it be.

'Something funny?' Smit asks.

Jaap's turn to shrug.

He settles his eyes on the photo of the suspect, pinned squint to the dashboard between them. Francesco Kamp is mid-thirties, his name and curly black hair courtesy of his second-generation Italian mother, height from his Dutch father.

Where he gets the propensity to kill young women is anyone's guess.

Kamp, a train driver for the NS, had a wife who died in childbirth just eight months ago, leaving him as the sole carer of their baby girl. It was through one of the social workers assigned to him that Jaap had got a feel for just how angry Kamp was. Jaap's not a psychologist, but he knows first-hand how grief can unleash things you never knew you had inside. He'd been through the grieving process himself, his daughter Floortje dying two years ago, and if it wasn't for Tanya helping him through it, then he doesn't know what he might have done.

And now he and Tanya are expecting their first child together.

Sometimes he marvels at how fast things have happened between them, at how he's now standing on the cusp of the rest of his life. There are days it makes him giddy. Others when the enormity of it almost makes him sick.

His leg's tingling less now, and he tenses the muscles for a few seconds before releasing them. It helps, so he does it again. And again.

Their phones are stubbornly silent, and the sun's bullying them from the sky. It's starting to make Jaap feel smothered, suffocated. His finger finds the button, a little indent showing him which end means down, and he presses it, hoping for a breeze on his face, the cleanliness of it, a new beginning.

But the air outside is humid and still, a solid, inescapable presence. Even the leaves have given up and are now hanging limp, as if exhausted from their wasted attempt to communicate.

Smit's phone buzzes. He takes it up to his ear, a puppet who's just had a string jerked.

'Talk to me,' he says like this is his case, like he's been the one working hours so long the days blurred into each other and he started waking at two in the morning terrified he couldn't breathe.

Jaap tunes out. He should feel resentful of Smit's intrusion, but really, what's the point? The police force is at heart no different to any other organization. As in, you take the shit, your superior takes the glory. That's just how it is, how it always will be, for ever and ever. Amen.

'Halle-fucking-*lujah*,' Smit finally says, hanging up.

Jaap takes a breath, expands his lungs and holds the air there, forcing calm, the pressure something to push against, anchor to, a moment of stability in an unstable world.

'Let's do it,' he says, breathing out.

It's way too hot for stab vests, but they pull them out of the boot anyway and Velcro them on. Smit inspects his gun, pops the clip and Jaap hears the double click as the slide's pumped. Satisfied, Smit slams it back together with the heel of his hand. He checks the sight, like there's anything he can do about it if it's not right, then ends his virtuoso performance with a nod and a quick purse of his lips.

'Been a while since you fired one of those?' Jaap asks, hoping Smit gets the implication, *you desk-bound bureaucrat.*

Smit eyeballs him, is just opening his mouth to say something, when he's interrupted by the whine of an engine pushed to the limit. Jaap's head's on a swivel, he sees a van from one of the major news networks sliding into the street so fast it's close to two-wheeling. They watch as it straightens up, just misses a side-on with a parked car, and stops fast, front end dipping hard as the brakes bite.

'You're kidding. How did they know?' Jaap asks.

Smit shrugs, rubs a small area on the gun barrel with his finger, as if there's some dirt there which needs removing.

The engine cuts out.

Sparrows chirp.

Jaap suddenly sees the answer to his own question. He's known Smit for over five years, so really he shouldn't be surprised.

He hears the rumble and hollow reverberating slam of a sliding door and glances over towards the TV crew.

They're setting up, a woman reporter and a bearded guy hefting a camera on his shoulder, looking for all the world like a dirty jihadist readying a bazooka.

As the man turns Jaap feels like he's in the firing line. He imagines cross-hairs on his chest.

From a parked car one of the surveillance crew gets out, starts ushering them back.

'Bad idea,' Jaap says, nodding towards the reporters, the woman arguing with the surveillance guy.

He knows it's not going to achieve anything, but he can't help himself, can't help needling his boss. Sometimes it's the only way to get through the day.

But Smit, if anything, appears relaxed.

Relaxed as in, doesn't give a shit.

'It's called media relations,' he says. 'Maybe you didn't notice but they've been all over this case. Now we need to show them the resolution. And it's better if we're in control of them.'

Jaap checks his own weapon again, doesn't say anything.

'Yeah, I know you don't give a fuck,' Smit says, seeming to take offence at Jaap's silence. 'But that's why I'm station chief and you're not. From where I'm sitting I see a bigger picture.'

'That management course you went on, how'd that work out?'

Now it's Smit's turn to be silent.

Jaap makes one more last-minute check on his gear, decides now is the time.

'Stay in front of me where it's safe,' Jaap says as just across the street a woman steps out of the house next door to Kamp's. She's medium height, long brown hair tied in a high ponytail which bounces as she neatly hops over the low wooden fence and presses the doorbell. She has an apron on, dusted with flour.

'Fuck's she doing?' Smit asks.

Jaap's debating ducking back to the car or running forward, but before he can react the door opens, their target standing there in the newly opened gap. He's obviously in the middle of some DIY, a screwdriver held in one hand.

He looks at the woman, then quickly, almost involuntarily, his eyes search the street.

Jaap and Smit don't have time to get out of sight. Kamp sees them, and acts. He leaps forward, the door swinging closed behind him, and grabs the woman, spins her round so Jaap can see the shock and confusion on her face.

Then, as she feels the tip of a screwdriver touch her neck, it turns to fear.

Somewhere down the street a mower rips into life, a once familiar sound taking on a menacing cast.

Menacing because Jaap doesn't want anything to tip the balance of Kamp's mind, anything which could destroy the delicate equilibrium of the moment, spur him into making the wrong choice.

'Take it easy,' Jaap calls across to Kamp. 'We can work it out.'

Out of the corner of his eye Jaap sees Smit, weapon out, edge one step closer. It's been less than thirty seconds since Kamp grabbed the woman, thirty seconds in which he and Smit have got into position, backed up by the surveillance crew.

Kamp's breathing hard, he seems more panicked than the woman he's holding, the hand with the screwdriver trembling.

And Jaap knows that in situations like this, panic is a killer.

'Just breathe,' he says. 'Breathe and it'll be OK.'

Smit takes another step, thinking he's out of Kamp's field of vision. But somehow Kamp senses the movement and zeroes his eyes in on him.

Jaap thinks of the game they used to play as kids, the aim was to sneak up on someone and freeze in place when they turned. If they saw you moving, you were out.

'Put it down,' Jaap says, staying put for now. 'Put it down, and we can talk.'

Kamp's not stupid. He knows the score, knows he's not getting out of this. Knows that the word talk is code for *arrest-and-prosecute-to-the-full-extent-of-the-law-you-dirty-piece-of-murdering-shit*.

Movement in the corner of Jaap's eye. He risks a quick sideways glance, and sure enough they're filming, edging closer to the action, the man supposed to be keeping them back focused on Kamp, his own weapon drawn.

In journalistic terms this is like winning multiple lotteries all at once. In police terms, it's the exact opposite.

'Go away,' Kamp yells, the first time he's said anything, his voice tight, ratcheting in his throat. 'Go away or I'll do it.'

He pushes the screwdriver harder, Jaap can see the dent it's making in the creamy skin of the woman's neck.

A drop of blood swells up as the tip punctures.

He tries to catch her eye, tell her with just a look that it's going to be all right. She squints slightly, either telling him she's understood, or in reaction to the pain, Jaap can't tell.

He doesn't want to take the shot, but his options are rapidly depleting. He's close enough, Kamp's head appearing over the woman's shoulder, face unreadable.

His finger, flat against the body of his Glock, curls down to the trigger, testing the resistance gently.

So much can happen in a simple millimetre.

'This is your last warning,' Jaap says. 'Put it down.'

Kamp's agitated, his eyes jerking around, a cornered animal searching for escape.

Jaap takes a step closer, just to let him know escape's not an option.

Kamp holds out for a few seconds more, then starts to lower the screwdriver. He releases his fingers, the tool clattering against the doorstep tiles. He shoves the woman hard, she stumbles and it takes her a second to realize that she's actually free, that it's not a trick. Then she rushes forward, into the arms of one of the surveillance team, who whisks her quickly away.

'On your knees, hands on your head,' Jaap yells as he starts moving forward. He steps up the path, past flowers and a fibreglass water feature desperately imitating rock, and reaches Kamp, waiting on his knees. Stepping behind him, Jaap goes for his cuffs, finds they're not on his belt.

Fuck.

Smit whistles; when Jaap looks up he tosses over a pair. Jaap catches them one-handed and cuffs one wrist then the other. He hauls Kamp up. There's a kind of damp heat coming off him, his whole body vibrating.

As they move down the path a baby starts crying from

the house behind them. One of the surveillance crew heads towards the door.

Smit, now the danger's passed, steps up and bear-mauls Jaap's shoulder.

'Good job,' he says.

Jaap can see the camera crew moving closer. He glances at them, only they're not playing the game, they don't stop coming.

'I'll handle this,' Smit says.

He turns and intercepts them before they get too close. Jaap knows it's because Smit wants *his* face on the news, announcing they've finally got the killer, taking the glory.

But somehow he doesn't care, he'll leave the politics and media relations to Smit. All he feels, now he finally has Kamp, is a rising anger, surfing the wave of his adrenaline rush. He grabs Kamp by the upper arm and guides him towards the surveillance van.

They reach the back, out of sight of the camera, and Jaap opens a door and shoves Kamp into a sitting position.

He pulls out photos of each victim and holds them in front of him.

His phone's going off in his pocket; he ignores it.

'Why did you do it?'

It's like his head is the same polarity as the photos – wherever Jaap places them Kamp's face moves away.

A shadow precedes Smit appearing round the corner of the van.

'Don't do this here, we'll take him back to the station. We need everything to be official.'

Jaap ignores him, his focus fully on Kamp.

'Why did you kill Dafne Koster and Nadine Adelaars?'

The second name pings Kamp's central nervous system; he jerks like he's just been stung. His eyes swing round and catch the photos. From the house the baby cries out again, a long, high-pitched wail. Jaap's phone stops ringing, then immediately starts again.

'No . . . nononono . . . I only . . . not that one . . . not her.'

'You killed both these women, you drugged them and then—'

'Inspector Rykel, urgent call for you.'

One of the surveillance crew's moved into his peripheral vision, tentative because he can see this isn't the time.

'Kinda busy here,' Jaap says, eyes still on Kamp.

'I know, but I've been told to tell you it's *really* urgent. Like, drop-everything kind of urgent.'

'Get it,' Smit says. 'I'll take him back to the station, question him there, and the surveillance crew can seal off the house till patrol get here. Also, get Protective Services in for the baby.'

Jaap stares at Kamp, his face pale with shock, before pulling his phone out, the station dispatcher's number on the screen.

'I'm in the middle of something,' he says, 'so this had better be good.'

The reply's a triumph of modern technology, Daleked beyond recognition. He starts walking away from the van, searching for better reception. He finds it and asks for a rerun. He can see a uniform walking out with the screaming baby in his arms.

'Case came in, raised a flag.'

'What flag?' Jaap says, a cold sickness seeping through

17

him. He only has one on the system. One which shouldn't now be raised again.

'Young woman found dead on a remote beach up on Vlieland. Died of suffocation, had been chased beforehand. Looks the same as your other two.'

'Time of death?' Jaap asks. For a split second he hears Kamp's denial.

Not her.

'Not official yet, but sometime round lunchtime today and—'

A gunshot explodes into the air. The world crystallizes for a fraction of a second. Jaap can feel the hard edges of his phone against his fingers. Everything's still.

A second shot joins the first.

He spins round, races back towards the van. When he gets there Smit's about a metre away, half-standing, half-crouching, his weapon held out in front of him. He can't disguise the wobble in his arms, the loose panic in his eyes.

Jaap stops dead, his mind a kaleidoscope of conflicting thoughts.

Kamp's body is sprawled on the road just behind the van, one arm above his head, the other stretched out like he's directing traffic, cuffs dangling from his left wrist, one section undone.

Just out of reach of his hand, on the blistering tarmac, lies a gun.

Not a model used by the police.

As he gets closer Jaap can hear Kamp trying to say something, his breathing in overdrive.

'I . . . I didn't kill them both . . .'

Kamp's whole body judders, he bites the air once with a strangled grunt. Then he's still.

A wound on his chest blossoms like a time-lapse flower.

Something moves in Jaap's peripheral vision. He turns to see his own face reflected in the cameraman's lens, a red dot flashing just beside it.

2

'Jaap, that's awful, are you OK?'

He's in a car, being driven by someone else for once, and after all the chaos of the last few hours he'd suddenly realized that what he *really* wanted to do was talk to Tanya.

She's down in Rotterdam, on secondment to a large and seemingly never-ending drugs case, and he's been missing her more and more.

'Yeah, I think so,' he says, still not really sure. 'The whole thing's a bit of a mess though, I—'

A thought hits him, stopping up his mouth like a ball-gag. He glances up front, the driver a random uniform simply doing an assigned job. Though he had been assigned it by Smit. Jaap wonders if he's being paranoid.

'Look, it'll be easier if we talk later, I'm due to land there in about an hour, I'll try and call you then?'

'Sure, I'm just heading out to get some food, I seem to be craving bacon.'

Tanya loves bacon, always has, always will.

'Yeah, yeah. Let me guess, pregnant craving?'

'Of course.'

'And you're not just using that to legitimize your bacon fetish?'

'Inspector Rykel, your cynicism is *very* disappointing.'

Quarter of an hour later the car pulls into a helipad in

Harlingen, where a search and rescue chopper is due to take him over the water to Vlieland.

Only the place is deserted.

He steps out of the car, walks the short distance to the centre of the large H and scans the skies. Nothing. The sun's dipping towards the horizon where he knows the island of Vlieland lies, and beyond that the North Sea.

'You want me to wait?' calls the uniform.

Jaap ignores him, is about to pull out his phone, when he spots something high up, off to the north. He watches for a moment, decides it *is* heading his way.

'No,' Jaap says. 'You can go.'

As the car pulls off he finds a rusty oil drum slightly away from the helipad and sits down. His presence startles something in the long grass behind, whatever it is rustling away without being seen.

The scene he'd left behind in Amsterdam was a mess, no question, and he still doesn't understand how it had gone so wrong. He's been wracking his brain, trying to work out if it was all his fault, if he'd somehow, in the anger which he'd not reeled in enough, made mistakes.

After the shooting Smit had been in shock. Turns out that unlike Jaap, who has been forced to kill in the line of duty, he'd never shot and killed anyone before.

And that's not something to be taken lightly. Doesn't matter if the guy deserved it, even if in the dark hours of the case you end up fantasizing about doing it to whoever preyed on the young, extinguishing their fragile potential as if it was nothing. Ultimately it's still killing another human being.

Smit, of course, has the law on his side. There's no

question of that. But just because it's the law, doesn't make it right, doesn't make it any easier when you close your eyes and see the person you shot dying again and again, the actual moment when consciousness disappears into an infinity of nothing.

So the fight they'd had afterwards, after Smit's initial shock wore off, wasn't a surprise. Neither was the news that there will be an investigation.

And Jaap knows that he's going to be on his own when that all kicks off.

There's more rustling in the grass behind him, maybe whatever it was he'd scared off earlier has come back with reinforcements.

He plays the scene again, every moment from when he stepped up to Kamp and cuffed him. Can he be sure that both cuffs clicked together? Could he have missed one? And, worryingly, no matter how hard he tries, he can't seem to dredge up a memory of checking Kamp for weapons.

Fuck, he thinks. Fuckfuckfuck.

All of which is bad. But it's only a distraction from the thing which is pulsing inside his head, his whole body, tearing at his mind.

Kamp denied killing the second victim, Nadine Adelaar.

The rhythmic thud of the chopper saves him from his thoughts, and he soon has to clamp his hands over his ears as the fluorescent yellow machine comes in to land, the downdraft buffeting him, making his progress towards it difficult.

The door slides open and the pilot, little more than head-phones, flight goggles and an arm, motions him inside.

They lift off, the lurch in Jaap's stomach reminding him he's not eaten for hours, and the chopper circles round till they're heading out over the water separating the mainland from the string of islands which follow the north Netherlands' coast. Of which his destination, Vlieland, is the second one up.

Jaap tries to clear his mind and just enjoy the sensation of flying above the water, but no matter what he does it keeps going back to the case.

Specifically Kamp's denial. He didn't deny both murders, which Jaap could understand, but only one. And yet both bodies, despite the minor differences in their deaths, had something in common which was incontrovertible: large amounts of scopolamine in their blood.

When it had come up in the extended tox report, Jaap had not even heard of the stuff. After some fruitless research, calling round the various labs the police used for their forensics, Google filled him in.

'Dragon's breath' they call it in Columbia, where the drug originates, processed from the seeds of a genus of flowering shrub called *Brugmansia*. They're primarily grown for their flowers, which hang like somnolent trumpets from the branches, giving off an intense, some say intoxicating, fragrance. But the beauty is all surface; scopolamine, once refined from the seed, has been used for years there to rob people, to rape them, to do any manner of things a sick mind does when confronted with the opportunity.

Victims of scopolamine – those that are lucky enough just to be robbed when under its narcotic influence – describe the same thing: they all just did what they were

23

told. A man might be slipped some in a drink by a prostitute and before he know's what's happening it's the next morning and he finds his bank accounts have been emptied, and quite possibly everything in his flat or house as well. In fact, the only thing the victims usually have left at this stage is no recollection of what happened, and the mother of all hangovers which pounds their heads for days. Though it turns out *not knowing* what happened to you in that gap in memory is far worse, and far more persistant. The *not knowing* is what haunts the victims.

And if it was administered to a woman, well, that's just going to be worse. Much worse.

Despite this, the only time the drug usually surfaces outside of Columbia is in minute doses in a prescription patch for extreme travel sickness, where it's listed as Hyoscine hydrobromide. But when Jaap had asked the question the response came through that a body would have to have been covered head to toe in the things for months to get the kind of blood levels seen in both victims.

The rarity of scopolamine was in itself enough to link the two deaths; add the suffocation and it was reasonable to assume the killer was the same. Jaap had enough on Kamp for the first death, Dafne Koster, but it was really the scopolamine which clinched it, linking him to the second.

But maybe that was wrong, he thinks now. Maybe I should have dug deeper.

They're heading into the sun, and soon he can see a slip of land rising from the water up ahead.

His phone buzzes in his pocket, he fishes it out and

reads the message confirming that a patrol car is waiting for him on Vlieland.

In the water below he spots a yacht, tilted at an angle, the taut sail turned golden by the sun. He snaps a few quick photos, selects the best one and sends it to Tanya.

As the flight continues he starts to feel his breathing slow down, and as they get closer, with the sky turning red and the land darkening, Jaap is surprised to find himself humming Ride of the Valkyries.

3

The dune path is flanked with swaying grasses, seed heads desperate to reach out and touch Jaap as he moves past. The ocean's briny tang pushes against his face as he starts out across the beach.

In front of him the dying sun bleeds into a vast sea.

Hours earlier he'd been on the cusp of cracking what was thought to be the Netherlands' first serial-killer case of the twenty-first century, a case which had exploded into the headlines, the after-shock reverberating there for months.

I didn't kill them both.

Kamp's last words, unease pricking Jaap's brain.

He sees him lying on the road, dying in front of him, he feels Smit's quiet panic, the fear of what could have happened, the fear of what did happen.

And the loose cuff, evidence that he'd fucked up.

Now he may never burrow down deep enough to know what really happened.

Because Jaap can't figure out why Kamp would admit to one killing, but not the other.

Unless Kamp was speaking the truth.

Which could, given he's about to walk up to a possible third body, rip open the guts of his near-finished case.

Thirty or forty metres ahead, dark figures silhouette against the vibrant red. They're at the water's edge, standing by the body like a guard of honour.

Right now he expects to hear the whirling cry of gulls above him, but it seems eerily quiet, as if the water, earth and sky are all watching him, waiting to see what he will do. Judging him on his actions.

Beneath his feet the sand is a tricksy lover, yielding unpredictably to his shoes. As he walks, unusual muscles in his calves and ankles are forced into an intricate choreography just to keep him upright.

Ahead the muted thump and hiss of the waves, behind him darkness sucks away at his back.

One of the uniforms turns as he approaches the group, revealing a sheet lying on the sand. Small waves the colour of blood and fire wet the fabric's seaward edge with exploratory laps. The unmistakable configuration of peaks and troughs tells him that under the sheet is a body lying on its back.

He glances out to sea, something catching his eye, and for a second he thinks he sees a gull, flying low, a wing tip skimming the waves on a turn, a dark mark streaming across the bloody sun.

He blinks and it's gone.

'What have we got?' he asks as he comes to a stop, wanting to search for the bird but tearing his eyes away, back to the figures. He now sees one of them is a forensic, Max Bakker, who he's worked with before.

A case just over two years ago. The same case which led to his daughter Floortje's kidnapping, and ultimately her death.

The memory stings hard, lighting up the wound all over again. But, he notices with a kind of amazed detachment, it's not as intense as it used to be, as if the voltage has lowered over time.

And there's a kind of guilt implied in that. Something inside urges him to feel it more.

The last slip of sun bleeds away, and the sky darkens, as if mourning its passing.

'Hang on,' Max says, peeling off a glove and thumb-typing something on his phone. He holds it out from his chin, as if he were long-sighted. Elongated shadows streak up his face from the sickly light.

It reminds Jaap of a camping trip he'd been on as a kid; buckled down in their tent, he and several others had taken it in turns to hold the torch and try and frighten each other. It hadn't worked.

Now, years later, and given all that he's seen, Jaap wonders why anybody would actually *want* to be frightened.

Max is still working his phone. He's probably the only person in the universe who's left the clicker sound on for typing. Jaap's not sure if he's writing notes on the crime scene or just texting a friend, arranging a post-body drink.

But, he decides, he doesn't mind either way. Things will start soon enough. He thinks of the argument he'd had with Smit, adrenaline pitting them against each other. Smit's tirade of accusations, Jaap's robust defence of himself.

Because he'd never be so sloppy.

But was I? he thinks, going over it all again, trying to work out if the surge of anger he'd felt when he'd arrested Kamp had forced him into making mistakes which could have cost him his own, or Smit's, life.

A wave reaches out and strokes the sand. Jaap watches as it returns to the sea. Watches as one more comes to do the same. And another.

Smit had been lucky, no question, Kamp's shot going wide, allowing his boss to retaliate.

And yet with that bullet, he realizes, standing here on the beach with the sea and the earth and the dark sky, his chance of finding out what really went on may have died.

'So,' Max says, putting away his phone, his face disappearing into the darkness. 'Wanna see? We kept it fresh for you.'

Max pulls out a torch, runs the beam along the sheet from the feet-end up, quietly singing the *Jaws* theme, *da dum*, *da dum*, *da dum da dum* then *daaaaa* as the light reaches the head and dances around in a frenzy. Jaap shoots his hand out, grasping Max's wrist, forcing it still. Max gives in and holds the torch steady. In response Jaap releases his wrist as a uniform's gloved hand reaches into the cold light and grips the end of the fabric.

Jaap feels like looking away.

The darkness all around is immense and suffocating at the same time, and he's suddenly aware of his hands, heavy and ripe with blood.

The glove whips away the sheet, the torch beam remaining steady.

Jaap scans the body: a young woman, sandals, tight jeans ending just below the knee, and a sleeveless pink T-shirt with a cartoon kitten on the front, paw raised in a wave, head cocked to one side, eyes slits.

Her arms are behind her back, forcing her torso off the ground so that for a second Jaap thinks of a woman doing yoga on the beach.

He looks at the head.

'Nasty, isn't it?' Max says.

29

But Jaap hardly hears, sound receding into the background like he's just plunged head first into the nearby sea.

He moves in closer, feels the magnetic push and pull of death.

In the victim's mouth is some kind of round plastic tube, though it's not hollow, the end covered with a narrow lattice. Silver tape wraps round her head, holding the tube in place, making a perfect seal round her mouth, and another stretch of tape completely covers her nose. Another young woman, killed in a different way, but ultimately the same: being deprived of the oxygen the body needs to burn fuel efficiently.

None of this is conclusive, he tries to tell himself. Not unless she tests positive for scopolamine.

But somehow he just knows what the report will say, can see it already, the positive mark next to the name of the substance he'd not even heard of three months ago.

He squats down, getting a closer look, the toes of his shoes slowly sinking into the sand, moistened by earlier waves.

'Bloods?'

'Pulled earlier. They were due to be picked up by the chopper which dropped you off. Results back in the morning.'

Jaap holds out his hand and Max places the torch in it. Jaap grips it overhand-style, and brings it closer to the woman's head.

He's starting to make sense of it, even though part of his mind is resisting.

'You know what it is?' Max asks, jolting Jaap back.

'Yeah, all right,' Jaap says, straightening up, feeling the vast void in his stomach. 'Tell me.'

'It's a valve,' Max says. 'A one-way valve.'

'So you're saying . . .' Jaap says, not wanting to hear it.

'I'm saying . . .' Max pulls out a cigarette and attempts to light it, cupping his hand round the Zippo to stop the flame writhing around like it's in pain. He finally gets it lit and looks straight at Jaap. 'I'm saying she could only breathe out.'

4

'So you're the hotshot?'

Station Chief Wieland Stuppor is a single *syrupwaffel* away from a major coronary event.

And the fact that Jaap's been parachuted, almost literally, into his island fiefdom doesn't seem to be helping much.

They're outside the island's station, a building Jaap has yet to set foot in, but he can tell from where he's standing that it's little more than a converted bungalow with a blue POLITIE sign tacked on to the wall.

The night is cooler here than the sweltering density of Amsterdam. The welcome too is turning out to be downright frosty.

'Inspector Rykel,' Jaap says, holding out his hand.

Stuppor doesn't take it. He has a face like a statue from an island thousands of miles away in another ocean. An island, Jaap remembers, where the population were so smart they used up all the resources available to them and ended their genetic legacy by killing each other off completely. Jaap imagines the last one alive, howling into the darkness on an island devoid of food, and with no trees left to build an escape raft.

'I'll need everything you've got so far,' he says, retracting his unshook hand.

Midnight can't be far away and he still doesn't know

where he'll be sleeping. Stuppor stares at him for a moment then nods him inside. Jaap follows, past the front desk, which isn't manned, and into the main room at the back. Three more desks – two of which are being driven by uniforms – and morgue-like strip lights that hang from the ceiling and illuminate the general air of decay.

Through a door is Stuppor's office, which looks out onto the car park at the back and two cones of light shining down the wall of a building on the far side. They go in and Stuppor settles behind his desk.

Jaap looks around for something to sit on.

He's somehow not surprised when he comes up with nothing.

This is just petty.

Then again, he figures there's a reason Stuppor's ended up in charge of an island where birds outnumber the population ten to one. Not that he really knows anything about the place; he just assumes from what little he's seen of it in the last few hours that it probably *is* the kind of terrain where wildlife makes a bigger contribution to the carbon cycle than humans.

'Here's what we know—' starts Stuppor.

Jaap walks out. He selects the free chair, which happens to be at the furthest desk, and drags it across decaying lino the colour of used dishwater. One of the men, heavily tanned and not looking like police at all except for the uniform, jerks off a bit of air and nods his head towards Stuppor's office.

As Jaap tries to get it through the narrow doorway he gouges the door frame with a chair leg. Dry paint flakes off, showering the floor.

'Oops,' he says, positioning it opposite Stuppor's desk. He sits down.

'You were saying?' he prompts. He wishes he had a *syrupwaffel* to offer Stuppor.

'Body was discovered at 13:12,' Stuppor says after a power-game pause. 'Young couple going for a romantic stroll.'

From Stuppor's tone it sounds like he regards a romantic stroll as somewhat akin to a full BDSM orgy with a hefty dose of transgender chem-sex thrown in for good measure. He shuffles some paper on his desk, eventually finding what he's after and holding it out to Jaap, forcing him to lean forwards.

It's a transcript of the call, and a few sheets detailing the first officer to the scene's notes. He glances through it before dropping it back on Stuppor's desk.

'Says here the victim was wearing a bracelet with the name "Heleen" engraved on it. Has she been ID'd yet?'

'No. We're checking that now.'

Jaap spots a map on the wall to his right and turns to scrutinize it. The island's a thin, lazy sickle shape, one of a chain broadly mirroring the shape of the mainland. The west coast, where the body was found, faces out into the North Sea; Oost-Vlieland, the only ferry port, sits on the east coast, sheltered from the tide and prevailing winds.

'How frequent are the ferries to the mainland?'

'This time of year, every couple of hours.'

Given his perfunctory answers, Jaap feels like Stuppor's not totally invested in the process.

'Say the killer wanted to get across the island quickly, how long would it take for them to get to Oost-Vlieland?'

'If they had a bike they could do it in about half an hour.'

'By car?'

'Visitors to the island can't have cars, only residents are allowed them.'

'And you're sure it's not a resident because . . .?' asks Jaap. 'Actually, what I'm more interested in are the people who were booked on the ferries set to depart after the body was found – where did you keep them?'

Jaap sees that it might not even take a *syrupwaffel* to do the business. He also feels that he's getting to the bottom of Stuppor's lack of co-operation.

'OK, you're telling me you didn't stop the ferries,' Jaap says, not even framing it as a question. Because he knows the answer, both to that and the reason for the warm welcome.

Nobody likes to be caught out on a colossal fuck-up.

Which is, Jaap can see, exactly what's happening here.

The image of Kamp dying on the road with only one cuff done up makes a brief appearance, aligned with the word 'fuck-up'. He pushes it aside just as Stuppor comes clean.

'There was a ferry which departed at 15:00 for Harlingen. Unfortunately it wasn't stopped,' Stuppor says. 'The person responsible has been reprimanded.'

Jaap decides he needs to check just how long the surveillance team lost sight of Kamp for.

'Well,' he says, getting up, 'that's good. Looks like we're going to have some fun here. Where am I staying tonight?'

Stuppor smiles for the first time since Jaap met him. 'Don't worry, that's all taken care of,' he says, gesturing to the door.

The reason for the smile soon becomes obvious. Turns out he's staying somewhere which doesn't even hold one star.

The island's cell block. Which contains two cells, both of them empty.

'Tourist season,' shrugs Stuppor as he shows Jaap to the nearest one, where a fresh set of towels is folded neatly on the solid bed. 'The whole island's booked out for the summer holidays.'

'Thanks,' Jaap says. 'Looks comfortable.'

5

So comfortable he decides to head out for a walk.

He hits the main road, a stretch of tarmac with no centre line and edges decaying into the sandy grasslands all around. It's deserted, and doesn't have any street lights. The stars are bright though, and the tip of a fat moon is just oozing off the horizon, spilling a greasy yellow slick onto the dark water separating the island from the mainland. He can hear the distant surf as well, a kind of muffled roar.

It's idyllic, a million miles away from the jumbled solidity of Amsterdam's centre.

Jaap thinks of the girl on the beach, the one-way valve taped into her mouth.

Suddenly he's not sure he likes idyllic.

He checks his phone, hoping for a message from Tanya. There isn't one, so he sends her a text. The progress bar falters halfway, hangs there for ages before zooming to the end in a fit of enthusiasm.

He's missing Tanya, hopes she'll be posted back to Amsterdam soon. They're going to have to start preparing, a big change coming their way. It strikes him suddenly that the change may be bigger than either of them thinks.

His phone goes off and he pulls it out, expecting to see Tanya's face on the screen. But it's an Amsterdam number he doesn't recognize.

'Inspector Rykel, I'm Chief Superintendent Laura Vetter,' a voice tells him. 'I believe you were involved in an incident earlier in the day, the death of a suspect, Franceso Kamp. Is that correct?'

Jaap's suddenly aware of the back of his neck.

'There was an incident earlier today,' he concedes, wondering why he feels on full alert all of sudden.

'Right. Well, as you know the death of a member of the public caused by a police officer is a serious matter, and I've been tasked with looking into this.'

'Kamp wasn't a *member of the public*, he was a murderer.'

'Not until he's been convicted in a court of law.'

'He's dead, so I guess that's not going to happen.'

'Precisely, which is why I have to get to the bottom of this.'

Jaap had once gone to an exhibition of M. C. Escher's work; he remembers the staircases leading back round to each other. He takes a deep breath before replying.

'OK, what do you need?'

'We've already taken a statement from Station Chief Henk Smit, and I need to take a statement from you as well. Then we can go from there. However, I've heard that you're in the middle of a case and you're out of town this evening, so we can meet tomorrow at ten a.m. at your station. Does that suit?'

Not really, no, thinks Jaap as he hangs up, having agreed. He doesn't even know if he'll be off the island by then. In fact, all things considered, it seems highly unlikely, but he decides he'll deal with that in the morning.

He goes over the whole scene again in his mind, trying to work out how he'd managed *not* to do the cuffs up properly. And the gun. How could he have missed it?

Fucking idiot, he thinks.

Headlights appear out of the darkness behind him and for a few moments his shadow shows him to be a towering giant. He feels like putting his hands up beside his head and growling like a beast from a kids' horror story.

Instead he steps off the road and the car slows, pulls up beside him. A window cranks down and Jaap recognizes the tanned uniform from earlier. Except he's no longer in uniform.

'Hey,' the man says, leaning out the window. 'I'm Arno Janssen, didn't get introduced earlier.'

'Jaap Rykel,' Jaap says as they soul-shake awkwardly through the car's window.

'Thought you'd be staying in, enjoying your accommodation.'

'It's kind of luxury overkill,' Jaap says. 'Your boss going through the male menopause or something?'

Arno laughs, puts the car into neutral, the engine shifting pitch. Jaap notices the hand on the gearstick has a tiny glowing ember floating just above it.

'Don't think you can blame it on hormones,' Arno says. 'I think he's got asshole coded in his DNA.'

'A wise man once told me you only need one asshole in your life. More than that's just not necessary.'

'Agreed. C'mon, you can stay at my place. Long as you don't mind a sofa.'

'A sofa will be just fine.'

The glowing tip isn't a cigarette, Jaap discovers when he gets in.

'Uh . . .' Arno says, holding up the blunt, 'I'm off duty.'

'Yeah, but they stopped that a while back, didn't you

hear? They said that police officers have a duty to uphold morality even when off duty.'

'Morality, fuck. It's just cannabis, not krokodil.'

Jaap stares at him, reaches out and takes it. He notices the tattoo on Arno's wrist, a circle of intertwining thorns. He winds his window, the car so old it has to be done manually. It creaks on the way down.

'Don't, that's the last of my—'

Jaap lifts the blunt up to the window space. He takes a hit. A big one.

He's not done it for years, not his kind of scene. But the day's been shit, and he feels like he needs some help with it. He keeps the smoke in his lungs, the urge to cough growing urgent, but just about manages to hold it down.

He hands it back. 'Fuck it,' he says, blowing an aromatic stream of smoke out the window, 'we're not paid for twenty-four hours, are we?'

'No,' Arno says, putting the car into gear and lurching it forward. 'No, we're not.'

Jaap discovers the seat he's in is actually quite comfortable, the world seems softer suddenly, more rounded, and he finds himself relaxing into it, enjoying the movement as the car heads into the night.

He starts to feels more welcome.

6

'Fucker,' Bart says. 'Where is he?'

Kees Truter takes one last hit, holding the smoke in till he feels the burn. He releases it, and flicks the cigarette away, ignoring Bart's question.

The flaring orange tip spirals in the darkness before extinguishing in the water below. He thinks of a fish, darting up as if alerted to a fly, cold lips clamping round the sodden butt.

You're welcome, he addresses the fish telepathically.

He's found he's losing the taste for smoke, but he's not sure why.

Maybe it's the drugs, he thinks.

Beside him Bart shifts, releasing the deep animal funk of old leather. Kees feels tired and wired. It's been a rough few days, three jobs in a row, and they had to break off at the last minute yesterday and race up to Amsterdam-Zuid, where he'd been told to sit tight in the car Bart had stolen especially – the one Kees had had to drive like his job description said 'Chauffeur' – whilst Bart went inside the house.

Kees is used to being kept in the dark, it's only natural. It takes time to get deep undercover, and it's not a process you want to rush. One false move leaves you exposed, and Kees has absolutely no desire for that to happen here. As it stands, on Station Chief Henk Smit's guidance, he's

41

been working his way into Van der Pol's gang for the last year, inching closer to his ultimate goal.

But yesterday had been a reminder that he's still got a way to go.

He'd been tired and wired then too, sitting in the car waiting. He'd also had that ache which told him he needed to piss badly, the urgency not helped by the constant trickle of water from some cheap rockery plonked in the house's front garden. It'd got so bad he'd actually been searching the car for some kind of container when Bart reappeared with a face which said job's a good 'un.

'So what was that yesterday?' Kees asks.

Bart grins. Then he actually winks whilst making a *click* sound out of the side of his mouth.

Kees doesn't think much of Bart, especially as he's spent the better part of the last year paired up with him. Not that he has any choice in the matter. It's not like there's an HR department he can go and complain to. For a moment Kees imagines walking into Van der Pol's Portakabin office and saying he'd like to work with a different team member. Realistically, doing that would be little more than a death sentence. Probably, knowing Van der Pol's twisted mind, he'd be dead within the day, pummelled by Bart and his baseball bat.

But he *is* alive, the drugs helping with that. They also mask some of the pain, but not all of it. He's got another appointment with his specialist booked in later next week. Kees is not sure he can face going.

'Secret,' Bart says eventually.

Jesus fuck, Kees continues his telepathic conversation with the fish. The fish, maybe having choked on the cigarette butt, or averse to Kees' choice of words, doesn't respond.

'No, seriously, I'd like to know. We do all these jobs, and they're all kind of the same, but yesterday was different. What am I missing?'

Kees had caught a glimpse of the man, tall with dark curly hair and a scared look on his face.

'The question is, what'll you be missing if you keep on asking questions.'

End of.

Actually, Kees is impressed. Given that he assumes Bart would be out IQ'd by even the non-responsive fish, his reply was surprisingly eloquent.

Regardless, Kees still wants to know. Needs to know. He'd had a message two days ago telling him to watch for anything out of the ordinary and report back. That's his job. His *real* job.

Which for the moment means he has to do as Bart tells him.

Which right *now* means not asking any more questions.

He focuses on the building they're watching across the water, the single-storey prefab with round porthole windows blaring light out into the darkness.

It's the only building for miles around, racks filled with slender canoes off to the right, two SUVs parked to the left.

They're half an hour outside of Eindhoven, on a drainage canal, and surrounded by nothing. They'd had to leave their bikes on a dirt track and trudge across two fields to get here, one full of sheep ambling around like zombies, the other dotted with rows and rows of some kind of summer cabbage. Bart had made a point of using the plants like stepping stones, flattening each one with a soft crunch.

Kees knows that was stupid – why *try* and leave evidence, for fuck's sake? – but hadn't said anything, even though it had made him burn inside.

He thinks of one of the quacks he'd been to who'd told him his disease was caused by repressed emotion, probably anger, and that to fully heal he'd have to let go of it.

Kees had told him to fuck off and left without paying.

Maybe . . . a voice pipes up – Kees is unsure if it's the fish finally come to life or his own thoughts – *maybe he was right after all*.

Across the water figures flit behind the portholes.

The moon, which has been lighting the sky from out of sight, starts to rise behind the building. It comes up fast, revealing three flag poles on the building's roof. From each one hangs a limp flag. To Kees they look like victims of a lynch mob left hanging as a warning to others. Though what the warning's about remains unclear.

'Here we go,' Bart says in a whisper as dirty as the Harley he rides.

Kees reckons Bart could get a job as a voice-over artist if this gig doesn't work out.

Then again, he's not convinced Bart can actually read.

They watch as a door opens at one end, light spilling out in a wedge. Shadows slice into it, then figures step out, one by one moving towards the two SUVs parked a little way off to the left.

Kees counts five, three men and two women. Their target is amongst them, unmistakable by his girth.

Kees had been briefed earlier, and though he'd forgotten the name of the guy, he knows that he's the fat one, a minor player who'd made the mistake of encroaching on part of Van der Pol's extensive turf.

In other words, tonight's all about a little gentle persuasion.

The headlights catch the women as they clamber into the lead SUV, ducking their heads just as their hems rise. Bart stirs beside him. They're just his type, long leather boots, short skirts and a history of being traded from an Eastern bloc country to here.

Where they have important jobs in the service industry.

Kees suddenly thinks of Tanya. He wonders what she's doing, if she's still with Jaap. Then he wonders how Jaap is. The last time he'd seen him he'd just found out his baby daughter and her mother had been killed. Kees had seen the mother, Saskia, thrown off the boat and he had swum out to her whilst Jaap chased the man who still had his daughter. But by the time Kees got Saskia to the shore and was pumping her chest and blowing into her throat, mouth pushed against her cold slippery lips, it was clear she wasn't coming back.

For a moment, and not for the first time, Kees marvels at how things have got so fucked up.

'Let's go,' Bart says as the SUVs pull out, nothing but two pairs of red lights bobbing away from them erratically on what must be a bumpy track.

They make the way back across the cabbage field, Bart crushing a few more just for the hell of it, and through sheep which have separated into smaller groups, each a small cloud in a dark sky.

They're not hurrying, they'd scoped it all out before and know they've got at least another five minutes to get on their bikes and round to where the fat man's SUV will pass on its way back to Eindhoven.

Kees doesn't like the plan; he thinks that doing this kind of job on the road, even if the road runs through a small wood, is too exposed a place. Predictably, when he'd brought up his concerns, Bart had called him a pussy and told him to suck it up.

The way their relationship works is this, Bart's more senior, he tells him to suck it up, Kees does.

For now.

Bart's bike growls into life and then broods in a rhythmic idle.

One day, thinks Kees as he fires up his own bike and flips the headlight on.

The beam hits a sheep which turns to see what's disturbing the peace. Kees stares at its eyes, the beige iris slashed with a black horizontal pupil, and for a split second doesn't know who he is or what he's doing.

They reach the designated spot a few minutes later and Bart pulls up on one side of the centre line, Kees bringing himself level on the other. They kick their bike stands down, the noise like a mouthful of grit. They kill the beams.

Now all they have to do is wait for the flicker of headlights through the trees to their left.

Kees reaches for his gun, Bart bends forward and clasps the handle of the baseball bat attached to the special clips he's had installed on his bike. Kees doesn't understand how a living person can be such a cliché.

46

But, he has to admit, Bart wields the thing with a certain grace.

And effectiveness.

Most of the people Kees has seen it introduced to find the whole experience motivational enough to change their behaviour – often permanently.

Attitude adjustment, Bart calls it.

And tonight the aim is definitely for a bit of that. The same as pretty much every day. Van der Pol has a lot people whose attitudes need adjusting. Only yesterday the guy Bart met with – 'met' being code for 'putting pressure on' – had looked, to Kees' eye, like a civilian.

He thinks back to the message, *Watch for anything out of the ordinary.* Then something out of the ordinary happened. Only Kees doesn't know what it was.

Next to him Bart coughs something up his throat and spits it onto the concrete.

'The guy yesterday, did he agree?' Kees asks.

'Agree to what?'

'Agree to whatever you went to tell him.'

Bart turns and looks at him, his long straggly goatee luminous in the moonlight filtering through the trees.

'All right. You wanna know? How's this? The guy yesterday—'

They hear a sound, both their heads snap up in time to see headlights strobing through the trees. They watch the SUV's progress until it rounds the corner less than thirty metres away. As it straightens up, Kees and Bart flip their lights on in unison, two lasers firing right at the incoming vehicle.

Brakes scream into the night, and the SUV swerves,

then skids sideways. The back end swings round and crunches into a tree. Kees is already off his bike running, gun trained on the driver. Bart's by the passenger door, surprisingly swift and agile given his size. He hauls out their target and throws him to the ground. A phone clatters against the tarmac. Bart starts with that, grinding it with his heel like he's a dancing hillbilly.

The driver hasn't seen Kees, he's fiddling under the dashboard for something. Kees fires a shot wide into the wood.

Muzzle flash sparks across the windscreen.

Now the driver sees him, he raises his hands and puts them at eleven and one o'clock on the wheel. Kees nods at him, *That's right*. He keeps the gun trained, trying to ignore the sour taste in his mouth and the blood pumping through his throat.

He listens to Bart explaining what he wants. The man refuses. Bart goes to work, the thud of the bat and a grunt telling him the man is trying to tough it out.

Just give in, Kees thinks. It'll be easier.

Then he hears something else, the sound of an engine. He glances towards Bart, but he hasn't heard it, too immersed in his work. The man on the ground's trying to protect his already beaten face with his hands. Bart goes in for a sideswipe, knocking his head left.

Kees hears the sickening crack, followed by a wet splat.

Bart had chosen this spot as it was pretty remote; the chances of someone else being here at this time of night were slim.

He'd said.

But lights are stabbing through the tree trunks, along

48

the same stretch of road the SUV had come from. Kees yells at Bart as headlights swoop round the corner. Kees can see it's the other SUV, the one which should have been taking the women back to Schijndel, in the opposite direction.

Something's gone wrong.

Now Bart reacts.

They're both running towards their bikes, Bart just ahead, when Kees hears the shot.

Or he doesn't hear so much as feel it, like a missile screaming past his ear.

Ahead, Bart's head explodes.

The second shot comes and misses.

Kees finds he's on his bike, tearing into the night, unable to stop the slo-mo action replay of Bart's head rupturing into a wet mess of gore unfolding in his brain over and over like a video in a contemporary art installation.

Later, when he's sure he's outrun them, Kees eases off the throttle, the wind softening on his face. He watches the repetitive on-off-on-off of the broken white line running along the middle of the road.

He's mesmerized by it.

He's not even sure if he's breathing or not.

Then, as he accelerates, the broken line blurring to solid, streaming at him out of the darkness ahead, the fish finally responds.

Day Two

7

Now there are gulls.

They're mobbing a small boat out on the choppy water. Jaap watches them wheel and dive, their cries carrying landward on the breeze, screams of drowning sailors.

He'd woken on Arno's sofa worried he'd been tied in a knot, his spine complaining about the working conditions, and in the midst of an intensely erotic dream featuring Arno's girlfriend, Kim. She'd been asleep when they'd turned up but had been woken by their pathetic attempt to enter the property quietly. She'd not seemed that surprised, had made the sofa up for Jaap then headed back to bed, Arno joining her.

After he'd shown Jaap around his home-grow operation.

Arno had explained that there was only one real dealer on the island and as he couldn't, as a police officer, buy from him, he'd figured it would be less complicated to grow it himself. In the grow tent there were four plants coming into flower, the smell intoxicating when he'd unzipped it, pungent and almost overpowering.

Jaap had drifted off not long after, the soft fan from the grow tent lulling him to sleep.

The extra few hits he'd taken before turning in hadn't hurt either, had mellowed things out nicely.

He breathes in and starts moving, down the same path leading to the empty beach as if it's a rerun of the previous night.

He'd called Max first thing, checking up on the blood tests, but had been forced to leave a message.

He soon finds himself at the spot where the body was found. It's no longer there, taken away after they'd finished, the location marked by four poles, a single strand of red-and-white police tape strung round the top.

He stares down into the marked-off area, his mind a jumble.

It looks to him like the sea has moved up several feet overnight and back again. Nothing really, but already the impression the body left in the sand is gone, a faint indent just beyond the waves' reach the only clue she'd been there at all.

In the past he would have started thinking about the metaphor, how each individual's life was like that, a tiny mark which would soon enough vanish as if it had never been there.

But all that had ended with the death of his baby daughter. The searing grief had consumed him for months, but it had also purged him somehow, made him less introspective, more alive to the moment.

He'd been seeing a grief counsellor – the department's meagre apology – who'd been surprised when he confessed this to her; it was almost like she didn't want him to have found a sort of peace, like she wanted him to struggle for longer. He got a strong impression she fed off other people's sorrow.

After that he stopped going. Tanya had been what got

him through; without her he doesn't know what would have happened.

The breeze, up until now soft, toughens slightly and pushes at his face like the touch of invisible hands. He feels a speckle of spray, lifted off the waves, tiny micro-dots pinging any exposed skin. The gulls crescendo into an orgy of piercing shrieks and swooping sharp cries. The boat is moving – he can hear the *blatblatblat* of the out-board now – turning to the shore fifty or so metres up the beach.

The craft itself is small and made of wood, the hull painted white with an orange stripe running round the top. Jaap walks up the beach to intercept. The outboard is churning water at the stern like a jacuzzi. Gulls follow in frenzied hope.

Jaap watches as the man cuts the engine and the boat coasts forward until it's close to the sand. He jumps over the side into the water and wades round to the front, haul-ing the boat landwards.

By the time Jaap reaches him, the bow's well past the waterline and attached to a rope the man's pulled out of the sand, stretching back in a taut arc to a stake anchored in the dunes.

As Jaap steps up, the man's back in the boat, busy trans-ferring lidded barrels over the vessel's side.

'Hey,' Jaap says, having to raise his voice to compete with the gulls.

'Morning,' the man says. He doesn't stop, keeps on off-loading barrels.

'Let me help,' Jaap says as the man picks up one larger than the rest. The man nods and once he's got it over the side Jaap takes the weight. It's heavier than he'd thought it would be, and as he's lowering it, one side sliding down the boat's hull, he feels it starting to tip. He pushes hard against it, trying to jam it between him and the boat, but it's not enough. It slips onto its side and the lid flies off, releasing a slick of silver fish, spreading out on the sand in a wet slither of flashing eyes and scales.

This is *exactly* what they've been waiting for; the gulls dive down, jabbing and pecking, each bird for itself, the noise deafening. The man jumps over the side with a loud roar, waving his arms about, knocking the birds up in a frenzy of wings, orange feet and dark glossy eyes.

Satisfied, he starts shovelling fish back into the barrel. Jaap goes to help, the gulls keeping close.

'I got it,' the man says, picking up a particularly large fish. He holds it up to Jaap and there's movement, the gills vibrating fast, eyes twitching back and forth, aware perhaps that this new world it's seeing for the first time is hostile. 'Spent twenty years trading stocks, but this is better.'

'I bet you keep that quiet.'

The man shrugs. 'Everyone hates a banker,' he says. 'But really, hating bankers for being greedy is like hating a shark for eating baby seals. It's what they do. The real people everyone should hate are the ones who allow the sharks to get anywhere near the baby seals in the first place.'

'I've never liked politicians much either.'

'Bunch of fuckers, they're the real problem.'

He grabs more fish and tosses them in the barrel. Each one lands with a wet, slippery slap as they join their fellows.

He's probably ten years or so older than him, Jaap decides, and has stubble on the cusp of graduating to a beard and a thin nose with peeling skin.

'What made you change?'

'My wife died. About six months later I took out everything, cashed it all in. Turns out it was a month before the crash. The plan was to travel the world, but I somehow ended up here.'

'Life does that sometimes,' Jaap says, finding a crab has scuttled in from nowhere and is challenging him to a fight, claws held aloft ready to strike, eyes, literally, on stalks.

'Yeah, everything's normal then one day, bang.' The man slaps two fish together, a bit of water or fish slime hits Jaap's cheek by his right eye. 'It all goes crazy. Kind of like what you're doing, I guess.'

The man looks at him; Jaap sees he has green eyes. Which makes him think of Tanya, guilty about his earlier dream.

'What *am* I doing?' Jaap says, rubbing the slime away. He's not sure if the question is directed at the man or himself.

'The murder, that's what you're here about, isn't it?'

'Small island community, no secrets, right?'

'Living here, the best thing is not to have any, then you don't get caught out,' he says, tossing the last two fish into a barrel. 'Hey, that's pretty profound, you think I should tweet it?'

'Did you see anything?'

A lone gull breaks away and makes a desperate dive.

'No,' he says, fending the bird off successfully. 'I already spoke to one of your guys last night. I think the girl was a tourist, pretty sure I saw her a couple of days ago, hanging out with some of the surf crew up there.' He points north along the beach.

This goes along with the briefing notes Arno had taken him through earlier. The fisherman was also mentioned, but had been dismissed as he'd been over at a shop on the mainland picking up several new nets at the time of the killing.

'Any trouble with them?'

'The surfers? No. In my day it would have been all drugs and stuff. Now? They're all clean-living types, into Paleo and meditation, and they worship their bodies just so they're fitter for surfing. Youth—' He shakes his head with a grin '— totally wasted on them.'

'How far?'

'Fifteen minutes or so, the beach curves round. There's an underwater shelf out there, so they get better waves than here. You'll see a shack up in the dunes where they keep all their boards, but I'm sure you'll find some out in the water already. They live by the tides.'

Jaap thanks him and starts walking, leaving behind the victorious crab.

The sky's massive overhead, a few clouds relaxing in the blue expanse, just happy to be floating there, gazing down on the craziness below. Waves stroke the sand and the sun warms the right side of his face, and he finds it working on his body and mind, a temporary sense of respite.

A wave, not content with just working the sand, reaches for him with flecked foam, and he sidesteps further up the beach to avoid its touch. Disappointed, but no doubt willing to try for him again, the wave recedes, leaving dark sand behind it.

He stops, takes his shoes and socks off, and carries on walking just as an F-16 fighter jet storms out of the sky, right over his head, surely no more than five or so metres above him. His hands are over his ears but it's still deafening, the whole world suddenly vibrating. He turns to watch it head south, curving up and to the left in a fast, smooth arc.

He knew there was a military training ground on the southernmost tip of the island, a vast expanse of beach which tourists were strictly forbidden from entering. What he *didn't* know was that they flew the planes so goddamned low.

Once it's out of sight, his ears still ringing, he carries on walking and soon he can see them out on the water, sitting on their boards, rising and falling on the growing swell. Which is much bigger here, the fisherman was right on that.

He pauses and wipes all the sand he can off his feet before slipping on his socks and shoes. Properly shod, he watches as one of the surfers lies down and starts paddling, head swivelling over their shoulder to check the incoming wave, arms windmilling the water. It grows behind, from slight bulge to yawning mouth, and the figure springs up just as the wave breaks, a flurry of foamy white as the water peels over and splits. The surfer rides it in, all the way to the shallows, finally stepping off their board as the wave loses momentum, melting back into the sea as if nothing had happened.

Jaap calls out, but the wind stuffing the words back into his mouth, right down his throat. He thinks of the one-way valve.

Miraculously the figure hears and turns, putting a flat hand across their brow to block out the sun, which is cresting over the dunes behind him. He sees it's a woman, a girl really, and he waves her over.

She hesitates for a moment, glancing back out to her fellow surfers, then pulls her board round and walks out of the sea, a loop of cord attaching her ankle to the board dragging behind her. Blue stripes run down the arms and legs of her black wetsuit, and her hair, plastered back on her head, is long and probably blonde when dry.

'Heleen?' she asks, once Jaap has introduced himself and she's told him her name is Kitty Paumen.

'You knew her?'

'Hardly,' Kitty says. 'I'd met her a few times, seen her around here.'

'Surfing lessons?'

'I think Piet took her out a few days ago. He's just finishing up a lesson, want me to get him?'

'Yeah,' Jaap says, his phone starting up.

A male voice, thick with tar, introduces itself as Max's assistant.

'Tell me,' Jaap says.

'Yeah,' says the voice, then falls silent. Jaap wonders if their connection has broken.

'Yeah what?'

'Scopolamine. Her blood was damn-near saturated with the stuff.'

*

60

Boards lean up against the walls of the shack.

Jaap's on the wooden deck, the surface coarsened with sand, both wet and dry. An old brown dog lies wiry-haired by the door. It raises its head, decides Jaap's not the food-carrying type, and rests back down again. Piet shrugs out of the top half of his wetsuit, leaving two arms dangling down to the ground whilst he towels off his very short hair. His face and neck are tanned hard, but below the line of his wetsuit his skin is like milk.

'Seriously, she was a bit weird, you know?'

Jaap doesn't know. He asks for clarification.

'Just . . . I dunno. Not quite right. Too quiet, like she was holding something in.'

'Was she with anyone?'

'At the lesson? No. Just her.'

'Didn't we see her yesterday? Wasn't she with some-one?' Kitty says, stepping out of the hut having changed from her wetsuit into denim hot pants and bikini top. She obviously spends a bit of time trying to even out the dis-crepancy between neck and body colour that Piet has, but she's still two-tone. She puts her head to one side and wrings out her hair, a thick gush of water hitting the deck. Jaap thinks of a horse peeing.

'Someone?'

'Yeah,' Piet says, nodding his head slowly at first, then getting into it. 'Yeah, you're right. Just over there, she was walking with this guy I'd not seen before.'

'This was when?' Jaap asks.

'Yesterday, would have been about twelve, twelve-thirty.'

'You're sure?'

'The tides wait for no man,' Piet says, though Jaap can't

tell if he's being ironic, can't tell if he's just playing the part of a surfer dude or he really *is* a surfer dude. He decides it's probably a combination of both, like some New Age mantra, you become what you think. 'That's when the tide turns, waves flatten out for a few hours. Someone was screwing around with one of those remote-control flying things, we could hear it buzzing but couldn't see it.'

'That's when we saw her,' the girl says. 'When we were looking for the flying thing.'

Jaap pulls out Francesco Kamp's photo, the one he'd had pinned to the car's dash yesterday.

'This the guy?'

They both lean in to peer at it.

'Hard to tell, bit too far away,' she says.

'Any reasons it couldn't have been him?'

Piet and the girl confer with their eyes. The wind shifts direction.

The old dog sleep-barks once, then stretches out all four legs with a soft groan.

'No,' she eventually says. 'I guess not.'

8

'Here,' Arno says, handing him a sandwich.

Jaap decides Arno will go far. Assuming, that is, he keeps his horticultural hobby in check.

He holds his hand out, still staring through the window which looks across the car park to the cell block where he'd been due to spend the night. 'Thanks,' he says, turning his swivel chair. 'You know Piet, the surfer?'

'Went to school together,' Arno says. 'Same class. Nice guy, we used to surf together a bit.'

'Used?'

Arno grins, and takes a bite of his own sandwich. 'He had a thing for Kim.'

Jaap remembers his dream. He has to admit that Kim is pretty. As in, pretty hot.

Jaap thinks of Tanya, down in Rotterdam, with their baby growing inside her. He struggles to surf a personal wave of dizziness.

'What about the mainland?' he asks once it passes. 'Any CCTV from the ferry terminal?'

'It's on its way, and a passenger list.'

Jaap wants to see Kamp's name on there.

Then again, Jaap *doesn't* want to see Kamp's name on there.

In truth, Jaap can't figure out what he actually wants to see on that list because really there's no good outcome.

On the one hand, if it was Kamp then Heleen's death is on him. He should have stopped him sooner. If on the other – and this one's really not going down well either – if it wasn't Kamp, then just who the fuck was it? Who has somehow come up with a remarkably similar way of killing young women, using suffocation and scopolamine?

Not for the first time Jaap asks himself how that's even possible.

Kamp was a train driver, for fuck's sake. He had a young child, everything to live for, and yet he somehow managed to procure one of the world's most terrifying narcotics, and killed two, possibly three, women whilst they were under the influence of the same.

He just doesn't get it.

This isn't the kind of drug your local dealer gets you, not least because recreational use is anything but recreational. Jaap's even checked out the dark web, logged onto the most popular marketplaces for drugs, and found not a single listing, not a single seller who was offering the stuff.

And when he adds all that to Kamp's denial of the second killing yesterday, he's left with . . . well, Jaap doesn't know what he's left with.

'Any update on where she was staying, who she is?' Jaap asks Arno, suddenly aware he's been zoned out.

Somewhere behind him a phone tries to get some attention.

'That might be it,' Arno says as he goes to answer.

Jaap turns back to the desk, stares at the scribbles he'd put down on paper earlier, but they look foreign to him, like he'd written in another language. Then he remembers

64

he needs to check exactly how long the surveillance crew lost Kamp for yesterday. He needs to rule out that Kamp could have got to the island, killed Heleen, then got back to his house all in the time he'd been AWOL. He puts a call in to his station back in Amsterdam and requests the information. He's promised a call back.

Behind him he hears Arno asking questions, then listening to very long answers.

He starts unconsciously opening the sandwich, his hands on automatic, finding the edge of the wrapper with his fingers without looking at it and peeling it off the soggy bread. Then he stops and looks down.

It appears to be beef and mustard, but that's not the problem. The problem is the cling film reminds him of Dafne Koster's death, all those months ago.

And the fact that yesterday he caught her killer. But now . . .

'I didn't get anyone to spit in it,' says a voice Jaap recognizes as Stuppor's. 'Or maybe it's not fancy enough. Filling not organic and grass-fed enough? Not like the kind of stuff a high-flyer like you is used to getting down in Amsterdam.'

Jaap wraps the sandwich back up and places it on the desk. 'I may have got something,' he says, ignoring Stuppor's jibes. 'Want to hear it or not?'

'Let's talk in my office.'

Jaap follows him across the room and regrets his earlier barefoot walk in the sand. He'd obviously not managed to get all of it off, grains now flaying skin between his toes.

They enter Stuppor's office and Jaap is immediately disappointed.

Because the chair he'd dragged in yesterday is gone.

'So, let's have it,' Stuppor says, sitting behind his desk.

Jaap briefly explains what he's found out so far, and finishes with a request to get someone to look for anyone flying a drone in the area yesterday. 'They often film with those things, if so I'd like to see what's on there.'

'You think they got the murder happening?' Stuppor sounds incredulous, eyebrows riding high.

'I don't think anything,' Jaap says. He slips his right shoe and sock off and leans against the wall as he goes about emptying sand from them both, having to turn his sock inside out. He's only slightly embarrassed by the socks, they're actually a pair of Tanya's he'd found at the back of a drawer when he'd been searching for some clean ones of his own. They looked like they'd never been worn; the colour's not too bad, a kind of navy blue, but they have a little ring of pink and white flowers going round the top. Of course, when he'd pulled them on, he'd only had a vague notion of where Vlieland was, still less that he'd be on the island showing off his socks to a station chief. 'I'm investigating, which means I look at everything I can, anything which may give us a chance at—'

'Pretty slim chance,' Stuppor says.

'Well, if the ferries off the island had been stopped as soon as the murder was discovered then we might be having a different conversation,' Jaap says, putting his sock and shoe back on, then doing the same with the other foot. 'But they weren't, so we aren't.'

'Listen, you have—'

The door behind Jaap swings one-eighty and crashes into the wall.

'Found it,' Arno says, unable to hide the excitement in his voice. 'The house where Heleen was staying.'

'Take me there,' Jaap says, scrambling to get his shoe back on. He walks out of Stuppor's office without even glancing at him. Then he turns back.

'Whilst we're gone, get someone to put that chair back in here. Or better yet, do it yourself.'

9

Tanya Vandermark can't find anywhere to park.

And now her appointment's in less then seven minutes. She's been crawling round and round the car park for the last twenty at least, scanning for any sign that another car is leaving. And she's not the only one, she's part of a long line, a lazy snake of cars, each with a driver probably getting as worked up as her.

She wonders how many people die out here.

Maybe the hospital has a crew which runs through once a day, carting off those who don't make it to the large incinerator whose chimney towers over the complex. For all she knows it might have been planned this way, maybe car park fatalities don't count towards hospital statistics, so they can weed out the weakest ones before they even set foot in the hospital and mess with their numbers by dying inside.

Well, maybe.

The sun's out in force and the temperature's already hitting unbearable. Petrol fumes from the other cars aren't helping, she can see their distorting haze all around, making solid objects wobble gently. And to cap it all off, the air con in her car's not working.

She'd taken it to the garage last week, and they'd charged a full seventy-five to re-gas the thing. She sees now that she might as well have kept the money and fanned herself with it instead.

Checking the time on the dashboard she notices her appointment's now in six minutes.

When she'd first pulled in she'd been breezy about it, she'd find a space and she'd be on time, no problem. But now the digital display on her dashboard is gloating at her, each diminishing digit jacking up her stress levels, shallowing her breathing out. And her fingers – all except the two which don't work so well any more after the bullet had torn through the ligaments – are gripping the wheel like they're trying to snap it in two.

She consciously releases them, tries to breathe deeper. The fumes bite, she goes back to shallow breaths.

Five minutes now, which is just enough to get into the hospital and up to the third floor.

But only if she parks. Right. Now.

Four and a half minutes and she sees it. A car off to her left, reversing lights coming on. Even better, the red Lexus she's been following has just gone past it. The space is hers. She has to reverse a bit to let the car out, but just as she does the Lexus slams into reverse, sneaking into the spot with the kind of practised ease which shouldn't be allowed.

Tanya slams her hand on the horn, holding it there whilst a guy gets out, pretending not to notice.

She knows him.

Or at least, she knows his type. Late-fifties businessman who wants everyone to know how successful he is: designer jeans, open shirt with sleeves rolled up, and a watch the size of a sundial on his wrist. For a split second reality fragments and she actually believes it's her foster father, Ruud Staal, risen from the grave to punish her for his death.

A sharp stab of fear in her gut reconfigures reality.

And that just makes her angrier.

'Hey!' she yells, getting out of the car.

He looks up as if surprised, as if he's only just noticed her, as if he hadn't just swung back and, against the convention which keeps the world from descending into an all-out bloodbath, swiped someone else's parking space.

'Yeah?'

'That's my space.'

As the words are out of her mouth she can't quite believe it's come to this, standing here about to get into an argument over a rectangular piece of tarmac.

'Sorry,' he says, with a shrug which shows he's anything but.

For a moment she finds she's wishing he's ill. Terminally. Like in the next two minutes. *After* he's moved the car.

'Move it now,' she says, reaching into her pocket.

'Fiery redhead. I like that. So if I don't move it, you gonna slap me?'

His grin is pure cartoon, and he *does* look like her foster father. He really does. She has to fight down the panic as she pulls out her ID, steps forward and shoves it right in front of his face.

He glances at it for a few moments.

'You're not in uniform.'

'Undercover. We suspect one of the doctors who does the physical prostate examination of enjoying his job a little too much.'

'How did you—?' he says before catching himself.

Got you, thinks Tanya, as she smiles the smile of the innocent.

'I'll move it,' he finally says.

'Don't forget to rebook,' she calls out after him, waggling a finger when he looks at her. 'Next week should be safe.'

Once inside the hospital Tanya makes her way up to the waiting room, and even though she's a few minutes late the appointments are, thankfully, running even later. She's checked in by a Filipina nurse who speaks better Dutch than she does, and is directed to a row of plastic seats pinned to a steel bar running along a wall.

She sits – turns out the seats aren't that well attached as they move disconcertingly – and, now the focus of arriving on time is gone, tries not to think about the reason she's actually here.

Which is of course, like resistance, futile.

The pain started up a few hours ago, just a small tingle to begin with, but it had quickly grown into something which wasn't possible to ignore. Even so, she'd tried her best, told herself it was indigestion, nothing more. But in the semi-light, just as the birds were staging a dawn riot outside the window of her rented apartment on Peppelweg, it'd kept getting worse, expanding, nagging, demanding attention until it was the only thing she could think of.

Eventually, exhausted, she'd called the hospital.

The nurse she'd spoken to hadn't sounded concerned – though that was probably a result of her training – but had booked her in for an emergency scan, just in case.

She'd wanted to call Jaap, had even picked up the phone and tapped his name, wanting to hear his voice, to be reassured by him. But she knew it was just going to worry him, so she left it, hitting red before it even connected.

It's hard being down in Rotterdam, being split geographically from Jaap, but her posting is, in theory, only temporary. Once completed in the next month or so she should be free to go back.

That is unless Henk Smit, her boss, has other plans for her. She knows Smit and Jaap don't get on, and wonders if her secondment down here has anything to do with that.

'Tanya Vandermark?'

The voice jolts her out of her thoughts, and she's aware of the woman standing in front of her holding a medical chart and smiling an efficient smile.

'I . . . sorry, I was just thinking,' Tanya says as she gets up and follows the efficient smile down the corridor and into a room which smells of cleaning fluid and alcohol.

There are no windows, the only illumination coming from a single lightbox in one corner of the room.

They go through the usual questions then start the scan itself. She lies back and feels the ooze of cold gel and the sweep and slippery push of the ultrasound scanner.

As she's dressing the woman reviews the images, still efficient, but minus the smile.

'All OK?' she asks, noticing the slight pleading quality which her words have taken on as they expand out into the dead space of the room.

She gets no answer from the woman, but finds her phone is buzzing in her pocket. She pulls it out and sees it's Harry Borst. She answers, vaguely remembering something about not using mobiles in hospitals.

'Tanya, I need you here now, we've got a break and we're going to have to move fast.'

'I'll be there in twenty,' she says and hangs up.

'So?' she prompts the nurse, who is still staring at the screen.

'I'll have to get Dr Bruggen to look at them and give you a call.'

'Sure,' says Tanya, trying to ignore the freezing hand which has just gripped her throat, the whole room malevolent suddenly, all the soulless equipment there to work against her, cold hard machines devoid of emotion. 'When will I hear from him?'

'He's not in until the late shift,' the woman says. She turns to look at Tanya and the smile is back. It's more efficient than ever. It's now positively uber-efficient. 'But I'm sure you'll hear today.'

10

'Jesus,' Arno says. 'Really?'

They're in the car, heading to the address Arno found, and Jaap's just filled him in on his case, the two murders and Kamp's death yesterday.

'Yeah, I know. Thing is, he admitted to the first death, but then baulked at the second one. It's not like it would have made much difference to his sentence, so why deny it?'

'Unless he didn't do it, but then . . . fuck. There can't be two people running around doing the same kind of killing, can there?'

Something catches Jaap's eye out to sea. At first he thinks it's a bird but then he sees it's another fighter plane heading landwards. He shakes his head.

'I don't know. I can't decide what's worse.'

'Right,' says Arno. 'I mean, Jesus.'

The cottage itself is easy to spot when they turn up; it's the only one wrapped almost entirely in red-and-white crime-scene tape, round and round like the person doing it was trying to hide the house completely. It's one of fifteen, all identical, all laid out on a grid, and sits in a row of three which look out over the dunes to the sea beyond. A loose tape end flaps inland, powered by the sea breeze. The lone flapping somehow makes it feel desolate.

'Bit overkill, isn't it?' Jaap says as he turns off the ignition.

'The guys don't get to use this stuff much out here,' Arno says with a lopsided grin that reveals a chipped canine. 'Must've got carried away.'

They're at the front door when Jaap's phone goes off.

'Max, what've you got?'

'A winning personality and a bright future.'

'Besides that.'

'Actually, it's something you're gonna have to see for yourself.'

Jaap gets the address Max is at and hangs up.

They snap on gloves and search the cottage quickly, the air inside stale like it's been used too many times already. Jaap catches a trace of herbal-cheesy weed. For a moment he's worried it's on his own clothes.

Turns out the bedroom's where it's all at, a black zip-up suitcase on the floor half-filled with women's clothes, probably Heleen's given the size and styles. At the bottom Jaap finds a phone, all glass and metal. He tries to turn it on. It's dead. He bags it up, scans the rest of the room. The bed's a double and looks like it's been the scene of a pro-wrestling event, covers and pillows strewn all over.

He picks up a hair he finds on the sheet, just below one of the pillows. It's dark and curly. Kamp's name pops into his head, makes his heart beat a little faster.

'Pube?' Arno asks from the wardrobe.

'I'm not sure,' Jaap says, bagging it up as well.

They leave the house, next stop Max.

Turns out the only refrigerated place to store a body is a private funeral firm in Oost-Vlieland, the main – pretty much only – town on the island. Just as Arno's pulling into the car park Jaap's phone goes off again.

He sees the time just as he answers, knows what's coming. He had genuinely forgotten.

'Yeah?'

'Inspector Rykel, we're ready for you now. Are you in the building?'

'No.'

In Amsterdam, Laura Vetter pauses. 'We had agreed to meet to discuss the events surrounding Francesco Kamp's death. I believe we'd said ten a.m.?'

'Events have moved on, I'm going to have to give you a call.'

'Inspector, I realize that you're busy and this all seems to you like a pen-pushing exercise—'

'If you can read my mind so well then can't we just do this remotely, save me the time?'

'—but it's important that we get your story down, particularly given the accusations made against you by Station Chief Henk Smit. So I suggest—'

'OK, I got it. I'm about to see a dead body so I'll have to call you back later today to arrange a time.'

Jaap hangs up, the word 'accusations' leaving a nasty imprint on his mind. He doesn't know exactly what Smit's been saying, but he can make a pretty good guess.

Max is standing in the car park, just across from the drab building housing the funeral home. On the main road an old man creaks past on a bike, his straw hat held in place with a leather chin strap, eyes focused on the road even though it's empty.

They reach Max who seems lost in thought, staring out over the harbour below. The great evolutionary triumph

76

of opposable thumbs is being put to good use, a cigarette clasped tight.

'Need help?'

'Hey,' he says, turning to look at Jaap. 'Didn't get to chat last night, not seen you for a while.'

'Missed you. Moved out here?'

'Yeah, just over on the mainland. It was like I had to get out of Amsterdam, y'know?'

'But the bodies seem to be following you anyway.'

Max makes a *pfff* sound. 'The bodies don't bother me,' he says. He brings the cigarette to his lips and tries to suck all the air left in the world through it.

'Let me guess, the living do?'

A large hearse noses its way into the car park like a dark and shiny predator.

'Got it in one,' Max replies, voice tight from holding in all the smoke. 'And when you see what I've just seen, then I think you'll agree I'm pretty justified.'

As they head towards the building Arno, who, Jaap's noticed, has started to appear nervous, clears his throat.

'What's . . .' Arno says.

'Awww . . . first time?' Max says as if talking to a child. 'Do you want to hold my hand?'

'It's never easy,' Jaap replies, thumping Max on the arm. 'But you get used to it. And if you think you're going to throw up, don't try and tough it out, just get outside. Fast.'

As he's stepping inside his phone goes. He can see it's his station.

'Go on, I'll follow,' he says.

He answers and a desk sergeant tells him he's got the surveillance logs he'd requested. Jaap asks him to read them out, then email him. Once he's heard what he needs he hangs up, plays around with Google Maps on his phone and pulls up the ferry company's website.

Then he steps inside, knowing that in the time the surveillance team had lost sight of him, Kamp could conceivably have made it out to the island, killed Heleen, and got back home.

11

Kees steps out his front door, sits on the dusty step and takes a sip of the Coke he's just found in his hand. It's the real stuff, curved glass bottle with proper sugar in it, not the cans or plastic bottles junked up with high-something-or-other corn syrup. Yeah, sure, it'll make him fat and give him diabetes and leprosy, cause his hair to fall out, his penis to shrivel and, quite possibly, eat away at his brain. But what the hell. For some reason sugar and caffeine help with the pain and generally how shit he feels in the mornings. And lately, with his disease going the way it is, he needs all the help he can get, all the positive energy the world can muster if he's not to walk over to the road and throw himself in front of the next speeding vehicle.

Talking of energy, there's always the sun. But right now he's not experiencing it anywhere near as positive enough for his liking. It's bright, way too bright, and he's squinting so hard he wonders if his eyeballs will implode.

His hand forms the peak of a cap and his eyes relax a little. He glances across the patch of grass he's not cut since, well, since he moved in over a year ago. Doesn't even own a mower, in fact.

But who's complaining?

Most of the properties along the road are the same, junk piled high in one, the carcass of a rusting, cannibalized van in another.

He watches as the man opposite leaves his house and walks down the street in a full white gown. Kees knows there's a specific name for that, but he can't remember what it is. There's a lot of stuff he can't remember these days, though he *does* remember the specialist saying the drugs may cause some slight memory dysfunction.

He'd also said that Kees shouldn't worry.

Which, as is pretty much universally acknowledged, is *much* easier to say than do.

He doesn't know what the man in the white gown does for a living, but he clearly does something, because he appears to bring in enough to feed a family of at least six children. Kees wonders if there are a couple of wives tucked away in there somewhere as well.

His bike stands on the cracked concrete driveway, exactly where he'd left it last night. The custom paint job glitters in the sun. Faded patches of oil dot the concrete.

No one's going to steal one of these, the consequences would be too high, so he never needs to garage it or even chain it up.

Hell, he could probably leave the keys in the ignition if he wanted to.

The neighbourhood cat sits near the front wheel, tail curled round its front paws like a serene Buddha.

He takes another sip of Coke and thinks. About the panic attack he'd had the night before.

It had hit him the second he'd pulled up and turned the engine off, his hands shaking, his legs subjected to a private earthquake. He made it inside, but collapsed in the kitchen, the corner of the table having a go at his cheek on the way down.

He'd been lucky. He remembers the night he found Tanya standing over the man's body, in shock at what had happened, how he'd died from catching his head on a table corner too.

He reaches up and feels it, the scab formed already. The urge to pick at an edge and pull it off nags at him.

The panic attacks had started a few months ago, and he'd assumed it had something to do with his illness.

Maybe not, he thinks now. Maybe it's to do with my lifestyle.

Always wondering, always looking over my shoulder.

Because he's feeling the pressure, like something's trying to crush his head the whole time.

It's at its worst when he's with Van der Pol. He's started having nightmares that the man can see right through him, see what he really is. And the consequences of that are not worth thinking about. If Van der Pol had even an inkling that Kees was working undercover the retribution would be swift and brutal. Actually, he thinks, it probably wouldn't be swift, it'd be drawn out, designed to cause maximum pain.

A couple of kids cruise by on skateboards, one of them with a grazed arm, a rash of grit still embedded under the skin. He watches them head down the street, their youthful energy, the knowledge that all is right with the world and that they'll never have to grow up positively reeking from them.

Kees suddenly feels old. And he's only just coming up to thirty-five.

Maybe today's the day, he thinks, taking a sip and, not finding it satisfying, switching over to gulps. Maybe this is it.

*

He spends twenty minutes or so looking for his keys, only to discover that he *had* in fact left them in the ignition. Now riding out, the vibration of the motor tremoring through his body in an almost therapeutic way, he starts to feel a little better.

He's cruising past fields, a tiny dot in a flat landscape under a vast sky.

White clouds billow in the blue and he's the only one on the road. For a second he gets the weirdest out-of-body sensation, like he can see himself from above.

He pulls into the petrol station, an old concrete block with a small shop inside and only two pumps, diesel or unleaded. It's one of the few places left in the area which has a payphone, a box attached to the wall round the side of the building, right next to the toilet door. The machine guzzles the couple of euros he feeds it and he punches out a number. It goes straight to voicemail, as it always does. There's no message, just a short beep telling Kees when to speak.

'We need to talk,' he says, his voice rising, speeding up till his lips trip over the words. 'We need to talk right now.'

He slams the phone down, turns and leans against the wall, which appears to be the only thing in the world not currently spinning. He bends forward from the waist, tries to catch his breath. There seems to be air all around, he just can't get any of it.

The spinning gradually slows, and when he feels safe, he straightens up and fumbles out a cigarette. Finally he gets it lit. But the second the smoke hits his lungs he feels sick all over again and tosses it onto the ground. He watches it roll in a loose circle on the concrete, the tip smouldering.

'Hey,' a voice jabs at him, 'are you trying to blow us all up?'

Kees looks at the man who'd stepped out of the shop, presumably heading for the toilet. He's from Bangladesh or somewhere, his face showing a kind of hurt anger. His green and yellow T-shirt has a round logo of a large oil corporation splattered on the fabric. Given its position it looks like a diseased nipple.

The guy's obviously new. No one talks like that to one of the crew.

Because there's such a thing as consequences.

'Word of advice,' Kees says. 'You see that symbol on my bike over there?' He points to the pair of wings flanking a human skull. 'That means you shut the fuck up. For your own safety.'

Van der Pol's base is a legit business just outside of Eindhoven, a haulage company which he never uses for anything illegal at all. The books are all in order, the drivers never drive a second over whatever the EU regulations stipulate, and if you're looking for a firm to transport your contraband around then you'd just better look elsewhere.

Van der Pol often jokes that it's the only logistics company in the country *not* moving stuff they shouldn't be.

In general, Kees doesn't like it when Van der Pol jokes. It creeps him out. In fact, there's something about the man Kees finds downright disturbing. Something aside from the fact he's singly responsible for a gang which now operates a large part of the criminal enterprise in the

Netherlands and beyond. That he imports women for the sex trade, and probably whole hosts of stuff Kees isn't high up enough to know about, only adds to his unease.

The main offices, the official ones, are in a block at the back of the lot, but the shipping container, plonked on the tarmac along with a few others, is where the real business goes down. Kees steps up to the container. Cort is leaning against it mulling over a thorny problem in his self-funded PhD study on gravitational waves and their effects on dark energy. Either that or he's working out just how he'll eventually kick the living shit out of Kees.

If Cort was a dog, it would almost be admirable. As Cort is a man, at least of sorts, Kees finds his devotion to Van der Pol bordering on the psychopathic.

'You're late,' he says when Kees is close enough.

'Yeah, your mum says hi.'

Kees had found himself slipping into the speech patterns and predictable insults that abound in Van der Pol's crew with alarming ease.

Cort gives back some response which undoubtedly has to do with something shoved in an orifice of Kees' non-existent sister, only Kees can't be fucked to listen to it. Pleasantries over, Cort swings open the door and points him in.

The door clangs shut behind him and Kees can see Van der Pol isn't alone. He has Dirk Rutte with him. Dirk Rutte's fairly high in Van der Pol's pecking order. They're sitting facing each other at a Formica-topped desk, and Kees steps closer. It's only then that he realizes Dirk's in trouble.

Van der Pol is holding his hand and manoeuvring a

pair of secateurs onto Dirk's first finger. They're nice secateurs, the type those freaks who are into roses have, carved wooden handles and steel blades which, though worn, have been looked after. Dirk's trying to tough it out, but he's starting to tremble. Two men are standing by, just in case Dirk decides he'd rather not comply.

Van der Pol gets the blades round Dirk's finger, his actions smooth, unhurried, as if he were arranging a flower display at the local church, mulling over the perfect cut angle.

'Please, no,' Dirk whispers.

Van der Pol shushes him, then, with Dirk's finger still caught between the blades, looks up at Kees, catches him studying him.

Van der Pol's shorter than Kees, and whilst many, if not most, of his crew indulge in all the illicit world has to offer, Van der Pol is lean and clean, his eyes never shrouded with alcohol or drugs.

Which, considering some of the stuff Kees has heard about him, and seen him do first hand, means he has to be just about the most coldhearted motherfucker in Europe.

'So what happened?' Van der Pol says to Kees, ignoring Dirk for the moment.

Van der Pol does what he does for two reasons that Kees can see. One is to keep the empire he's built at the top. The other is because he flat-out enjoys it. Enjoys the beatings meted out by people like Kees and Bart. On more than one occasion Kees has been asked to film Bart going to work on someone so Van der Pol could watch it later.

So Kees tells him what happened, not leaving out a

single detail, knowing that Van der Pol will push him harder if he suspects he's holding anything back.

'Really?' Van der Pol says, laughing when Kees has finished. 'His head exploded?'

His two goons are laughing as well, and eventually Dirk joins in.

Kees is feeling that weird pressure again, his scalp tingling, shrinking. 'Yeah, it was . . .' Kees can't think.

'Wish I'd seen it,' Van der Pol says, still laughing, though his eyes remain cold.

The goons, of course, are finding this shit *hilarious*.

'Right,' Van der Pol says two seconds later, having killed his own laughter as if it'd never been there. 'Bart was on a job tonight, so you'll have to do it instead, seeing as he's indisposed.'

Deep in Kees' brain Bart's head explodes for the millionth time.

'The thing is . . .' Kees says, trying to shake the image and thinking of the message he'd left, wondering when he'll get a response.

'You'll have to do it,' Van der Pol says. 'And it's a big one, so don't fuck up. Like Dirk here did.'

Van der Pol stares at Dirk for a few more moments, then pulls back the secateurs, leaving Dirk's finger free. He smiles at Dirk, who breathes out. The room mellows.

Van der Pol takes a moment, then leans across the desk and stabs Dirk in the throat.

As Kees leaves on his bike the scream is still ringing in his ears.

12

'Got a charger for this?'

Jaap shows him the bagged phone he picked up at Heleen's rental. Max takes a look.

'Ancient. Luckily so's mine.'

He rifles through his kit bag, pulls out a lead and hands it over. Jaap hooks it up and plugs it in. The phone buzzes with pleasure as current surges through its innards.

'Also this, can you get it to the mainland lab and DNA'd?'

'Oh man, a pube?'

He takes it anyway.

'Ready?' he says after he's catalogued it.

They're in a small room at the back of the building, the air clinically cold and the lighting even worse. On a table lies Heleen's body, and all three step up to it.

Max leans forward, gloved fingers exploring Heleen's head like scuttling albino spiders.

The spiders find the edge of the tape and start unwrapping it. Max has to lift her head gently to assist them. The tape unspools, a soft noise just audible above the quiet hum of refrigeration, the lowest layer pulling the skin up before finally parting from it. Once it's all off Jaap steps closer and looks at her face.

The skin that was under the tape, across her nose and mouth, is wrinkled, like she's spent too long in water, and it makes her look freakishly old. Or like one of those acid-attack victims who sometimes pop up on the news.

'Nowhere for the perspiration to go,' Max says, dropping the dangling tape into a waiting evidence bag.

Then Max goes in for the tube, which is still in Heleen's mouth. He works it loose, knocking it against one of her teeth on the way out, and holds it up for Jaap to see. It's about fifteen centimetres long and made of white plastic.

Max inspects it. 'Hey, I was right. It's a one-way valve, hospitals use them all the time.'

'What for?' Arno asks.

Jaap wonders if he's doing it just to prove he's OK, because frankly his voice sounds a little shaky.

'Anytime you want the patient to breathe into something you can use one of these. Air goes through but won't come back out, means infections don't spread.'

'So whoever did this has a medical connection, or can you just buy these things?' Jaap asks, peering at it, trying to make sense of the whole thing.

'You can get anything on the internet, I'm sure you can buy these too. Wanna try?'

Max puts down the valve, switches gloves, and then rummages around in his bag. He tosses a small pack right over Heleen's body. Jaap catches it. It's an identical-looking valve in a sterile wrapper.

'Go on, it's a blast,' Max says.

Jaap rips it open and inspects it. Then he puts it in his mouth and tries to breathe. Like Max says, breathing out is fine, but in is another matter. If he really tries he can suck a small amount of air in. He stops, his head already spinning.

'So you can get a little bit through, but it's not enough to keep you alive indefinitely. And if she'd been running, well, that would simply have jacked her need for oxygen up even higher.'

'How long from insertion?'

'You'd have to get someone to run some tests, but I'm guessing it'll have been hard to survive with one of those strapped across your mouth for more than ten minutes or so.'

Ten minutes. Not long at all in the greater scheme of things.

But a hell of a long time to know you're going to die.

'So what did you want to show me?' Jaap says, putting the valve down, suddenly not wanting it anywhere near him.

'Yeah, there *is* something. But first the other stuff. Her wrists had been tied.' He picks up an arm to show a thin line of bruising. 'The usual plastic tie, given the diameter of the marks, so no useful bits of fibre to help you.'

Jaap nods. Whilst it's important to get these details, in his experience they are often overrated; the main way to find a killer is to find out *why*, not the minutiae of how. The whole CSI thing? thinks Jaap. *Way* overrated.

'Also, there's no sign of recent sexual activity.'

'Anything else before you tell me about whatever got you all worked up?' Jaap asks, knowing that none of this was really why Max had called him.

'Man, you're impatient, anyone ever tell you that?'

'It's been mentioned before. Just get on with it.'

'I noticed this last night, it was hard to tell under torchlight but I had a look just before you got here and . . .'

He eases up the victim's pink T-shirt, the waving kitten bunching up until it's unrecognizable.

The whole room sucks in a breath.

Jaap's finding *he* can't breathe now. He stares at the exposed midriff.

Lines run across her belly, a criss-cross of old scars and one fresher cut. He tries to count but keeps losing track. There are so many.

For a moment he feels like reaching out and running his finger over the scars, like it's a kind of Braille which will reveal what he wants to know.

'I've seen this before,' Max says. 'Self-mutilation. There are whole forums on the internet for people who do this, they even post photos to egg each other on.'

Liquid suddenly gushes against a hard surface in the corner of the room.

'I'm not clearing that up,' Max says, eyes flicking over to where Arno's bent double, still heaving.

13

Even before she gets to the conference room she can feel the buzz.

Tanya checks her phone one last time. It seems she's been checking it every minute or so, but there's still nothing from the hospital. She keeps feeling it vibrate in her pocket but when she pulls it out there's no call or message. Reluctantly she puts it away again and steps into the room.

It's on the fifth floor of a building overlooking a particularly industrial part of the Rotterdam ports. Out the window she can see numerous piers jutting off a central spine, each loaded with an ever-changing array of shipping containers; today for some reason they're all Maersk. The room has been refurbished in the last six months. Tanya doesn't know what it was like before, but now it's all glass, stainless steel and white paint. There's even wood-effect flooring, only given away by the fact you can see the pattern repeating, and the way it gives slightly underfoot.

It's standing room only. Tanya squeezes past several cops she doesn't know and leans against the wall at the back. There isn't just excitement in the air, there's a heavy, woody aftershave, like someone's bathed in the stuff. It's so strong Tanya finds her eyes watering.

At the far end of the room there's a large map of

Rotterdam and she looks at it, tracing her morning route in. Her place on Peppelweg looks out onto Meidoornweide Park, a flat area usually full of people jogging in the mistaken belief that strenuous, monotonous exercise is actually good for them. She's sat on her balcony a few nights and watched them go round and round. But she's enjoyed it, being up high on the third floor.

Not that that's really high, but back in Amsterdam she lives with Jaap on his houseboat, which has a permanent mooring on one of the city's prettiest canals. And Amsterdam, at least the centre, *is* pretty. All those old houses nestled close, the sinuous whale-back bridges and the lime trees dappling the canal waters with shadow. The glories of the Golden Age, museums, small cafés and brick-lined streets . . . the whole place is almost too chocolate box.

Rotterdam on the other hand is a city which commissioned a massive bronze statue of Santa Claus holding aloft an enormous butt plug, and what's more is actually *proud* to display the thing in public.

Which, thinks Tanya, tells you all you need to know.

But she's got used to it, and has grown slightly fond of the place. Rotterdam has no pretensions, and she admires that.

A few more stragglers make their apologetic way in, and a man stands up.

He's Station Chief Derek Huisman, and he's big. That's to say he's big physically – the Dutch hammer back so much dairy that they're now officially the Tallest Nation in the World, not bad for a race which only a few generations back were, by all accounts, rather small swamp dwellers – and big in terms of reputation. Back in the day, Huisman was military, serving in Kosovo, and had come back after a lengthy tour to receive the Bronzen Leeuw medal. Unfortunately for him, the day it was presented was the same day that Dutch troops in Srebrenica looked the other way as Ratko Mladić started up his massacre, and for some reason the two news stories got entangled, one tabloid in particular holding him personally responsible. He'd got his lawyers to issue a statement, but then decided that suing for damages wasn't fitting and retired from the military. Six months later he turned up in Rotterdam, and had been at the helm every since.

He doesn't look ex-military to Tanya. For one he has cheekbones a wannabe supermodel would claw someone's eyes out for, but which on him look odd. His limbs don't have that military pump either, but then he probably doesn't see the need to work out these days. He is liked by his staff though, something which Tanya's own boss, Henk Smit, mostly isn't.

'OK,' he says once the room's excitement has come down to a simmer. 'Operation Leda.'

This is the reason Tanya's down in Rotterdam. When she'd been assigned she'd looked up what Leda meant and was surprised to find she was a Greek who'd been raped by a swan who then turned out to be Zeus. She'd no idea what that was supposed to mean, other than possibly that Greek civilization had pre-empted the Netherlands' stance on drugs by many hundreds of years. Or it's simply some sick wish-fulfilment of whoever came up with the story in the first place.

'As most of you know, Borst and his team have been working on this for months and today we've got a bit of interesting news. Harry?'

Harry, who'd been sitting close, takes over.

Tanya's been reporting directly to him, which has made her uncomfortable. She has to admit, she finds him attractive. What makes it worse is that she's pretty sure Harry feels the same. As in, he finds *her* attractive, not himself. Though there is a touch of arrogance about him, so he probably does find himself just a teeny bit attractive as well.

Harry pulls out a large photo and pins it up on the wall behind him.

'Most of you know this man,' he says, eyes roving the room. 'Van der Pol, probably the biggest piece of shit in the country. For anyone who's been living in a cave, Van der Pol controls a massive operation which goes from drugs, extortion, right up to the sex trade and more. Basically, if it's illegal and nasty, he's in it. He's also got to be one of the most careful criminals we've ever dealt with, we've never had anything concrete enough on him to even bring him in for questioning. But all that's about to change.'

He does the whole dramatic-pause thing, stretching it out as much as he can.

'Because three hours ago an informant gave us the time and place of a major transaction. If the info is correct then we're talking the biggest drugs haul in the Netherlands' history. And it's all going down tomorrow night. Whatever plans you had are now cancelled. Parents' evening, your flower-arranging class or your Monday-

94

night bondage club . . .' He pauses to make sure he's got their attention. 'It's cancelled.'

He walks to the map.

'The whole thing is due to take place here—' He points to a spot north-east of the city, necks crane to see '—and we think we've got a tactical advantage. So over the next twenty-four hours we're going to be planning this out in detail. We'll meet back here first thing tomorrow, but I'll probably be speaking to many of you individually today as the plans progress. Questions?'

Tanya's starting to find the aftershave suffocating. The few questions raised are dealt with quickly, and Huisman takes over for a final word.

He stands tall, sweeps his eyes around, and says: 'Go get the fucker.'

It's a kind of ritual. At first Tanya had thought it silly, but it clearly works as Huisman runs a great station and Smit doesn't. Smit would never think of having a running joke with anyone.

'And for God's sake,' he adds, 'whoever drowned themselves in aftershave needs to go clean themselves up.'

Laughter breaks the meeting up, the energy high, everyone excited but trying to appear professional and jaded at the same time. Most of them don't manage it.

Tanya knows this will be big. If they pull it off. A few careers could get a major boost. She suspects there'll be a fair amount of jockeying for position, everyone's going to want to be on the ground crew tomorrow night.

But for her the news is exciting for another reason: if this case gets done then she'll be free to head back to Amsterdam.

And Jaap.

She checks her phone, only to see she has a voicemail.

Her fingers tremble slightly as she hits play and holds the phone to her ear.

A voice bursts into life.

'Our records indicate you may be due compensation for your accident. Please call us now—'

14

Heleen's dancing on a beach, her arms above her like she's reaching for the stars, her whole body swaying in a fiercely loose rhythm. There are other people too, all moving, dancing, surrendering to the moment like there's really nothing else, like the world's an illusion so the only thing to do is go for pleasure.

But the camera's not interested in them, the camera stays on Heleen, a greedy lens which can't get enough.

'You recognize the beach?'

Arno nods. After the funeral home they'd stopped off at a store and Arno had dashed in for a bottle of mouthwash. Jaap had watched whilst he'd swigged, swished and spat onto the sandy verge.

'Yeah,' Arno says, and Jaap can smell the minty alcohol. 'It's on the north-western coast, party central.'

From the booking forms submitted to the cottage rental agency they'd got her surname, Elders, and they've spent the last hour or so digging furiously.

Heleen Elders was twenty-three when she died, and was on holiday from her job as a check-out girl at the Albert Heijn supermarket chain. On the face of it she had no connection to either of the previous two victims. She rented a small flat in Hilversum, where she lived alone. Both her parents had died when she was fourteen in a senseless car accident. None of this told them much; they were still trying to find a next of kin, but it was her Facebook account which opened things up a bit. She'd posted the video there herself yesterday morning, with no comments, just a smiley.

'You know what the question is, right?'

'Who filmed her. I'll get on it.'

Jaap plays the video again. There's no sound for some reason, and it's weird seeing people dance without the music. But maybe that's better, allows him to concentrate, search for any hint that the girl enjoying herself, enjoying the freedom of movement, of being outdoors with people engaged in the same activity as her, also enjoyed closing the bedroom door on the world and slicing open the skin on her belly with a sharp knife.

Max had said he'd seen such things before, and had explained the possible routes to it. One is deep-set stress. The world's a scary place, constantly changing, events outside of your control continually rushing at you, throwing you off balance, taking away your power. The only way to reclaim it is to be able to grab back some of that control, and by taking a blade and parting your own flesh, you regain some semblance of being the one in charge.

Why? Because you decide when it happens, and when it stops.

In this case, Max had said, the pain is incidental, though through repetition you can become classically conditioned so that the feeling of intense pain is linked with the relief of gaining back control; pretty soon you crave not just the sense of power, but the sting of the knife as well.

The second route could be numbness, a lack of feeling which in extreme cases gets classed as anhedonia. For the person who doesn't feel much, the pain can be a welcome reminder that you are, in fact, alive.

Jaap had asked Max how he knew so much. Max had blustered a bit and muttered something about his medical training. Jaap left it at that.

She doesn't look like she's the anhedonia type, at least from the video. There's a grace and intensity to her movements which, to his eyes, make it look like she's feeling the pleasure of dance. He presses pause and stares at the smiley, the last trace that she left of herself on social media, her parting shot to the world.

Cyberspace is filled with the traces of dead people, he realizes. The internet is a vast network of the living and the dead. For some reason he finds the thought makes him uneasy.

He switches view, going through Heleen's friends, which on a quick estimate must run well into the hundreds. A small amount nowadays, but not really a sign that she was some kind of loner who stayed at home with sharp objects for company.

But he's not naive enough to think people don't hide things.

Francesco Kamp, for example.

On the face of it he was just a normal guy going about his business. He had a wife, they were married six years ago in a ceremony in a church in Leiden and last year she gave birth to a baby boy. The birth had been difficult, his wife had died and the baby had spent the first eight weeks in an incubator, cut off from the world while the doctors waited to see if the complex systems of life would win through. Kamp had taken time off his work as a train driver, made the hospital his home, until it was clear their baby would be fine.

So maybe he wasn't just a regular guy, maybe losing his wife had reconfigured something, or maybe unleashed a latent sickness within.

Jaap shakes his head at the unknowability of others.

He's just about to power the computer off when Heleen's phone buzzes softly on his desk, Max's charger having done its job.

Jaap picks it up, takes a brief run through what's there. All the usual apps, emails, several games. Then, swiping onto the third screen, he notices the WhatsApp icon showing an unread message. He opens it up, noting the time as yesterday morning. His eyes fall on the text of the message itself, held in a cartoon speech bubble:

I CAN'T W8 2 CUT U

15

It's like some Zen koan, Jaap thinks.

If you're asking someone else to do it, is it still self-mutilation?

He's in the Vlieland station car park, sitting on a low concrete wall, throwing stones at a crushed Coke can. So far he's not hit it once.

Seeing the message on WhatsApp had thrown him an unexpected line of enquiry, one which he'd turned over to Roemers, head of the Digital Crimes Unit in Amsterdam. Roemers, famous for his bad taste in music, had a redeeming feature, an almost supernatural understanding of, and skill with, technology. Jaap hopes that understanding and skill will bring him a name.

The name of whoever likes cutting young women's flesh.

A patrol car turns into the car park. For a moment Jaap's afraid it's going to hit the can and deprive him of his target. But the driver, a uniform he's not been introduced to, manages to avoid it.

Jaap throws another stone; it bounces just to the left of the can, missing by a centimetre or so.

Damn.

Jaap's somehow convinced himself that if he does manage to hit it everything will work out. He's on his last stone, more a bit of grit really. He tries again. This time he's out by more like ten centimetres.

Fuck it, he thinks.

He bends forward, gathers a load more stones. The sniper approach didn't work, so now he's going for the sawn-off strategy.

'Your guy just called.'

Jaap turns to see Arno walking towards him.

'What he get?'

'A name, and an address.'

'Kamp?'

'No. A Daan Brouwer. He owns a house on the island.'

Jaap throws the full handful.

'I can't believe it,' he says once the stones have settled. 'Did you see that?'

'Weird, it's like it's got a force field around it or something.'

Jaap shakes his head. 'All right, let's go.'

A few minutes later Arno's proving men can multitask, flooring it down the east-coast road *and* filling Jaap in on Daan Brouwer. Though there's not much to tell.

'Born 1971, moved here about ten years ago according to the land registry, and nobody I've asked about him knows much. Keeps himself to himself apparently.'

'So you're saying, mid-forties male, lives by himself?'

'Looks that way. Classic weirdo material if you ask me.'

The road dives into an oak wood, serrated leaves like a jumbled-up jigsaw you could never hope to finish.

Arno reaches out and clicks the radio on.

'Figured I'd see what the press are up to,' he says.

It's a local station, broadcasting out of a building just north of the harbour in Oost-Vlieland. Guitars twang under a male voice which sounds like impending throat cancer. When the song ends the DJ switches up and spins on an English punk, singing about a girl called Amy who worked in a bar in Exeter.

'Love this song.'

Jaap doesn't know what it is, but he's finding being in different surroundings is changing his perception of things. The song wouldn't normally even feature on his radar, but out here on the island, he sort of agrees with Arno.

The song finishes and the news comes on. Arno cranks it up and they both listen to the reporter giving a brief overview of Heleen's death.

When it's finished Jaap clicks the radio off.

'They've not got any real details,' Arno says. 'They don't seem to have linked it with the other killings.'

'Won't be long now,' Jaap says. 'Someone always leaks.'

They leave the trees behind them and a few minutes later they reach the house.

'So, what's the plan?' Arno asks as he parks.

16

The plan.

Like all the best is simple: walk in and talk to him.

But it's foiled by one basic fact. Daan Brouwer's not home. Or if he is he's seen them coming and isn't answering. Arno's fingering the brass nipple but it's not yielding much in the way of door-opening action.

Arno relaxes his finger, looks round.

'Break it down?' he asks.

'Sure,' Jaap says. 'But let's see if it's open first.' He tosses over a pair of gloves he'd taken from Max earlier.

Arno pulls them on and tries the door handle. It turns.

'Experience, huh?'

'I had a colleague once, good cop but he had some problems, one of which was he loved to smash things. He'd never check a door, he'd just knock it down. Got to the point that if he was assigned to a case, whoever was in charge budgeted some extra for breakages.'

'Did he ever stop?'

Jaap thinks of Kees. He usually tries his best not to, a whole world of sadness there he doesn't quite understand.

'Last I heard he was in prison.'

'For knocking doors down?'

'No,' Jaap says as he steps through the door and into the house. 'Well, maybe. Just not the right ones.'

They check the house, moving from room to room,

but it's clear Brouwer's not home. As they start going over the place several more things becoming apparent: Brouwer lives alone, likes boats – he has at least ten painstakingly built models, impressive in their detail, complicated rigging like spiderswebs – and doesn't go in much for cleaning; the place is full of sand, blown in from the front door, which he must leave open on hot days.

In the kitchen, a large room to the back of the property, Jaap pokes around, finding in the sink a bowl, the bottom smeared with a milky residue. Dotted round the rim are what appear to be bloated flies, though when he gets closer he can see they're individual grains of a chocolate-flavoured rice cereal.

A glass stands by the sink. Jaap probes the inside with a gloved finger. The orange juice residue is tacky, not fresh.

None of which goes any way to answering the questions they've come to have answered.

But as they step into the room tucked in the eaves on the first floor, Jaap's hopeful that they might start getting somewhere. There's a desk, dark walnut top, with a wireless track-pad and keyboard, and a real wireless. A mug with the red and white livery of Ajax football club sits next to it. Above the desk, attached to the wall and angled into a broken curve, are three screens.

Arno finds the tower under the desk and presses a button. The screens load fast, the computer way more powerful than anything Jaap gets to use at the station, and Arno starts nosing around, clicking through folders, delving deeper and deeper into the beast.

Jaap walks to the west-facing window. From this

elevation he can see past the grasslands to the beach and sea beyond. Heleen's body was found not far from here. He reckons about fifteen on a bike. Twenty tops.

'He's a trader,' Arno says. 'That's why he doesn't appear to have a job. Just sits here and plays the markets.'

Jaap walks over, peers at the screens, which now show some kind of trading platform but with an error message saying NO FEED.

'Does he have WhatsApp?'

'Can't tell. Internet's not working, that's why I'm getting this No Feed bollocks,' Arno says. 'The router's on, but the computer just isn't picking it up. I kept getting the same thing at home, drove me crazy.'

'How did you fix it?'

'Honestly? I didn't. Kim did.'

'Get her on the phone,' Jaap says.

Arno checks the time. 'Might just catch her before she goes out.'

He gets Kim on the line and she starts talking him through whatever hoops he's going to have to jump through just to make a bit of technology, which has been designed to make people's lives easier, work.

Jaap leaves him to it. He wanders through the house, taking another look at the boats, realizing that Brouwer probably made them himself. One in particular catches his eyes, different from the rest, with three masts and red sails. The wood has been varnished to look old, and there is no dust on deck. Not a single speck.

Back in the kitchen he starts going through the drawers, thinking about Heleen, about the message she'd received. Skin on his arm goose pimples up.

He's just closing the third drawer down when he stops and pulls it open again. Right at the back, hidden under a bunch of wooden spoons stained with use, is a handle made of dull metal, two bits of wood riveted on each side. He pulls his phone out, snaps photos from several angles.

Because he knows what he's just found.

He takes it out carefully. It's an old-fashioned cut-throat, the type you see in films when a director wants to add a touch of cheap tension, the blade scraping up a man's neck, clearing off a frosting of white shaving foam. Will it, won't it?

Jaap opens it up, the action heavy but smooth, like it's been used regularly. He inspects the metal, holding it up into a jet of sunlight he finds near the window, tilting the blade back and forth so it winks on and off.

It's clean to the eye, no blood residue.

Which doesn't mean much.

The sheer amount of cuts on Heleen's stomach had been staggering, and had been done over a period of time. The knife would have been cleaned off properly after each session. He bags it up, places it on the kitchen table, and puts a call into Stuppor, telling him to put out an alert to the ferry company.

It's a long shot; Brouwer could have been gone for hours, right after breakfast, and there'd probably been three or four ferries since then, but Jaap's not going to make the same mistakes Stuppor has.

'Got it,' calls Arno from upstairs just as he hangs up.

Jaap's heart is racing when he reaches the top of the stairs and steps into the room.

They open WhatsApp.

Sure enough, the message is there.

Jaap leans forward, puts his hands on the desk, moving the mug out of the way.

It's warm.

Warmer than ambient.

He reaches out and clicks on the radio. The name of a station scrolls across a small screen and a pounding beat fills the room.

'Same one?' Jaap points to the station name.

'The only one,' Arno says.

Jaap swears. Brouwer was at his desk listening to the radio, and heard the same newsflash they had.

They've missed him by a matter of minutes.

17

'So how long are you going to be there?'

Tanya's on the phone, and her retinas are burning up.

Jaap called her whilst she was in the office, and, not wanting to have a conversation with a bunch of cops eavesdropping, she sought some privacy outside.

Where the sun is, hence the retinal damage.

'Not sure,' Jaap replies. 'Won't be that long if the station chief here has anything to do with it.'

'Doesn't like you?'

'Understatement, Station Chief Stuppor's a solid gold—'

'Stuppor? Wieland Stuppor?'

'Uh . . . yeah. You know him?'

'He was my boss at Leeuwarden. He's . . . well, you obviously met him. I think he had a thing for me but didn't know how to show it. You remember that first case we worked on together when he came down and tried to take me back up as he hadn't given me permission?'

'He's the one you cuffed and left in the snow?'

Tanya thinks back to that. Not her finest hour. But it *had* saved lives.

'The very same. Send him my love.'

'I'll drop it into the conversation later. It'll be fun.'

Hearing that name again reminds her of her years spent up north, when she was trying to make inspector. Those years are like a dream to her now, she was someone else back then, lost and scared. Scarred too.

Because of what Ruud Staal had done to her.

But she doesn't want to think of the past now; she wants to think of the future.

A pang in her stomach reminds her she's still not heard back from the hospital.

And that she's not told Jaap about her visit earlier this morning.

'You still there?'

'Yeah, I'm here,' she says.

'I think we should come up to the islands sometime, once the baby's born and settled in.'

'I'd like that,' she says, trying not to think of the hospital. 'Yeah, let's do that. Listen, I . . .' she says before something chokes her voice off.

Just tell him, she says to herself.

'Yeah?'

Do it. Do it.

'Nothing, just I miss you.'

'Miss you too.'

I should have told him, she thinks a few minutes later as she's walking away from the police building.

Her phone buzzes and she checks the screen, thinking it's Jaap calling her back. Like he'd been able to tell there was something wrong and he's calling to find out what.

But it's Harry Borst.

'Turn round,' Harry says.

Tanya turns.

'Look up.'

She looks up the police building, instinctively going to where Harry's office is on the third floor.

'Higher.'

Then she sees him, standing right on the edge of the roof.

'What's up?' she asks when she's made it up there.

The roof's flat, and the view out over the harbour is impressive, if not exactly beautiful. She can just see the top of the butt plug, glinting merrily in the sun.

'Real operation's on tonight, and I need you in the team.'

Tanya eyes him up. 'So all that stuff about tomorrow?'

'Bit of a diversion,' he says. Something must have flown into his throat as he coughs a little.

'You've got a leak,' Tanya says.

'Maybe,' he shrugs. 'Maybe not. Maybe fuck yourself.'

'Good film,' Tanya says. 'I prefer the two it was based on though.'

Harry laughs. 'You know, you're the first person to get that reference. I've been using it for years and I think everyone so far just assumes I'm being an asshole.'

'Surely not.'

'Yeah, hard to believe.'

He turns to look out across the harbour. A large crane plucks shipping containers off the quay and places them onto the deck of a waiting ship with a kind of balletic delicacy.

'So . . . I've got a small team working tonight, all people I completely trust.'

'How come?'

'How come what?'

'You trust them all.'

'I've borrowed them from stations all over, they don't know anything about the operation. As far as they're all aware it's a training exercise they've been specially selected for.'

'I got a call the other day,' Tanya says. 'They said I'd been *specially selected* for the opportunity to invest in some luxury flat development somewhere on the harbour front.'

'I got one of those as well, think they overestimate how much we get paid.'

'Mind you, this goes down right . . . who knows?'

His phone goes off, he feels like a slave to it. 'So,' he says, checking the screen, 'you in?'

'Sure,' Tanya says, with a creeping sense that she should really be saying no. 'When are we going?'

He looks at her, having to squint into the sun which is over her left shoulder.

'Right now.'

18

Kees stares at the foil blister pack.

There are ten individual blisters, and all of them have been punched out bar one.

He hates them, hates that he's dependent on them to keep his own body from destroying itself.

But the alternative is . . . well, there is no alternative.

He also hates that they are in packs of ten. It makes no sense; seven yes, fourteen yes, but for fuck's sake why do they do them in tens?

He pushes his finger under the last one, watches as the pill's shape starts to form and then, as the foil splits, the pink pill itself emerges, like some sick alien life-pod.

He flips it into his mouth, the bitter pill, quite literally, bitter.

He upends the Coke he has clutched in his hand, downs the lot, and gives himself a bad case of brain freeze.

The bar's quiet, dark and smells of exhaled alcohol and the ghost of dead cigarettes. It's the ideal place to field calls. Which is what he's doing, waiting for incoming.

They have a complicated system set up: he calls and leaves a message, then he gets a text message with a time to be at the bar and he has to confirm or deny to another number, via text. Then he deletes the text message itself.

At first Kees thought it overkill.

Now he's worried it's not overkill enough.

He finds his finger drumming on the bar's surface, like a woodpecker on crack.

The strange thing is, he doesn't remember asking it to do that. He tries to stop it. Nothing happens, the finger carries on – a touch faster, if anything. None of his other fingers are moving, he notices, it's just the one. Now it's going so fast it's like a blur. Sweat oozes down his back, and his neck feels like a long thin pole, his head teetering dangerously on top. It's taking all his concentration to keep it there, thousands of micro adjustments a second.

And his scalp's shrinking fast.

The sound's getting louder, he can hear it now, hear little else, and he glances round to check if anyone else is noticing, see if the bottles are shaking on their shelves, or jumping off to certain death on the floor below.

Is this it? he finds himself calmly wondering. Is this how it ends?

'Hey, for you.'

The voice snaps him out of whatever it is he's locked into.

He swings his vision back to his finger. It's still, innocent, like it hasn't moved.

The barman's holding out a phone to him on an oversized curly cord, something uncomfortably umbilical about it.

He takes the receiver, the plastic slicked up with a sheen of sweat from the man's hand, and steps round the corner, stretching the cord as far as it will go.

Suddenly he doesn't know what to say.

'We . . . we . . .' he says.

'You need to piss?'

'We need to talk,' Kees says. 'Face to face.'

And hour and a half later Kees is scrambling down a tree-covered slope. It's steeper than it looked from the top, and he slips, reaching out a hand to steady himself on a nearby trunk. The bark is rough and dry against his palm.

He's in a wood outside Gouda, and in less than three hours is supposed to be gearing up for the job Van der Pol's put him on.

Unless . . . he thinks as he reaches the bottom of the slope.

The ground's covered in dry leaves, and he looks around, spotting the man leant up against a tree less than ten metres away, acting like it's perfectly normal to be meeting like this.

Kees has not seen him for over a year, and he looks fitter, younger somehow. Looks like he's taking good care of himself whilst Kees is just rotting away.

He steps over, the rustle and crunch of leaves almost deafening in the quiet wood.

'Hey,' Kees says. 'Didn't think you'd come.'

'Oh ye of little faith,' replies Station Chief Henk Smit, stepping away from the trunk. 'But charming as this all is, I would like to know why it's necessary.'

Not changed a bit then, Kees thinks.

A bird chirps behind him, a rapid-fire series of notes at the same pitch, the last one longer than the rest. It does it again. And again. For some reason it reminds him of a speeded-up version of Dirk's scream as the secateurs plunged into his neck.

Kees thinks of his finger, drumming insanely.

'I need out,' he says.

Smit looks at him, eyes unreadable.

'Suits you,' he says. 'The whole biker thing. Looks good. Earring's a nice touch too.'

For a second everything around Kees seems to freeze. He feels empty, present, but only as an observer.

It feels good, like there *is* a respite from it all.

From life. His own life.

But then it all speeds up, anger surging, bubbling in his blood like a diver with the bends. He explodes forward, grabbing Smit and ramming him up against a tree.

'This isn't funny, you fucker,' Kees screams in his face. 'I'm the one doing this. I'm the one risking—'

Smit stomps on Kees foot hard and the pain makes Kees loosen his grip just enough for Smit to get free.

Before Kees can react he's face down eating leaf, with Smit's knee pushing into his spine. His right arm's twisted up behind his shoulder blades, held there tight.

Oddly, Kees is finding it hard to breathe.

'You're getting soft,' Smit remarks, voice steady, no emotion.

'I need out.'

Smit releases his arm then stands up, lack of knee freeing up Kees' breath.

But he doesn't feel like breathing now. What he *really* feels like is crying.

Jesus.

Something crawls past his ear.

He rolls over onto his back and looks up at the branches clawing at the sky.

A lone raptor, wings outstretched, spirals upwards on a lazy thermal.

'I don't understand why you don't just arrest him. Surely I've given you enough for that? Just arrest him and get it over with.'

'Soon, but I need a bit more.'

'So what're you going to do, wait till he finds out who I am and kills me? Arrest him for that? Will that be enough for you to take him down?'

'Kees, listen,' Smit says. 'I know it's tough. You've done well so far, I just need you to stick with it a bit longer. A few more days.'

'I could just walk,' Kees says. 'Walk away right now.'

Smit holds his hand out. Kees looks at it, then struggles up on his own. Smit inspects his palm, as if to see why Kees refused it.

'A couple of days,' Smit says, finishing the inspection and swinging his eyes back to Kees. 'That's all I'm asking.'

'Then I'm out?'

The repetitive cry of the bird starts up again, piercing the quiet. Kees listens to it.

'Then we'll talk,' Smit says.

19

'Ready?'

Jaap's standing on a small mound swelling out of the grasslands behind Daan Brouwer's house, the only place he could find strong enough reception. As a result his view is wide-screen, ultra HD. Turning in a circle he can see the whole sky, bruised by the sinking sun.

'Hit me.'

'Not really my kind of thing,' says Roemers. 'But anyway, I've looked pretty much everywhere and I couldn't find any real connection between Kamp and Brouwer.'

Jaap breathes out. It must be audible because Roemers carries on.

'But . . . one of my guys came across something.'

Jaap stops turning, finds himself facing the beach where Heleen was found.

'What?'

'Check your phone, I'm sending you a file right now.'

Only it gets stuck downloading, the wheel spinning tirelessly. He calls Roemers back. Roemers has gone AWOL. Probably plugged in headphones for his fix of late-sixties Krautrock.

Jaap decides to speak to the neighbours while the ones and zeros sort themselves out.

Of the two remaining houses the first has no one

home, the other's occupied by an old woman. She answers the door and Jaap notices the skin on her inner wrists, marbled with veins like mature blue cheese. He talks to her, she's surprisingly lucid considering she's just turned ninety-one – the number gives Jaap a passing touch of vertigo – and she tells him what little she knows about Brouwer: he's quiet, keeps himself to himself, and she can't remember when she last saw him.

Not revelatory. He thanks her and checks his phone again to find the file is finally there. He heads back to Brouwer's house, reading it.

Up until now there was a slim chance the killings weren't related. Granted the whole suffocation thing could be passed off as a coincidence, and maybe the scopolamine could as well at a massive pinch. Say some entrepreneur imported a load and put it on the market, telling clients exactly what it's good for.

But given what's on the screen in front of him, the chances that they're not linked are slipping rapidly away. Because it looks like Francesco Kamp and Daan Brouwer had, briefly, lived on the same street in Haarlem back in the early nineties. It's not proof of anything, nothing which could stand up in court, but for Jaap it means that there is something to dig at.

Back at Brouwer's house Jaap finds Arno slamming his phone down on the desk.

'I didn't mean for you two to argue over it,' he says.

'Not Kim, Stuppor,' Arno says. 'On his way over, mumbling something about how we're making a mess of it. Due here any minute now.'

The only surprise Jaap feels is that it's taken so long.

Sure, the man was insulted by having Jaap sent in, but if he'd been cooperative from the beginning . . .

Jaap brings Arno up to speed then asks, 'The last ferry has gone, right? So even if Brouwer left right after the newsflash he'd not've had time to get there.'

Arno checks his watch. 'There's one more ferry due in about half an hour's time. It'll take another forty to turn it round.'

'We can get there before then?'

'Take us ten. We've got time. Look at this though, all sorts of stuff on his computer – ready?'

Arno clicks on a file, a new window opens on the screen, and he starts opening individual files.

Brouwer's politics are based on what could loosely be called hate. There are articles about neo-Nazis, anti-Islam groups, a whole subfolder dedicated to the killer who'd gone on a shooting rampage in Norway, and another on Theo van Gogh, the filmmaker shot and stabbed to death by a Dutch-Moroccan Muslim now spending life in jail. A third is on Pim Fortuyn, the gay far-right anti-Islam politician who in the early 2000s was making such significant inroads that he was on the cusp of becoming a major political power. Pundits thought the post of prime minister was within reach, and the bookies' odds reflected this.

That is, it was within reach until he was assassinated by, of all people, a militant vegan, whose beef with the politician was never quite clear. Jaap had been the arresting officer, the case a media spectacle only outdone by his current one.

He leans in and takes over the track-pad, clicking on a

few more files. He finds what they are looking for: a video, taken from who knows where on the internet.

Jaap hits play.

A girl's thigh is centre camera, already slashed by multiple cuts.

Like Heleen's, some are healed over, just raised scar tissue, and some are fresh.

Particularly the one which is trailing behind a blade, blood dripping in its wake.

They watch the whole thing in a kind of suspended silence.

'Money shot,' Arno says.

He's right. A head moves into view, face pixelated, tongue reaching out like a starving alien.

It licks a trickle of fresh blood off the knife's edge.

20

'Tanya, we're ready.'

Tanya nods, gives Harry the one-second gesture.

She's been on hold for over ten minutes now and is starting to wonder if she'll have to go back to the hospital for radiation poisoning. And yes, she knows that using a phone whilst pregnant isn't good, but with life today, what can she do?

A voice comes on the line, the same nurse who'd put her on hold.

'Dr Bruggen's been called away urgently, but I've left him another message so I'm sure he'll call you back as soon as he can.'

'OK, but is there anyone else who can have a look at it? I was in first thing and . . . and I want to know if anything's wrong.'

'There's no one available, but I'm sure Dr Bruggen won't be too long.'

Tanya thanks her, even though she doesn't feel like thanking anyone, and hangs up. She walks across the cracked concrete, tiny oases of weeds pushing through the gaps, to the low warehouse with the corrugated roof where Harry's standing, waiting for her by a red metal door.

'Everything OK?'

'Just some personal stuff.'

Inside, eyes adjusting quickly to the relative lack of light, she follows Harry through a series of flimsy partitions. There's a fat seam of rancid fast food in the air. They track it down to an area with ten or more people inside, all looking uncomfortable. The partitions, which look like they're made of asbestos, are too thin to lean against. The lucky few have managed to rest up against a small desk with tubular legs. On the desk is a box labelled RAT POISON.

There are seven or eight men and three women, Tanya counts. One of the men is shovelling down the source of the smell, some kind of meat which has been rendered, processed, stuffed with chemicals and then finally encased in puff pasty. Flakes scatter on his shoes.

'Where are the chairs?' Harry asks to a general round of shrugging.

He makes a call, argues with someone, then hangs up.

'OK, we'll start without.' He picks up the box and hands it to the nearest man. 'Phones,' he says. 'All of them. You'll get them back once the operation is over.'

The first man hesitates then draws his out, drops it in then passes it on. It circles round, reaching Tanya. She has no choice but to drop hers in.

As she does she can't help thinking about Dr Bruggen.

Harry's already talking. She resolves to speak to him later.

'. . . the thing about it being a training operation isn't true. You're here to work.'

He has their attention now, even the man with the sausage roll stops mid-chew.

'We're short on time, so I'm going to give you a quick

123

briefing then lay out a plan for the operation, for which I'll be assigning you into teams. Once we've done that we'll be moving out to the location. Questions before we get started?'

'What's the operation?'

'We're intercepting what could be one of the biggest drug hauls in the Netherlands' history. Good enough for you?'

'Why us?' one of the men says. He's taller than the rest with a moustache melting down either side of his mouth.

'Well, it wasn't for your looks,' Harry says to laughter from all but the moustache. 'Seriously though, two reasons. The first is you've all had at least partial Arrestatieteam training.'

Tanya had started the SWAT training several years ago before deciding inspector was a better route for her; she'd completed the first round but not taken it any further.

'And the second is none of you have any prior connection to this case.'

'You've got a leak,' says one of the women, short and stocky with military hair, dyed blonde.

Harry shrugs. 'It's possible, and this operation is too important to take a risk. So now we've got that out of the way, let's look at exactly what we'll be doing.'

The noise of someone banging on a door reverberates around the space.

'That must be the chairs,' Harry says. 'Let's get them in, then we can make a start.'

They're taking a break, and Tanya manages to catch Harry out on the expanse of concrete. The sun's not far off the horizon now, the increased angle taming its earlier ferocity.

'What do you think?' Harry asks as she approaches him.

'Uh . . . about what?'

'The plan? The whole thing we've just been going over?'

'Oh, that.' She forces out a laugh, which even to her ears rings false. 'Yeah, it's good. I think it's going to work.'

'I hope so, I've been trying to catch him for years. I really don't want this to get fucked up.' He glances at his watch, as if undecided about something. 'Listen,' he says, 'this isn't really the right time, but I've been thinking, or wondering . . .'

Tanya's heart sinks. Harry is forthright and confident. So his sudden dithering can only mean one thing.

'How about a drink sometime,' he says before she can think of a way to head it off.

'Harry, I'm with someone.'

'Hey, just a drink, nothing serious.'

He's hiding it well, but she can tell he's feeling the burn.

'Yeah,' she says. 'Just a drink. That'd be good.'

Harry nods, looks around for something to distract from the moment. 'Better get back,' he says. 'Transport will be arriving soon.'

'Harry?'

He turns to look at her. 'What is it?'

'I'm waiting for a really important call, and I was wondering if I could just check my phone . . .?'

He's still all of a sudden, eyes oriental. 'I can't make any exceptions, everyone will be asking if I let you.'

'I know, it's just . . .' she says, a wave of fear rushing up from nowhere. She's suddenly worried she's about to cry.

Harry clearly is as well. He takes her by the elbow, walking her a few steps. 'OK, what's going on. I'm sorry if the drink thing—'

Before she can stop herself she finds she's telling him about the scan, and how she's waiting for a callback.

'Whoa,' he says when she's finished. 'If you're pregnant there's no way I can let you do the operation tonight. It's way too dangerous. You should have told me before. It's too late to get someone else in now.'

She feels miserable, like she's really screwing things up. Everything she does, every decision she makes is a bad one. The thought that it all goes back to Staal shudders through her. Like what he'd done to her had somehow made her less able to cope, less herself.

He stole from me, she suddenly realizes. He stole something from me and I don't know how to get it back.

She's about to tell him to forget it, forget it all, ready to just walk away, when he speaks again.

'OK,' he says, giving her arm a quick squeeze, 'here's what we're going to do.'

21

As far as trading ports go, Oost-Vlieland had once been big time. Back in the seventeenth and eighteenth centuries it was part of the Hanseatic League, a confederation of merchant guilds who controlled trade in the Baltic and beyond. But since then its fortunes had been more mixed, the port eventually having to be bought out by the government's Waterways and Public Works Department when the locals were struggling to keep their island from sinking into the sea. With the new ownership, sea defences were built and managed, and the island was able to look for new opportunities. They found one; the trade which now keeps the island afloat is tourists who own boats and need somewhere to dock them.

The marina is to the north, a forest of masts just visible, but when the ferry terminal was built they needed better access to open water. This is where Jaap is now, the town sloping gently up away behind him, the ferry terminal – basically a stretch of concrete with a booking office – below.

A deep horn rumbles out over the water; he feels the waves of it in his chest. He looks up to see the ferry he's been waiting for heading towards the island.

Everything's in place, all available officers – for which read five, including Jaap and Arno – are deployed in plain clothes round the ferry terminal, one of them actually in with the person selling tickets. Jaap's across the road, sitting on a bench, trying not to look like a cop.

'Caught anyone then let them go again?' Smit asks when Jaap answers his phone.

'Not quite,' he replies. For a moment he wonders why it is he always seems to be working for assholes.

The phrase 'problem with authority' floats into his head. He brushes it aside.

Henk Smit got to his exalted position by battling his way up from patrol and taking charge of a small crime-riddled district outside Rotterdam. The results he'd got in a few short years – a near eighteen per cent reduction in crime – meant he came to the attention of people higher up the chain. He was duly promoted to Amsterdam, getting his own station at the very early age of thirty-eight, a fact that endeared him to pretty much none of the people who had the pleasure of working for him. Jaap was one of those people, but they'd found a way to work together. After all, Smit likes good clearance rates, and Jaap's are consistently high.

'So,' Smit asks, 'putting aside yesterday, are the deaths linked?'

Jaap thinks of the cuts again. There's something about it all, something disturbing beyond the usual. But also out of character with the two previous deaths.

'I thought so at first. Tox test confirmed scopolamine in the victim's blood, and she died like the other two by suffocation.'

'Could it have been Kamp? Was there time for him to get over there and back?'

'The timing works out, the surveillance crew lost him

for long enough that he *could* have done, but I don't know if he did. You remember when I showed him the photo of Dafne, and he admitted to that, but then denied killing Nadine?'

'Not really—'

'He did, and I'm starting to believe him.'

Smit ruminates. At least that's what Jaap assumes his silence means.

'Multiple killers running around,' Smit says eventually, 'using the same basic method? Means they've gotta be in touch somehow, any evidence of that?'

Jaap fills him in on what he got from Roemers, and his current situation.

'All right,' Smit says, digesting it all. 'Keep me updated. And Inspector Rykel?'

Somehow Jaap knows what's coming.

'Yeah?'

'If you get the guy,' Smit pauses for effect, 'make sure you cuff him right.'

It's childish, but Jaap gives his phone the finger. Arno, who'd walked up to the local supermarket to get a drink, reappears before he's finished.

'Having fun?'

'Yeah,' Jaap says. 'Yeah, I am.'

The ferry's made it into the harbour without crushing any smaller vessels, and is now inching in sideways towards the dock. A small blonde girl, dressed in shorts and bright orange T-shirt with the same waving kitten as Heleen's, stares at him, a frown pulling her face down.

Jaap wonders what life has in store for her.

Then decides it's best not thinking about.

'Anything?'

Jaap's been keeping an eye on the queue which has been forming outside the ticket office on the quay. They'd found a few photos of Brouwer on his computer – nothing dodgy – so know what he looks like: bald as an eel and a sharp face like, well, an eel.

'Not so far.'

The ferry terminal is a one-storey building which to describe as functional would be to overstate its beauty. The queue outside is twenty strong now, and the flow of passengers disembarking is starting to dry up.

'I'm not seeing him,' Arno says.

Neither's Jaap.

They watch as the last of the queue get on, an old couple wearing identical white panamas, shoulders hunched, steps shuffling but determined. Jaap finds he's drumming his foot. If Brouwer's not here then he's going to have to call in a full search team to go over the island. Which isn't going to happen by tonight. His phone goes off, he sees it's Superintendent Laura Vetter back in Amsterdam. He leaves it.

'Fuck, I thought he'd be here.'

He looks north, the masts in the main harbour suddenly sparking something in his head.

'If he owned a boat himself—' He's thinking back to a moment of unease he'd had whilst updating Stuppor earlier '—it'd be moored there, right?'

He points just as another fighter jet – or maybe the same one which buzzed him yesterday – glints out to sea.

Arno nods. 'Only place on the island.'

'Any way to find out if he does?'

'Harbourmaster has the logs, should be able to tell us.'

Jaap looks back at the ferry, a sailor now unleashing the moorings, the queue all aboard. Brouwer's not coming. He suddenly remembers the model boats at Brouwer's house.

'Fucking idiot.'

'What did I do?'

'Not you,' Jaap says. He should have thought of this earlier, shouldn't have focused just on the ferry. He suddenly feels this case it getting to him, forcing him to make bad decisions. 'Me.'

22

The inside of the van is cramped and hot.

Tanya can feel the heat forming a layer between her skin and her clothes. She's in jeans and has already stripped down to just a T-shirt. She has no more moves left. Though the guy next to her probably wouldn't complain; she's found that, in general, men never tire of tits. The internet, she's pretty sure, is founded on that very principle.

In front of her is a whole bank of monitors, the computers running them presumably only adding to the heat, and beside her the surveillance expert whose name she's been told but has instantly forgotten.

Harry adapted the plan when he'd heard her story, dumping her in the surveillance van out of harm's way. She wishes she'd not said anything now. Especially as it hasn't even gained her access to her phone.

Voices crackle in her earpiece and she adjusts the frequency, twisting the dial till they come into focus. The building complex is just that, complex, and so they're having a few signalling issues.

Which is bad, because if the informant is right, the whole deal is due to go down any minute now. An advance crew inserted cameras at key locations, though given the size of the place they'd not been able to get eyes on everything. They had managed to hack into the site's own

CCTV though, so of the twenty screens in front of her, seventeen are showing live feeds.

'Confirm positions,' says Harry's voice in her ear.

One by one the teams sign in with their codes.

'Listen to them,' the man next to her says. 'It's like they're all acting in a movie or something.'

Tanya hears the excitement in their voices too, some hiding it better than others. But why not? So much of a cop's life was mundane, and she feels the anticipation herself, even if she'd prefer to be out there, taking part.

For a long moment the question of what she's going to do when the baby is born looms in her head, demanding answers. Will she have to give up being an inspector? Will she stay at home whilst Jaap goes out to work?

'Mind you—' the man next to her saves her from the questions which are starting to take on a menacing tone '—I've heard about Van der Pol. Some of the shit he's rumoured to be into . . .' He shakes his head. 'There's one rumour that used to do the rounds, said he was into having people killed, and filmed it happening.'

'Urban myth,' Tanya says. 'The whole snuff thing.'

'You reckon?'

Tanya shrugs. Now that she thinks about it she's not so sure. What her foster father had done to her hadn't been so far off. In terms of suffering it was probably more; she was still living with it. She thinks back to the last time she saw him, the light disappearing from his eyes as he died.

'Nine,' he says, letting Tanya back into the present.

She doesn't want to relive that night. Not now, not ever.

But the images stab at her just the same: his body lying, blood leaking from his head where it'd hit the table corner as he fell, the expanding moment when she saw that it was final, that he wasn't coming back.

'You OK?'

'Sure, I was just thinking of something,' Tanya says, alarmed that she'd clearly zoned out long enough for him to notice.

She fights it off and checks screen nine, and sure enough a small convoy of vehicles, two cars and at least eight bikes, are entering the compound.

'Subtle, huh?' the man says.

He's right, thinks Tanya. It *is* like something out of a movie. It never ceases to amaze her just how many criminals go out of their way to *look* like criminals. She's seen this scene countless times before, and knows what's going to happen; the convoy will pull up, suited dark-glassed men will get out of the cars and spread out, before a smaller man, usually in more casual clothing, emerges.

They follow the progress from screen to screen, the convoy stopping in a small square between four buildings.

Tanya sees with disappointment that it's one of the spaces the crew had not managed to get a camera in. Harry had noted this and put the man with the moustache on the roof. He'd complained a bit. But when he got there and saw the roof was pitched and that he'd have to be hanging off the spine, he'd complained some more.

Now it looks like it's going to pay off.

'I've got a visual,' he whispers through the comms.

'Good,' Harry replies. 'Just hang in there.'

Because to do a deal you need two parties, and so far only one's come to the table.

Two minutes later they get some movement, this time three SUVs, all approaching with their lights off.

'The eagle has landed,' says the man next to Tanya.

'Are you kidding?' Harry comes back, clearly annoyed.

'Sorry, couldn't resist. They're here, roof guy should be able to see three SUVs right about . . . now.'

'Got them.'

'Exit teams in position, everyone else standby,' Harry says.

Now it's a waiting game. Moustache on the roof has to give them the signal that goods have exchanged hands, or at the very least that he has a visual on the goods themselves. Moments pass.

'We pull this off then we're going to be moving up,' whispers the surveillance guy.

Suddenly noise bursts through their earpieces, a kind of leathery scrabbling, like someone stroking a microphone. Two seconds later there's the unmistakable *pop pop pop* of gunfire.

'Hold positions,' yells Harry.

Tanya watches the screen closest. Muzzle flashes light up walls, creating mad shadows. She can see a biker using his Harley as cover, popping up to release a hail of bullets then ducking back down again.

An SUV skids round the corner, back into full view of the screen, two more following close behind.

'Exit teams, you're up!' Harry shouts.

The third SUV breaks away from the others, skidding round a tight corner into a narrow alley between two buildings. It stops, the back doors fly open, and a figure jumps out.

He starts running hard.

Tanya watches him, calculating that soon he'll be passing just one building away from the van. She should try and alert someone, but the gunfire and noise of engines and shouting means their comms system isn't holding up too well.

He's going to be passing in less than a minute.

If she's going to do something she needs to do it now.

She's frozen in place, at war with herself.

Then she rips the earpiece out, grabs her gun, and jumps out the back of the van.

The movement feels good, a release, and she makes it round the edge of the building just in time to see she was right, the figure with a rucksack rushes past, no more then twenty metres ahead of her.

She's already going flat out.

But she pushes herself harder.

A thought flashes through her mind, the baby being starved of oxygen.

She's now at the corner the figure ducked round moments before. She goes round it and immediately sees he has a problem. He's reached the perimeter of the complex, a chain-link fence reaching up to the stars, topped by a curl of razor wire picked out by a security light.

'Police!' she yells, slowing down, pulling her weapon up into position.

The figure freezes for a second, not looking back, then dives off to his left, doubled over and running like an ape, swinging one arm up to fire blind behind him.

She slams into the wall next to her, giving her some cover, then looses off a single shot as he's making it to a row of vertical columns, made up of chaotically stacked tyres.

From the scream she knows she's hit him.

Her breathing's ratcheting through her chest now, and she takes a second to try and slow it down. She listens out for movement, but the ringing in her ears from the shots means she can't rely on audio.

One last breath and she sprints forward, swinging round the first column of tyres, gun out ahead of her.

The security light is dazzling and her hand shoots up to protect her eyes.

As they adjust she can just make out the figure, moving to the right. For one fraction of a millisecond she thinks she catches a glimpse of his face.

It's like a bullet's hit her full in the chest.

They lock eyes, he gestures to the backpack which she now sees he's ditched, and he disappears, limping round the corner of the next building.

Once the crew has been rounded up, two casualties being attended to by the ambulance on standby in the local village, Harry asks to see her in the van.

She clambers in, and he tells her to pull the doors closed.

His face is hard, anger tightening muscles under his skin, and she wonders how she was ever attracted to him.

'You sure you're OK?' he asks without much concern in his voice. At least, not to Tanya's ear.

She nods and Harry stares at her for a few moments, just long enough for her to feel uncomfortable, then turns to the bank of screens.

He stabs a few keys and points to a screen which has started playing.

They watch in silence, and when it's done he hits pause and turns back to her. 'As I've been alerted to this by your colleague it will have be admitted into evidence. I can't just get rid of it.'

Evidence? thinks Tanya. What? 'I'm not sure I—'

'The trouble is, it looks bad. He was limping, so you could have caught him easily. Or taken another shot – he had fired at you so that would have been justified. But you let him go.'

'But I got the backpack, and you got the rest of the crew. Why's he so important?'

Harry reaches down beside him and pulls up the backpack itself. He unzips it, and empties the contents on the narrow desk below the screens.

Small furry things tumble out, spilling onto the surface and beyond.

He picks one up and shows it to her. Then he squeezes it and the rat squeaks.

'They're stuffed, right?' she asks.

He has a knife in his hand, Tanya doesn't see where he got that from, and he turns the thing over, slitting its furry belly. He pulls out foam and the squeaker mechanism, and nothing else.

'No,' he says, 'they're not.'

Tanya stares at the toy rat, one of its whiskers bent at an odd angle, the screens next to it distorted in its black beaded eyes.

She thinks about the face she saw.

Was it really him? she thinks. Could it be?

It was dark and there was a security light shining right in her eyes so she couldn't see that clearly.

Harry picks up the rats and starts stuffing them back into the backpack and she suddenly realizes why the whole thing had seemed like an episode on a TV crime drama – it had been a set-up, a show put on just for them.

Orchestrated to meet their expectations.

Basically, to fuck with them.

Harry speaks again. 'So, you wanna tell me what's *really* going on?'

23

Where is it?' Jaap asks. He's scanning the skies, ears primed for the thundery hum of the SAR chopper which is supposed to be heading his way.

Stuppor's co-operation factor went up by a multiple of ten once he realized that Jaap needed to get off his island. He checks his phone again.

'Five minutes out.'

The run from the ferry terminal turned out to be a waste of time because the harbourmaster was able to confirm that a boat, a forty-two-footer called *Vrijheid*, 'Freedom', registered to Daan Brouwer, sailed half an hour before.

The light's failing fast. Jaap needs to be in the air. Now.

He'd expected the police to have their own launch, but Stuppor had explained that cutbacks meant they shared with the coastguard, and it was currently out, a fishing vessel had sent out a distress call from the North Sea. Jaap dialled the mainland, and two boats had already been launched, but they're still, according to the dispatcher, at least half an hour away.

Jaap's also sent out an alert to all ports within a two-hour radius, but he doesn't want to wait. And he'll still need the chopper, because if Brouwer does put in somewhere and gets arrested by a local patrol then he wants to be there in as short a time as possible.

Arno, who Jaap had sent to the local supermarket, turns up just as the chopper appears on the horizon.

As it's coming down Arno hands Jaap a bag. Jaap thanks him, delves inside and hands the single-wrapped *syrupwaffel* to Stuppor, who takes it suspiciously.

'Fuck's this?' he shouts, the chopper just touching down, the sound beating at their ears.

'A present,' Jaap yells back. 'From my partner. Inspector Tanya Vandermark. I believe you know each other?'

Credit cards can buy you stuff, but the look on Stuppor's face? Priceless.

And from the look on Arno's, he's enjoying it as much as Jaap.

As the chopper springs up into the air the sun seems to slide lower, making the sea a cauldron of gold. The pilot corkscrews, giving them three-sixty views, but neither manages to spot anything resembling the *Vrijheid*.

Half an hour into it, the pilot gets a call. Jaap's eyes are strained; he's been scanning the water, hardly noticing the change from golden down to a much darker hue as the sun slips away. And still no boat. They'd headed north, hugging the coast of the next island in the chain, Terschelling. Three separate boats had spiked Jaap's heart rate, but each time, on closer inspection, it was clear none of them were the *Vrijheid*.

'For you,' the pilot says, flipping a switch. 'Go ahead.'

'Inspector Rykel,' a new voice says. 'This is Chief Inspector De Zoet of the Terschelling force. I hear you're airborne.'

'Yeah,' says Jaap, suddenly spotting another vessel, way

off to the right, only just visible in the failing light. He nudges the pilot and points. The chopper veers, then straightens up. 'We've just spotted a possible boat, heading towards it now.'

'Had a call from the harbourmaster here on Terschelling, he's been in radio contact with a man piloting the Vrijheid. Apparently he wants to dock. What do you want us to do?'

Jaap nods to the pilot who swings the helicopter round. 'Just sit tight,' Jaap says. 'I'm coming.'

24

Kees is worried about dogs. Tracking dogs. And he knows he's not going to get any forewarning as they don't bay like the hounds chasing foxes. The dogs the police use are a different breed, Malinois, and they work silently like sharks in the night. Sniffing out spilt blood.

Of which there's plenty around. All of it Kees'.

He's pulling a strip off his T-shirt and wrapping it round his leg, tying it as tight as he can, trying to stop the flow. He's in a ditch, the sides wet, the bottom even wetter.

There's no pain, though. Which is odd.

The bullet seems to have gone straight through his calf. He could probably stick his finger through the hole if he felt so inclined. But, strangely enough, he doesn't.

He finishes off the knot, checks to see how he's doing, if anything else needs any work. It's hard in the dark, though the moon is giving him a bit of help.

Looks OK, he thinks.

He lies his head back, wondering what's going to happen. The police will be trying to find him for sure. If he's caught then he'll direct them to Smit, and this whole nightmare will be over. But seeing as he'd shot one of their own then he was pretty much fair game. Meaning they'd probably shoot first, and not even bother to ask any questions after.

And to top it all off, the cop he fired on wasn't just any cop.

When he'd seen who it was he'd thought he'd been hallucinating. It was only a glimpse, her hand held up to block the light shining right at her, covering a part of her face. And he was running on adrenaline.

Plus, if he was honest, he'd not been feeling that stable since he'd watched Bart's head explode into a thousand tiny fragments of gore. Or the secateurs plunge into Dirk's neck.

But still, he was sure it had been her.

He shifts a little, a stone or something hard digging into his hip. A rush of emotions swirl up from nowhere and for a moment he wonders if he isn't just going to vaporize from it all, from the conflict, from the sheer fucking irony of what's going on.

A bullet has ripped through his calf, shot by the woman he loves, the woman he'd gone to prison for.

He thinks about the last time he'd seen her, walking off into a field of tulips at the crack of dawn, her hand bandaged from the gunshot she'd sustained. That night, within the space of a few short hours, Kees had discovered Jaap's daughter had died, and had then found Tanya at her foster father's house.

When he got there it was obvious the foster father was no longer alive.

This was the same foster father who, she'd confessed to him two days previously as they'd sat on a skate ramp smoking dope, had abused her over and over.

The law didn't make provision for private justice, they as cops both knew that, so Kees had tidied up the scene as best he could and got her the hell out of there. But no matter what he did, in the end she would be caught.

Then Smit had turned up with his offer. Which wasn't really an offer at all.

Kees had agreed, he figured with his disease she had a life and he didn't, so he took the fall.

And thinking of Smit, something which has been bothering him, an annoying tingle at the back of his mind, grows more intense until it morphs into a question – he'd seen Smit earlier so why hadn't he warned Kees about the raid? What the fuck was he playing at?

An engine noise brings him back to the ditch. He turns his head to watch the double beams cutting through the darkness, heading his way. He puts a hand up, his head just above the ditch's lip, but they're dazzling. He can't tell if it's a cop car or not.

Earlier he'd made a call, giving his exact GPS coordinates as displayed on his phone, so it had to be them, not the cops.

A third possibility strikes him.

Maybe it's Tanya, he thinks. Maybe she's come to get me, but not as a cop.

There'd been times – both in prison and since he'd got out – when he'd wondered if he'd done the right thing taking the fall for her. He didn't even know if she knew he had, until he'd finally asked Smit several months ago. At first Smit refused to answer, but then he'd given in. No, he said. She didn't know what sacrifice he'd made for her.

And with that simple answer Smit had blown open a fantasy which Kees knew was stupid but which had nevertheless sustained him through some tough times.

Because it turned out Tanya wasn't waking up every morning thanking Kees silently, awed at his amazing sacrifice.

A car door opens and Kees holds his breath.

He doesn't know if he wants it to be someone from Van der Pol's gang, or the cops, or Tanya.

'What, you want me to carry you?' says a voice from behind the headlights. 'Get your sorry ass over here, we need to get moving now. Or you can just lie there and die in a ditch. Pretty much the same to me.'

Kees thinks it over.

Maybe that's best, bleeding out, right here under the night sky, the end coming before the dawn.

His disease is getting worse, and really what does he have left?

'Seriously, are you coming or what?'

As Kees struggles up and starts limping to the car, he can't help feeling that somehow he's just lost.

25

'Welcome to Terschelling.'

Chief Inspector De Zoet's a more skilled, and willing, host than Stuppor.

They shake, then climb into the back of the waiting patrol car. Space restrictions mean the chopper wasn't able to put down right by the harbour itself; the pilot had taken one look at it and said 'No way.'

'Food? Drink?' De Zoet asks, having given the driver the go-ahead. He hands Jaap a paper bag, folded neatly across the top.

Jaap takes it, suddenly aware he's ravenous. He pulls out a bottle of chocolate milk and some kind of pastry which looks like it's studded with rabbit droppings.

'Cranberries,' says De Zoet, noticing Jaap's scrutiny. 'You just can't get away from them here. Every damn thing you eat has a fucking cranberry in it.'

Terschelling, the pilot had told him earlier, was famous for very little, the exception being that in the mid-nineteenth century a barrel of cranberries had washed ashore from a nearby shipwreck. An enterprising local had decided to see if he could cultivate them and soon found that the tart berries liked the climate and soil. Now the island produces cranberry-everything in a desperate attempt to differentiate itself in the minds of tourists from its rival islands.

'You're not from here then?'

'Rotterdam, born and bred. The old story, fell for an island girl. Only back then I didn't mind the whole cranberry thing so much. Sixteen years in, I'm starting to mind. I've gotta say, though, I've never had a UTI, so maybe it's not all bad.'

Jaap takes a bite, decides it really isn't so bad. Especially as he can't remember the last time he's eaten. The pastry disappears, the chocolate milk loosening the dry crumbs sticking in his throat.

'So,' Jaap says, dropping the empty bottle back into the paper bag, 'tell me.'

'The boat you're after, the *Vrijheid,* called into the harbourmaster here about twenty minutes ago.'

'Saying?'

'Saying they wanted to dock. He gave them the OK, then got on the phone to me. I've got men there in case it comes in before we arrive.'

Three minutes later they pull up by a red-brick building, the harbourmaster's office. De Zoet turns off the engine and radios his crew. The message comes back that a boat is just now entering the harbour itself.

'Tell everyone to stay out of sight,' Jaap says, getting out of the car, feeling the strong offshore breeze.

De Zoet gives the order and walks with Jaap over a rickety wooden bridge onto the floating jetty. It's about 200 metres long, with shorter jetties running off at right angles. At the junction of each, a pair of ground lights stand guard, illuminating a small patch of boards and the odd hull.

De Zoet nudges Jaap with his elbow, points out into

the darkness. It takes a few seconds for his eyes to adjust. But then he catches it, the outline of a boat moving in, the mast bare, the sound of the engine hidden beneath the wind. They move quickly along the jetty, heading for the only free mooring spot, right up at the end.

The boat beats them there, and they watch a figure leap ashore. He busies himself tying up, and is finishing by the stern, his back to them as they approach. Jaap can see the boat looks the same as the *Vrijheid,* though it's too dark to read the name.

'Daan Brouwer?' he shouts into the wind.

The figure stiffens, then straightens up and pivots round, rope coiled at his feet like a snake.

His face matches the photo. It's Brouwer.

He takes in Jaap, and De Zoet next to him in full uniform, his eyes widening in shock.

'Inspector Jaap Rykel, Amsterdam Police. We need to talk,' Jaap says, moving forward.

Brouwer takes a step back.

His left foot slips off the edge of the wooden jetty. For a moment he's impersonating a windmill with his arms, then he goes over backwards, a foot catching the rope he'd been tying the boat up with.

A brief lull in the wind allows Jaap to hear a strangled cry cut short by a thudding impact.

He rushes to the edge, De Zoet there with him, and grabs Brouwer's foot which caught in the rope. Brouwer's hanging upside down, his head against a vertical iron support, rough with rust and molluscs. There's no movement as they drag him up and over the lip.

They lay him face down, and De Zoet flicks on a torch.

It's clear why there's no movement. The back of Brouwer's head is partially crushed, bone splintering on impact with the hard edge of the iron. There's blood everywhere.

They flip him on three. De Zoet obliges with the torch, illuminating Brouwer's face.

Jaap presses two fingers into Brouwer's throat whilst De Zoet calls in medical. There's a distinct lack of pulse. Jaap looks up at De Zoet and shakes his head.

'Dead,' he says.

The paramedics arrive quickly, and confirm the diagnosis. Jaap is standing a few feet away when he feels his phone going off; he sees it's Arno.

'Been doing a bit of digging,' Arno says when he answers. 'You know the video of Heleen dancing? I've been talking to a few people who were on the beach that night, and they remember the guy filming her.'

'Brouwer.'

'Uh . . . that's the thing, I showed them a photo of him, and they said not. For a start the guy had hair. But there's worse.'

'Worse how?' Jaap asks, wondering how it is he's seen two suspects die in front of him in as many days.

'I did some background on Brouwer. He's guilty of the mutilation, it's clear that he and Heleen were in contact. But he can't have killed her.'

'Why not?'

'He was on the mainland when it happened; he didn't step off the ferry back onto Vlieland until two hours after her death had been called in. I've got it all on camera.'

It's like his head's been invaded by junk. None of this is making any sense.

'I'm gonna call you back,' he finally manages.

'Bad news?' De Zoet asks.

He doesn't know if it's been minutes or hours when his phone goes off.

De Zoet had got him a room in a small hotel just off the harbour, and he doesn't even remember falling asleep.

He reaches for his phone, noticing he's still fully dressed, and squints at the screen, which is telling him two things: the first is that it's past midnight, the second that the person calling him is doing so from the Police Commissioner of Amsterdam's office number.

'Sorry to call you so late,' says Commissioner Bergsma when Jaap's answered.

'Early,' Jaap says.

'What?'

'It's early.'

'OK then, early. Where are you currently?'

'In bed.'

'In bed where?'

'Some island. I can't remember what it's called because I've been working straight for—'

'Well, you're going to need to get off that island and onto the mainland. If you tell me exactly where you are I'll get a helicopter out to you.'

Jaap sits upright.

Tanya, he thinks.

Maybe that's why he's not heard from her. Maybe something's happened.

'What's this about?' he says, his heart thudding, the pressure in his head immense.

'A body of a young woman was discovered in Gelderland earlier this evening. Given the circumstances of her death the local inspector called it in to us.'

Jaap sinks back onto the bed, the cheap springs squeaking in displeasure. His mind's working. Gelderland is about as far east as you can go in the Netherlands without hitting Germany, which means . . .

All of a sudden he knows what's coming next, and is about to speak but the commissioner gets there first.

'The girl died of suffocation. And they ran an urgent tox test, which came through ten minutes ago.'

Jaap's up, the weight of his body monumental but his mind cranking to life, already going back to what Arno had told him earlier, what this means, what . . .

'Don't tell me,' Jaap says. 'I don't want to know.'

Day Three

26

Tanya can't breathe.

The panic's sharp, intense, her heart pumping double time.

She finds herself standing in the bathroom of her flat, the light on, her own face frightening her in the mirror.

For some reason she can't begin to fathom she has the strongest urge to touch her reflection, as if that'll be key to allowing air to flow once more.

And somehow it works, the cool touch of the glass on her fingers freeing up something and she's gasping big lungfuls of sweet air. Her hands are trembling, in fact her whole body is trembling as she tries to fight it, retain control, claw back from whatever she's just been on the edge of.

It takes a few minutes for her breathing to normalize, and she cranks the tap on, cups her hands under it and splashes water over her face, sucks some into her mouth, letting the cool water dribble down her throat.

Back in the bedroom, she collapses onto the bed, over the peak now, onto the slow come-down.

It's been so long, Tanya thinks. And yet it never goes away.

Ruud Staal had abused her for years before she finally ran. She'd done her best to forget, fallen into the old cliché of burying herself in work — well it was either that or drowning her sorrows in drink, but Tanya had too much drive for that – and she'd gradually found a kind of unstable balance which allowed her to live.

But expunging something from the mind is hard, Tanya discovered years later, when she found herself actively seeking out the man who'd caused her all that pain, driven by some force she didn't fully understand.

And she'd found him.

The same night Jaap's child had been killed and a bullet had flown through her hand as if it were no more solid than butter, she'd gone to confront him, convinced that it was the only way to finally break free from her past.

Memories of that night are still vivid, the jumbled emotions as she'd stood outside Staal's house and rang the doorbell, her hand throbbing hard, the makeshift bandage sticky with blood.

It was her last chance, because she knew that the very next morning Staal was booked on a plane to Thailand, where he planned to spend the rest of his life.

Presumably doing to others what he'd done to her.

Tanya couldn't let that happen. She just couldn't.

He'd been slow to answer, and with each passing second she'd felt the urge to turn and flee grow stronger and stronger until she was visibly shaking.

She was still shaking when Staal finally opened the door just a crack, a suspicious eye roving up and down her body. Then it flared as recognition kicked in, and he tried to close the door.

All these years later she's not sure how she did it, but she'd managed to force herself in before he got the chain latch on. They'd stood in the hallway, facing each other. Tanya had felt a wave of sickness which threatened to knock her off her feet, sap strength from her muscles, and once again make her a victim of the man standing in front of her.

And it was like he could read minds, because he caught her eye and a smile split open his mouth, widening further and further till Tanya wanted to scream.

The rest of it's hazy even now, but he'd attacked her and they'd somehow ended up in the front room, Staal on the ground, bleeding from a wound on his forehead. He was moaning, trying to say something, and it took her a few moments to understand.

She had leant forward; maybe this was it, maybe he was apologizing for what he'd done to her, deeply sorry for everything, asking for her forgiveness. But as she got closer what he was saying registered.

'*Cunt*,' he'd whispered like it was a mantra which would keep him alive. '*Cunt cunt cunt*.'

It was then she'd felt a hand on her arm, and turned to see Kees Truter standing there, taking in the scene.

Seeing Kees – who'd somehow worked out what was going on and had decided to check up on her – had punctured whatever bubble she'd been existing in, and he'd got her out of there as fast as he could, clearing any potential evidence against her as he did.

He'd told her it would be OK, that he'd made it look like the man had simply fallen, he was old after all, and hit his head on the coffee table on the way down. And even though she'd spent months expecting a knock on the door it seems he was right, the case was never pursued.

She'd had panic attacks in the months afterwards, but they'd gradually tailed off until she hoped they'd disappeared for good, allowed her to finally put it behind her and think of starting a new life with Jaap.

And yet, she's just had one again.

She gets up, suddenly ready to be busy, get on with the day, with her life, anything to distract herself. The attacks will become less frequent over time, she knows that, she has to *believe* that, in order to keep going.

As she leaves her flat, she catches a glimpse of herself in the mirror.

I can do this, she thinks. I can.

The whole world tilts dangerously to the left, the skyline tipping as if on scales.

As the helicopter banks, Jaap looks out the curved glass at the shifting world below.

Twenty-four hours ago he'd never been in a helicopter, now the novelty's worn off. He's got earphones clamped over his head like a vice, so there's no escaping the pilot's voice as it bursts into his ears, telling him they're almost there. Really, he doesn't need to be told, a huddle of police cars on the sparse land ahead indication enough.

It's only a few hours since a cataclysmic series of knocks crashed into his unconscious state and brought him back to the real world. He'd been in a haphazard dream, constantly shifting from one thing to another, but he remembers part of it, the feeling that there was something wrong with his heart, a slow failure which could prove to be fatal.

Before he was fully awake he'd found himself being driven through the pre-dawn to the chopper which the commissioner had arranged for him.

The flight itself – they'd taken off just as the sun was busy cracking the horizon they're flying towards – had given him time to think, to try and absorb just what had happened yesterday. He'd spoken briefly to Arno, who confirmed that Brouwer couldn't have been responsible for Heleen's death. What's more, Arno continued, clearly having been working through the night, it turned out Brouwer was visiting a friend on Terschelling, something he did once a week like clockwork. In other words, he hadn't been running from anyone. It was doubtful he even knew Heleen was dead, if he'd missed the radio broadcast, which Jaap has to admit is possible. So Brouwer was clearly guilty of the mutilation – there was a long history of messages between him and Heleen going back two years – but not her murder.

All of which, Jaap thinks, leads to what? Who is doing this?

And then there's the electric ping he keeps feeling in his stomach whenever Kamp's denial comes into his head. Which is often.

On the ground ahead there are cars, people, and a triangular area, taped off between three trees, all the accoutrements of a classic crime scene.

And in the centre lies a body, looking like a dark stain spilt on pristine ground. They're banking again, swinging round the site as if the body's the centre of a whirlpool and they're being sucked in.

Figures are looking skyward now, and as the turn deepens Jaap glimpses an airbase huddled up against a band of trees running north–south. Deelen airbase, the pilot told him earlier, was once used by the Nazis when the Netherlands had been occupied during the war, but was now a training ground for helicopter pilots. The pilot trained there himself before shipping out to Iraq where, he'd told Jaap, he'd not even been scrambled once.

'We could land there,' the pilot says, pointing in the

general direction of the base itself. 'Easier to set down. I'm sure they can get you a car?'

They're on their second circle now, the figures no longer watching.

Jaap doesn't see the point of having a helicopter unless it takes you door to door. He shares this opinion with the pilot.

'OK,' the pilot says as he breaks the circle and looks for a place to set down.

'Not too close,' Jaap says. He doesn't want some forensic chewing his ass off because his mode of transport kicks up a cascade of dust and debris. It's not rained for three weeks now, and it's starting to show. Much of the Netherlands is built on reclaimed land, the water table high, so the soil will stay wet even if it never rains again and the sun shines 24/7. But here inland is different, the ground already cracking like dried-out skin on an old man's heel.

The pilot's looking for a suitable spot and Jaap thinks about all four deaths, all in open locations – a contrast to where he's spent his career, in Amsterdam, the tight alleyways a million miles from the expansive beach on Vlieland, or the openness of the land here, part of the Hoge Veluwe National Park.

He'd checked up on his destination during the journey. The land had been bought in 1909 by a wealthy industrialist couple who wanted a country estate where they could invite guests to blast away at various species of animal because, really, what could be more fun? They'd built a house large enough to show off their ever-growing collection of contemporary art, and their guests had hunted by day and partied by night, even as storm clouds gathered over Europe.

Like most parties, this one ended up with a colossal hangover. Worsening economic conditions meant they eventually had to relinquish the estate, donating it to a foundation which turned it into a national park. The only shooting allowed these days was done with cameras.

They suddenly drop fast, and he's thankful his departure was too rushed for breakfast. De Zoet had seen him off, and handed him a brown paper bag which Jaap has yet to open.

Dust balloons round them as one rail touches down gently, as if testing the ground is solid enough before fully committing with the other. The motor whirrs down the octaves, a high whine settling out into lower beats as the blades slow from a single entity to individual parts.

Jaap pulls his headgear off, hands it to the pilot and springs out, ducking instinctively even though the blades are well above head height.

He heads towards the only man not in uniform, but clearly the one in charge. Leadership's in the way the body's held, not the flimsy, and fakeable, covering.

'Jesus,' the man says when Jaap gets close. 'You must be the fucking cavalry or something.'

Jaap shrugs as if it's nothing, as if he spends his days being ferried around the country in his own helicopter, and holds out his hand.

'Jaap Rykel,' he says.

The man in front of him clearly got the memo about dairy. Jaap is six-two but this guy's off the chart, the top of his cowboy hat damn near scraping the sky. He's at least ten years older than Jaap, with a face that hasn't seen much of the inside of an office. His sunglasses are the mirrored lenses of a seventies airline pilot. In them Jaap catches a glimpse of himself, his body hourglassed, head too big, the dry landscape stretching out behind him.

Jaap wonders if he's going to be like Stuppor, the pissed-off obstructive local. He doesn't seem to be making many friends at the moment.

But the man smiles suddenly, shoots his hand out to take the shake, removing his sunglasses with the other. In a swift motion he has them folded up and hooked onto the front of his shirt.

'Frank Ploumen,' he says. 'Just glad you could make it. Shall we?'

They walk over to the nearest stretch of tape, shadows still long on the ground. Frank has the habit of blowing air out of his nose in occasionaly puffs, as if trying to dislodge a fly. Jaap expects Max to appear at any moment. He catches a glimpse of a nightmare future where all he ever does is roll up to dead bodies, Max appearing again and again, only under the sheet he whips away each time there's a different body.

He shakes it off, ducks under the tape held up by Frank and takes the vinyl gloves offered to him.

Yesterday he'd hoped Heleen was the last dead body he'd have to deal with, and now, before he could tie that up and quit, there's another.

They make it over and Jaap crouches down, the still, inland air pungent with the bacteria already eating the body from the inside out, breaking it down into simple molecules which will slip back into the crazy carbon cycle some people call life.

If he's honest he'd prefer the beach. At least there was movement there, both to take away the smell and to give a feeling of life. But here it's still, way too still.

A shadow flickers across the ground, over the body and away. Jaap glances up to see a bird hanging a tight right, bringing its wings up to soften its landing just on the far side of the body.

Once terrestrial, it tucks its wings and glances around with a jerky head. Before Jaap can stop it the bird jabs the body's face. Jaap shoots his hand out and the bird retreats, gives him the head-cocked one-eyed stare, then insolently flaps its wings and takes off slowly.

'Bitch needs to show you some respect,' Frank says.

He may not spend time indoors during the day, but by the sound of it he spends his evenings watching American box-sets. Frank does a double snort with his nose for emphasis as Jaap processes what's in front of him.

The girl's head is encased in a clear plastic bag, gaffer tape wrapped round and round the neck making the seal tight.

The inside of the plastic's beaded with condensation, distorting the view of her features.

She's dressed in white jeans, covered with long patches of dust and one knee torn, as is the skin beneath, the wound clogged with powdered soil and dry grass. Her top's a blue hoody, two tassels of orange-and-white cord used to tighten the hood both frayed at the end. One of them lies across a breast, the other on the ground like a poisonous snake in wait.

Her wrists have been tied, then released, and just like in Vlieland the marks are thin, with no trace of what they'd been tied with. Classic indicator of cable ties.

'Give me a minute would you?' he says to Frank, who's been standing a few feet to his left.

'Sure,' says Frank. 'We think we're close to getting someone, just waiting for something to be confirmed. Take whatever you need, I'll let you know once we're ready to go.'

Jaap waits until he hears the scuff and rasp of his footsteps recede.

The sun's on him now, he can feel its warmth, its power. The source of all life, but no longer for this girl, no matter how long she stays out here, or how strong the sun becomes.

He reaches out, gently picking up the hem of her hoody to see she doesn't have a T-shirt on underneath. He holds it slightly higher, his eyes having to adjust to the interior shadow.

Her stomach is untouched. No cuts at all.

He releases his fingers, the fabric settling slowly as if in respect for the dead.

Jaap hadn't expected to see cuts, he'd understood that was coincidental to the killing, but he'd had to check nonetheless. Because right now he feels like he's grasping for something which can make it all make sense, but is slipping through his fingers like liquid silk.

Frank's on the phone so Jaap decides to take a walk, get a feel for the area, but just as he's ducking under the tape his phone goes off.

'Hey, finally caught you,' Tanya says when he answers,

her voice competing with a background hum doing something to his insides. It's always the same, a subtle repositioning of all the atoms in his body, like each one glows a little brighter.

'Yeah, I'm kind of busy these days. Flying round the country, you know how it is.'

'My hero,' she says in an awed voice.

'So, Rotterdam's done?'

'Nearly, but it didn't end well. I've got to debrief this morning. I'll tell you about it when you're back. Which will be . . . ?'

Jaap looks out across dry earth to where the body is being fussed over by a forensic.

'I'm not sure, this case is . . . well, it's nasty.'

'You're OK?'

'I'll be fine, I just want to . . .' He doesn't need to finish, Tanya knows what he wants. The same as any investigator on a case. He wants to find out why. 'Listen, I've got to go, when do you reckon you'll be back?'

'Uh . . . probably this afternoon.'

'Great, you can get some rest—'

'Look, I'm pregnant, I get it,' she says, 'but I'm not a fucking invalid, OK?'

The problem with wanting a woman like Tanya, Jaap thinks, is that you've basically got to handle with care. 'I know. I'm sorry—'

'People keep telling me to rest, you know? It's all this over-the-top concern—'

'Hey hey hey, I'm sorry, OK? Forget I said it.'

'Yeah, OK,' she says after a few moments. 'Sorry. I got

a bit worked up, had some stuff go wrong on this case . . . I need a case of my own.'

'Take mine.'

'Maybe I will, I never get cases where I'm flown round the country in helicopters. I'll let you know when I'm back. Remember to call me, OK?'

Twenty minutes later Frank's taken him through everything he knows. The victim is Kaaren Leegte, a twenty-five-year-old retail assistant at a jewellery store in Hoenderloo. She's not currently in a relationship, and has no criminal record. Which doesn't surprise Jaap, because if she did then she wouldn't be working at a jewellery store.

'So this is where I'm at,' Jaap says. 'We've already had three other killings in which scopolamine was used, and each victim also died from suffocation in remote areas. Kaaren's death fits the pattern. Day before yesterday I went to arrest the man who we thought killed the first two victims, and, well, you heard the news.'

Frank nods. 'The press are loving it; murder suspect shot by a senior police officer? They're coming in their pants.'

'What they don't know is that just before Kamp died he admitted to having killed one of the victims but not the other, which is when I get a call about the third body out on Vlieland, which Kamp could have been involved in, because he'd ditched the surveillance team long enough to do it. Only now there's yet another body, and she was killed well after Kamp died. You see my problem?'

Frank whistles, then shakes his head. 'Any chance it's all coincidence?'

'All killed in wide open spaces, suffocated, and all testing positive for scopolamine? I'd love to think that was the mother of all coincidences. But I'm not sure I believe it. There is something linking all these deaths. I just don't know what it is.'

Frank's phone rings. He answers, listens, then gives a few orders.

'Right, it's on,' he says to Jaap. 'We got CCTV of a car leaving the road the victim's house is on, and the timing matches up. Just had confirmation of the owner, we know where he is. And given what you've just told me, it looks like it's going to be your arrest. Maybe this is going to be the missing link.'

28

The whole concept of pain as simply the body's way of alerting you to something which needs attention had been explained to Kees when he was a kid by a doctor with grey hair and a gruff manner which fooled precisely no one.

It'd been during the summer holidays, on one of those days perfectly balanced between the end of school far behind him and the start of the new term miles out in front, and he'd decided that climbing the tree at the end of their road was the only thing he wanted to do in life. It was an old oak, and held its branches with a lazy solidity, its bark pitted and rough like the surface of an alien world.

The thought of climbing it hadn't developed over time, or at least not consciously. As far as Kees remembers, it came fully formed one day as he passed it on his walk to the bus stop, like someone had simply beamed the ready-made thought into his head. He'd stopped, looked up, and realized that one day he was going to sit in its higher branches, see what the world was like from there. He'd kept the thought secret, not telling anyone, and he'd been nursing it for weeks until he woke up one morning and knew that today was the day.

The hardest bit was getting onto the first branch, but as Kees walked towards the tree, which now seemed twice as big as it'd ever seemed before, he could see someone had parked a car right under the lowest branch. Before he knew what he was doing he was standing on the metal roof, not feeling quite safe, and hauling himself up onto the branch itself. From there it had been easier going, and he'd managed to reach about two-thirds of the way up before anything went wrong.

Which it did, in the form of a weak branch, hollowed out by insects or fungi or just cruel fate.

He'd been found by a passerby on the pavement, with scratches all over him and a leg which didn't move.

At the hospital, lying on a stretcher with a doctor examining his leg, he'd complained of the pain, cried and said he just wished there was no pain in the world. The doctor had stopped what he was doing and told him that pain was simply a message, simply a way of the body saying, 'Hey, I need a bit of attention here,' and that in a world without it you'd end up dead very quickly.

And now, years later, with his leg feeling like a nuke has gone off in it, Kees wonders again if ending up dead wouldn't be the most attractive proposition. As long as it meant the pain went away.

His leg has taken on a life of its own, throbbing with every heartbeat.

Though Kees hopes it's not, because nobody's heart should be going that fast. Should it?

He tries to sit up, propping his elbows against wooden boards, and looks around. He'd been brought here last night by one of Van der Pol's crew who he'd seen around but never knew what he did. Now he knows.

The guy had laid him on the sagging sofa, given him a shot of something, then told him to get some rest.

Which was a fucking joke if ever he'd heard one.

Get some rest, like he's Florence fucking Nightingale.

Only Kees isn't laughing as the shot's worn off and he feels like a nuke has gone off in his leg. Has he already thought that?

Fuck it. His mind's not working properly.

He hears voices, movement, footsteps and a door scraping open.

'This the one?' a voice Kees doesn't recognize asks.

'I don't see anyone else with their leg shot to shit, do you?'

'OK,' says the first voice, coming into view.

Kees can see he's scared, youngish with short brown hair and a politician's face, instantly forgettable. Probably a junior doctor who owes someone a favour.

The man snaps on blue gloves and starts unravelling the remains of the T-shirt Kees had tied round his leg the night before.

He tries to tell the man that he wasn't in pain last night, so he doesn't know why he is now.

'Shock,' the man says, working efficiently despite the fact he's clearly scared out of his wits.

'I'm going to have to do some work here,' he says, having finally got the fabric off. He gently probes the wound with a finger. Kees sucks air.

Once finished, the doctor leaves Kees propped up on the sofa. The guy who'd brought him here has gone out, saying he'll be back later. As he left Kees heard a key turning in a lock.

A TV across the room is on silent, a news show, words

171

scrolling fast along the bottom. The view changes from the anchor to a street scene, a row of houses, one of them taped off with police tape.

Kees sits up a little straighter.

He knows the street – that's where he and Bart had been two days ago. He looks around for the remote, finds it and hits unmute.

Now the screen's changed again, the face of a man, black curly hair unmistakable. It's the man they'd gone to meet.

'. . . *and sources close to the police are saying that the man shot and killed yesterday at his home in Amsterdam-Zuid by police was being arrested for the deaths of Dafne Kosters and Nadine Adelaars. As with any shooting, an internal investigation has been launched, though when the results of that will be released remains, as yet, unclear.*'

Kees brain is in overdrive. He doesn't know what's going on, but he needs to call Smit. Only he's locked in a room, fuck knows where, and has no way of getting him a message.

Across the room there's the noise of a key being inserted in a lock. The door opens and the man steps back in.

'Boss wants to see you,' he says. 'Now.'

29

Can it be as simple as this? Jaap wonders.

They're in a car driving towards a milk-processing plant located in the countryside east of Apeldoorn where a man called Pieter Groot works. Frank's been taking Jaap through the steps which have led him to believe Groot's their main suspect. CCTV images caught near Kaaren's house turned up five cars within a time-frame which could work, given that she'd got back home at just after five yesterday and had been found dead at half-past nine, when one of the park rangers was doing the final round, checking no tourists were wandering through the park lost and about to be locked in.

Of those cars, three were listed as belonging to locals. A Citroen and a Fiat were registered to people Frank didn't consider serious contenders. The Citroen's owner is known to Frank's men, an eighty-year-old who causes endless road-rage incidents by driving no faster than twenty-five kilometres an hour, dogmatically sticking to that speed, never wavering, as if it's his final *fuck you* to the world. The Fiat is owned by a single mother, one of whose three children is seriously disabled. Which leaves the Audi.

'Pieter Groot, does he have a record?'

'Nah, face of it he seems clean, got a young kid, steady job. No reason to think he'd do something like this.

Though his wife left him not long after the child was born, so he's on his own.'

'Anything on why she left?'

'Far as I can work out she joined some kind of yoga cult, moved to India, an old tea plantation in the Keralan hills.'

'Pretty unusual – the man walking I can kind of see, but a new mother?'

'Post-natal depression. I knew someone who had it, they didn't run off and join a cult, but I think it was pretty rough on them.'

Great, thinks Jaap. Something else to worry about.

He puts thoughts of Tanya aside, she's too strong for that kind of thing he tells himself. She's not really a quitter.

'But,' Frank says, pulling out a stick of gum – Jaap didn't know they even made them any more – 'given what you told me earlier I had one of my men do some checking and he discovered that two days ago Pieter wasn't at work, he'd booked a day off.'

'Could have driven up to Vlieland and back.'

Frank shrugs. 'Just sayin'.'

Jaap thinks a minute, then gets Arno on the phone.

He gives him Groot's details and the car reg, and asks him to check for sightings, not least on the ferry over.

'I'm going to get you a photo of Groot, when it comes through can you check with the people who saw Heleen being filmed dancing, see if any of them recognize him?'

The plant rises off the flat land ahead of them. When Frank said Groot worked at a milk co-op, Jaap'd had images of a small farm, happy cows grazing in pastures and occasionally ambling over to a small shed to willingly give up their cow juice.

But this is something totally different. For a start it's vast, a metal building the size of at least six football pitches, with tall conical tanks two storeys high clustered in a section to the south of the building. The road leading to it glints with a tailback of tankers. The ones at the front of the queue have large tubes attached as if they are metal cows being milked themselves.

They nose past them, heading for the main car park, where they take a slow cruise round until Jaap spots the Audi.

'Let's go and have a word,' he says.

Inside they're greeted by a guy on reception who has attitude but not enough intelligence or drive to get out and find a better job. He treats their request for an audience with the manager with a massive dose of silent contempt. Frank administers a lesson in civic responsibilities and gets him jumping, and soon they're being ushered into the office of the woman who runs the plant.

She's early fifties, grey hair pulled into a tight bun, and is shockingly like an old neighbour Jaap used to have, one houseboat over. The woman – he's not sure he ever knew her name – had lived there for years with a white cat, and had suddenly vanished one day. The cat, sensing a lack of food, transferred its affections to the nearest person available, Jaap, and he'd left it scraps on deck every day for a year until it developed leukaemia and got booked on a one-way to the local euth society. Jaap had teared up like a baby when that went down. And he'd not even liked the cat that much; despite taking Jaap's food it'd always eyed him with frank suspicion, leaving him with the feeling he was being used.

They explain what they're wanting to do – Jaap having to restrain himself from asking her if she has a sister – and the woman's eyebrows ride up her forehead. But she keeps calm, gets her PA to pull today's rota and their file mugshot of Groot. She then escorts Jaap and Frank through the vast plant, having first insisted they don regulation white coats and hairnets. 'Health and safety,' she says. 'Can't have any hair in our milk. Product recall is pretty much the end of the world around here.'

As they walk, Jaap marvels at the sheer scale of the operation. High-tech, stainless steel pipes are everywhere, and the smell of antiseptic is a constant in his nostrils.

'Through there is the area he'll be in,' she says, stopping at a solid-looking door.

'How many others?'

'Three on shift at any one time. It's mostly automated, but there needs to be a skeleton crew in there just to oversee it. Go past the first set of pipes and you'll find the computer terminal, most likely he'll be there. They do have to make occasional rounds though.'

'This the only exit?'

'Yes.'

Jaap thanks her and moves forward, pushing open the door and stepping into another vast area, Frank following close behind, the occasional snort letting Jaap know he's still there. A deep hum pressurizes their ears. Jaap undoes his lab coat so he has easy access to his gun.

As they walk on the polished concrete floor, angled towards a thin drain running along the centre, Jaap hears voices up ahead. A man and woman talking.

'Seriously, what's he thinking?' demands the woman. 'That's the whole batch gone to shit.'

'He's usually pretty reliable. Maybe he's ill or something?' the man responds.

'Mentally, perhaps.'

Jaap can see them now, two figures standing by a tank, both holding clipboards.

'You're harsh, you are,' he says, turning towards Jaap. 'Give him a—'

Jaap steps forward. This is not the man whose mugshot he's just seen.

'Pieter. Where is he?'

'The control booth, over there,' the woman points. 'Who are you?'

Franks flashes them. Their eyes bulge at his ID.

'I need you to leave the area now, got it?'

They got it real good.

Once Jaap's sure they've made the door he heads in the direction the woman pointed, following yet another set of pipes to where they right-angle round a corner. He can see the control booth now, a glassed-off section with a massive bank of screens, complicated flow diagrams covering them.

But what interests Jaap is the man sitting in a chair with his feet up on a desk, watching the screen intently. His face is in profile. It matches the mugshot.

177

The glass door is out of Groot's current line of sight. Jaap steps over and pulls the vertical steel tube which serves as a handle. His gun is in his hand. Frank is beside him, weapon also drawn.

He steps inside.

Groot doesn't react.

'Police,' says Jaap.

He sees the exact moment Groot's body primes itself for flight. It's like an electric shock's just run through his body, every muscle tense, taut with power.

But he doesn't run.

His body relaxes, shoulders lowering. He swings his legs off the desk and uses them to propel himself round in the chair.

Jaap's seen many killers, seen how the killing doesn't achieve close to what they had hoped for, how often remorse is there, just waiting to burst out.

But as he stares into Pieter Groot's eyes he realizes he's never seen something like this. Groot pushes himself up from the chair, weary like he's an old man, and slowly, as if in a dream, he holds his hands out in front of him, wrists together.

Ready to be cuffed.

Jaap steps up and puts them on.

And this time he quadruple-checks they're done up right.

30

She's done this hundreds of times, possibly thousands.

Tanya walks into the cell and sits down opposite the man already occupying the other side of the desk. Over the years she's honed her interview technique, learning from other inspectors she's worked with. Jaap's favourite – the Routine he calls it – is good, a whole elaborate display designed to depersonalize the process, but it's not the only way.

She likes to play on her feminine charms a bit, assuming the person she's dealing with is male – and let's be honest here, the vast majority of criminals she deals with *are* male – and try and make them a bit comfortable. Like this is all a misunderstanding, we can clear this up in no time if we can be friends. Get them to soften up a bit.

Then she hits them hard. Switches up from girl-next-door to über-bitch.

She's actually quite proud of it, it seems to get results. But in this case she's not sure that's going to work.

Because for the first time ever, she's the one being interviewed.

The guy opposite is clearly of the Jaap school of thought, totally ignoring her, going through some notes which are probably just some bullshit football league statistics but which look impressive nevertheless.

It starts to dawn on Tanya just how effective the not-knowing-what-they-have-on-you thing really is.

Minutes tick by. She can hear his slightly laboured breathing, like he's naturally a mouth-breather but has been told about it so tries to breathe through his nose. She focuses on keeping calm.

It doesn't work; by the time the door opens she's just about ready to break down and confess to whatever they've got going. But when she looks up and sees Harry stepping into the room she toughens up.

They go through the prelims, she learns that the mouth-breather is called Inspector Cremers, and is with Internal Affairs. He's the one doing the questioning, for now.

He starts with the basics then pulls out a laptop, positions it on the table so all three can see it, and brings up a video.

It's the same one Harry'd shown her last night, and they watch, Cremers hitting pause just as she picks up the backpack and lets the limping man get away. Luckily her face is too much in shadow to pick up what emotion it had been displaying, though she's not even sure herself what it might have been at that moment.

She's been thinking about this all night, in a way glad to see the video again, hoping that it might confirm or deny her suspicions.

But his face isn't visible either, so she can't tell if she really did see what she thought she saw, or if her imagination was simply fucking with her.

'The thing is,' Cremers says, 'we had, as I understand from Harry here, an informant give rock-solid info, and yet it turned out to be a sham. And then we have you letting one of the key players in all of this get away. So you see our problem.'

Tanya sees his problem all too clearly, though it's nothing to do with the case. She'd been told first thing that everyone there last night is going through a similar debrief, normal protocol for any operation of this size. But now she's not so sure. Because this is starting to feel like they're going all Salem on her.

And Harry's driving it, she's sure of that. Since the moment he'd shown her the rats he's been aloof, a coldness creeping into his manner which she knows all too well how to read.

And she gets that, she really does. He's been working on this for months, years, and the best chance he's probably ever going to get just blew up in his face.

But it's not her fault. They're looking for someone to blame, she thinks. But it's not going to be me.

And there was the rebuff also, maybe that's playing a part too? Wounded male pride can be a dangerous thing.

'I see your problem,' says Tanya finally. 'I just don't know what it has to do with me.'

'From where I'm sitting—' Cremers points to the screen '—that looks like collusion. You let the guy go. You must have had a reason to. And unless you can tell us what the reason is, it looks a lot like you're the one who tipped Van der Pol off.'

'From where I'm sitting it looks like you're making a bunch of shit up,' says Tanya. 'What about the informant, are you sure he didn't set you up? Feed you false info? Or that they'd been fed false info to flush them out? Seems to me you're not asking the right questions because you just want an easy solution.'

'You're changing the discussion. Right now I need to know why you let the man go.'

He stares at her like he's a robot. The standing joke is that anyone applying to work at IA has to undergo special training to remove any last vestige of humanity which may still be lurking in their biological shell. Tanya's starting to think it's not a joke.

She stares back. They want to hang her? Fine. She's just going to have to dodge the noose. Her chair creaks as her posture follows her mindset.

'The reason I "let the man go" is that I suddenly had a really bad pain, and I couldn't move for a few seconds.'

Harry, up until now granite, stirs.

Tanya looks at him. Oh yeah, you know what's coming. He catches her eye. It's clear he doesn't want her to play that card.

But backed into a corner even the friendliest dog bites, she thinks.

'Pain?' says Cremers, seemingly confused by the word. It's like he's never heard it before.

'OK,' Harry says, standing up, 'I don't think we need to take this any—'

'What sort of pain?'

'Well—' Tanya stares at him '—maybe you better ask Harry about that.'

Ten minutes later she's walking out the station and getting into her car, free to go home, back to Amsterdam. She sits for a moment, the air thick and heavy, and tries to clear her head. She doesn't want to think about the shit-storm she's just stepped out of, Harry's attempt to scapegoat her – because that's what it was – blowing up in his face with IA now investigating why he'd allowed a pregnant officer on the operation in the first place.

But by suppressing those thoughts she finds the old nature-vacuum thing is real, because her mind is now flooded with thoughts of the hospital.

Because, unbelievably, she's still not heard anything.

So instead of heading straight for Amsterdam, she finds herself turning off for the hospital.

The parking is just as bad, if not worse, than the day before, so she finds a place near the entrance which isn't going to block any ambulances and parks up. She leaves the blue lights in the grille going.

She presents herself, doesn't take no for an answer, no matter how efficient the smile, and a mere twenty minutes later is sitting down in a consultation room with the exalted Dr Bruggen.

Bruggen turns out to be a man in his early sixties, the buttons of his white coat done up out of sync. A fact that's not inspiring her with a huge amount of confidence. He's got a serious comb-over, probably a world record if he ever gives the guys at *The Guinness Book of* a call, and thick black-framed glasses like he's a Bauhaus architect, not a gynaecologist in Rotterdam.

'Right,' he says pulling the scans out of a file.

He peruses them, Tanya gets the feeling for the first time, and then puts them down.

'It's nothing to be worried about,' he says.

Which doesn't make the last twenty-four hours any easier to bear, she thinks. But she doesn't say anything.

'I'm just a bit concerned with one of the heart valves,

the mitral valve. It's too small to see here really, but I'd like you to go to someone up in Amsterdam. A colleague of mine who's good at this kind of thing.'

'What kind of thing?'

'Really, it's nothing. I'm just being ultra-cautious. There's a very rare defect which can occur, meaning the valve doesn't form properly, and we just need to rule it out.'

'And if you can't?'

He writes something on a bit of paper then turns to his computer, moving the mouse around and clicking a button. She wonders if he's playing solitaire.

It's karma, she thinks, panic flushing her skin hot and cold at the same time. This is payback for Staal's death. An eye for an eye.

'Don't worry, the nurse will give you a letter,' he says, as if he's not heard her properly.

'So the pain I had, was that connected?'

He shrugs like the human body's a mystery to him. 'Could have been anything, it happens. Can you go up to Amsterdam?'

'I'm going there today,' she says, her homecoming, the things she's looked forward to for months now, feeling like a death sentence, a death sentence for her own child.

He tilts his head up so he can see her through the glasses, which are way down his nose. Tanya can see a rich curly thicket of nose hair which would be white if only nicotine didn't stain so well.

'Excellent,' he says, eyes swimming behind the lenses like fish in bowls. 'Excellent.'

On her way out she gets a glimpse of the screen.

The fucker *was* playing solitaire.

31

Below him Amsterdam's opening up like an old lover. He even spots their houseboat on Bloemgracht as they make their approach to the station.

Jaap's worked out of the building since it was commissioned in '96, and he never knew it had a helipad on the roof. As they near it Jaap can make out two uniforms waiting to take his charge.

The roof isn't that large, but the pilot brings them down with skill, and Jaap gets out, taking Pieter Groot with him. He's cuffed behind his back, but he's shown no fight at all. Jaap keeps seeing in his mind the way he brought his wrists up, like he was offering himself up for sacrifice. The uniforms take Groot, the helicopter pilot gives Jaap a casual salute, then takes off, the downdraft almost enough to scoot him off the roof.

But he stays. The uniforms are going to process Groot, and Jaap's in no real hurry to start the interrogation. He feels like he could use a rest, feels like he needs to take some time off. A few years perhaps.

He walks over to the edge of the roof, a small wall no more than three feet high running round the perimeter. Looking north he can see the helicopter, nose dipped, powering away. Higher in the sky a languid plane smudges the blue with a white line.

Jaap watches the vapour trail as it slowly expands,

dissipating into nothing. He'd once arrested a murderer who believed in chemtrails, believed that chemicals were being sprayed on everyone as part of some massive mind-control conspiracy, and that the killing he'd perpetrated – the brutal stabbing of a fairly minor player in local government – would reveal to the world the true extent of their enslavement. Last Jaap heard the guy was still in jail, and a whole movement of crackpot conspiracy theorists took his conviction as positive proof that the government was fucking them, and had made him the figurehead of their internet community of truth-seekers.

A jangle of birdsong explodes in the treetops just below him, evaporating any further thoughts of the craziness of things.

His gaze swings round until he can see the roof of his houseboat. It makes him think of Tanya. With any luck he can get this done so they can spend the evening together, make the time to be just a couple expecting their first child. For a second he feels like shouting out, an intense rush which he realizes must be a kind of joy.

His phone massages his leg. He doesn't want to check it, too wrapped up in the moment. But old habits are nigh on impossible to kill.

'I may have something,' Arno says. 'The guy you have, he wasn't the one who videoed Heleen, no one recognizes him, but I've found someone who fits the description of the man who did, got CCTV of him at the ferry port. Got his plates as he drove away on the mainland. I'm outside his address now.'

Jaap's thinking about Groot's silence since the arrest. He's not said anything, his eyes surveying a world Jaap can't see. It has to be him, he has to be the one who killed Kaaren and possibly Heleen. Frank had also confirmed that Groot wasn't at work when Nadine had been killed.

And yet he's been wrong before.

How many murderers are there in this case? he wonders. What's the link?

He fills Arno in on Groot's arrest before asking if Stuppor knows Arno is on the mainland.

'Uh . . . not exactly. I took the day off and . . .'

I was right about him, Jaap thinks. He *is* like me.

I'll get someone local to go with you, this has to be official. If you're not happy with his answers then bring him in. Send me the address and sit tight until they get to you.'

Jaap waits for him to agree, then kills the call. A text comes in from Arno giving his exact location. Jaap only has a dim awareness of where Warmond actually is. Once he's found it on his phone – a small town just north of Leiden – he starts towards the door leading into the station. He'll get a local inspector to meet Arno. But just before he descends he has another thought. He calls Tanya. She answers.

'Are you near Leiden?'

'Just passed it, why?'

Jaap hesitates for a second, he doesn't want to jeopardize their evening by making her late. But it shouldn't take more than an hour at most. There'll be plenty of time, he thinks.

'I could use a hand with something.'

'Sure, what is it?' she says, her voice faint over the background hum of car interior.

He tells her.

'Jeez, he sounds like you,' she says. 'Need me to hold his hand?'

'Yeah—'

'Is he fit?'

'I wouldn't know . . . he did say something about genital herpes though.'

'Hands off then.'

'Hands most *definitely* off.'

32

Really, it's not so bad.

At least that's what Kees tells himself as he gets out of the car, tentatively putting a bit of weight on his bandaged leg. He'd been told to rest it, but Van der Pol had requested to see him. Kees doesn't think Van der Pol's the kind to take much heed of a sick note, even if the scared doctor had been willing to write one.

He'd been driven by the same guy who'd been with him since last night, and he still doesn't know what his name is. All he knows is he has a shaved head, a full lumberjack beard and that he looks like he can turn a human into mincemeat with one hand alone. And despite it all, despite the pain and the fear, Kees is feeling something else deep in the pit of his stomach. Something triggered by what he saw on TV, the man they'd been to see two days ago now, shot by the police, and who turns out to be responsible for the killings which have had the nation buzzing for months. He's got to call Smit, but so far Lumberjack's not left him alone for one second.

And now this summons.

It's a tranquil spot, a lake somewhere with a bench metres from the water's edge and a beat-up old motorhome parked beside it. The motorhome's windows have orange net curtains.

Kees is back to bipedal now, a triumph of evolution,

and the beard directs him to the motorhome itself. Tiny bolts of intricate lightning flash through his leg for the ten or so metres, but he makes it across, forehead beaded from the strain. The door opens and he struggles up the steps, watched by everyone inside, no one rushing to his aid, no one saying, let me help you with that, or just putting an arm out for him to grasp.

Nice, thinks Kees. I took a bullet for you shit-bags.

The interior has been ripped out, a long low bench riding along one side the only furniture. Van der Pol's sat on that. Everyone else stands.

Kees glances around, seeing these are Van der Pol's right-hand men, the long-timers, people who over the years have proved themselves loyal, each gaining a part of the country to run. Rumours about these guys are crazy. The one Kees had heard repeated most often was that once a year Van der Pol would take them on the equivalent of a corporate away-day. Only Kees is sure they don't go paint-balling or fire-walking, and they sure as hell don't attend a vegan yoga retreat in the Atlas Mountains.

Truth is, no one really knows what they do, but Kees has no doubt it's sick.

And here he is, in a motorhome in the middle of nowhere, with all of them.

Kees gets the feeling they've all been talking, but stopped now that he's here.

Van der Pol motions to the bench next to him. Kees makes it over and lowers himself down, on the one hand glad – it takes the weight off – on the other less so, proximity to Van der Pol not high on his bucket list.

'So,' Van der Pol says once Kees is settled.

Light filters through the net curtains, turning everything orange.

'Last night,' Van der Pol continues, 'tell us what happened.'

'We got lucky,' a man called Axel Hof says. He's shorter than Kees, with military hair and a face unlikely to inspire a painter. Kees has seen him work, and knows he's one of the most brutal of the men in the room. Which is saying a lot. 'We heard the police were onto us about an hour before, gave us just enough time to contact the other side, get them to make the switch. Whilst the cops were busy being heroes the real deal went down fifty kilometres away.'

This is news to Kees, but not, seemingly, to the rest of the motorhome. It also means he took a bullet for literally nothing. No reason. He was just a decoy. He'd been told there were kilos of meth in there, he'd given it up to Tanya to make sure it never made the street.

'The firefight . . .' Hof says as Van der Pol just stares at him, 'I don't know why that happened, we'd agreed to make the whole thing clean, just hand over the bag of rats and get out of there, but then one of them started firing.'

'I told them to,' Van der Pol says.

This *is* news to everyone.

'Shit . . . why?' Hof asks. 'I've got three of my crew arrested. They're going to be out of action for months now, possibly years, depending on how hard the judges decide to hit them. That's three guys not earning and—'

'Chill,' says Van der Pol, raising a hand and channelling a stoned reggae master. 'I wanted there to be a shoot-out so the cops were kept busy.'

This doesn't make any sense to Kees. Nor to any of the others, by the looks of things.

Van der Pol clearly doesn't care. He's not an elected leader. This is not the Democratic Republic of Van der Pol.

He winks at Kees.

Kees' balls sack tightens.

'I'll get you replacements,' Van der Pol says to Hof, like this is the last he wants to hear of it.

'But I'm going to need to pay them regardless. If I don't then I'm going to be exposed.'

'Maybe you're better off without them, sounds like they're not that loyal.'

'Loyal? Fuck. You think they'll be getting poled in the shower and thinking of loyal? No way. I've gotta stand by them or I'm in shit.'

Kees feels the others all tensing, the motorhome itself holding its breath, waiting to see what'll happen.

Van der Pol is still, silent, like a viper waiting to strike.

Then he laughs. The space eases off.

'We'll find a solution which protects you,' he says.

Hof senses he's stepped over the mark but got away with it. He thanks Van der Pol, seems about to say something else, presumably apologize, but Van der Pol waves him off.

'But we're not here for this, fun as it's been,' he says. 'We're here because yesterday we found out we've been compromised. Someone ratted.'

He takes in all their faces, one by one.

Kees feels the gaze on his is the longest.

He has an overriding urge to swallow. That and the urge to get the fuck out of there as fast as possible.

'Luckily,' Van der Pol says, the heat of his gaze now elsewhere, 'I've got someone in the police. Have done for years. He's the one who told me about last night, allowed us to make the switch in time. And now he's working on finding out who they have here. I reckon we'll know in the next forty-eight or so, and when we know we're going to have a bit of fun.'

He's looking at Kees again.

General laughter round the motorhome. Because this motherfucker is *funny*.

Kees' nuts are now pulverized.

'One more thing,' Van der Pol says. He nods to a man next to Hof.

Kees sees the blade in his hand, short and serrated. The man steps forward. Kees is getting ready.

Then the man swings round and plunges the knife into Hof's stomach.

Again and again and again in a sticky frenzy.

Even some of the crew start to look a little uneasy.

Kees becomes aware of Van der Pol talking again. He tunes in.

'Chill,' he's saying, as if shushing a baby to sleep. 'Chill.'

33

Downstairs the station's buzzing, though he's not sure if it's to do with the result he's got, or something else. He checks in on Pieter Groot, finds he's still being processed, so heads to his desk and makes a start on the notes which will end up as his final report.

His desk phone interrupts him. He answers and immediately wishes he hadn't, because the voice drilling into his ear is that of Michiel Berk, the chief crime reporter for *De Telegraaf*. Berk has the persistence of a junkie chasing heroin, only with far less charisma.

'Hear you're in charge of the cling-film killer?'

'No, I'm not in charge of it.'

'No?'

'No, sorry. Try the press office,' Jaap says as he puts the phone down. He knows that was stupid, it'll only make Berk push harder, but he doesn't want to deal with it.

The phone rings again. He whips it off the cradle, taps a button, and leaves the headset on the desk.

When he'd started his career the police didn't care much about their image, mainly because the press still reported on them with a fair amount of reverence. But over the last fifteen years or so that reverence has slipped away, the teddy-bear press turning into a snarling grisly. Newspapers have gone into decline, the smart ones have switched models and now live to drive traffic to their website, trying to convert clicks into cash. And does deferential get you web traffic? The few who tried that found out pretty fast that it doesn't.

The answer, discovered fairly early on, was lurid reporting. The more lurid the better. Which was when the police suddenly found themselves not only fighting crime, but fighting to keep themselves out of the headlines. Panic at the top led to the hiring of a series of PR consultants who guzzled massive amounts of public money just to show the police how to make themselves look better in a world which suddenly seemed intent on destroying them.

But Jaap doesn't like dealing with the press for a more personal reason: he'd once been forced into a press conference by Smit to announce the successful completion of a murder case, just as the news came in that another body had been found. They were on live TV; Jaap had looked like an ass. The event had done little to endear either the press, or Smit, to Jaap.

Someone calls his name and he looks across the office to see one of the uniforms who'd taken Groot away.

'All yours,' he says.

Smit's down by the cell, looking through the small glass window.

Jaap flips into stealth mode, gets close behind Smit before opening up.

'Lawyer in with him?'

Smit jumps. Sure it's childish, but at the same time Jaap finds it hugely gratifying. Smit turns and glares at him. They have a long and rich history of antipathy, but Jaap finds he suddenly no longer cares.

'Said he didn't need one.'

'Really?' Jaap says, his hand on the door handle already.

'Really. He was strongly advised, but he still refused. So go in there and destroy him.'

Jaap goes in. He's planning on using the Routine.

The Routine is simple: move into the room like you own it, ignore the prisoner totally, like they're not even a speck of shit on your shoe. Pull out a chair, stop halfway to inspect one of the legs, pull it out further. Test it, make sure it's not going to collapse the moment you sit on it, check that there's no wobble. Sit on it. Get up and move it a centimetre to the left. Test it again. Think for a minute. Decide it's OK. If you've got a toothpick, then a quick bit of dental hygiene won't go amiss.

Basically do everything you can to ramp up the tension and fear in the suspect's mind without actually acknowledging their presence.

But Pieter Groot's got other ideas.

'I killed her,' he says before Jaap's even had time to get to the chair.

Jaap sits down before answering, studying his face. It's collapsed in on itself, a face that even before the spread of whatever internal sickness had turned him into a killer, would look defeated.

'Both of them, you mean?' Jaap says, pushing photos of Heleen and Kaaren across the table.

Jaap has to check there's no one in the room firing off a Taser, because Groot looks like he's just had the two prongs jammed into his flesh and the power whacked on high.

'What do you . . . ? No, not her!' he says, staring at the photos, his eyes expanding as if he's being pumped full of gas. 'No no no, I only killed the other one . . .'

Jaap looks at Groot, his skin now translucent like wax. 'You didn't kill Heleen Elders, on Vlieland?'

'I . . . no . . . I—'

'The two women were killed in the same way and you expect me to believe that you only killed one of them?'

Pieter Groot doesn't answer, he's just shaking his head from side to side.

'You've just admitted to me in a formal interview which is being recorded that you killed Kaaren, so why not admit what we both know, that you killed Heleen as well? It's not going to make any difference to your sentencing. You're going to prison. That's a fact. You *are* going to prison and nothing can change that. So why don't you tell me why you did it, why you killed Heleen first, and then Kaaren?'

Groot's shaking his head more violently now, back and forth.

'Where did you get the scopolamine?'

But Groot's done talking, he's rising up out of his chair, flailing like he's engulfed in a swarm of stinging bees. He throws himself against a wall.

Jaap's up, grabbing Groot by his T-shirt, and finds himself screaming in his face. 'You're gonna tell me, right here, right now, where you got the scopolamine.'

The door opens behind him, a rush of uniforms taking over, prising him off Groot.

He steps out of the room, trying not to hear the wail coming from Groot, a muezzin on speed. It gets cut off abruptly as the sound-proofed door slams shut.

He takes a few moments to breathe, to really get some air into his lungs, try and work out why it's happening again, why he has a man admitting to one death, but not another. Cold unease seeps through him.

As soon as he's out of the cell he calls Tanya but her phone goes straight to voicemail. Then he tries Arno, gets the same. He leaves messages, asking to be called back instantly. Then he dashes up the stairs, he has too much energy to walk now, and heads for his desk, finding someone's left a large photocopier right by it.

'What's this?' Jaap asks the room at large.

'Broken, there was this guy taking it away.'

'So why's it here?'

'Dunno,' says the officer who'd answered, looking like he wished he'd kept his head down. 'Maybe he went to get something?'

Jaap starts shoving it away from his desk just as Smit appears round the corner and catches a foot on the copier's corner.

'Fuck!' he yells, looking down at his shoe.

Jaap follows his gaze, sees the fresh scratch on the patent leather.

'What are you doing?' demands Smit, inspecting the damage, then spitting on his finger and rubbing the mark. It doesn't go away.

Just then a man dressed in grubby overalls appears and, oblivious to both Jaap and Smit, starts to haul the photocopier away.

They watch him go then Smit turns back to Jaap.

Jaap's never much liked Smit's face.

But he likes it even less now, because he can tell it's bad news.

'My office, ten minutes.'

34

'Tanya Vandermark,' she says, bending down and looking through the passenger window.

It's taken her longer to get there than she'd hoped, her phone running out of reception several blocks away. As she finally found the road she saw a cell tower – constructed in a pathetic attempt to disguise it as a tree – being felled.

Arno leans over and opens the door, then offers his hand once she's in.

Tanya thinks of Jaap's comment just before clasping it – awkwardly, given the angle. He looks younger than she'd imagined. On his wrist she notices a tattoo, a circle of intertwining thorns.

'So, tell me about it,' she says.

He points to a house across the street, a detached property in a row of detached properties. Front gardens all neat, flowers looking like they'd been colour-matched, as if the whole thing was controlled by some committee hell-bent on making the place look nice. And safe. It's the kind of place an ad agency would set an advert for washing powder.

The sun beats down, tarmac shimmers.

Arno hands her a photocopied sheet. In the top left corner there's a passport-sized photo.

'This is the guy that lives there, he's called Stefan Wilders. He was renting a cottage in the same holiday camp Heleen's cottage was in. And he was seen by a kid leaving the beach where she'd been killed round about the same time.'

'You think he did it?'

He shrugs. 'Jaap says he's got the killer, but maybe Stefan Wilders saw something? Might help get a conviction if he can ID the killer.'

Tanya thinks it unlikely. The news had exploded onto every platform earlier in the day, she'd seen it scrolling across a screen in the motorway stop she'd made on the way out of Rotterdam. The media was frothing like a crazy person, the news of a young girl being killed on a holiday beach just the kind of story to whip them into a manic frenzy of indignation heaped on wild speculation. In other words, the chances of Stefan Wilders not having heard the news is basically zero. And if he had heard then surely he'd've come forward already.

'It's a weekday, why's he going to be here, not at work?'

'Yeah, that's kind of tragic. His wife died not long after their kid was born, rare type of brain cancer, so he stays at home with their baby.'

Tanya doesn't think about her own baby or the hospital. She doesn't. Because on the drive up from seeing Dr Bruggen she made the decision that she's not going to worry about it at all. It's fine, she'll go and see the specialist and it will all turn out to be nothing more than an overcautious medical professional. So she tries to funnel her mind away and it slips down a related route; assuming everything is OK and she gives birth to a healthy child she realizes that she's still going to want to go back to work. She wonders if Jaap will turn into the house-husband type. She gets a glimpse of him meeting her at the door with an apron and a baby slung on his hip.

'What's funny?'

'Ah . . . nothing,' she says. 'If you're ready, let's go and ask him what he knows.'

They make their way across the street, only to find no one's home.

In the garden two doors down an old bow-legged woman stalks a rosebush with a bottle of insecticide and a look of intense determination.

They wait.

Then they wait some more, eventually starting to head back to their cars when Arno motions to her. She looks up to see Stefan Wilders turning into the street with a cluster of shopping bags. They watch as he makes it to his front garden. Tanya crosses the street, Arno on her heels. She calls out to him and he turns on the doorstep.

Tanya's shocked by the complex emotions which swirl across his face. She might be reading this wrong, but she's sure they settle into a kind of relieved fear. Which makes no sense.

'Stefan Wilders? I'm Inspector Vandermark, I just wanted to ask you a few questions.'

Stefan's a head taller than her, dressed in combat shorts with pockets stuffed like hamster cheeks. He's wearing a black T-shirt, a universe of sweat under each arm and a galaxy of dandruff on his shoulders. He also badly needs a shave, the designer-stubble thing not doing him any favours. At least in Tanya's view.

'Sure,' he says. 'Let me just offload this stuff. You want to come in?'

They do.

He puts down the bags and searches a pocket for his keys.

As the key nears the lock a baby squawks from upstairs and Tanya instinctively glances up.

At the same moment Stefan slams his body back, right into Tanya, knocking her off balance, her foot catching on something behind her. She goes over backwards, tailbone taking the brunt, right into a patch of flowers. The surprise and shock of it grips her lungs tight.

Stefan's ducked inside, the door slamming shut just before Arno's shoulder hits it hard. He tries again.

'Round the side,' Tanya manages to say once she's sucked in enough air to make her lungs function properly again, pain lighting up her whole spine till it practically glows.

'You OK?'

'Just go!' she says, her voice stronger now, struggling to her feet.

'Fuck,' Arno says, hesitating before deciding on the left.

Tanya's on her feet and can feel the adrenaline taking over, killing the pain more effectively than any drug. She starts out round the opposite side to Arno as a voice in her head tells her she shouldn't be doing this, she should be calling for back-up.

She's wavering between following Arno and dashing back to the car to get her radio, when she hears the shatter of glass.

And a scream.

Which sounds like Arno.

She runs faster, rounding the house. The pane on a large bifold is missing, Arno's lying in a glittering sea of glass and blood. She sees him getting to his feet, a massive cut down his right arm bleeding badly. Behind him Stefan's running across a large lawn, a shard of glass stuck in his right calf making him limp like a gangsta rapper.

He reaches the fence, a head-height wooden slatted job, and starts trying to climb, his feet scrabbling as he hauls himself up.

She sprints across the lawn, reaching him just as he has one leg over, riding the fence like a horse. She lunges for his foot, grabs it, and, working on the principle that innocent people don't assault police officers, yanks down hard.

He screams, head thrown back, and now he's riding bronco. She yanks again. Underneath his second scream she hears something else. A crack, like wood splintering.

Arno's voice flies out at her from behind, but she can't make out the words.

The fence starts to topple towards her.

She releases Stefan's leg, tries to back-pedal, but it's picking up momentum now.

Everything slows down.

The sun in the sky darkens as Stefan's form moves towards her.

Seconds before impact she knows she's fucked up.

He hits hard, and for a blinding, crushing moment she thinks she can hear bones snap. It occurs to her that she might never be able to breathe again.

Seconds later the pressure releases. She's dimly aware of Arno hauling Stefan off.

Something's wrong. She knows it, but she doesn't know what *it* is.

Arno has Stefan a few feet away now, shoving him to

his knees. Stefan's facing her, she follows the direction of his gaze.

Now she knows what's wrong.

Her gun has been knocked out of her holster. She tries to move but Stefan slams his head back, knocking Arno full in the face as he's ducking to get his cuffs.

Stefan lurches forward, reaching for the weapon.

Fear kick-starts her; she's moving towards it as well.

But Stefan is there. He has it in his hand.

He points it right at her.

Eyes lock.

They're blue, she notices, and the left one has a tiny imperfection in the iris, a smudge of yellow. Behind him Arno's getting up, hands on his face, a torrent of blood gushing from what must be a smashed nose. Behind him the house, the broken patio door the only thing out of place.

This is it, her mind tells her over and over. This is it. This is it.

All she can think about is the baby in her stomach, growing there with an imperfect heart.

Stefan's mouth is moving but she can't make out the words. He's saying something over and over again. She starts to make sense of it.

'I had to do it,' she thinks she hears. 'I had to protect her.'

Then Stefan turns the gun round, bites down on it, his eyelids screwing tight.

When the gun goes off, her eyes are closed.

She feels warm spray all over her face and neck.

35

Jaap's watching Smit's mouth move. He guesses that means he's still talking, forming words – there'd been no reason to go through the funny sequence of movements otherwise – but for some reason he can't hear them.

Because Smit started off with a word-grenade which exploded in Jaap's head and now his ears are ringing in the aftermath.

His mind keeps going over what he's been told, that Pieter Groot's not lying, he couldn't have killed Heleen as he had a rock-solid alibi for the time of her death.

Frank's crew had been working hard on background, and found evidence which planted him miles away at the time of the murder.

'Are you listening?' Smit asks, the ringing tapering away from Jaap's ears.

'No,' Jaap says, 'I'm not.'

They're in Smit's office, sun layering through the window to Jaap's left. He looks down, one foot is in the light, the other in shadow.

'Least you're honest,' replies Smit. 'I was asking, what now?'

Which is the question.

Jaap's mind goes into overdrive, thinking of possibilities, a bright anger forming in him. He leaves the room, ignoring Smit's call, and walks down the corridor. By the time he reaches the stairs he's running, down three flights, to where Groot's being held.

'OK,' he says as he kicks the door open and walks in, the anger more than bright now, it's *blazing*, 'you're going to tell me what the fuck is going on. Right now.'

But Groot's got other plans. He may be cuffed and restrained, in a cell, facing a life in prison. He doesn't have much control over his life, or what's left of it. The one thing he does appear to have control over is whether he's going to talk or not.

And it becomes clear that he's decided he's not saying another word.

36

Jaap's spent the last fifteen minutes walking the streets, trying to make some sense of things. Usually cases follow a logical progression of sorts, you accumulate evidence which leads you in a certain direction, then you accumulate more and it clarifies things. This case is the opposite, each step, each new bit of information, only seems to complicate matters, throw him further and further off balance.

'Boss wants to see you,' says the desk sergeant as Jaap walks back into the station.

'You haven't seen me,' Jaap says, walking past him.

He's at the top of the stairwell, heading back down to Groot, when his phone goes off. Arno.

'Turn up anything?' Jaap asks.

'I . . . yeah, we've—' Arno's voice crackles through the speaker. Jaap moves out of the stairwell, hunting for better reception.

'Where are you?'

'Listen, don't freak out but I've got some news. We found the killer, he's dead. And Tanya's OK, she really is, but they're taking her to hospital just in case and—'

'What? Tanya? What happened? Fuck. Where are you?'

The desk sergeant's watching him closely now.

'She's fine, really. Just a precaution. We're going to the AMC at Bijlmer.'

'I'm going there now, how long?'

'Twenty.'

Jaap's running down the stairs, past Groot's cell and on to the car pool.

This is his fault. He's not been paying proper attention.

And the result is he's put her in danger.

Fucking idiot, he thinks as he grabs a set of keys from the officer manning the car-pool desk, ignoring his requests to sign, and jumps in a car, firing up the engine and slamming it into reverse.

He scrunches the car beside it as he swings round and lines it up for the exit ramp.

Sirens scream, blue lights strobe the concrete walls, and his foot stomps the pedal.

The cell door closes with a clang as the man steps out.

Pieter Groot's not really aware of him leaving.

He's not really been aware of much the last few days.

He remembers the feeling he'd had as a teenager when a dentist had pulled two teeth out, the strange numbness of his lips, which were there, but didn't really feel like they were.

He's got the same feeling now, or similar at any rate, all over his body. And his mind too. He feels like he's detached from himself somehow, just a passenger in his own body.

He forces himself to think. Because he knows he has to do it now, he may not get another chance. And he has no choice, that much is clear.

The T-shirt slides off his back and over his head.

He twists it up, as if he's wringing out a towel, tightening with each turn.

He knows the reflex is going to be his enemy, and he takes a moment, seeing if he can override it in advance.

As he feels the fabric settle into position, the gagging start to kick in, he thinks of his son.

He pushes harder, twisting the T-shirt more to help it screw further down his throat, until it blocks it totally. He can feel the lack of air start to build.

Again he thinks of his son.

And as things start to darken, he asks for his forgiveness.

Ceiling tiles are coming and going, each one a dull square sliding from above Tanya's head to well past her feet.

Shoes squeak, rubber wheels purr, and a distinct metal rattling adds to the whole. It's starting to feel like a piece by Steve Reich, simple but complex at the same time.

Her ribs are aching, and she keeps having this weird sensation which is both hearing *and* feeling at the same time. The crack when Stefan landed on top of her. Though it's now getting confused in her mind with the sound of the gunshot. And somehow it's only adding to all the other sounds, building the piece up into something relentless.

Breathing's difficult as well, painful, an effort to keep it going.

She knows she's in shock, but that doesn't stop her mind jumping around, getting stuck on something repeatedly – *crack crack crack* – before veering off onto something else.

Now it's the lights, thin strips two panels long. She

tries to see a pattern, but just as she thinks she's got a handle on it, broken the code, it changes.

She keeps on watching them, until they slip away.

The traffic is there purely to stop him.

There is no other reason for all these people to be out on the road, driving slowly, obeying speed limits, getting in his way as if it was their goddamned right.

Jaap's got the full whack going – lights, sirens, and he's hitting the horn too. And yes, cars *are* moving out of the way. Just nowhere near quick enough.

All he can think about is how he's put Tanya in danger.

As he's skidding into the AMC's car park in Bijlmer he's offering up prayers to a god he knows doesn't exist, offering anything at all in return for Tanya's safety.

He spots Arno down a corridor and runs towards him, dodging round a bed carrying a man with so many tubes coming out of him he looks like a science experiment. The nurse pushing the bed calls out in protest but Jaap ignores him.

'Where is she?'

Arno's nose is broken. He's got tape across it like a young Jack Nicholson in *Chinatown*. Minus the hat.

'They've just taken her away, she's unconscious. I think they're going to do an X-ray on her chest—'

'Which way?'

Arno points along the corridor.

Jaap takes off. He can see Radiology signs. He follows them down three corridors before reaching a reception area. His body's all over the place, he feels like he has more limbs than he should, and he's not fully in control of them all.

The nurse on duty listens to what he has to say and quickly checks her computer. The air con hums. A strident voice calls for a Dr Vos in Cardiology. Down a distant corridor a child is crying.

'Room three,' she finally says, pointing the way.

Jaap can't breathe, he reaches the door. A warning light is on: DANGER RADIATION DO NOT ENTER.

He throws it open.

She's there on the bed, a mechanical arm holding a bulbous form hovering above her body.

He runs forward, hits it out of the way.

'What the fuck—'

'She's pregnant!' yells Jaap at the tech who'd emerged from a separate room. 'Tell me you didn't do it.'

37

There's some international conspiracy whose tentacles reach into every hospital in the western world, one which decrees that the walls have to be painted in strange pastel colours which, if you weren't sick already, are certainly going to push you that way through a creeping osmosis. The corridor in which Jaap's talking to the surgeon, who hasn't even bothered to remove his face mask, is such a colour. Jaap finds himself wondering what the name on the paint tin would be. Faint Apricot Vomit is about the closest he can come up with.

'Bottom line,' the surgeon's saying as Jaap pushes away his weird thoughts, 'there's a chance one or more of her ribs have snapped and are interfering with the lung. I'll have to get in there to have a look.'

Jaap's standing stock still. His legs feel like glass, one movement and they'll shatter. 'But the anaesthetic—'

'Not ideal, agreed. But neither's a collapsed lung or internal bleeding.'

Jaap's phone is going off in his pocket. It's like something from another world. He ignores it.

People are moving around them, beds being wheeled, nurses hurrying from one place to another, relatives fearing the worst in plastic chairs.

'Yeah, OK,' Jaap says. 'Can I see her before—'

'No time,' the surgeon says before disappearing through

a set of double doors. Jaap watches them swing back and forth, his eyes on the ever diminishing glimpses of the corridor beyond.

Tanya's going under the knife. They're going to open her up, slice flesh with a scalpel. And he's standing here doing nothing.

Because there's nothing he can do.

And it's all his fault. He put her in this position. He'd not been paying attention, too wrapped up in the case to spot the danger.

His phone buzzes again. Again he ignores it.

He turns and walks away down a corridor, not knowing where he's heading, trying to control the blaze of anger inside.

As he passes through a doorway a nurse points out the hand-gel dispenser.

Jaap glances at it. Then reaches out and rips the box off the wall.

Somewhere close by a man's screaming.

As he smashes the small box against the floor he realizes it's him.

38

'He knows about me, you fuck.'

Which is no way to talk to a superior officer.

But right now Kees isn't up for a whole lot of decorum.

The only thing Kees *is* up for is making sure he stays alive.

'Impossible,' Smit says, voice breaking in and out thanks to low reception. 'No one knows about you.'

'He does, he fucking does know!' Kees yells, unable to keep his voice down. 'And he says he has someone in the police who is checking up.'

He's standing in the middle of a field with a burner he'd bought less than an hour ago. Thin strips of cloud, so pink they look artificial, drift in the fading sky.

The heat's easing off, but Kees' body feels like it's cooking from the inside out, his heart doing its best to crack a few ribs.

He'd dialled into Amsterdam and demanded to speak to Smit. All of which was a total break in protocol.

'Kees, I'll be honest here. No one *can* know about you because I kept you off the books. Completely. There's not a single shred of evidence that you're anything but a piece-of-shit biker along with the rest of them.'

The sky darkens exactly one notch. Kees feels the vast space around him.

He's not sure if what Smit's just told him is true.

He's not sure Smit *actually* just said what he thought he said.

'I just watched one of his long-term men get carved up right in front of me. You get that? Van der Pol sat there and fucking *joked* about it. You think if he finds out about me he's going to go any easier? The man is a fucking psycho and I've given you enough to put him away. Why can't you just fucking do it?'

Silence.

The light notches down again, the landscape and sky merging into a colourless gloom, pink clouds now drained of colour.

'Listen,' Smit says finally, 'here's what you're going to do.'

Kees is listening, expecting a plan, a carefully crafted exit strategy, preferably one which involves him leaving right now.

'Stick at your job and wait till I tell you it's over.'

39

'He said *what?*'

Jaap has just listened to Arno's account of what happened. Smashing the gel dispenser had been stupid, but had released some of the tension. Now he's starting to feel guilty about it.

'It was hard to hear, but it was something like *I had to protect her, I had to do it.*'

They're standing outside the hospital entrance where a bunch of in-patients have given up on the wonders of modern medical care and have chosen to self-medicate with nicotine. A cab pulls up. They watch the driver take a wheelchair out of the boot and try to unfold it – he's not having much luck, you'd think the thing was a Rubik's Cube – and a backseat window rides down. The passenger, a man with Einstein hair, gives him instructions through the window.

The sun's aiming for the horizon, dropping into a patch of clouds, rays poking through the odd gap. It looks like the cover of a cheap Christian prayer book.

Jaap's mind's been on Tanya, but what Arno's just told him raises questions.

I had to protect her, I had to do it, he thinks. But from what? And who is she? Heleen?

Was the killer so sick in the head that he thought there was something so bad she needed protecting from that death was preferable? Or was 'she' someone else?

The cab driver now has the wheelchair assembled, and he's helping the passenger into it.

I can't do this, thinks Jaap.

He watches Einstein wheel himself away from the cab, manoeuvring with a kind of technical grace.

He feels his responsibility is with Tanya. He suddenly realizes there's no way he can carry on with the case. Not now.

'Listen, I'm stepping off this case. But I can put a word in for you, would you be up for carrying on? Not as lead, but working with whoever gets it?'

Arno looks at him, excitement under the surface. He seems so young, Jaap thinks. Which makes him feel old.

'Yeah, I'd like to do that.'

Jaap slaps him on the shoulder. 'Thought you'd say that. Bit of advice?'

'You're not old and grizzled enough to be handing out advice.'

'Maybe. But . . . oh, for fuck's sake.'

He reaches for his phone, which has been going off constantly for the last ten minutes, part of his thigh massaged into a painful numbness. He doesn't know why he'd not just turned it off.

The number on the screen is Smit's.

Do it now, the quitting voice says.

An ambulance pulls up, the crew rushing a gurney out the back.

The gurney's moving fast, flanked by three paramedics. Jaap tries to catch a glimpse of the person lying on it.

He hits green and is about to speak, but Smit's already talking.

'Pieter Groot tried to kill himself, he should be arriving at the AMC any moment now.'

Jaap turns and watches the hospital doors slide closed behind the gurney.

It takes ten minutes to find the room where Groot is being treated. He's just stepping up to it, reaching out for the door handle, when it swings open and he nearly collides with a nurse bustling out. The nurse glares at him – he has something wrong with one of his eyes, a kind of scar or birthmark which gives one eye a half-closed look – but he carries on past Jaap down the corridor without saying anything.

Inside, the room looks out over a central courtyard, the windows opposite slicked golden with the last of the day's light.

Groot's lying in the bed, hooked up to an IV.

Jaap thinks of Tanya in surgery, and wonders why his world has suddenly narrowed to one building.

Groot's eyes open, recognition flaring there for a second.

Jaap grabs a chair and sits beside him. He's sent Arno to the surgery waiting area so he can call him the second there's news on Tanya. He figures he might as well try and take his mind off it by talking to Pieter Groot.

He pulls out his phone and starts recording.

'Ready?'

Pieter doesn't respond.

Jaap reaches out, shakes his shoulder, his grip maybe firmer than he'd intended.

'I had to,' Groot croaks. 'I had no choice. He made me do it or he said he'd . . .'

'Who? Who's *he*?' Jaap says, leaning in closer.

Groot's eyes have closed again. Jaap shakes him.

He notices something on the floor, a dark shadow creeping out from the bed, already touching his toes.

He leans over Groot's body, finds the drip tube stuck in his arm. It's hanging down the far side of the bed so he'd not noticed it. The end trails to the floor, spilling Groot's blood, a whole lake of it expanding quietly outwards, the surface a dark sheen reflecting the fluorescent lights from the ceiling.

His life literally draining away.

Groot had tried to kill himself at the station but had been stopped.

Now he's tried again by reversing the IV.

Jaap rips the tube out and presses down on Groot's arm, a fluttery panic taking over his body.

But he already knows it's too late.

40

The sheet whooshes like a sail catching the wind, then sinks gently down, the shape of a person gradually emerging as it settles.

They tried their best but Groot didn't make it.

The staff seem subdued but philosophical. You win some, you lose some.

Jaap steps away from the room, and finds his way out of the hospital. It's all too much to deal with, especially as half his mind's on Tanya, still in surgery.

He walks fast, not aware of his surroundings, running through all the bad possible outcomes. A few minutes later, he stops dead.

He's on a main road. It's dark, cars rushing past him, the people inside them caught up in their own lives, unaware of what he's going through.

When he'd been driving to the hospital he'd found himself offering prayers up to God, saying he'd do *anything* if only Tanya was allowed to live, unharmed. This was ridiculous because he'd never been religious, but in those moments of fear his rational mind seemed to dissolve, and he knows that right now he'd do *anything* to protect her, save her. Anything at all.

He stops dead.

Kamp had no wife and a young baby to look after.

Pieter Groot's wife had run out on him, leaving him with a child.

He can feel the rush starting, he knows this is it, what he's been looking for. His fingers are trembling as he gets his phone out and dials Arno.

'The guy who shot himself, Stefan Wilders, did he have a child but no wife?' Jaap asks when Arno picks up.

'How'd you know that?' Arno says.

'So no wife?'

'No, she died.'

Jaap hangs up and takes a few more seconds, the whole thing zooming into focus.

He suddenly sees what it is he's missed all along, why he's been doing nothing but chasing his tail, why this whole case has been a rapid-fire series of events which have been way out of his control.

He imagines someone handing him a gun, telling him the only way that Tanya is going to live is if he shoots someone in her place.

A deep shiver surfs down his spine.

He'd assumed the crimes were based on hate. But now he knows that's not true.

The key to this is something far stronger.

The key to it is love.

41

The spade hits a stone, sending a judder right up Kees' arm into his neck and shoulders.

It's not the first.

There've been countless stones already, and, if he knows anything about life, there will be many more.

Because even though he's been working on this for over an hour – his back pouring with sweat and aching only slightly less than his leg, the blisters on his hands surely going to burst soon – he still hasn't managed to dig a hole big enough to bury a large dog, let alone Hof's body.

Which right now is crumpled up in the boot of the car parked twenty metres or so outside the woods he's digging in. Also in the car, though sadly still alive, is the Lumberjack. He's the one who's driven him out here and ordered him to get digging whilst he sits and smokes a joint and watches porn on a smudged iPad.

Kees reaches down into the hole and tries to work loose the stone with his fingers, dirt already packed tight under his fingernails.

The moon's up; it has a yellowish tinge which makes Kees think of pus, and he can just see the stone has a sharp edge running along one side. It also seems to be much longer than the others he's pulled out so far, widening out where it disappears into the soil at the edge of the hole.

He scrapes earth away from underneath it, scooping it

out in handfuls, then works the spade underneath, trying to prise it up. He applies pressure. Nothing.

He tosses the spade aside, gets back down and scrabbles at it with his hands like a mad burrowing animal, like evolution hasn't happened.

He comes out of the frenzy to find his hands aching like everything else in his body, but he's got used to that over the last couple of years.

The morning he'd gone to the hospital is a vivid memory, fresh and untainted, presumably because he's tried ever since not to think about it, kept it in the dark to protect it from scrutiny. But it's all unwrapping now, unfurling like an evil tentacle, and he can smell the disinfectant, feel the churning in his stomach as he sat next to a man in a large waiting area. The man's body was contorted like his back had twisted up wrong, curled in on itself, and his breathing was laboured, rasping in and out of his mouth like each breath was a struggle. He had white flecks on the side of his mouth, lips taut in a grimace.

Kees had been on a night stake-out when the call had come in. He and Jaap had been working a case where a woman was suspected of knifing her abusive boyfriend then torching the house to try and hide the evidence. Kees was stuck with watching the woman's closest relation's house on the off-chance she'd try and seek refuge there. The night had been long, and although he'd been to the hospital a few days prior, he'd been doing a great job of putting it out of his mind. The uniform who was supposed to be relieving him at 9 a.m. was late, and when his phone had gone off he'd been expecting the person at the other end to apologize and assure him he was just round the corner.

Instead he'd listened as the woman, after verifying who he was, asked him to please visit the hospital as soon as possible. He'd replied he could probably make sometime next week.

There'd been a pause before the woman had wondered out loud if he could make sometime that very day.

So once he'd got off shift, the uniform finally having turned up with some bullshit story about how one of his kids was sick, instead of driving home and trying to get some catch-up he'd motored over to the hospital, his mind trying to block out all the possible scenarios that were crashing around in his head.

And then his name had been called and he'd jumped up and made his way to the specified room, it was all going to be good, because he was young, something minor, nothing like any of the truly sick people he'd been sitting around with in the waiting area. They'd give him a drug perhaps, and then he could just go about his life.

All would be well.

But the doctor's face when he stepped into the room told him otherwise.

Kees had sat in the chair placed to the side of the man's desk as he talked. For at least half of it Kees had felt like he was underwater, his ears only picking up a quiet roar whilst the man mouthed his way through something, like he was eating an invisible meal.

He had picked up enough though.

The basic message was that his immune system was attacking his own body. Kees had never heard of such a thing, it didn't really make sense. Why would it do that? The doctor didn't know, but said it seemed to be accelerating and that the only thing they could realistically do was give him some drugs to shut it down.

Kees had asked if that wasn't dangerous long-term.

The doctor had talked about a rock and a hard place.

He'd also informed Kees that long-term was, in his opinion, unlikely.

The stone gives a little. Kees stands up, grabs the spade and wedges it under. He leans on the handle and the stone shifts a couple of millimetres. Then it stops dead.

Kees pushes harder. Still nothing. Jesus *fuck*.

He goes back to it with his hands, pulling more and more dirt out of the hole. But the more he removes, the wider the stone seems to get, like it's an iceberg, the tiny tip above the earth, a colossus below.

Something jabs the end of one of his fingers, deep enough to get past the numbness, and he jumps back. He grabs the finger with his other hand. He can feel blood seeping out. The same blood which is transporting whichever part of his immune system is doing the damage round his body.

He feels like howling but snatches up the spade, jamming it under the stone and pushing down with all his weight.

Nothing else is important now. Nothing else matters. He just wants to move the fucking stone and be done with it.

The wooden shaft creeks. Then it cracks.

A bird detonates out of one of the trees behind him.

'Fuck was that?' a voice says.

It belongs to Lumberjack, who must've got bored of the pair of smoothly shaved lesbians on his iPad licking each other like they're nutrient-starved.

Kees doesn't bother to answer as Lumberjack steps up beside him and inspects the hole. He smells of weed and damp clothes. He pulls something out of a pocket. Kees sees it's a torch.

The beam light-sabers on and is guided towards Kees' work, sweeping back and forth until it settles.

'Seriously,' Lumberjack says, 'he's not a pygmy. We're gonna need a bigger hole.'

42

He sees Smit outside the station, leaving for home.

Jaap doesn't feel like preamble. He steps over.

'The killers don't want to kill,' Jaap says. 'They're being forced into it.'

Smit stops. He stares at Jaap, the orange streetlight making his features look ghoulish.

'What do you mean, forced?'

'That's why none of this has made sense,' Jaap says. 'Whoever it is is picking people and forcing them to kill for him. Groot said he had to do it to protect someone, and Stefan Wilders, who shot himself when Tanya tried to question him, said something similar. It's their kids, someone's threatened their kids, maybe even held them until they've done what they wanted—'

'Hang on,' says Smit, his face getting visibly paler. 'Hang on a minute.'

Jaap hangs on, but Smit seems to be lost in thought. He's massaging his jaw, eyes looking out over the car park.

'Fuck. What else?' Smit finally says.

'I think he also tells them that if they're caught and they say anything then he'll still get their kids. They're all single fathers, the kids will go into care, so it'd be easy to convince them you could get to their kids somehow, even from prison. That's why they're choosing the only way out they can see. They may even have been *told* to kill themselves rather than talk if they were ever caught.'

'Fuck,' Smit says, earning him a glance from an old man walking past, sucking on his vape. Smit turns his back on him, lowers his voice. 'Why not come to the police when they're first threatened? That would be the sensible thing to do.'

'Someone threatens to kill your kids, you don't think straight.'

Smit shouldn't need to be told; he knows that Jaap's own daughter had been kidnapped by a man desperate to get someone released from prison. He'd tasked Jaap with getting that man out, and told him if he spoke to any of his colleagues about it then he'd never see his daughter again. Jaap had done as he was told, busting the man out of the International Criminal Tribunal in Den Haag. Only things had gone wrong, his baby daughter paying the price, along with her mother. Jaap had never felt such fear, and knew that it had clouded his judgement in a way that no one could understand.

They stand for a few moments more, both men feeling like they're on the edge of a cliff, like the next gust of wind will determine their future, whether they fall off it or move back. A tram clangs its bell, and a distant siren sounds once, dying mid-swoop.

'Fuck,' Smit says again. 'I'm going to have to call the commissioner, we need more people on this.'

43

Jaap had once, at the end of a six-hour meditation session at the temple in Kyoto, caught the most fleeting glimpse of what he'd gone there to find. For a second or so – it was hard to tell as time got so distorted in those long sessions in the main hall – he realized that his ego wasn't him.

Sure, he knew the theory, knew that this was the kind of lightning strike they called 'Satori', the Awakening. But Zen wasn't about theory, Zen was all about discovering it for yourself.

He'd never managed to get that feeling again, no matter how long he meditated. His old Zen tutor, Yuzuki Roshi, would give him the 'don't try' type of Zen bollocks, but that didn't work either.

And now, holding Tanya's hand in his own, the hospital room clinical around him, he's glad he's not managed to rid himself of ego.

Because if he had he'd not be able to love Tanya as much as he does.

It hurts, it's true, but it doesn't matter because, fuck it, life hurts. Without that, without love, what is there?

In the corridor outside a pair of nurses cruise past, laughing quietly at some private joke, looking forward to getting off shift.

He wishes Tanya was awake, but the doctor said not for another hour or so.

He sits there listening to her breathing and before he's able to stop himself he's thinking about the case. About the men, bereaved at what should have been the most joyous period of their lives, being manipulated, petrified into killing to save their children.

But by who? And why?

A knock at the door surprises him, so wound up in his thoughts he's not heard the surgeon's footsteps. He steps out into the corridor.

'Good news,' the surgeon says. 'One rib had made contact with the lung, but the wound's minimal. It'll heal quickly. The rib's cracked so it's going to be painful for a bit, but again it's not really a problem. I was able to do it keyhole as well, so the entrance wound will also heal fast. We'll keep her in overnight, but assuming all goes well she can probably leave tomorrow. She was lucky. Damn lucky.'

All the tension and fear and worry surge up and Jaap finds he's got tears in his eyes. The surgeon puts a hand on his shoulder, squeezes it, then walks away before Jaap can thank him.

In the bed Tanya stirs, her mouth moves slightly and her eyelids flicker for a moment before settling again.

Watching her, Jaap makes a promise.

I'm never going to do anything which puts you in danger again.

Day Four

44

Jaap's deep underwater, the shimmering surface far above him. He kicks hard, his legs working against the water which seems to frustratingly absorb their force, his lungs burning with the desire for air, fear lighting up his reptilian brain. He knows he's dreaming, and he knows the surface is the idea which is going to tie this whole case together, knows it's purely symbolic, knows that once he can break through he'll find the answer. Just a few metres more and his head breaks through, air filling his lungs. And—

He jolts, like his whole body's been shot, just before the idea disappears. He tries to chase it, dive back down to the watery depths of sleep, but as he lies there on the hospital floor next to Tanya's bed, a towel rolled up into a makeshift pillow, he knows that full consciousness has just obliterated whatever it was.

He gets up, feeling heavy and stiff, and checks on Tanya. She's still asleep, her red hair splayed out on the pillow as if she's the one underwater, and he reaches out to touch her. She murmurs, seems to be saying something. He leans closer and catches a name, Ruud somebody? Staal, maybe. It means nothing to him, and Tanya's never talked of anyone called Ruud. Maybe it's someone she'd met down in Rotterdam. For a second he feels an insane pang of jealousy.

*

Jaap leaves the houseboat, where he's pit-stopped for a shower and quick change of clothes, and walks down Bloemgracht, turning left at the bottom. On the Lijnbaansgracht bridge he spots the homeless man out begging for money. He'd first appeared years ago and initially Jaap had ignored him, avoiding eye contact, each pass more guilt-ridden than the previous. Finally, on a thick foggy morning in November, water condensing on the bare branches and dripping into the canal like an insane symphony, Jaap had ducked into a shop and bought the man a couple of pastries and a cup of soup. He'd handed it all to him, a feeling he couldn't quite categorize, a kind of noble upswelling expanding in his chest.

The man took the goods offered, inspected them one by one and then looked back up at Jaap.

'What, ain't you got any bloody money then?' he'd said.

This morning he's actually asleep, his accumulated clothes bunched around him like the shell of a snail, and Jaap drops him a couple of euros as he goes past. It'll probably go on drugs, but if it gives him a few moments of pleasure then Jaap's not sure he really cares.

By the time he gets to the office the nightshift inspectors are bleary-eyed and clock-watching, willing the phones they'd wanted to ring all night to stay silent long enough for them to get out of there and head home for sleep. They've got another hour to go before the sun comes up and their relief arrives, so Jaap doesn't fancy their chances.

After an intense bout of caffeination Jaap starts scribbling notes, trying to let them flow freely, not to self-censor, hoping that somehow whatever he'd glimpsed in his dream was still there, buried in his unconscious mind, and might emerge on paper. But after a while he has to admit defeat. Whatever it was has gone.

The room's humming as he steps in.

Smit's call yesterday to the commissioner had yielded results. Purse strings have been loosened, money has flowed down the chain, and now Jaap has a team of six waiting to be briefed.

He recognizes a couple of them: there's Lisa Oosterhuis, the youngest in the department and the chain-smoking champion of the whole station, and Erik Verbaan, who's arrogant but capable of good work. The other four are new to him, he'll have to learn their names, but right now he doesn't have the mental capacity for it.

Also in the room are Arno – his clearance had come through earlier from a begrudging Stuppor – Smit and Thomas Haase, the force's main criminal profiler, who'd once spent a few months with the FBI at Quantico and has built a career on the back of it ever since. It's never been clear to Jaap what Haase actually did during those months – for all he knows he could've been there sweeping the floor or scrubbing the toilets till they shone, ready for some big-dick *real* agent to swing in and sully the thing all over again. Jaap's had the benefit of Haase's expertise on a couple of cases, though none of the man's insights has, so far, led to an arrest.

None of which stops Haase from frequently appearing on TV, exposing complex aetiologies for crimes which made the headlines, a service he undoubtedly gets well paid for. He'd even brought out a book which for a brief, heady moment had hit the bestseller lists, but though the public seemed to love him the running joke in the station is that you don't need a highly paid specialist to tell you a sadistic killer is a sick fuck.

Smit's sitting at the back, arms folded across his chest, and Haase's managed to get a space slightly apart from the group as if to emphasize his rarity and importance.

'Right,' Jaap says. 'Let's do it. Two murders in the last three days and two older killings.'

He starts with Dafne and Nadine, takes them through the investigation which led them to Francesco Kamp. After a five-minute break, coffee for all except Lisa who hurries outside for a cigarette, he ploughs on, hoping the team can keep up with all the detail he's throwing at them. When he gets to the arrest and subsequent shooting he can feel Smit's eyes on him, but he glosses over it, powers on to Heleen and Kaaren. He pins photos of each on the board and goes through the circumstances of their deaths.

'From this it all looks like a classic serial killer, but—' He pulls out photos of Kamp, Groot and Wilders and pins them up as well '—meet the killers. Stefan Wilders was seen filming Heleen on Vlieland, and Pieter Groot killed Kaaren the next day. Logically these two must have known each other somehow, or have some kind of link, but we can't ask them. This guy—' He points to Stefan's photo '—well, he introduced his brain to a bullet, and Groot, after nearly choking himself with his own T-shirt in our cells downstairs, had a second go at the hospital. He somehow reversed his IV and bled to death.'

He whips out a crime-scene photo showing the mass of blood staining the floor and pins it up too.

'But before both of them died they each said something. Arno, can you tell us what Wilders said?'

'"I had to protect her," ' Arno says. ' "I had to do it." '

'And then Groot said something similar.'

He pulls out his phone and plays the recording he'd made in the hospital room.

When it's done the room falls silent.

'So now we're getting down to it.' Jaap points to Wilders' photo. 'He had a daughter, just over a year old. Mother died in childbirth. Kamp also had a daughter and Groot had a young son.'

Jaap lets all that settle in.

'Thoughts, anyone?'

He's asking because he knows he doesn't want to be the one to say it out loud, but he feels the time has come to let loose what he, Smit and Arno already know. He'd once heard the most infectious agent of all is a thought, so he stares at the people he's about to infect.

'Right, so here's the theory. Someone is effectively blackmailing these people into killing for them. And I reckon he's using their children's lives as the bargaining chip.'

The room sucks the news dry.

Most of the people in here should be pretty much unshakeable, having seen enough stuff in their careers to keep a shrink in business for life, but he can see this is new to them. The infection has taken hold.

'So—' He draws a question mark in the centre of the board, lines radiating out to the photos '—there is someone out there, a serial killer, who is getting other people to kill for them. And it's now our job to find who they are.'

'What about their spouses?' Lisa asks. 'I mean, apart from Wilders. What do they say?'

'That's where it gets interesting. I think this is going to be our way in. The three killers actually have *two* things in common: they each have a young child, and their wives are dead or, in the case of Groot, AWOL. So these men are on their own, and whoever is forcing them into killing is targeting them specifically because of this. They're clearly vulnerable, and angry, and I think the killer is using that to his advantage. But the question is, how is the killer finding them? How is he finding men who have a young child and a dead or absent spouse? Is he looking at death records and screening from there, does he have access to hospital data, how else could he be finding them? Have they been on dating sites looking for new partners? We need to find out how he knows, how he picks them.'

'And what about the women, is the killer choosing them as well, what's the link there?' asks one of the men Jaap has yet to put a name to.

'So far there's nothing which links the women, or the women to the men who killed them, apart from physical proximity. So we need to dig on that front too. Is the killer choosing the women to be killed, or are they leaving that part of it up to the men themselves? There are a ton of questions here, and we need to get some answers. Quickly.'

Jaap breaks the room into three teams of two, assigning

Arno to work with him as the fourth. The first team, headed up by Erik, is to work on Heleen and Stefan Wilders, the second, led by Lisa, has Kaaren and Pieter Groot, and the third is to focus on Nadine. They take their assignments and get to it, leaving Jaap with Arno, Smit and Thomas.

'I want to be kept in the loop every step of the way,' Smit says, standing up and fiddling with his cuffs. 'The commissioner's all over this one, he's watching us and we need to get it right.'

Jaap waits till Smit's gone before turning to Haase.

'I know you've only just seen all this, but anything strike you so far?'

Haase, the personification of minimalism from the way he dresses, the trimness of his nails, and his air of detachment, clears his throat delicately.

'The suffocation is interesting,' he says adjusting his rimless glasses, the lenses hexagonal – or something with lots of edges on because really, who's counting? – and clearing his throat again. 'If the mystery man is forcing the men into killing for him and giving specific instructions as to how to do it, then . . .'

Jaap and Arno wait, watching him tap a finger gently against his lips.

'Then?' prompts Jaap when the tapping gets annoying.

'Then I'm going to have to think about it. It'll be more useful to you than if I give an off-the-cuff first impression now which might not be right.'

'Live a little,' Jaap says. 'Sometimes a first impression is the best thing.'

Haase looks at him and nods slowly.

'OK, my first impression is Smit doesn't like you very much.'

'Give the man a prize. Now tell me what you think about the case.'

'Oh the *case*,' he says, allowing himself a little minimalist smile. 'Well, my first impression of the case is that whoever is forcing people to kill for him in such a specific way is a total sick fuck.'

45

Jaap's never been much of a team player.

That's partly him, and partly the department. Because most murder cases are handled by at most two inspectors, mainly for pecuniary reasons.

But now that he has a team backing him up he feels a vague sense, not quite of relief, but a loosening perhaps, a feeling that now he can start to explore more deeply instead of just reacting to events.

His revelation yesterday was a major breakthrough, no question, but there's still so much he doesn't understand. Why had the particular women been chosen? Had they been chosen by whoever is forcing the men to kill, or had the men been free to choose their own victims?

He pulls up the files on Heleen and Kaaren. He's been meaning to go through them again, see if there's any connection between them, or anything which might point to why they'd been chosen. Yesterday he'd tasked Roemers with getting him access to all the victims' and killers' social media accounts, a simple enough task for someone who seems to know how to crack any password online. Jaap checks his email, and, sure enough, Roemers has got passwords for Heleen and Kaaren's email, Facebook, Instagram and WhatsApp accounts. He promises the rest later.

Jaap starts with Heleen, tracking her across social

media, looking for connections, red flags, anything which might help him progress. He's just about giving up on it when he comes across some emails – luckily Heleen was quite old-fashioned and actually used the archaic form from time to time – from the address psychonaut@dmt. com. Reading through the string of messages between Heleen and Psychonaut, who signs himself off as 'RV', it becomes clear that Heleen is wanting to quit her lifestyle, stop self-mutilating, and that Psychonaut appears to be helping her. There's talk of progress during their last session and plans for another one soon. But what really catches Jaap's attention is their last communication, from Heleen, and it simply read

YOU SHOULDN'T BE HERE, LEAVE ME ALONE.

It was sent the day before she died.

So was Psychonaut on Vlieland? Jaap wonders.

He moves on to the men, looking for a way in, looking for something which will crack this thing wide open.

'Turning into a shit-storm, huh?'

Jaap looks up to see Roemers, clutching a mug emblazoned with the words I'M GREEN. He has the uncomfortable feeling that Roemers has been standing there for ages watching him scribble away.

'Doing my bit, y'know?' Roemers says, seeing Jaap's gaze. 'Even though it's kind of pointless, the whole planet's fucked, we all know that.'

'You need to do something about your relentlessly optimistic attitude,' Jaap says, thinking it's way too early to start talking about global warming and the demise of mankind. 'Get a bit of balance, see the negative side of things.'

'Thanks, I'll try that. Passwords good?'

'Yeah, thanks. But I notice I don't have anything for Groot or Wilders yet . . . ?'

'Fucking hell, only just got here, two hours earlier than usual, I might add,' Roemers says, before lightly punching Jaap on the arm and promising he'll have them shortly.

Jaap goes back to his thoughts, the feeling he's over-looked something lurking in his brain. For the next twenty minutes his mind turns in on itself, twisting and churning, trying to tease it out.

'Inspector Rykel?'

Jaap looks up. A thin woman with a file tucked under one arm is standing where Roemers was before. She's tall, fifty-ish, with neat grey hair which frames her face, and a core of steel.

'Not me,' says Jaap, recognizing the woman as Super-intendent Laura Vetter. 'I'm just borrowing his desk.'

'Well, I'll have to make do with you then, whoever you are. Got a moment?' she asks in a way that strongly implies *yes* is the correct, and only, possible response.

46

Small actions have large consequences. There's the old butterfly theory, something about its wings flapping and causing a hurricane on the other side of the world – which Jaap has never really understood because, let's be honest, there are a whole load of butterflies around, and yet the world doesn't seem to be a perpetual clash of competing hurricanes. Or at least not physically. Mentally though, well, Jaap's starting to wonder if the theory has a point.

'Finally,' says Laura Vetter, settling into the chair opposite Jaap.

Jaap knows her only by reputation, he's never dealt direct. What he does know is that she is seen as fair, her own woman, prepared to stand against the tide, no matter the cost.

The biggest case she'd ever worked on was back in 1992, when a cargo flight, El Al 1862, took off from Schiphol at 16:20 and crashed into a massive housing complex in the Bijlmermeer neighbourhood of Amsterdam at 16:35. A total of 43 people were officially killed, 39 of them on the ground, though that number was thought to be three or four times higher as the housing complex had a high number of illegal immigrants who weren't on anyone's records. Given the ferocity of the impact, explosion and resulting fire many of their bodies didn't leave much of a trace. The investigation never came to much of a satisfactory conclusion. But that wasn't what Vetter was involved in, at least not directly. The case she ran stemmed from the fact that on the list of victims crushed and burned in the building that day – and whose body, along with many others, was never found in the wreckage – happened to be a police officer suspected of being involved in collusion with a criminal gang. The officer had been trailed for months, and Vetter was just about to pull him in and use what she had on him against the rest of those involved.

Only he ended up in a building which got hit by a plane and died.

Not even the wildest, most rabid conspiracy theorist on YouTube could formulate a credible story whereby a few bad eggs in the Amsterdam PD had facilitated, or at least known about in advance, a catastrophic plane crash and found a way to make sure a colleague of theirs, who they suspected of turning on them, just happened to be in the building at the very moment 500-plus tons of aluminium, jet fuel and four unfortunate crew would crash into it.

But Vetter could see something else was going on. She had no body, only police logs which showed he'd being going to visit a suspect at the very building that the plane came out of the skies and obliterated. The more she dug, the more she came to believe that he hadn't actually gone to the building, but had been taken, or worse killed and the body disposed of somewhere else, and the story of him going to see a suspect was being used as cover to hide his murder.

In the end no one was ever prosecuted, but the rumour was that the whole experience had left Vetter with a bad taste in her mouth and, as physiologically impossible as it may be, a hard-on for any *hint* of a bent cop.

And that's what she thinks I am, Jaap realizes as he sits

down in an office next door to Smit's. He has a quick image of Smit, an empty glass bridging the gap between the wall and his ear.

'So this is just a quick chat, nothing formal at this stage, although we will require a full statement later on,' Vetter says.

She hands Jaap a series of photos, various shots of Kamp dead on the ground, the gun just out of reach.

As he sifts through them a thought hits him. Kamp had held the woman hostage with the screwdriver he'd had on him when he opened the door. But why not just use the gun?

'Trace on the weapon?' Jaap asks.

'Look, in this situation, really it should be me asking the questions. I'm in charge of investigating his death—'

'The death of someone who killed at least one person, possibly two, and is at the centre of an ongoing case. My case.'

Yesterday Jaap had been ready to step off the case. Now look at me, he thinks.

'I understand,' Vetter says. 'Which is why I've cut you some slack on this. Really I should have had you back in on the day, but I realize that the situation is somewhat . . . unusual. Two things we need to deal with, the gun and the cuff.' She picks up a sheet and reads something quickly, as if reminding herself of something. 'So, did you forget to do it up?'

'Honestly, I'm pretty sure I did it up.'

Having spent years trying to detect lies in others, Jaap thinks that maybe he can get away with it. Because *honestly,* he's not sure, the exact moment lost in a stew of adrenaline and anger.

'You've checked the cuffs themselves, right?' he asks.

Vetter pulls out a pair of cuffs and hands them to Jaap. 'Go ahead, they've been through forensics already.'

They look like the ones Smit tossed him on the day, a black oxide version, less shiny than the nickel-plated ones uniforms are issued with. If you're not in uniform discreetness is important, and the black oxide finish is non-reflective. As inspector, these are the ones you'll get issued.

He works each cuff; the action's normal, the male and female parts joining with a satisfying series of clicks as a central hole reduces. He tries to break them apart, seeing if maybe the latch mechanism's faulty, but they're rock solid.

Vetter watches him, a benevolent predator.

'Would you say they're fine?'

For some reason, Jaap feels like refusing to speak and asking for a lawyer.

'Look. I don't know what to say.'

Vetter watches him for a moment, then writes something down.

'And the gun. When you arrested him, standard procedure is to check the arrestee for weapons. Did you check Kamp?'

The room feels hot suddenly, way too hot.

Vetter waits a few moments. Once it's clear Jaap's not going to say anything more, she again writes something down.

The scratch of her pen on paper is the only sound.

47

His desk has about ten sticky notes on it when he gets back, all callback requests from Berk, the reporter at *De Telegraaf.* Somehow he's surprised it's taken so long, but he hasn't got time for this now and decides that the best way to dodge any more distractions would be to go down to the basement where Roemers runs the DCU.

It's a series of interlocking rooms, each housing three techs. Jaap asks for a desk with a terminal and Roemers sets him up with one near him.

'Only thing is, I'm listening to music now, you're gonna have to put up with that.'

'Haven't you got headphones?'

'Yeah, but the left one started giving me weird distortions. I'll keep it low. Ish. And anyway, you're gonna love it. Group called Can, they're the—'

'Roemers, I have to work.'

'That relentlessly fun-loving nature of yours, you should give it a rest sometimes. Get serious, know what I mean?'

Jaap gives him the finger. Roemers smiles, cranks the music up.

So, accompanied by Can, Jaap starts trawling through everything he can on Kamp.

Francesco Kamp was thirty-four when he died. He'd worked for the NS, the national train service, since he'd left school, first as a ticket-seller before being accepted into the driver training programme. For every place in the programme about thirty people apply; Kamp was one of the lucky ones, getting through that first door.

Reading the reports from this time Jaap can see he did well, he was studious, diligent, polite, all the things the train company wanted, and he passed the course with the third highest marks in his group. That was only the beginning though, because then start the years of shift work, and you can bet the rookies get the jobs no one else wants. So Kamp put his head down – after all, he was getting a decent wage, and so what if the hours were irregular and he often found himself hauling freight up from Rotterdam at four in the morning, or being the man responsible for taking late-night revellers from the centre of Den Haag out to their suburban homes where they could sleep it off.

It was during this period he met Famke Reijn, a social worker from Haarlem who was pretty in a plain way, matching Kamp's expectations. Their combined salaries were enough to get them on the property ladder, and they had been paying off the mortgage on their property in Amsterdam-Zuid ever since. Kamp steadily rose, his pay now at a level which most people would describe as comfortable, if not stellar.

The couple decided the time was right, they were finally secure enough to start a family. The pregnancy, from the medical records Jaap pulled, seemed to pass easily enough, no drama or hints of what was to come.

Because on a clear night in February, whilst Kamp was on a run down to Leiden, Famke was tidying up the kitchen, clearing away the remains of her meal, when a pain so sharp she caught her breath seared through the left-hand side of her stomach.

The transcript of the emergency call is a dry representation of what actually went on, the operator getting the details as quickly as possible, and goes nowhere near explaining the horror and fear that must have been going through Famke's head. The ambulance crew were there in three minutes, having just finished a job nearby which didn't require transporting anyone to the hospital, and within eighteen minutes of placing the call Famke was being wheeled into the AMC in Bijlmer.

Everything had worked as it was meant to. The system, designed to be as efficient as possible, proved itself. She was in the best possible place. But that's when things started getting tricky. Assessments were made, tests done, she was prodded and measured and questioned, and then the decision was kicked up to the next level, a surgeon named Huisman. There was no hint of the surgeon's drinking problem in his record at this stage, no colleague raising a flag about gin on the man's breath as he worked, no complaints from anyone about punctuality or a shaking hand as incisions were made. All that came after. The official investigation which ended in him being disbarred didn't mention the death of Famke Kamp, largely because what had happened wasn't necessarily the surgeon's fault. Going under the knife is always a risk, doubled up when the aim of the surgery is to extract a living being from the body of another.

The post-mortem explained that a cut in the bowel wall had bled, and a clot, forming quickly to stem the flow of blood, had broken loose and travelled through her veins until it reached the main artery leading to the left lung, blocking it fully. Pulmonary embolism was recorded as the reason for death.

Kamp clearly saw otherwise.

He saw medical malpractice, and driven by grief, anger and a sense of injustice that his carefully planned life had turned into a world of pain, Kamp pushed his case as far as it would go, all the while caring for his newborn, a girl named after her mother.

So he was angry, Jaap thinks, surfacing from his research, the room coming alive around him with the smell of coffee and stale air and printer dust, and Can still powering from Roemers' speakers. And anger could be a trait useful to someone looking to force another person into killing for them.

Next he turns his attention to scopolamine. Given its rarity he'd originally thought it would be easy to find the source, but during the months after Dafne and then Nadine's deaths, he'd not come up with much of anything. There were no mentions of it on the system anywhere in the Netherlands, no dealers arrested with it on them, no other reports of its use. Given he now has four dead bodies with it in their blood, finding out where the stuff is coming from is getting more and more critical.

'Music finally got to you?' Roemers asks as he gets up and heads for the door.

'No, it's beautiful.'

'Really?'

'Yeah, I could stay all day listening to it.'

'But . . . ?'

'But I've got to go and meet a friend. One who likes drugs.'

48

'You've got various levels. There's your basic, just a new ID card. It'll be enough to get you out of child support, but you can't travel abroad.'

'I may need to leave the country,' Kees says.

After burying Hof's body last night, Kees made a decision. He's getting out. Fuck Smit with his 'just one more day' attitude, and fuck Van der Pol and his tendency to extreme violence. He'd wanted to know who it was Bart had intimidated the day before he was killed, but now he's seen that that man had ended up dead, shot by police whilst trying to escape arrest for the murder of two women, he feels the time has come.

'Right, so you need the complete package. New ID, passport, financial history going back ten years. Takes forty-eight hours to get done. Ten thousand euros payable up front, twenty on delivery.'

'Cash?' Kees asks.

His back is on fire, each vertebrae seemingly fused to the next, creating a solid spine of pain which resists all his attempts to move around in a normal fashion. His hands aren't much better; the protective blisters which had formed against the spade's green plastic handle had burst overnight, exposing soft, weepy skin.

'Cash? You think I'm a fucking amateur? Thirty thousand euro equivalent in bitcoin. And you'll need to tumble them first, I don't want coins which can be traced back to you.'

Ten grand might just be doable as a deposit. But twenty on delivery is definitely in the realms of fantasy.

But the alternative is . . . what?

'OK,' he says. 'I'll sort out this bitcoin thing. Is it easy?'

'Just Google it. Call me when you're sorted. And I'll need a set of passport photos.'

'Can't you do those for me?'

'Sure. Costs extra though.'

Kees hangs up.

49

When it comes to drugs, the authorities are not to be trusted.

They claim all sorts of stuff to make you not take them, how you'll become addicted, how the chemical hooks they contain will fuck with your brain, how they'll bring on mental illness, that taking them is a shortcut to misery and ruin and destitution, all because they're scared. Scared of what you might see, how in reality we're nothing more than a resource which the elite feed off, how we spend our lives in toil and paying taxes and shitting and fucking and consuming, striving for more possessions, all so the few people at the top get to live their lives in extraordinary ease and luxury, when all we really need to do is just stop and listen, marvel at the beauty and wonder and intricacies of the world around us.

At least that's the view of Sander Nuis, an old friend of Jaap's who decided early on to take a different path in life.

Jaap's not sure of Sander's world views, especially as they can get quite long and complicated, dotted with words and phrases such as 'Authoritarianism', 'Quantum Coherence' and 'Ontological Design', and can stretch out into such a convoluted Theory of Everything that frankly you'd reach for the shrooms just to make your head stop hurting.

But he is sure that if anyone knows anything about scopolamine, and it's clear from his research that no one in law enforcement really does, then it's going to be Sander. Because, being a connoisseur of altered states of consciousness, Sander has tried just about any method which might get him there, legal or not.

He lives in a small flat tucked in the eaves of a building on the pedestrianized Koestraat, right in the heart of the red-light district. To get to it there's a complicated series of doors and rickety stairs which Jaap finds hard enough to navigate, and his mind's not under the influence of psychedelics. Trying to find your way whilst tripping on whatever exotics Sander's into now would probably drive a man crazy.

He hadn't called ahead, partly because he's not sure Sander has a phone, and partly because he *is* sure Sander doesn't get out much. As in, not out of his flat, but definitely out of his head.

Of course in Sander's mind, Jaap's the one stuck in a bad trip.

On the door, painted black, someone's written in white paint in a loose, flowing hand:

Those who dance are considered insane by those who can't hear the music.

It makes him think of the silent video Heleen posted of herself dancing.

Sander gets to the door on the fourth knock, and greets Jaap like a long-lost soul brother from another life with a lazy bear hug. He's shorter than Jaap, and looks surprisingly healthy given his lifestyle. They spend a few minutes catching up, Jaap trying to ignore all the stuff lying around which, in his duty as a fully paid organ of the state, he really should be confiscating, before he gets on to the reason for his visit.

'Drink?' Sander suddenly asks.

'Yeah, nothing psychoactive though.'

Sander grins and heads through to the kitchen. Jaap hears a fridge door open and the clink of bottles.

He looks around. The room is pretty much as he'd expect. Mismatching rugs on the floor, fractural wall art and, on a long wooden shelf, a world-record collection of bongs and vaporizers. In a corner, balanced on a low table with mid-century turned legs, an oblong glass box sits. The floor of the box is covered with twigs, and lying on them is a chameleon-like creature. Only it's not like any chameleon Jaap's seen before, because its scales are white, giving the creature a ghostly feel.

'Friend of mine breeds these,' Sander says, having appeared with two bottles of Coke, handing Jaap one. 'It's just an albino chameleon, but he sells them for a fortune, has a waiting list two years long last time I checked. It's all to do with that TV series, the one where all the characters are always walking from one place to another. Either that or they're fucking and fighting dragons, y'know it?'

One of the benefits of living on a houseboat is that Jaap's yet to get a fast enough internet connection to actually stream anything, and he'd thrown out his TV years ago. He shakes his head.

'It's crazy, this friend bred these things, then got a mutant which he rebred and now gets these all-white versions. At first he thought no one would want them, but he called them ghost dragons and put them on his website along with the normal ones, and within a day he'd had so many enquiries he knew he was onto something. Thing is, he doesn't mention that they only seem to live half as long as normal, but so far no one's complained. But I tell you, watching that thing when you're tripping? Wild.'

Behind the glass the ghost dragon moves an eye, taking Jaap in then going back to being still, as if to say, Watching that guy trip watching me? Really wild.

Jaap turns away and starts telling Sander why he's come.

'Man, that stuff is nasty. I mean, really nasty,' Sander says, shaking his head when Jaap finishes up.

'You've tried it?'

Sander's relaxing in an old-fashioned deckchair which serves as the main seating in his flat, the fabric predictably a multicolour tie-dye. Above him on the wall a framed bit of paper proclaims:

THE ONLY WAY TO DEAL WITH AN UNFREE

WORLD IS TO BECOME

SO ABSOLUTELY FREE THAT YOUR VERY EXISTENCE

IS AN ACT OF REBELLION.

Below it is a child's picture of a flower.

'Yeah, last year. And really, it's funny for me to be saying this, but in the case of scopolamine then you really should Just Say No.'

'So from what I've read, people given it tend to lose their free will, is that what happened to you?'

'The whole free-will thing? Who's to say we're free?'

'All right, but philosophy aside, when you took it did you feel anything like that?'

'You know how they say you can't be hypnotized into doing something you wouldn't normally do?'

Jaap nods.

'Well, scopolamine's obviously different.'

Sander rolls up a sleeve. On the inside of his left bicep is a tattoo which Jaap can't quite make out. Sander sits forward, allowing Jaap a closer look. It seems to be some kind of alien, the elongated face and smooth features so beloved of Roswell fanatics. Only in this rendition it's auto-fellating.

'Jesus, what *is* that?'

Sander shrugs, rolls his sleeve back down. 'Fuck knows, I had it done when I was taking scopolamine. Didn't even remember. Woke up and could feel something hurting my arm, then I found this. Took me months to work out where I had it done, but I eventually found the parlour, this place on Kinkerstraat, fuck knows what I was doing there. Anyway, I finally spoke to the guy that did it. He said I'd come in with someone and they'd told me to get a tattoo, and I agreed. Just like that.'

'Who were you with? Was it the same person you got the scopolamine from?'

'I . . . look, there are people you don't really want to mess around with and—'

'You're forgetting I'm a cop. And I'm dealing with a case in which men may have been forced to kill young women. I think I can handle it.'

Sander thinks for a bit, or else he's just stuck in an acid flashback, because his eyes don't really seem to be present. Then he snaps out of it.

'All right, I'll get his name for you, may have to make a couple of calls. But on one condition.'

'Don't worry, I won't say you gave me their name.'

'Nah, it's not that. I was going to say, the one condition is that you give that fucker a *real* hard time.' He rolls his sleeve up again, leans forward, deckchair creaking, and points to the alien, nearly stabbing himself in the arm with his finger, his face angry now, hippy bliss long gone. 'For this. I have to live with this shit. And sometimes it really does my head in.'

50

The station's got that heavy, somnolent mid-afternoon bloat. Jaap's called the team together to see if they've managed to get anywhere. One by one each pair has gone through what they'd got, which so far isn't much. He's just about to break it up when Lisa puts her hand up.

'Yeah?'

'I've been doing some digging on Kaaren. Found something interesting, though I'm not sure if it's relevant to the case.'

'Let's hear it.'

'Seems like she made money online, working as a fin-dom. Last year she cleared over thirty thousand euros.'

'Back up – what's a "fin-dom"?'

She looks surprised that Jaap doesn't know. 'A financial dominatrix.' She gets up and hands Jaap a few sheets, print-offs of various private conversations. He reads them quickly.

'So she just says "Pay me five thousand euros, you dirty little man," and they do?'

'Bank records match up with those chats.' She hands him another few sheets, transactions highlighted in pink. 'She gets paid in bitcoins and transfers them to real money.'

'Sounds like my ex-wife,' says one of the men at the back. 'She's always demanding money.'

'That's called *child support*,' Lisa says. 'You know, when

you ran off with that other woman and the court said you had to contribute to your children's upkeep? Not the same thing at all.'

A burst of edgy laughter before everything settles again.

Jaap hands back all the sheets. Maybe it's good that he can still be surprised.

'Anyone else got anything, any link between any of these people?' he asks, pointing to the board.

But nobody has. Each time that happens Jaap knows it pushes the case closer to being the sort which never gets solved. If there's really no link, no logic behind it, then there's nothing to work out.

And if there's nothing to work out, Jaap thinks, how the hell am I supposed to work it out?

'All right, back to it. Anything comes up let me know immediately.'

He makes his way to the outer office and over to his desk, which is now covered in yellow sticky notes like some stupid viral video. He looks around but no one's paying him any attention.

'Hilarious,' Jaap says to the room at large.

'Look, if you called him back then we wouldn't have to keep fielding calls from him,' shouts Schuurmans, the oldest inspector in the department, and one whose aversion to hard work is legendary.

Jaap clears them all, and sits down, feet on desk. He's supposed to be going back in to see Vetter in twenty minutes, she'd said she wasn't satisfied and wanted to drill down harder into his story. Jaap doesn't want any harder drilling going on, but realistically he doesn't have much choice. So he's using the time he has now to let his mind go where it wants, not guiding, just seeing what trail it'll follow if left to its own devices. Years of meditation help with this – even though he stopped the practice after Floortje's death – he's adept at detaching himself from his thoughts, becoming a bystander, seeing if anything good comes up . . .

'Nice,' says a voice. 'Wish I could have a nap.'

Jaap opens his eyes, sees it's Arno.

He gives him the finger, suddenly realizing he's been doing that a lot recently. He makes a mental note to cut down.

'Whilst you were out Roemers came up, said he had something. Here,' Arno says, dropping a stack of paper on the desk.

Jaap looks at it, then closes his eyes again. 'Give me a recap.'

'Well, he reckons he's found your Psychonaut guy. The RV stands for Rogier Vink. And he has a record, prison for sexual assault of a minor back in '91. Seems he got into self-harm whilst inside, but once he got out he turned his life around and started up a type of therapy to help people quit. But that's not the interesting part. The *interesting* part is that Rogier Vink was on Vlieland, and left the island the day Heleen died.'

Jaap's feet hit the floor. 'You know where he is?'

'Got his address right here.'

Jaap checks his watch. He'd promised Vetter he'd make an official statement right about now.

Fuck it.

'Let's go.'

51

Arno's at the wheel, getting his first taste of Amsterdam traffic.

'Missing Vlieland yet?' Jaap asks as he gets caught between a chaotic gaggle of cyclists and a thundering tram, ringing its bell like the country's being invaded from the east.

'Jesus,' Arno says, achieving the double victory of not getting mangled by the tram *and* allowing the cyclists to live. 'Is it always like this?'

Jaap's phone's ringing. He's realistic, this is the modern world, and the phone is damn useful, speeds up investigations no end and keeps him in touch with Tanya when they're apart. But sometimes he just wishes his life wasn't lived in thrall to an oblong bit of technology which is almost certainly, and against the feeble protestations of both phone companies and governments, right this minute giving him cancer.

He answers, and listens to a request from the commissioner's office.

The commissioner would like to speak to him in person, at his earliest convenience. Turns out the commissioner feels that all the extra cash being thrown Jaap's way entitles him to some face-time with the lead investigator.

Jaap shakes his head whilst agreeing, then hangs up.

'Bad news?'

'It's not bad, but I can't run an investigation if I have to keep breaking off to brief people on the lack of progress,' Jaap says. 'Mind you, maybe he's just got the bill for the helicopter. Right here.'

Arno hangs a right as if he's back on the island. Jaap can see a cyclist shaking a fist at them in the wing mirror.

'Should be along here somewhere,' Jaap says when they reach the street. It's just west of Vondelpark, a war zone studded with SUVs larger than WWII tanks, the uniform of choice a Zegna suit. They park and walk up to the house.

'Maybe I should give that therapy thing a go,' Arno says. 'Looks like it pays.'

He has a point. Because the building is big, a large red-brick overlooking the park that would be so far out of Jaap's bracket it's not even worth thinking about.

Jaap remembers he's been on this street before, interviewing a man who'd been suspected of kidnapping a child and killing her parents. Turned out the guy was a serious asshole, but rather unfortunately innocent.

The front door's all studded wood with brass decorations, flanked by two long-stemmed bay trees.

Jaap presses the bell, the sun strong on his back.

As expected there's no answer.

It takes seven blows before there's any movement, another two before the door finally gives way. Jaap toes it open and their shadows race ahead of them into the long hallway, the floor a mosaic of falafel delivery leaflets and religious circulars. There's the odd one for mid-level call girls as well.

If the place is impressive on the outside the inside's less

so. Sure the bones are there, but as they move through the building the whole feeling is one of neglect. The kitchen has had all the units ripped out, a microwave plugged into a socket and resting on a small table. Full, tied black bin bags line a wall. Mostly microwave empties, Arno discovers once he's pulled on some gloves and done a bit of untying.

Which probably accounts for the smell.

And the flies.

They go through floor by floor, the place pretty much empty. The general feel is that Rogier Vink's not a man to keep up appearances.

That or he has no guests to keep them up for.

Seems he's not been present for a while either, the leaflets downstairs and the air holding a dull stillness that only uninhabited spaces can muster.

Jaap finds it in the bedroom, tucked away at the bottom of a cheap set of drawers, the handles mismatched.

He pulls out the plastic bag, and holds it up to the deluge of light flooding in from a window overlooking the Vondelpark. Inside it is a sheet of blotting paper perforated into tiny squares. The whole sheet is printed with a kaleidoscopic background, and a black swan right in the centre.

'What's that?' Arno asks from the doorway.

Jaap holds it up for Arno to see.

'Wow,' Arno says. 'Have a nice trip.'

'Nine hundred trips,' Jaap says after a quick count.

The house yields nothing else of interest so Jaap tells Arno to bag up the stack of leaflets, see if there's some real mail amongst it.

They're out the door when Jaap becomes aware of a low growl. They turn to see an old guy exiting the house next door. He's rocking mustard cords and a tweed jacket, complete with suede elbow patches. His hair is thinning and whiter than white. He has a leash in one hand, wrapped tight round his fist.

The source of all the noise is at the other end of it. A dog which is basically a mini Jabba the Hutt.

Jabba pulls the old man their way, eyes bulging.

'Have you come to arrest him finally?' the old man asks, having scanned them both, clearly deciding that Jaap looks like the one to address questions to. His eyes are washed out, like an old watercolour, the skin round them pink.

'What for?' Jaap asks, keeping an eye on Jabba, whose front paws are scrabbling at the concrete in an attempt to get to him.

'Trying to kill him.' He motions to the dog. 'I reported it. Evil man. He just wants to play, that's all.'

Jaap looks at Jabba. The thing is stock still now, eyes on Arno, and his teeth are showing through pulled-back lips. The growl's much deeper than Jaap thinks is possible given its size.

'When was this?'

'Are you saying you're not here to arrest him?'

'When did you last see him?'

'A few months ago, that's when he attacked him. He should be shot. Animal abuser.'

The man, in his passion, lets the leash go slack. Jabba notices, lunges forward, jerking the leash out of the old man's hand, and launches himself at Arno, who's already powering backwards into the broken door.

Jaap stamps on the leash as it flies past him. Jabba hits

266

the end of it, spins in the air and redirects his attention to Jaap in a flash of snarling teeth. Jaap barely has time to snatch the leash up, holding it high and away from his body, forcing the dog onto its back legs. Front paws scrabble the air, eyes become even more bulbous.

The old man is shrieking now. Jaap's worried he's going to have a stroke.

Actually I'm not, he thinks. At least it would shut him up.

'Get your dog under control,' he says to the man. 'And I'm sending a team out to assess this,' he says, handing the leash over once the dog has finally calmed down. The man snatches up the dog, gives Jaap an evil eye, and shuffles away, cooing to Jabba.

'Thanks,' Arno says. 'Little fucker was going to bite me. And the guy says he just wants to play?'

'Play,' Jaap says.

'Nice move with the lead.'

'Someone taught me how to do that once, never thought I'd get to use it. She trains police dogs out near Utrecht. She's no more than five foot, but man, she walks into a field and those dogs snap to it like they're North Korean military. Any of the new recruits tries any biting on her, well, let's just say it's a one-time-only kind of deal.'

'Lesbian?' Arno says.

Jaap punches him on the arm. 'Don't they give you diversity training on that island of yours?'

52

Kees' plan had been to spend the next couple of days keeping out of Van der Pol's way whilst trying to work out where he'd get the extra money to pay the balance of his new ID.

But it's not working out too well. He got called in again, and is now waiting at the haulage company, a rented lot on a soulless industrial estate, to see the man himself, an experience which is more unnerving each time it happens.

He wonders, not for the first time, if he's going to be asked to dig another grave before being knifed himself.

Nah, he thinks. If Van der Pol finds out who I am he's not going to be content with a mere stabbing.

But Van der Pol, when he ushers Kees into the shipping container, seems to be relatively relaxed, pensive almost.

Which doesn't stop Kees' fight-or-flight reaction blasting on. But he manages to control it and takes the seat offered.

Van der Pol's desk is neat, a few piles of invoices which Kees knows Van der Pol insists on approving himself, and his cheap mobile which looks early 2000s at least. Kees is sure Nokia don't even exist any more. Maybe Van der Pol bought a job lot years ago to keep him in burners. He knows why Van der Pol insists on using these old phones – they're far less hackable than the newer 'smart' phones. Each layer of added complexity simply adds a layer of something which can be manipulated, more ways for people to hack in. Kees worked a case where a computer tech had turned on the mic of a suspect's phone remotely, allowing them to listen in on a conversation. The conversation had led to arrests, but the case had proved a massive headache for all involved, the defence making much of the fact that what they'd done was basically illegal.

Kees realizes the shipping container is part of this too, easy to sweep for bugs, and very difficult to listen in on, no internet in here, just a single electrical cable from the generator outside powering the strip lighting overhead.

'Job done?' Van der Pol asks as he finishes signing the papers on his desk. He puts his pen down, leans back in his chair and gazes at Kees.

'Yeah.'

Van der Pol carries on staring.

Kees sits and waits, returning the stare, concentrating on the end of his nose, hoping Van der Pol can't make out what he's doing. He's learnt it's easier than looking him in the eye.

'OK, here's the deal,' Van der Pol says, leaning forward suddenly. 'We're down a few, as you know. I'm going to need you to step up the next couple of days, there's a job needs doing.'

'I'm not sure I can dig any more holes,' Kees says, holding his hands up.

Van der Pol waves them away. 'No, this is less manual. More . . . cerebral, shall we say. I need you to find someone for me.'

'OK,' Kees says. 'Who?'

Van der Pol pulls a small file from under the invoices and slides it across the table.

Kees opens it up, sees a page or so of text with a photo on top. He looks at the photo. It's not anyone he recognizes, a middle-aged man with anonymous features, a slightly round face and trimmed hair, colour unknown as it's a black and white shot. But on closer inspection Kees spots something unusual by his left eye, some scar tissue maybe, giving him a squint look.

Van der Pol writes on a piece of paper and shows it to Kees.

'If you find him you'll get this, as a bonus.'

Kees stares at the paper.

He wonders if there is a God.

A cruel, malevolent one whose main purpose in existing is to continually fuck with him.

Because the number on the paper is pretty much exactly what he needs.

'Once I've found him, what do you want me to do?'

Van der Pol looks at him for a moment, then breaks into a smile. Kees is reminded of a nature documentary he'd seen years ago – some old guy lying in the jungle, explaining in a half-whisper that for chimps, a group of which were busy picking insects off each other's backs only metres away, a smile was a sign of aggression.

'Just find him,' Van der Pol says, Kees still seeing nothing but teeth. 'Then I'll let you know.'

Van der Pol's phone buzzes, he checks the screen and signals to Kees that they're done. Kees gets out of there as Van der Pol swivels in his chair and answers the phone.

He's ten feet away from the container when he realizes he didn't take the file, so he doubles back. Just as he's getting close he can hear Van der Pol, his voice raised, more agitated than he's ever heard him. He moves closer.

'. . . so you think I don't know *that*?' Van der Pol's voice stops, as if he's listening. 'I've got people on it. We'll get him.' Another pause. 'Yeah, well, get this. If I go down then you're coming with me, remember that.'

Kees hears something smash against the shipping container's wall, the noise reverberating through the metal.

He waits a few moments before retrieving the file.

As he's out of there – Van der Pol hardly glancing at him – he's starting to wonder just who it is he's meant to be finding.

53

If you took every piece of junk mail which gets pushed through every door all over the world every single day, Jaap's pretty sure the amount you'd end up with would be so vast that it might actually shame people into doing something about it. Like passing a law making it illegal to send out flyers advertising such non-trivial items as the Best Vacuum Cleaners in the World, or the latest, speediest stairlifts.

Luckily he has Arno to go through the mail they'd picked up at Vink's house, and, even more luckily, after a mere half-hour, Arno's found something. A statement showing Vink's monthly rent payment on a property in the countryside on the way to Utrecht.

They're heading there now, pulling off the A2 and cruising through an increasingly rural landscape, Jaap having to resort to his phone as the car they've signed out has a faulty satnav which every few kilometres tries to change their destination to a street in Nairobi. Which, it claims, will take them six days and eighteen hours. It also helpfully draws their attention to the fact that the chosen route includes a ferry crossing and tolls.

'Left here?'

'Seems to be saying that,' Jaap says.

Arno slows down and they both peer at the narrow track winding away from them into a thick wood. It looks too narrow for a car. It also doesn't seem like it's been used since the time of horses and carts.

'Fuck it,' Arno says, spinning the wheel and nosing onto it.

Branches scratch the car's sides, clawing at Jaap and Arno through the open windows, but Arno carries on, the car pitching and yawing like a boat on rough seas.

'We got enough to arrest him, bring him in?'

'We don't really have enough for a warrant yet; at a push we could use the LSD found at his house, though that's slightly tenuous. Let's wait and see what he's like – his reaction to us turning up will be telling.'

'You think he's the one forcing all those men into killing?'

Jaap thinks about it. 'I don't know,' he finally says. 'You got the team working on linking him to any of the other women?'

'Yeah, told them to call the moment they found anything. So far no call.'

A few minutes in, just as it seems to be narrowing further, the track suddenly opens out into a clearing.

'You have reached your destination,' the phone tells them.

Jaap checks out the clearing, sees the cabin. Horizontal overlapping planks of wood form the walls, silvered with age, topped by a sloping roof smothered with a low-spreading plant. A pipe leads down from the roof into a large plastic water butt on the left corner. The door is ill-fitting and worn.

At the edge of the clearing a squirrel spread-eagles halfway up a tree trunk, waiting to see what they'll do.

A car is parked to one side, the front windows fully down.

'Looks like he's home, you take the back,' Jaap says.

As Jaap approaches, the front door opens and he recognizes the man from the photo.

'Who the fuck are you?' Rogier Vink says.

He's thin, cheeks sunken. Shadowy pools of purple below his eyes show Vink's not getting his eight hours.

'Rogier Vink,' Jaap says, 'I'd like you to come with us.'

'What? What the fuck for? Are you *arresting* me?'

Jaap thinks for a moment, weighs it up.

'Yeah,' he says, 'I am.'

'What for?'

Jaap thinks another moment.

'Possession of drugs,' he says, 'and cruelty to an animal.'

54

Killers are like fruit.

At least that's what one of Jaap's early mentors had told him once when he was training to be an inspector.

They'd been working a case where a male prostitute had been hung from a branch, a rope tied round his feet, and his throat cut so he'd bled out like a slaughtered pig. The killer had actually captured most of the blood in a series of buckets and taken them from the scene. One of the techs had mentioned they'd had blood pudding and eggs for breakfast.

Jaap's mentor had dropped his wisdom-pearl when they finally caught their main suspect, who – even when presented with some pretty solid evidence against him – maintained his innocence. His mentor had barrelled the guy into a cell, saying that like fruit, killers needed time to ripen. Which is where the metaphor had broken down a bit, as he'd gone on to say that, once ripened to perfection, you splattered them against the wall, their guilt oozing down for all to see.

Jaap thinks back to that day and wonders if it hadn't been warning enough. Get out whilst you've still got your sanity, because clearly policing hadn't done much for his mentor's state of mind. It was only a few months later that a call had come in saying a man had been spotted naked, except for a pair of orange wraparound sunglasses, standing in Dam Square, his left shoulder twitching up to his ear seemingly at random. When Jaap turned up a huge group of tourists had been gathered round him, perhaps thinking it was some kind of performance art. Some had even thrown coins onto the ground in front of him.

When Jaap and a couple of uniforms had taken him, he was mumbling under his breath, eyes not seeing, and two days later he was signed off permanently for psychiatric reasons. He was, at least, given a full pension.

So now Vink's in a cell, and Jaap's letting him stew, rather than ripen.

Under guard.

He's not having anyone else in this case commit suicide.

He's in the main office prepping when Tanya calls to tell him she's been discharged.

'I'm just about to interview, I'll pick you up as soon as I've finished.'

'Really, I'm fine. I'll get a cab. And I think they need the bed, there's this nurse who keeps walking past and doing the *oh you're still here* sort of look.'

'Get their name, I'll have them arrested. And I'll send someone round—'

'Jaap, I'll get a cab. Least the department can do is spring for the fare. You go and get your guy.'

And she hangs up before Jaap can say anything else.

He grasps the handle and steps inside.

After dismissing the two uniforms and going through the prelims, Jaap starts by asking about Heleen.

'I already told you I didn't kill her or have her killed like you said. That's crazy. I was trying to help her.'

'Yeah, it's true. You did say that before. But I'm not convinced.' He pulls out a print-off of the email exchange, points to Heleen's last email. 'Read that out aloud.'

Vink hesitates then reads it out. '"You shouldn't be here, leave me alone."'

'Which to me says that she doesn't want your help.'

Vink stares at him across the steel-topped table, one hand cuffed to a low rail underneath the surface, his hollow cheeks and the dark rings under his eyes more pronounced by the overhead lighting.

'She was a patient of mine,' he eventually says. 'I got too attached, which is why I went to Vlieland. I was trying to get her out of that cycle.'

'The mutilation?'

'That's how I met her. I'd found her online, on a forum for people who were into that kind of thing. I got in touch with her and offered to help. She'd seemed receptive, you know? So we eventually agreed to meet and I started working with her, trying to get her to stop. A lot of these people have deep trauma in their lives, and the self-mutilation is a symptom of that. I can help them get to the bottom of it, help them see it for what it is, and move on.'

'Oh, I'm sorry,' Jaap says, shifting through the file he's brought with him on Vink's background. 'I must've missed the part where you spent years studying this. Like which medical school, that kind of thing.'

'You don't need to go to school to be good at something. Bit of paper showing you jumped through some hoops? Means shit in my world.'

'Right,' Jaap says, knowing that he actually sort of

agrees. A bit of paper is no guarantee. 'So you're self-appointed. And self-taught.'

'Fucking proud to be as well, that's why I get results. I guide them through a healing process, which is unique for everyone.'

Vink uses his free hand to pull up the sleeve of his cuffed hand. Jaap sees the scars, thin lines all running in the same direction, from the inner elbow upwards, heading for the armpit.

'This is my qualification,' he says. 'You got a problem, you'd rather go to someone who knows about it from a book and looks down on you, or someone who's been through it and come out the other side?'

Vink's not a fruit. And he hasn't ripened. Or stewed. Or whatever.

In fact, once he'd got over the initial shock of arrest, the opposite seems to have happened.

'And do you sleep with all the patients you manage to lure over the internet? Is that part of the *healing process*?'

Vink doesn't answer, he just stares at Jaap, defiance in his eyes.

'And these?' Jaap pulls out the LSD tabs. 'Is this part of your protocol as well?'

'Some of these people have been to psychiatrists before and been given medicine which seriously fucks them up. It's almost barbaric. This stuff?' He points to the tabs. 'Used right, this stuff can be seriously healing.'

'So you let them trip out on acid and they get better?'

'I've helped many people with this, so you can keep your condescension. Means nothing to me. I sleep at night.'

'Just having these could be life, you get that right?'

Vink shrugs, like life's part of life.

'I didn't kill Heleen. I haven't killed anyone. You want to charge me with possession then go ahead, but all you'll be doing is stopping me from helping other people.'

'The problem is this: as we discussed earlier, you don't have an alibi for Kaaren Leegte's death because after leaving Vlieland you were staying at your cabin, and according to your statement you were there till I found you.'

'I don't even know this other girl you've talked about. But if you want to find out who killed Heleen then you should be looking for whoever was mutilating her. All along I thought she was self-harming, that's what she told me, only I find out when we're on Vlieland that she has someone do it for her. That's the guy you should be looking for.'

'He's dead.'

'What?'

'The man who was mutilating her, Daan Brouwer, is dead.'

Jaap flips across a photo. Vink takes it in.

'Are you sure?'

'Yeah, he's definitely dead.'

'No, I meant are you sure that's the man?'

'Who mutilated her? Yeah, I'm sure. Why?'

Vink purses his lips, thinks. 'Because I saw someone hanging around the cottage a couple of times, I assumed he was the one.'

'What did he look like?'

Vink shrugs again. 'Y'know, average. But there *was* something, one of his eyes was a bit weird.'

'Weird how?' Jaap asks, the whole room swimming in déjà vu.

Vink bends his head down towards his cuffed hands, and with a forefinger and thumb pinches together a bit of cheek and eyebrow, narrowing his eye.

'Kinda like that? Like he'd got a bad cut and scar tissue built up.'

Jaap's thinking hard. Then he gets it.

The man leaving the hospital room where Pieter Groot had bled to death.

55

Built in the eighties, the AMC hospital is considered Amsterdam's best. So stuffed full of specialists both practising medicine and doing cutting-edge research, it really is *the* place to be if you're sick.

At least that was the perception, until three years ago a junior doctor had been caught emptying out the saline from the drip bags, filling them instead with a solution which contained a particularly nasty strain of gram-negative bacteria. The bacteria themselves were dead, but gradually released endotoxins, a nasty substance officially known as lipopolysaccharides. Patients who'd been admitted for simple procedures were dying and no one knew why. Until a young student pathologist noticed all the bodies showed a bunch of markers for endotoxin poisoning.

It'd taken months of work to find the culprit, and since then the hospital had incorporated a raft of new procedures and protocols to stop anything like that happening again. One of them had been the deployment of CCTV throughout the hospital, an expensive option but one deemed necessary by a governing board alarmed by their slide in the hospital rankings.

It's the CCTV Jaap's banking on.

Arno's really stepped up and got them there in record

time. Once inside Jaap sends Arno to work on Personnel whilst he tackles Security. The chances the man is actually a nurse here are low, but Jaap's feeling like he's been slack and wants to cover everything.

But before he goes to Security he finds his way to the corridor Pieter Groot's room had been on. He checks the corridor, fifty metres or so long, Groot's room almost exactly at the halfway mark. There are cameras at either end, blinking red lights showing they're working.

Once at Security he explains who he is and what he wants and things move fast. Soon enough he's sitting in front of a screen with a bald techie beside him manning the controls.

Down the corridor people move at double-quick time, trolleys – both empty and patient-laden – speed through until Jaap sees himself zoom up the corridor, the movements oddly stiff.

'Now.'

The screen slows down, fluidity returns, and a man steps out of Groot's room. Jaap watches as the collision happens, and the man carries on.

But instead of heading to the end of the corridor he turns left after about ten paces and heads through another door. The sign on the door is visible as it opens, the international stick man.

'Cameras in there?' Jaap asks.

'Nah,' the bald techie says. 'They talked about it but I seem to remember there was a human-rights issue or something. Privacy. I mean, they got a point, who wants to be watched while you're trying to heft out a big 'un?'

They keep watching. The door swings open and a

surgeon steps out, full hospital gown and facemask hooked round both ears. The bald man's clicking his thumb and first-finger nails together. Jaap's not finding it therapeutic.

Time ticks on, but the nurse doesn't appear.

Jaap watches himself burst out of Groot's room and the subsequent flurry of activity once he'd roused a few nurses.

And still the man hasn't left the toilet.

'Back up to that surgeon.'

Once they've got him on screen and freeze-framed the best shot they can get, Jaap leans in.

But because of the way the man has angled his head as he's walked towards the camera, only the right eye is properly visible.

'Follow him,' Jaap says.

They spend the next ten minutes tracking the man's movements through the hospital. To Jaap it looks like he clearly knows where the cameras are, as he seems to keep ducking his head when in range.

They're on the final stretch now, just heading towards the main exit, the suspect walking past a man on crutches. The man is obviously new to them, and a crutch suddenly slips away from him. He sprawls out, tripping the surgeon up. The surgeon recovers and makes it to the exit, not even checking on the man who's still on the floor, clearly in pain.

'Rewind.'

They play through the fall frame by frame, catching the surgeon's face in full as it twists on the way down.

And although the man's lower face is covered by the mask, and even though the image is black and white and blurred from the movement, Jaap can still just make out the eye. The left eye, the layered scar tissue giving it a half-closed look.

Jaap had bumped, quite literally, into the killer.

And I let him get away, he thinks.

56

Who is he? Jaap thinks as he opens the door onto the roof and is blinded by the sun, a half-circle cut by the horizon, hanging right in front of him.

He steps into it, then turns north, walking to the edge, hoping that being out here will clear his mind. The air's humid, evaporation from the canal below managing to reach five storeys up, making his skin feel sticky. All summer it's there, like a form of tinnitus, a background fug which you get used to but which you suddenly notice at random points throughout the day.

He's been working like someone possessed, getting the team onto the killer's image. They're still below, working phones, the internet, trying to piece together just who this man is.

The sun's sinking fast, basting the sky a golden-yellow. An invisible hand smears a few thin clouds above him.

Amsterdam's his city, he knows her streets and canals like they're part of his biology, almost as if he were part of her and she part of him.

The same way that he's a cop.

It's part of him.

A plane banks in the sky, the wings suddenly glowing as it tilts and catches the last rays. He watches as it circles south.

The thought strikes him that he's been an inspector all these years for the same reason the drunk drinks, the junkie jabs the needle into their arm and the sex addict chases those blinding moments of nothingness at orgasm – obliteration of the ego, however transient.

He glances across the tops of buildings, spotting Bloemgracht where their houseboat is moored, and further up on the corner the small café they sometimes go to for breakfast, on the odd occasion they both have a late start.

The sun's slipping away now, abandoning the world, light giving way to dark.

The baby's going to change things, he doesn't know how he's going to feel, how it'll be. And it's all mixed up with Floortje's death. He'd been a father for a brief few months which had ended in tragedy.

For a moment he feels giddy, like all his life he's been searching for something, though he doesn't know what.

It had taken him to Kyoto, the hours he'd spent there driving himself crazy with obscure Zen koans set for him by Yuzuki Roshi, which had eventually seemed to pay off. He'd come away from Japan with what seemed a better understanding of himself, of life.

Floortje's death shattered that particular illusion.

He relives that night, staring at the flames of a burning boat, Floortje dead, the realization that he didn't understand.

He still doesn't understand.

A craving for Arno's home-grow hits him with a sinuous intensity.

Down below a tram screeches to a halt; Jaap suddenly realizes it's fully dark. He glances over the edge, sees a man lying on the tram tracks – a metre more and the tram would have hit him. Several people cluster round, trying to work out what's going on.

He turns away and starts back towards the door when a thought mushroom-clouds in his head.

Pieter Groot was in police custody, he thinks. So how did the killer know where to find him?

He's standing still now, the question like an invisible wall he's just walked into.

The night shudders around him.

How did he know?

Day Five

57

Jaap wakes with an elbow in his eye.

He turns over, Tanya hardly stirring when he gently pushes her arm away, and lies in the fragile stillness of the morning, as if any sudden movement could break it all.

It's just before dawn; outside the porthole he can make out the outline of the canal-side houses, roofs rhythmically jagged against the sky.

Water laps against the hull. The boat creaks as if in pleasure, urging the water on.

He'd been at the station late, the team adding the question which had hit him on the roof – how had the killer known Groot had been transferred to hospital from the station? – to the long list of unknowns.

Jaap's never seen anything like it. The vast majority of cases are pretty straightforward, a linear progression of facts which lead you from the victim to the killer, often in only a few steps.

But this one's not like that. If a normal case is two-dimensional this one's like a multidimensional string-theory nightmare where everything is constantly shifting and changing, where each move he makes seems to open up multiple possibilities which spiral off on more tangents, spinning his mind into a tangled, twisted mess.

No wonder his head's pounding.

He gets up quietly. Tanya moves as his weight lifts off the

bed but then settles again. After dressing he steps through to the main area, closing the bedroom door softly behind him.

A large window makes up one side of the boat's living area, and he stands at it, watching the water. In a house opposite a light flicks on, the window ablaze, then goes off again. A distant tram rumbles.

Last night, when he'd finally made it home, they'd held each other for a long time. He'd been wound tight, but gradually all the stress and fear which had built up in him slowly began to dissipate.

In it's wake, guilt flowed freely.

Because it *was* his fault.

His fault Tanya'd been put in that position.

He'd apologized, but she'd brushed it off. Part of the job, she'd said.

The door opens behind him and he feels warm arms round his chest. Tanya reaches up and kisses his neck.

'Hey,' she whispers as she holds him, placing her face on his back. He feels her ear between his shoulder blades.

'Hungry?' he asks.

'Yeah, and seeing as I'm convalescing now, officially, I'll let you fix me some breakfast.'

She sits at the table whilst he clatters around the kitchen. Gas ignites under the frying pan with a soft *thwump*; then the brittle click of eggs on the side of the pan, the hiss as they hit foaming butter.

Next he gets the coffee going. He'd never drunk it until Tanya moved in. The morning after their first night together she'd been dismayed at the lack of coffee on board ship. He'd learnt pretty quickly that to avoid mutiny, it was wise to always have some on hand.

Tanya likes coffee. She likes it with a kind of raw passion, and he'd gradually picked up the habit. Initially it'd given him the jitters, but when he'd switched up to having it with a boat-load of sugar, as per Tanya's instructions, he found caffeine now makes him calm and focused. One of Jaap's colleagues had taken to having black coffee with coconut oil mixed in, some internet health fad which, apart from looking disgusting, didn't seem to be doing his health much good. Jaap had suggested sugar to the guy instead, and got a look like he'd just suggested shooting up heroin with his morning brew.

When the eggs have changed from liquid to a soft solid he slips them onto a couple of plates, pours the coffee, and reaches for the Tabasco.

Red dots hail down on the eggs and they start to eat.

'So what are you doing today?' she asks between mouthfuls.

'Briefing the team, then I'm seeing Haase.'

'Haase? You're really stuck then,' she says, reaching for the coffee and pouring in quantities of sugar which would give a nutritionist a diabetes-induced stroke just from witnessing it.

'Yeah, I guess I am. I've never had a case like this.'

'Take me through it.'

'Uh . . . no. You're supposed to be resting, you said so yourself. Convalescing's the word you used.'

'That was just so I could get breakfast made for me.'

'Like I never do it.'

'Don't remember it ever happening before.'

'Yeah, yeah,' he says. 'All right, what do you want to know?'

'Everything.'

He goes through it all, and by the time he's finished the sky's lightening, his voice running hoarse.

'Shit,' she says, when he's finally finished.

'That your professional opinion?'

'My professional opinion will cost.'

'Well, I'd rather be paying you than Haase.'

'My fee's not monetary. I don't think you'll want to be paying him the same way.'

'I think I'm going to throw up,' Jaap says.

58

Turns out Sander Nuis does have a phone.

Jaap's walking along Elandsgracht, two minutes away from the station, when he gets the call and Sander gives him the name of the man who'd sold him scopolamine.

And had suggested the tattoo.

'Thanks,' Jaap says. 'Have you thought about laser treatment?'

'Pricey. Might have to though, it's really starting to fuck with my head. I wake up at night in a cold sweat thinking about it. Then I was tripping the other day and all I could see were thousands of them, all . . . all doing the same thing. That's not good.'

Once in the office, a good forty minutes before the team's due to meet for his morning brief, Jaap gets on the database.

And there's a hit, proving that Sander hadn't merely hallucinated the name.

Jaap clicks on 'Bernard Kooy', waiting for the mugshot to appear on screen. He wills it to be a face he recognizes, the man from the hospital. But as the image comes into focus it's clear it's not the same man. He scrolls down a long list of his interactions with the police over the last fifteen years. Of which there are ten pages.

The office is virtually empty; a rash of calls had come in, cleaning out most of the inspectors currently on duty.

The only one left is on the phone right in the middle of a domestic, which, from what Jaap's heard over the last ten minutes, sounds like it's on a fast track straight to the divorce courts. He tries to tune it out and dig down into Kooy's past.

Kooy was brought up in Den Haag, and before he'd even left school he'd been known to the local force. The trajectory of his criminal career is one Jaap has seen before. First it's a warning or two, possession of narcotics, supply of the same, before the first full arrest at the age of eighteen. And from there things go downhill: drugs, violence, the same old story, his run-ins with the cops and justice system almost as regular as clockwork. Arrested, jailed, let loose. Then repeat it all again like some criminal groundhog.

Until three years ago when it all suddenly stops.

No more mentions of him on his file. Which might lead someone to think he'd either gone straight, or was dead. But given that Sander claims to have bought scopolamine from him well after the last arrest date, neither of those can be true.

Seems like he got smarter, Jaap thinks.

In the corner of the room a water cooler gurgles. He looks up to see the inspector he'd heard arguing on the phone sitting at his desk, head in hands. For a split second Jaap feels he should say something. But what is there to say? He leaves it.

The last mention for Kooy on the system is a driving offence, logged by two uniforms in Maastricht. A vehicle, a two-tone XKR, had been spotted driving erratically and reported by a member of the public. A patrol car was dispatched. They found a vehicle matching the description on a side road just off the A79. It was easy to spot, the report stated, because the car had somehow nosedived into a ditch. The driver, clearly not in the best state of mind, was still sitting in the vehicle, tipped well past forty-five degrees, revving the engine, the back wheels spinning uselessly in mid-air. When one of the uniforms stepped down into the ditch and knocked on the window, Kooy had apparently wound it down and asked him if he could see what was stopping his car from moving.

'Yeah, I remember him,' the officer says when Jaap gets him on the phone. 'He was out of it that day. But like you said, he seems to have cleaned up his act, we've not heard from him for a few years now at least. I figured he'd probably killed himself somehow, but there was a rumour going round he'd got a job.'

'Gone clean?'

'Not really, I think one of my colleagues saw him with some people . . . hang on.'

Jaap hears a conversation going on at the other end, but can't make out the words.

'You still there?'

'Yeah.'

'I'm passing my colleague over, he knows more.'

Jaap listens to what the new voice – a woman with the smokiest, most alluring voice he's ever heard – has to say.

'So who's he been seen with?'

'Guy called Van der Pol, big player. Covers pretty much the whole country. Drugs, sex-slaves, extortion, he does it all, he's like the Amazon of the criminal world.'

*

297

Ten minutes later Jaap walks into the room where his team's assembled. He brings them up to speed on Kooy.

'This is the guy supplying people with scopolamine; the chances are high that if we find him we can get to this man.' He points to the CCTV images of the man with the scar, pulled from the hospital yesterday. 'All right, that's me. Anyone else got something?'

Jaap looks around the room. Tired faces stare back at him. He suddenly realizes that some of them probably didn't go home last night, given the lack of shaving on a couple of the male team members.

The child-support dodger puts his hand up.

'I've been going through Pieter Groot's stuff, found a couple of things. First is that although his wife did leave him and go to India she's actually dead, died in a coach crash. Which leads to this.' He gets up and hands round some screen-grabbed sheets.

'These are private messages between Pieter Groot and an unknown person, username "HelpingHand". The messages were pulled from his account on a forum for bereaved parents. There was an email in Groot's inbox giving a weekly digest of the most popular posts, that's how I came across it. HelpingHand claims his partner died several years ago, and that he's spent much time since helping other people come to terms with the same tragedy. As you can see, there's quite a lot of back and forth between them, and eventually they agree to meet up. I spent some time in Vice, and the way HelpingHand gradually earns Groot's trust is pretty much the exact same way paedophiles groom their victims. So HelpingHand knows what he's doing, knows how to manipulate some-one's feelings, right up until he suggests they meet.'

Jaap scans to the end. The date of Groot's message arranging to meet is three days prior to Kaaren's death. Then there's only one more message from HelpingHand, the day before Kaaren's death.

The previous messages had been friendly, personal. This one is different. It simply gives the next day's date, a time and a location. The Hoge Veluwe National Park.

The very place Kaaren wound up dead.

59

Thomas Haase's office is, unsurprisingly, neutral.

It occupies the top floor of an east-facing townhouse on Prinsengracht, and consists of two designer armchairs, wooden floorboards, and a few harmless pieces of abstract art. A low bookshelf runs along one wall, the spines seemingly ordered by height and colour.

Haase had opened the door and invited Jaap to pick a seat.

Jaap's now choosing which one; for some reason he gets the impression that everything he does in Haase's presence is being monitored, catalogued and assessed.

The man himself is wearing ironed jeans, a blue shirt and a narrow tie with a sombre pattern.

Across the room a fly head-butts the window.

'It's not a test,' Haase says. 'I mean, it is when it's a client, but not now.'

Jaap chooses the seat on the left, immediately regretting the decision for some reason he can't quite fathom, but having to stick with it as Haase has taken the seat opposite. He crosses his legs and stares at Jaap.

'So if I was a client what would my choice have just told you?'

Haase smiles. 'Can't give away my secrets,' he says.

'Because there aren't really any?'

'You're the one here asking for help . . .'

Jaap wonders why this guy riles him so much.

The fly gives up and decides to explore the room.

'That fly's been driving me crazy,' Haase says. Jaap's not sure if that's meant to be a joke or not.

'So,' Jaap says, leaning back in his chair. 'What do you think?'

Haase takes his glasses off and holds them up to the window, inspecting them like an antiques' expert giving you the run-around. Jaap finds himself counting – they are octagonal, in fact – and Haase pulls a small blue cloth out of his shirt pocket and goes about polishing one of the lenses, his fingers moving in small circles. Without the lenses to hide behind Jaap sees that Haase is very slightly cross-eyed.

'There are a few interesting things,' Haase says, moving onto the next lens. 'But the main thing is the fact that the "killer" appears to be forcing others to do the killing for him. There could be several explanations. He could be repeating a pattern, something he saw in early life. Say as a child he witnessed a murder, or even what he mistook for a murder. The classic would be the father hitting the mother, or even witnessing them having sex could be constructed as violent to a young mind.'

'So you're saying he could be trying to recreate it?'

'*Could* be, yes.'

'Why?'

'Because an experience like that can act as a block, stop his development on a certain level. Part of his mind knows that he has to get over it for proper growth, but missed its chance. So he recreates it, hoping to get through it, but each time it creates more trauma, and so he needs to keep repeating it. Or another explanation is—'

'Power.'

'Exactly, he enjoys the power he has over the people he forces to do the killing. In which case the murder is incidental, what he's really after is the rush of watching someone buckle under his will.'

'So the victims would be inconsequential?'

'Pretty much.'

'So why were the victims all women in their early twenties?'

Haase finishes polishing, holds the lenses up again and, satisfied, puts them on.

Jaap notices the fly has landed on one of Haase's shoes. It rubs its front legs together like a miser gloating over a pile of money.

'There could be many reasons. Quite possibly, if what I said earlier is right, that was the rough age of his mother, or whoever it was he saw being assaulted – it's part of the recreation.'

Quick as lightning Haase slaps his shoe with a hand. They both pause for a second. The buzzing starts again.

'Thing is, despite the age of the women,' Jaap says, 'they all look quite different.'

'Might not be looks necessarily, might be anything else which sets off a memory in the killer, voice, scent, there could be many things which only make sense to him.'

Something's slipping through his mind, a hint of an idea. He tries for it, but it eludes him.

'What are you thinking?' Haase asks.

Jaap shakes his head.

'OK, question for you. Was anything taken from the dead women?'

'Apart from their lives, no.'

'Nothing? Even something small?'

Jaap knows the old theory, endlessly trotted out by books, TV and films, that serial killers often take something of their victim's.

'He doesn't seem to be the trophy-taking type.'

Haase nods, as if this is all very interesting, an intellectual conundrum, something to solve for a bit of fun. The fly's got caught in an invisible loop in the air just above Jaap, going round and round. It makes him think of something someone's said, but when he tries for it the thought slides away.

'The suffocation,' Jaap asks after a few moments. 'They were all suffocated, so whoever it was must have specified that. Why?'

'Again, could go back to something in his past. The suffocating victims might be a reflection of how he feels inside, he's slowly suffocating from not being able to work through whatever set him off on this path in the first place.'

The fly buzzes in a loose circle between them, landing on the floor. Both men stare at it.

Haase reaches behind him, slowly, and takes a book off the shelf.

He inches it forward in his hand.

He throws the book down.

They're both holding their breath. A bike bell tinkles on the canal path outside.

Just as Jaap's about to breathe out they hear a buzzing above them.

60

Tanya stands in front of the mirror and lifts up her T-shirt.

Just below her right breast, both of them distinctly starting to swell, a small square of bandage clings to her flesh. At its centre a tiny blotch of blood.

She finds the edge of the tape holding it in place and pulls it back, revealing the wound.

Which is not really as dramatic as it could be. She'd had images of some massive line of stitches, the edges of the flesh bunched up and mismatched.

But of course they'd done it keyhole, and she's amazed just how small it is. The bruising around it is far more impressive than the tiny mark itself.

Her finger gently probes the flesh and finds it tender, but not too bad.

She can still hear the crack of her ribs as the man landed on her. That seems to be affecting her more than the fact he'd then gone and blown out his brains.

Her hand moves down to her stomach.

Yesterday at the hospital she'd talked to the surgeon, told him about the referral she'd had and he'd contacted the specialist for her. Turned out to be a woman about Tanya's age who'd listened, then whisked her away for another ultrasound.

Afterwards she'd talked Tanya through it. She'd explained that, yes, it did look as if there was a hole there, but she said that it was early days yet. There's a strong chance it'll sort itself out as it grows, she told her. She'd also said that they were in time, they didn't have to make a decision about it yet. Tanya'd asked, in time for what?

Legally a foetus could be terminated up until twenty-four weeks, she'd told Tanya. She'd gone on to say the best thing they could do was to keep an eye on it, and she'd booked Tanya in for another scan the following week. She'd also told Tanya not to worry.

A boat motors past, the wake rocking the houseboat, their toothbrushes rattling in the glass by the sink.

She lowers her T-shirt.

I'm going to have to tell him, she thinks.

Her eyes catch her image in the mirror, hold her to account for a few seconds before she breaks away and leaves the bathroom.

She busies herself in the kitchen, clearing up breakfast, trying not to think. Once done she finds she's tired and lowers herself onto the sofa. It's her favourite spot in the houseboat, opposite the large window, and she loves to sit there and watch the water.

She finds a file Jaap must've left and starts flicking through it. It looks like notes on the case, a few pages of random thoughts, scribblings and crossed-out lines. At the back there are several photos and she flicks through them, finding one of Stefan Wilders. She stares at it for a moment, then moves to the next.

Her body's tense almost before she sees it, like it knew what was coming.

Her eyes scan the image over and over. It's a zoomed-in

CCTV shot, the man's face fuzzed with motion and twisted at an old angle.

Jaap had talked about the killer having a scar by his eye, but it hadn't rung any bells.

In this case, though, the old thing about a picture being better than a thousand words applies. Because although she'd not recognized the description, she's seen this man before.

She gets her phone, snaps a copy, and then searches her contacts.

Harry Borst is still on there. She should probably have deleted him after the stuff he pulled once the case had gone south, but she hadn't. She taps out a message and attaches the image.

Her finger hesitates a second before hitting send. She wills it on and watches the progress bar until it's full. 'Delivered' appears beneath.

She's just putting the phone down when it starts buzzing in her hand.

'Tanya,' Harry says, sounding out of breath. 'We need to talk.'

61

How did the killer know Groot was at the hospital?

Jaap's walking, hoping the movement will get things flowing, when his phone rings. It's Tanya, and she's going off at a hundred mph.

'Slow down,' Jaap says.

'—so I sent him the photo and he called me back right away. And I was right, I had seen him before.'

'You're sure?'

'Totally, and Harry is as well. It's the same guy, Jaap, no question.'

'Send me his number.'

Up ahead a man's kneeling in front of a metal gate fronting one of the townhouses. Beside him the tools of his trade, stuff Jaap doesn't even know the proper names of. The man's all business, his movements practised and precise. He slides his heavy visor down, adjusts the blue flame, then gets to work, festive sparks exploding when it touches the metal. Jaap doesn't look away quick enough.

By the time Jaap gets to the station the text's come through. And he can still see the outline of the flame, like it's got burned onto his eyes. He leaves a message and hangs up.

His fingers drum.

He's watching the phone, never a good sign.

It stubbornly refuses to ring. He tries to will it, imagine it ringing and him picking it up. Hopeless. He'd once heard a radio programme about how successful people used visualizations in their lives. So far it's not doing much good.

He spots Arno across the room talking to one of the team, the man who wasn't that into child support. He decides to call a meeting in the incident room in fifteen minutes, hoping that by doing so his phone will start ringing.

Smit walks past. 'Update?'

Jaap doesn't answer, still trying to make the phone ring. As he sits there a kernel of an idea starts to form.

Smit clicks fingers in Jaap's face.

'Earth to Rykel? Are you receiving?'

Jaap's staring at his phone, his constant companion, which goes everywhere he goes. 'OK,' he says. 'Your office.'

Smit raises an eyebrow, then nods.

'I'll be there in five,' Jaap says. He gets up and rushes downstairs to where the incoming are processed. The duty sergeant heeds his order and returns with a small cardboard box, taped shut. Jaap rips it open, finding Pieter Groot's wallet and house keys.

But he's not interested in these.

What he's interested in is the phone.

He picks it up, the screen black. But when he punches the home button it comes on and asks for a passcode. The battery icon's red. But the reception bars are full.

He drops it back in the box, heads upstairs.

'Which gives us a massive problem,' Smit says a few minutes later, once Jaap has got to his office and explained his theory.

Trees dapple shade through the window.

'Yeah, I'll get Roemers on to it, see if the killer's been tracing his phone somehow. My guess is that it *was* being traced and the killer knew he was here.'

'OK, I get that. But that doesn't explain how he knew he was taken to the hospital. Are you saying he waited outside, saw him being taken and followed him there? Kind of unbelievable.'

It doesn't work, Jaap knows it. But what else has he got?

'Yeah, I know, seems too . . . time-consuming on his part. Unless he knew Groot was going to try and kill himself, but . . .'

'What's the alternative?' Smit asks. 'That he's somehow got access to our internal information? I just don't see it. And seriously, if the police network has been hacked, well, we're fucked.'

For a moment Jaap sees Smit is genuinely concerned. And rightly so. If a criminal has managed to get access to their systems then they might as well give up now and let the country run itself into the ground.

But he still enjoys Smit looking worried. It's not something he sees very often. The dislike between them is a two-way street – always has been, always will be – although really, in the end, they're on the same team.

'I think it's worth getting Roemers to look into it,' Jaap says.

Smit breathes out long and slow. 'I'll get him on it,' he says once he's got all the oxygen out of his lungs. 'Anything else?'

Jaap fills him in on HelpingHand before moving on to what he's just learnt. 'It's looking like he's been associated with a large criminal gang, which should make getting his name easier. And once I've got a name—'

'Which gang?' Smit asks.

'Van der Pol's.'

Smit sits back in his chair. 'Really?'

'Like I said, just waiting for confirmation. Tanya recognized his face from when she was down in Rotterdam, working with Inspector Borst. I'm due to speak to him any minute now, chances are he's going to be able to give me a name, possibly more.'

'OK, this is big,' Smit says.

'Yeah, I think it could be what we've been waiting for.'

Smit stands up, steps over to the window overlooking the street below.

'Good work,' he says. Clearly it's painful. 'But before you go, there's something else. It'll not have escaped your attention that the press are starting to crawl over this like the shit-eating beetles they are.'

'Really?' Jaap says.

'Really,' Smit replies, eyeing Jaap. 'One in particular, Michiel Berk, has been kicking up a fuss, saying you're not returning his calls—'

'I don't work for that particular shit-eating beetle.'

'I know, but reality check here? We have to deal with them. Now, I had a call from Annie Meijer at RTL4. There's a slot this evening.'

'Is there,' Jaap says, noncommittal. Because he knows what this means.

'There is. And I'd like you to do it. You'll need to call her back to confirm – here's her number in case you don't have it.'

'I have it.'

'Just think, if you've managed to find the killer by then you'll be a hero, on live TV.'

'I can't wait,' Jaap says.

'And now—' Smit reaches for his phone—'I'm going to have to make sure anytime anyone is brought into the station their phone gets turned off.'

62

From complexity comes simplicity.

The vast, swirling galaxy of chaos is speeding up and taking form. Jaap can feel it, sense that he's finally on the right path.

'He goes under several names,' Borst says once he and Jaap connect on the phone. 'The most recent one was Alex Haanstra, and he was, or still is, involved with a fairly large criminal enterprise I've been working on for years.'

'Van der Pol.'

'Yeah. Thought we finally had him, but it's like he's got some kind of guardian angel. Every time we get close the fucker is one step ahead.'

'What does Haanstra do for Van der Pol?'

'That's the thing, we've never been able to pin it down. He's only been spotted a handful of times over the years, and not recently, which is why I didn't know for sure if he was even still around. The last sighting was logged three years ago. But it seems you've seen him recently.'

'Bumped into him the other day. If you had to guess, what is, or was, his role?'

'There were rumours he'd been with Van der Pol from the start and was his original enforcer, dishing it out to whoever needed it.'

'Dishing it out meaning beatings, or going the whole way?'

'The whole way. The irony is, when Van der Pol started out he basically got rid of all the competition. All these criminals started disappearing and the crime rate plummeted because he made sure his guys operated out of sight. Worked out well for the police chief of that district, boosted his career. Everyone thought he was doing great, but the reality is that it's competition which causes most of the problems; if you've got a massive monopoly you can just get on with it. So the police got complacent, they kept getting low stats, whilst Van der Pol expanded. It's every cop's secret fantasy, someone going around bumping off the bad guys for you. I mean, killing innocents is one thing, but when it's scum you're less inclined to look, right?'

'So what's Van der Pol's main business, drugs? Have you heard of any of his people selling scopolamine?'

'Back then it was, but now he's into anything you can think of. I've not heard of anyone selling scopolamine, and a good portion of his stuff is legitimate businesses now as well. This guy is smart. I've been working on him for years and he's yet to make even a tiny slip-up which we could use. His model works pretty well, I guess. But back to your original question, I think that Haanstra may have been the one tasked with getting rid of the competition early on – one minor dealer I busted was running scared, wanted to do a deal with us, give us the name of who he thought was responsible for a bunch of killings. The description he gave must have been Haanstra. Too bad I wasn't able to make the deal, or I might've been able to get him back then.'

'What happened to the dealer?'

'We'd agreed to meet and I'd got the go-ahead to make

him an offer. Only I turned up too late. Knife through each eye.'

'And he specifically said Haanstra had killed someone?'

'Killed many. He didn't know his name, but he described the eye, the scar tissue. Showed him some surveillance photos, bang. So why are you interested in him?'

'I think Haanstra has been forcing carefully chosen men into killing women for him.'

Harry whistles. 'Forced? Really? Then again, anyone connected with Van der Pol ... well. We found a body yesterday, been stabbed multiple times and buried at the edge of some woods. Really bad job, whoever did it. The grave was way too small, but they still shoved the body in, dumped some coffee grounds on it to stop animals digging it up, and sort of made a mound with some soil. But, turns out it was right by a geocaching site. This guy was out with his two kids, they found the geocache and noticed the mound close by. One of the kids scoops a bit of soil off. That's when the father gave us a call. And it turns out the body is one of Van der Pol's inner circle, Axel Hof. Word on the street is that he'd annoyed Van der Pol. Like that's all it takes.'

'The chief inspector, the one who got lucky, who was it?'

'Can't remember, but I seem to recall he got promoted pretty quick. They probably wondered why he wasn't as effective at his next position, couldn't recreate the magic.'

'So the real question is, anyone we can talk to? Have you heard of a Bernard Kooy?'

'No, should I have?'

'I think he's connected to Van der Pol. He's a possible

for supplying the scopolamine which was found in all the victims' blood.'

'Doesn't ring any bells, but Van der Pol's organization is huge, he's got outposts all over the country so . . .'

'There must be someone in his organization we can lean on a little?'

'Let me think about it,' Harry says.

'OK,' Jaap says as he finishes up. 'I'll get you the details on our victims – can you run them and see if they crop up in connection with Van der Pol?'

'Sure, I'll have a look.'

So in the end it's simple, Jaap thinks.

A man called Alex Haanstra is forcing men to kill for him.

And I've got to stop him.

Simple.

63

Kees has got a way out.

And the irony is, it's Van der Pol who has given it to him. One last job will give him a big pay-off, enough to afford his new ID.

'. . . three . . . two . . . one,' says a disembodied voice.

Lights flash in Kees' eyes. He blinks, pulls back the rough fabric of the curtain and steps out of the booth.

The station is busy, full of normal people doing normal things like buying a ticket or getting a train. None of them, as far as he can tell, are living a double life. Although he's not sure that 'double life' is the right phrase, because really he doesn't feel like he's got double the life, what he actually feels like is he's on a half-life, or even less.

He stands there and feels invisible, despite looking different to them all, because no one glances at him. They are managing to give him a wide berth though, like there's a magical space around him which no one can enter.

Which, Kees thinks, might be the story of my life.

He's not sure how it's turned out like this, and for a moment tries to pinpoint the choices he made which brought him here. But in the swirling world of the past, where do you begin?

The machine hums, stutters, then regurgitates a string of photos into a metal tray, saving him from further introspection. He pulls them out, the paper still warm, and holds them up to get a better view. His own eyes stare off the photo in front of him. He has an intense moment of unreality, where he doesn't know which one he is, the one standing, or the one peering out of the image.

He folds the four into two, slips them into a back pocket and leaves the station, working through the tide of commuters. For a moment he's a salmon heading upstream.

Then he remembers that after spawning, salmon keel over and die.

A man in uniform is hovering by his car. Van der Pol had made it available to him, and Kees thought it'd make a change from the bike. Which if he's honest he's just not that into anyway.

Kees walks up, the man turns to look at him, ready for a fight, ready to protect his own livelihood because Kees is sure these people work on commission.

But he takes Kees in slowly, then scrunches up the ticket he was filling out and drops it in a bin as he walks away.

The roar of the car echoes off the station walls. He lets the pressure build up before releasing the handbrake and skidding out into traffic without even looking.

Lights flash and horns blare.

He doesn't care.

All he cares about now is getting on with the job Van der Pol has given him.

The file which had slipped off the passenger seat a moment ago hadn't told him much, a photo, a name, some other minor details, but Kees had done a bit of digging – he hadn't spent years being an inspector without picking up a few tricks – and reckons he knows where he's going to find him.

He's on the A4 heading towards Amsterdam. The thought of his choices comes up again and he finds himself unable to stop it.

He starts to go back, cataloging memories, trying to find the moment it all went wrong.

By the time he's done mentally lashing himself he's aware he's slowed down, the traffic dense around him. A kilometre or so of crawling and the reason becomes clear. There are major roadworks up ahead.

Used to be they'd put a sign up saying roadworks and leave it at that. But now everything has to be an emotional appeal. He passes a series of signs trying to get people to slow down by other means; one has two kids with the words 'Our father works here' written on it.

Just as he's finally easing past the last of the works and the road ahead is clearing he spots another, final sign. It tells him that somebody loves him, so he should slow down. For their sake.

He reads it, and is surprised to find he's laughing.

Then he hits the pedal and accelerates hard.

64

He's like a ghost, Jaap thinks, floating through the criminal underworld leaving barely a trace.

He's been tracking Haanstra through the system, finding possible mentions of him in cases all over the Netherlands. The database which had replaced the old HKS had taken a few years to really start paying off, but with more and more information being fed in it's starting to yield results.

Harry had emailed him all the names Haanstra has been suspected of using and Jaap's run searches for them all. He's slightly dismayed at the number of hits it gives him. But he digs in, knowing that it's sometimes the dullest work which can swing a case like this.

It seems Haanstra's never the main subject of any investigation, he's only tagged tangentially, but as Jaap goes through mention after mention a disturbing pattern emerges.

None more so than in the case he's looking at now, a murder which happened just over five years ago.

The victim was a twenty-year-old woman who'd worked at a facility for the mentally ill, and who'd gone missing from her parents' home – she'd been between flats – on the night of her death. She'd gone to bed as usual at just after ten-thirty. The next morning she wasn't there, her father raising the alarm at just past eight.

Her body was discovered three days later by a farmer who was rotating his flock of sheep, moving them to a new field so they could feed on fresh, luscious grass. The inspector attending the scene noted no obvious cause of death, but the PM had later concluded that she'd suffocated. During the investigation a woman came forward who claimed to have seen a man leaving the field who looked, her words, 'wild and out of breath'. Armed with a description, the investigators gradually built up a picture of a suspect, one which fitted an ex-patient from the place the victim worked.

The patient in question, Menno Helling, who'd been ordered to the facility four years previously after a violent attack on a random stranger, had been released eight months earlier, and whilst he was still on a cocktail of drugs prescribed by the psychiatrist at the facility – Jaap couldn't help but think of what Vink had told him about LSD – had been deemed 'low risk'.

A manhunt ensued, culminating two days later in a chase which led to a multi-storey car park in Dordrecht. The officer giving chase caught up with him on the third floor and approached, trying to keep the suspect, who was highly agitated, calm by talking to him.

Backed up against the railing, the man kept apologizing, saying over and over that he'd been made to do it. The officer, reasoning that if he kept him talking there was less chance of him jumping, asked who. It took several goes at the question but finally the man answered. A ghost, he'd said. A ghost called Haanstra.

Then he'd jumped, splattering the contents of his head all over the concrete below in front of a group of horrified shoppers.

Given the man's problems, and that the PM showed he'd not been taking any of the drugs prescribed, his final words hadn't been given much weight. There'd been no follow-up. The officer filing the report had put Haanstra's name in, which nowadays would immediately raise a red flag as it was already in the database. But the old system didn't do that. Unless the officer explicitly searched for Haanstra he'd be unaware of any other mention.

And clearly he hadn't.

Because a crazy person is reason enough – why try and make work for yourself?

Jaap sits back in his chair, his head starting to spin.

How many others are there? he thinks.

His phone buzzes towards the edge of his desk. He grabs it just as it teeters off.

It's Harry. 'There's someone we could speak to. Interested?'

'Yeah, who?'

Jaap listens to the details and hangs up. Harry's driving up, but it's still going to be a while before he gets here. Jaap grabs the photo he has of Haanstra and heads down to the cells where Vink is still being held.

'Recognize him?' Jaap asks as he hands the photo to Vink.

Vink, less cocky than yesterday – an overnighter in a cell can work wonders – takes it with a kind of alert fatalism. But when he looks at it something changes in his face.

'What?' Jaap asks.

Vink chews his bottom lip. 'Yeah, that's the guy I was telling you about, the one I saw on Vlieland.'

Back upstairs Jaap gets Frank down in Hoenderloo on the phone.

'Frank, I've got a face. Need you to show it around, check if any of the park staff recognize him.'

'Sure, get it over to me.' Jaap hears him pause to do the snorting thing again. 'And I may have something, I just got off the phone with one of the day staff, they said they'd heard a noise in the rough area where Kaaren was killed.'

'What kind of noise?'

'Well, he reckons it was a drone. One of those flying toys people have. Says he watched a video online last night which reminded him of it. Don't know if it's linked or important or anything, but I thought you should know.'

Jaap hangs up. The fly buzzing round and round Haase's office. A picture's forming.

One he doesn't like at all.

He spends a few minutes on the internet.

The picture is clearer now.

And he *really* doesn't like it.

Because it means he missed something fundamental, something which he should have been onto right from the start.

He calls the team together in the incident room.

'I missed something,' he says. 'At the time of Heleen's death a witness, Piet, a surfer on Vlieland, said he'd heard a kid flying a drone. And I've just had word that one of the park employees heard something similar right about the time Kaaren was killed.'

Jaap looks around, seeing if they're getting it.

'Haase was asking me about a trophy. As in, is the killer taking any? I said no. But he *is* taking a trophy.'

They know where he's going with this now.

The room settles into a crystalline silence.

'He's not only forcing people to kill for him,' Jaap says. 'He's filming them doing it.'

65

'This one here?' the salesman says, foaming with enthusiasm. 'This one here's the shit.'

He's in the nearest shop he could find which stocks drones, trying to get a handle on what they can do. Beats beat from hidden speakers, forming the template for Jaap's own heart rate.

A long central table stretches away from him carrying a huge range of different types of drone, each mounted on a stand. Prices range from very little to numbers which Jaap can't quite understand. Expensive toys, he thinks.

'How difficult is it to fly?' he asks, having to crank his voice up to compete with the music. He picks one up, noting how light it is, how fragile it seems.

'Seriously? A kid can learn it in a few minutes. It's easy. Though to be honest, I'm pretty sure most of the men who buy them for their kids end up using them more themselves.'

He opens a cabinet door and pulls out a control. To Jaap it doesn't look that different to one he'd had as a kid for a remote-controlled car. The salesman starts taking him through the various functions. Jaap cuts him off.

'What's the range?'

'On this one? This one can fly up to two kilometres away.'

'And the camera?'

'Full HD quality, 1080p. The camera's gimbal-stabilized

so there's no wobble. And you can lock it onto a moving target and the drone will follow it.'

Jaap thanks him, hands the drone back and walks out.

He gets into the car he's parked outside the shop on Kalverstraat, right next to an English-language bookshop, and pulls away, heading to his meeting with Harry.

Once moving, he dials Haase, catches him between clients. He explains what he's found.

'There's your trophy,' Haase says. 'And it kind of fits in with what I was saying earlier, about the killer being stuck, trying to relive the trauma in an effort to get through it. Watching it over and over might be part of that.'

Jaap kills the call. He's feeling a kind of light-headed calm.

Twenty minutes later he pulls up at the address Harry had given him, sees Harry's already there, leaning against his car. His phone goes off just as he's getting out of the car. It's Arno.

'HelpingHand has appeared again,' Arno says when Jaap answers. 'Stefan was also on a forum, a different one, but he had contact with a user on there called Helping-Handz, that's with a "z", and there was exactly the same pattern as before. He befriended him, then agreed to meet three days before Heleen died, and then the day before he got the location and time of Heleen's death.'

'I need you to get the team looking at every possible place he might be communicating with anyone else—'

'I already got them started. There are about seven different forums for bereaved people, I'd no idea there'd be so many. But we're going through them now. I'll call if we get anything.'

Harry's on the phone himself, gives Jaap the one-minute finger.

They're parked in an industrial estate south of the city; large trucks are driving in and out with alarming frequency. He's thinking about Haanstra, 'Helping-Handz', tries to imagine him watching recordings of the killings.

Violence on screen was nothing new, you only had to flick on the TV or fire up a laptop to know that whatever they might say, even normal human beings were drawn to it. Despite knowing it's acted it could still make you wince or cringe, sometimes even make you turn your eyes away in disgust.

Your mind knows it's fake, but your body reacts as if it's real.

But filming an actual death? Then watching it?

Maybe Haase's right, Jaap thinks as Harry finishes his call.

'So, who're we going to see?' Jaap asks.

Harry smiles. 'Bram Tolhoek, nice guy. I think you're gonna like him. He's on parole now, so I'm sure he's a reformed character.'

'Reformed from what?'

Harry hands him a file. Jaap flicks through photos of a man severely beaten, face barely recognizable as such, lumps swelling out in all different directions.

'He was in twice, once for battering someone half to death, and the second time . . . well, also for battering someone half to death. That's the second one.'

'Charming,' Jaap says. 'I can hardly wait.'

They locate the unit Harry's looking for, cleverly

named Amstel Bifolds. Like the rest, it's clad with grey corrugated iron and has a loading-bay door and another for foot traffic.

A large bike's parked outside, bodywork vinyl-wrapped to make it look like carbon fibre, the chrome exhaust pipes shining like a religious experience. By the fuel cap there's a skull with two wings.

Harry points to it as if to say, told you.

The receptionist inside is bored, prefers her nails to both Jaap and Harry, and calls through to her boss in the slowest way possible. She listens for a moment, nods, then puts the phone back down and invites them to look around the collection of doors and windows. The show-room is devoid of customers. Insanely jaunty music pours from hidden tinny speakers.

'Bet if you look at their books they're turning over a fair bit of money, despite no customers being here,' Harry says.

Jaap's inclined to agree, he's seen his fair share of money laundering operations over the years. And this one has all the signs of being another.

'Can I help?'

Jaap turns from inspecting the latest in triple-glazed thermal-efficient bifold patio doors to see a short man standing in a doorway towards the back. Harry, who's been turning a flyer on angled roof lights into a paper plane, looks up too. He makes a couple more folds, then launches the plane towards the man. It spins through the air and nosedives to the floor, skidding to rest at his feet.

'Just as well you didn't go for that engineering job,' Jaap says as they convene on the man.

Who, from the visuals, is clearly on steroids.

He's in jeans and a long-sleeve T-shirt so tight Jaap can make out the veins standing proud of his biceps like worms burrowing under his skin.

Jaap had once heard a theory that Neanderthals hadn't died out completely, that they'd occasionally mated with modern humans, so some people still carried a few Neanderthal genes. The man's face is probably all the proof required to turn that theory into fact.

Jaap walks into the man's office. Harry follows and closes the door.

He pulls out the headshot of Haanstra from the hospital's CCTV and holds it up for him to see.

Bram Tolhoek stares at it, shakes his head. 'This supposed to mean something to me?'

'Friend of yours?' Harry asks.

'Never seen him.'

'Really?' Jaap says.

'Really.'

Sometimes it's possible to draw people out, use their desire to cover what they're trying to hide by letting them talk too much and eventually make a mistake.

Tolhoek's not of that ilk.

'The thing is,' Harry says, 'you're on parole, right?'

Tolhoek gives him the stare.

'And I'm pretty sure that the first time you went to prison you'd been spotted with someone else at the crime scene. Only he was never caught. And you didn't give him up. That's nice, isn't it?' Harry says to Jaap.

'Yeah, I like that. Loyalty. Show's character.'

'Exactly. But the thing is, Bram, right now loyalty is

going to fuck you. Because I want to know everything you know, or we'll get you on a parole violation.'

'What violation?'

'I dunno,' Jaap shrugs. 'But I'm sure between me and him we can come up with something.'

He holds the photo up again.

Tolhoek stares at Jaap for a few moments.

Then he writes something on a piece of paper, hands it to Jaap. Jaap reads it, shows it to Harry.

'If you're not there in twenty minutes we're coming back for you,' Jaap says.

Tolhoek nods, scrunches up the bit of paper and slips it in his pocket.

'Get the fuck out of my office!' he yells.

66

He may be a Neanderthal but he's true to his word. Because eighteen minutes after he's made a show of throwing them out of his office, Tolhoek's bike is pulling up at the exact spot he'd told them to wait. Which is under a flyover. Traffic's rumbling overhead, freight trucks laden with shipping containers, but no traffic is on the road they're next to.

'The receptionist,' he says once he's killed the motor, 'I think she reports on me.'

He hasn't got off his bike, his feet only just touching the ground either side. It looks uncomfortable. And with his arms up on the high handles it also looks ridiculous.

'Back to Van der Pol?' Harry asks.

'Yeah, thing is, second time I got out I wanted to go straight. But I was *persuaded* otherwise.'

'Lucky we came along, this is your chance to do some good,' Jaap says. 'So tell me.'

'About the guy?'

'We're not here for your life story, just the bit which coincides with the man in the photo.'

Tolhoek looks away, and for a moment Jaap thinks he's about to gun the motor and ride off without saying anything.

'I went down for that fucker, both times I was the fall guy for him. Van der Pol wanted to keep him out of jail so

329

made me go instead. But I'll tell you this, that guy is a nasty piece of shit. Like, seriously nasty.'

'Name?'

'I just knew him as Alex.'

'Haanstra?'

'Could be, I don't really remember.'

Harry pulls out his phone. 'Maybe a quick call to your parole officer will ease your memory?'

'Jesus, you cops think you're the good guys,' he says, shaking his head. 'You have any idea what it's like to be trapped? Like really trapped so you have no choice? Of course you don't, you—'

All of a sudden Harry's a virtuoso violinist with a sad-clown face.

'Fuck you,' Tolhoek says when he notices.

'You had something to say,' Jaap says.

'OK,' Tolhoek says after a deep breath. 'It was about six years ago, I was working in Eindhoven, enforcer for Van der Pol's main drugs distributor there. It was a fairly new area and there was already an established dealer. But that never stopped Van der Pol, and we spent six months taking over. But the dealer wouldn't give in, no matter how many of his people we persuaded to flip sides and join us.'

'Nothing like loyalty, huh?' Harry asks.

'Van der Pol pays better than anyone else. You're the guy on the street for some of these other dealers you're not making a minimum wage most of the time. So someone comes along and offers you a choice – more money for yourself or a bullet in the back of the head? It's a no-brainer. But the main guy's stubborn, wants to maintain control, so I'm told we need to persuade this guy to step aside. Van der Pol calls me to a meet just outside of town where he introduces this Alex guy. Tells me I've got to go with him, and that I'm to take orders from him. So I have to spend the day with him, and really he's freaky.'

'Freaky how?'

'Like . . . I dunno. There's something not right about him.'

'This is coming from a two-time convict.'

Tolhoek gives him the finger. Harry smiles.

'Freaky in that there's this kind of stillness about him. Anyway, Alex seems to know where the dealer's gonna be, we go to this shit-hole flat out in Haarlem. Turns out the dealer's visiting some girl he's got hidden from his other girl, and we walk in on them. He's banging her up against the worktop, she's bent forward over it taking a line up her nose and he's got his tracksuit trousers down by his ankles. And he's going at it like double speed, it looked like a cartoon, all blurred and stuff. There's some loud music on so he's not heard us, he was pretty into it, y'know? And Alex looks around, gets a wooden spoon from a container by the stove, and walks right up to him, jabs it up the guy's ass.

'My brother used to work at an abattoir down in Tilburg, he took me around it once, showed me the whole thing, and I tell you, the way that guy screamed reminded me of that. So, Alex makes him get dressed and we take him for a ride, out to these playing fields. The whole time Alex is kind of . . . I dunno. It's like he's really still, but wired at the same time. We drag this guy out, there's no one around, and Alex tells me to have a go at him, just rough him up a little.'

'Which you did,' Harry says.

'You want my help or not?'

'Carry on,' Jaap says.

'I start, nothing serious, just a couple of hits, you know? But I kind of sensed something weird and I turn round and I find this guy is filming me on his phone. I mean, is he fucking stupid or what? That's evidence. So I tell him to stop filming. He pulls out a gun and tells me to keep going. Tells me to make the guy bleed. So I give the guy a couple more hits, like this guy's a piece of shit anyway, not like he's some civilian, and then I stop. Alex is still filming, and he tells me to carry on. The thing is, as I'm doing it I see that he's really filming me, like he has the phone aimed at my face.'

Another truck rumbles overhead. It seems to snap Tolhoek out of his story.

'Then what?'

'Then he told me to kill him. He wanted me to strangle the guy. I told him to go fuck himself and he put the gun right up by my head. And the whole time he's still filming. And he's got this weird look on his face. Creepy, just really, really creepy.'

'So did you do it?' Harry says.

Tolhoek swallows, looks away. 'Nah, I got lucky. A couple of cars turned up, turns out it was a well-known dogging site, so Alex had to put his gun away. But you know what? If they hadn't, and I'd've refused to kill the guy, I've no doubt he would have pulled that trigger.'

Traffic overhead has slowed over the last minute or so;

now there's a truck stopped right above them. A waterfall of exhaust fumes starts to choke them. Jaap's phone goes off, he sees it's Arno. He takes it.

'You need to get back here,' Arno says. 'We've found HelpingHandz was talking to someone else too.'

'You know who?'

'Not yet, Roemers is working on it.'

'I'll be there in fifteen. Right,' Jaap says to Tolhoek, 'how do we find this guy?'

Tolhoek shakes his head. 'I don't know, I'm not in the loop any more. I just front the window business. But one thing I heard was that Alex no longer works for Van der Pol.'

'Where'd you hear that?'

Tolhoek shrugs. 'I dunno, a rumour, I can't remember where.'

'That's pretty unusual, isn't it?' Harry says. 'Knowing how Van der Pol operates, not many people tend to leave. You being a good example.'

The traffic above starts to move, the truck lurches into gear and moves off.

'I don't know what to tell you,' he says. 'That's what I heard.'

67

Arno was right.

Jaap's staring at a reel of messages, the same pattern emerging, the gradual, sinuous befriending of the next man he believes will be forced to kill. The messages themselves are between HelpingHandz – Haanstra – and 'TL1980'. Roemers is working on finding out who that is in real life – shouldn't take long, given the rather obvious clues.

It's skilfully done, Jaap thinks, following right from first contact up until the present. It's taken over four months, the two gradually getting to know each other, sharing increasing confidences.

Haanstra claims to have two little ones who are at the centre of his life, even more so since his wife died of some long, drawn-out cancer three years previously. The medical team had basically messed up, although he's purposefully fuzzy on the details. He writes of how he went through hell, hinting at some very dark thoughts, the anger that these people had taken his wife away; but someone he met online helped him through it, made him realize just how much he loved his kids, helped him see that he *could* carry on. Haanstra also claims that he's doing that same thing now, paying back, willing to help anyone through the hell which he himself endured.

Jaap watches TL1980 walk right along with it, offering

up more and more details about his life, using Haanstra as a sounding board on bad days, telling him excitedly about the good ones.

All the while Haanstra is there for him, playing the line between too forward, too keen, and not interested enough.

In short, Jaap can see why the men had fallen for it.

The messages continue, and it looks like they'd agreed to meet up yesterday, with the kids, just for an afternoon.

The same pattern as all the others.

Which means, Jaap thinks, Haanstra has probably already threatened him.

'Got it,' Roemers says from behind him. 'Theo van Lagen. Lives out in Winterswijk.'

Jaap calls the team together, updates them on the latest. He tasks Lisa with leading the hunt for Theo van Lagen.

Back at his desk he's just about to close his computer when he notices there's been a message.

From HelpingHandz to TL1980.

It takes Jaap a moment to figure out they're GPS coordinates and a time, 18:00, just over an hour away. He punches the coordinates into his phone.

'Arno!' he shouts across the room. 'Get a car out. Now.'

68

Tanya's getting this restlessness in her legs, like whatever angle she puts them her knees still feel uncomfortable. The houseboat's too hot as well, the air evaporating off the canal making the whole thing like a Turkish steam bath.

Only without the massage. For a moment she misses her flat in Rotterdam.

And thinking of Rotterdam, since she'd spoken to Harry, her thoughts have been hovering around the night of the raid, and the face she'd seen. She's not really had much time to think about it properly, so much has happened since, but it has been bugging her sporadically, like a tick which has lodged its head in the back of her brain.

Now, though, the tick has regurgitated its stomach contents, because all she can think about is the face.

Which, despite part of her mind telling her to let it go, she's managing to convince herself was Kees.

She'd called the station a while ago and requested his file be sent to her, and she's waiting for it to arrive. Finally a ping from her laptop tells her it's there. She clicks on the attachment and finds the case which led to his prosecution.

She shivers, despite the heat.

Ruud Staal had been her foster father, and for years had sexually abused her. She'd finally escaped and had buried it deep, not wanting to face it, hoping that by ignoring it the whole thing could be made to go away, frozen out. But when she'd fallen for Jaap, in a period of her life when she should have been at her happiest, deep feelings started to stir, as if her new-found joy had awoken them, defrosted the emotion, which turned out to be as fresh and raw as ever.

She remembered the day she'd finally decided to track him down, confront him, make him see what he'd done to her. Why she'd hoped that might put an end to it she didn't know, but the alternative had been to go official, get him arrested and charged. But then it would all have come out, everyone would know what had happened to her, and a feeling, which she later identified as shame, stopped her. No, she didn't want everyone to know what had been done to her. Mostly she didn't want Jaap to know. As if he might reject her.

So she'd tracked Staal down, and the same night Jaap's baby daughter had been killed she'd gone to confront him.

She'd not meant to kill him. That had been an accident. He'd attacked her and she'd defended herself. Only he'd wound up dead. Kees had found her, sitting in his front room, staring at his body, and he'd cleaned the place up and got her out of there. She'd spent days expecting a knock at the door, convinced they'd come for her.

She should have handed herself in, but she had to be there for Jaap, see him through his grief, so she'd done what she'd done before, what she'd become good at doing. She buried it deep, kept it suppressed.

But reading Kees' file now she finally sees the reason

why no one ever came for her: Kees had gone down for Staal's killing instead.

Kees had taken the rap for her.

Only, just over a year and a half later, she sees him, out, and working for the biggest criminal network in the country. Is that possible?

She reads the file again.

Her breathing's all over the place.

She needs to get out. She closes down the laptop and gets ready.

As she's leaving the houseboat, the gangplank swaying gently as she walks across it, she looks up to see a white van parked on the canal side right by the boat.

This despite the sign saying NO PARKING. It's so close she barely has room to edge round it. Just as she's reaching the corner, one of the rear doors opens and a man in overalls steps out.

He turns towards her.

She looks up.

And recognizes his face, the scar tissue almost forcing the man's eye closed.

69

They're soon out of the city, driving fast along the A12, the sun low behind them, dazzling off the road signs ahead.

Jaap's driving now. They had to stop for petrol. All cars are supposed to leave with a full tank but somehow this one hadn't.

'How far away now?'

Arno's tracking their progress on his phone. 'Just under forty kilometres. How fast are we going?'

Jaap checks the needle. 'Hundred and sixty, slightly over.'

'So if we're doing that, and it's forty Ks away . . .'

'It's like one of those maths exam questions they used to ask at school, you any good at that kind of thing?'

Arno tries to work it out in his head. 'No,' he says after a few moments.

'Right, me neither. I'm going to see if this can go any faster.'

They'd alerted a local patrol but told them to stay away until called for. Nobody wants them crashing in there and ruining their chances of getting Haanstra.

'You think this is another one, another killing?'

'The location fits the pattern,' says Jaap, putting his foot down. 'So yeah, I do.'

The needle swings higher, Jaap feels the road through the steering wheel.

*

Twenty minutes later, Jaap'd had to slow once off the motorway, they're there. The coordinates point to a quarry, disused, and there are four approach roads. They've already picked the one most likely to give them cover; it weaves through a bank of trees south of the quarry. Where the road ends, a track continues through the copse. He parks, the car hidden from view, and they set out on foot. The ground rises as the trees thin out and the quarry itself, a gaping wound slashed across the landscape, emerges ahead of them.

The last ten metres or so are steep, and they resort to crawling up to the lip.

Jaap scans for movement, but so far there's nothing. It's strangely quiet.

The quarry is huge, the area of at least six football pitches. It's a rough oval, a wider end to the west allowing the low sun to stream in and light up the raw limestone till it glows gold. The rock's cut in terraces, studded with tracks where the machines had once moved back and forth.

In the lowest section, the valley floor, two large pools are filled with sky.

'See anything?' Jaap whispers.

'No,' Arno says, 'nothing.'

Jaap looks again. Now he's here he can see what the map hadn't told them: the main entrance is to the east, where a track tears through the rock and then turns south. If someone's coming along it, he really needs to be on the far side to see.

'Stay here,' Jaap says. 'I'm going over there.'

He retreats down the slope until it's safe to stand and starts running.

The ground's uneven, and several times he stumbles, just managing not to fall fully. There's a kind of tightness in his chest, but it's not from the exercise, it's from the excitement. Because he can just feel they're onto it, onto the killer he's been chasing for months. The rush isn't in full flow yet, but he can feel it there, building in intensity. He knows it's a kind of addiction.

By the time he's reached the far side and chosen a route up he's badly out of breath. He pauses for a few seconds before starting the climb. It's even steeper this side, and whereas the other slope at least had some grass on it, this one is made of rock, much of it loose on the surface. His feet keep slipping as he scrambles up, creating dry avalanches behind him.

By the time he reaches the rim he's managed to scrape a knee and has a wide graze on the palm of his left hand. He takes a breath and raises his head over, taking in the scene from the new angle.

The quarry seems just as empty as before.

He tries to make out Arno, but either he's moved, or he's keeping his head right down. He's chosen the right spot though, he can see down the entrance track, a gorge between two crumbling rock faces before it hits the main area.

He's aware of his blood, thudding through him.

As he's watching, something moves in the corner of his eye. He swings his head.

A car creeps through the narrow gap, towards the quarry itself.

His stomach flips.

He watches as the car inches forward on the potholed ground. It's in deep shadow thrown down by the quarry's side, and the driver flips the headlights on. Only one works.

Just before it reaches the main area, out of shadow so Jaap can now see the car is a filthy white, it stops. The engine noise he's just been able to make out in the still air cuts off.

Nothing happens for a few seconds. Jaap finds he's holding his breath.

The driver's door cracks open, sun flashing off the window as it swings in an arc.

But no one gets out.

Jaap becomes aware of a high-pitched sound. A buzzing really. He searches the sky for it, but even though the sound's getting louder he can't see it. He checks back on the car – no more movement.

The buzzing noise is louder now, and he can hear it's coming from behind him. He turns.

And there, swooping down from the sky in a graceful arc, is a drone.

It slows down, stopping a metre away from Jaap's face.

It has four sets of blades, one on each corner of its square body.

A round lens, the glass convex like an eye, stares straight at him. A miniature sun burns in the top left corner.

His phone goes off in his pocket. He pulls it out to see a text message.

Just one word.

SMILE

Then his phone rings.

70

Déjà vu has never been properly explained. There are all sorts of theories: the matrix we live in breaking down, a simple programme glitch which affects us for half a second or so before the system self-corrects. Or the theory that our lives are lived over and over in a continuous loop, the moment of déjà vu nothing more than a brief snatch of memory of what has already been. Or for those of a more prosaic bent, for whom repeating lives is just too *out there*, there's the whole rational neuroscience angle, the experience just a temporary mismatch between neurons firing in the brain, nothing mystical, nothing special, nothing to get twisted up in existential angst about.

Jaap doesn't know which it is, but as he's standing there, phone ringing in his hand, the drone hovering close, full of insectoid menace, he *knows* what's happening next.

He looks at the screen of his phone, caller ID unknown.

His finger takes an age to hit the answer button. The drone's eye tracks his movement as he brings the phone to his ear.

'Listen carefully,' says a voice. 'If you do exactly as I say then I won't hurt her. I see you brought a colleague with you. Too bad. Because you're going to have to get rid of him.'

'Hurt who?' Jaap says. The quarry starts a slow, sideways spin.

'Oh, I'm sorry,' the voice says. 'Didn't I say?'

The phone beeps three times, call disconnected.

A picture message appears on screen. The background is indistinct, but the foreground's visible.

Tanya tied to a chair, her mouth prised open, a ball-gag stuffed inside.

A tulip-shaped lamp's blaring in her face. The light means there's no doubt.

The phone rings again.

'I see you haven't moved yet,' the voice says. 'You really should.'

The drone tilts, moves round him a half-circle, the dark eye on him the whole time. Then it starts to herd him back down the slope.

Jaap slips and skids down the loose rock, slicing the same hand he hurt on the way up, the pain nothing, non-existent.

Because all he can think about is Tanya, tied up in a chair, at the mercy of Haanstra. They'd bumped into each other at the hospital, and it had taken Jaap too long to realize who he really was. If he'd been quicker on the uptake then he might not be here now, Tanya not being held by a stone-cold killer.

Jaap skirts the quarry, the drone following him, sometimes close, sometimes riding higher as if on lookout. But he realizes that it's not going above the lip of the quarry, purposely trying to evade detection by Arno.

Jaap pretends to stumble, and tries to pull Arno's number up on his phone but the drone swoops in as if in warning, the rotors an angry buzz.

He carries on, staggering over the rough ground, the image of Tanya burning through his head.

Just as he's nearing the last bend which will take him into view of Arno, his phone goes off again.

'You need to get rid of him. Knock him out if you have to. And I've a sound feed on so don't try to tell him anything.'

'*. . . so don't try to tell him anything.*'

The ball-gag is too big, it feels like the sides of Tanya's mouth are splitting from being forced open so wide.

She's in a chair, in a garage somewhere, a desk at one end with computer equipment and a large screen.

On the screen, she's been watching Jaap.

Even though part of her's been trying to close her eyes, spare herself the horror, she's glued to it like some moron watching a soap.

She'd fought, but Haanstra had had surprise on his side. That and a gun, which he'd shoved into her stomach, forcing her into the back of the van where he'd cable-tied her wrists and ankles. Then he'd pulled out the ball-gag.

On the journey she'd tried to follow the route in her head, keep track of where they were going, but when they'd pulled up to a stop no more than fifteen minutes later she had to admit she had no idea where in Amsterdam they were.

As he'd taken her from the van to the garage she'd managed to glance around, but nothing she saw helped, rows of garage doors on some industrial unit the only feature she could see. Inside the garage he'd dragged her to a chair, sat her in it, and secured her tight.

The fear had really started to kick in then, one of the

chair legs tapping the floor as it transmitted her shaking to the ground.

And that was before Jaap had appeared on screen.

She watches as Jaap starts up the slope, heading towards Arno.

72

Ten metres out, Arno turns, sees Jaap and then the drone.

'What the fuck?' Arno says, pointing to it.

Jaap slips on a patch of loose gravel as he steps towards him, the sound like fabric ripping. His heart's hammering in his ears.

All he can think about is the picture of Tanya.

'He's over there,' Jaap says when he gets close, pointing across the quarry.

Arno turns to look, following the line of Jaap's arm. Jaap slowly bends down, his left hand searching the ground.

'I don't see him, and this drone is making me—'

Jaap's found what he needs, a rounded stone. He takes a swing, the stone hitting the back of Arno's head. He hopes he's judged it right.

Arno's head jerks round. Jaap sees his eyes.

Fear. Surprise.

Then he swings again.

This time the lights go out, Arno crumples to the ground.

The stone falls from Jaap's hand. It starts rolling down the slope, knocking others into motion as it goes.

His phone rings. He almost doesn't hear it under the noise of stones cascading down the slope.

'Good,' Haanstra says. 'She's worth it.'

'Don't hurt her, you fuck. If you hurt her I'll—'

'Yeah, yeah, spare me the macho bullshit. Right now the only thing you have to do is whatever I tell you.'

Jaap's breathing's out of control.

He notices a trickle of blood behind one of Arno's ears.

'Look over the edge,' Haanstra tells him.

Jaap does, sees the car moving again. It creeps forward cautiously, then stops. The door opens, and this time a figure steps out. A woman he doesn't know.

White noise fuzzes up his ears.

Then the noise stops dead.

Everything is suddenly clear.

73

It's terrible watching him, imagining what's he's going through.

Tanya once again fights against her restraint. Haanstra notices, breaks away from the laptop and steps towards her.

'Keep still, bitch,' he says, slapping her across the face.

It stings hard, her eyes watering in response. But she keeps them defiant, stares at him as if to say, I'm not afraid of you.

Which earns her a second slap on the opposite side.

'You want some more?' Haanstra asks.

This time she ducks her eyes, and Haanstra nods before going back to the laptop.

She finds herself watching the screen again.

After Jaap had knocked Arno out he started picking his way down to the quarry floor itself, towards the car.

He's doing this for me, she thinks.

She's been watching Haanstra too, but apart from the one moment when he'd gone outside and held a conversation with someone, he's been at his laptop. Tanya can't quite see, but she thinks he may have the drone controls there.

The camera has swung out, giving a larger view of just what Jaap's up against.

She can see the route he's chosen is leading to a large drop, a sheer face of limestone which will be too high for him to jump down. A few metres above it he slips, feet shooting out, and he's scrabbling with his hands against the rough slope, speed gathering as he heads towards the edge. Stones and dust form a waterfall, marking out the route he'll soon be taking.

At the last moment he manages to grab a small outcrop, gets both arms round it and stops himself, just as his feet go over the edge.

Tanya can see him panting hard, and the drone moves closer again, getting right into his face, until it take up the whole screen.

It's so familiar, and yet she's never seen it look so twisted up with fear and anger.

He pulls himself up the slope, slowly, the drone moving in close before zooming right out again. This time he picks the right route, although it takes him another ten minutes before his feet finally touch the quarry floor.

74

All the sickness in the world pools in him as he descends.

But he fights it, fights the fear which he knows will make him weak.

He needs to be cold to get through this, needs to push down emotion, keep rational. He needs to *not* think about Tanya, sitting there terrified . . .

He's running as fast as he can, even though he wants to delay the moment, delay what he knows he's going to have to do.

As he moves, his mind is looking for escape, but there's nothing that can alter the fact that Haanstra has Tanya. He's been in a situation like this before, his daughter held, and although he'd done all he could she'd still died.

He can't believe the universe is doing this to him, repeating a pattern like his life's an endless cycle, a water wheel dipping into the same pool of suffering over and over and over.

He slips and goes down hard, his hip slamming against jagged rock. He forces himself up, and makes it down to the quarry floor. As his feet hit the flat another thought breaks into his head. The case which had ended with Floortje's death had been well publicized, the press had gone crazy over it and he'd had messages from agents in London and New York all promising him large sums of money for a ghost-written book telling his story.

He'd never returned a single call.

But now he realizes that Haanstra could, with a quick web search, have found out about his past, and decided to use it against him.

It's not the universe fucking with him, it's not some metaphysical conspiracy designed to bring him down.

It's just one man.

An evil man.

The thought's like a thunderclap in his head. It clears it out, gets rid of the self-pitying voice.

He's going to get through this, he's going to save Tanya, no matter what it takes.

He's running along the track where the car came in. The car, and the woman, are hidden from view, round a large outcrop. His phone's ringing, he answers whilst running.

'I've made it easy for you,' Haanstra says. 'She's an addict, so you don't need to feel too bad about what you're going to do. I even told her to bring her own roll of cling film. She thinks you'll be giving her drugs in exchange for it, desperate bitch.' He laughs, then adds, 'Just remember, we'll be watching you.'

Jaap can see the drone, hanging in the dying light.

He's just at the outcrop now. He knows, if she hasn't moved, that she's only fifteen metres round the other side.

He stops for a moment, tries to still himself, then steps round.

Haanstra was right. She is an addict, wasted away, hollowed out. The kind of condition there's no coming back from. In her hand she's clutching a roll of cling film, the brand Albert Heijn, the supermarket where Jaap buys his groceries.

He looks at her, and feels the world fall away from his feet.

She starts out towards him, her eyes hungry for the fix, the roll held out like an offering.

The drone buzzes closer.

75

Jaap wants to tell her to run.

He knows he can't.

He's standing by one of the pools he'd seen earlier. Its surface is calm, serene, reflecting the sky, vast and untroubled.

The woman's within five feet now, her eyes wild and bloodshot, her face sunken, as if being pulled towards whatever it is inside her, whatever weakness or trauma or fear that turned her into what she is right now.

Jaap's mind is trying its best.

She doesn't have a life, she'll be dead in six months. Maybe slightly more, most likely less.

And Tanya's worth more than that, Tanya's alive, vital, carrying his child.

So it's two lives, not one, he'll be saving.

It's not personal. One dies so two can live. Simple.

The drone buzzes closer again.

'Where is it?' the woman says, her voice cracked and harsh. She holds out the roll of cling film, a beaten relay runner passing on the baton.

Again, the drone moves towards him, pushing him, daring him not to.

Oh fuck . . .

Jaap steps forward, grabs her wrist and drags her to the

ground. He flips her over, pins her arms with his legs, and reaches out to grab the roll where she's dropped it.

His phone falls out of his pocket, he doesn't notice.

He tries to find the edge, spinning the roll round, running his nail on the surface, hoping it'll catch. Finally it comes.

The woman's squirming, shrieking. The cling film hisses as he starts to stretch it out.

76

Tanya knows he's being driven by love.

Love for her.

He's on the screen, the camera far out enough to capture the whole scene, but close enough to read his face.

Haanstra's behind her. She'd caught a glimpse earlier, he seemed to be controlling the drone remotely. She doesn't know how that can be, at such a distance, but right now she has more pressing concerns. She's discovered that the chair isn't bolted to the ground, and she's been waiting for Haanstra to move close enough for her to try and ram him.

Desperate? Sure. But what else does she have?

So far Haanstra's been keeping out of range, though, as if he's read her mind.

On screen Jaap has the cling film stretched out, but he's still not started. The woman's writhing but he has her pinned down too well.

Tanya's breathing is getting out of control, she has to act before it's too late.

She starts to scream, the noise stifled by the ball-gag, but it's enough to annoy Haanstra. He steps close behind her and sends another breathtaking, stinging slap across the side of the face.

Now! she thinks. *Do it.*

All the strength in her legs boosts her back, and she

feels herself crashing into Haanstra, knocking him down. She lands on top of him, and he grunts hard like he's winded badly. She can feel the back of her head against his chest, and she scrabbles her legs, lifts her head, preparing to bring it down on his face, if only she can get into position.

But before she can she feels herself flipping sideways, Haanstra shoving her off him. Before she can do anything he's up, grabbing her, hauling the chair she's in upright.

She blew it. The chance to save herself, save Jaap from what he's being forced into.

He's still behind her, and she's waiting for the blow which she knows will come.

But then there's a loud knocking on the metal door behind them, the sound reverberating round the space. On the screen Jaap's still working, his face twisted in disgust.

Haanstra shoves the back of the chair, tipping her forward onto the concrete floor, her knees hitting just before her face. The top of the chair rams her in the back of the neck.

She hears Haanstra's footsteps heading towards the door.

77

Kees is back in Amsterdam for the first time since he'd been released from the Bijlmerbajes prison and relocated down to Rotterdam to start the long process of working his way undercover into Van der Pol's organization.

Right now he's asleep in the car he'd driven up in. A noise wakes him and he starts; for a full two seconds he can't remember where he is.

Then it all clicks.

He's watching a row of garages. The one he's particularly interested in is ten down. The noise he's heard is someone walking towards it, their back to him, a dark baseball cap on his head. The figure stops outside the tenth.

Kees has tracked down the man Van der Pol had wanted found, knows that the garage is paid for in cash by someone answering the man's description. And it looks like he was right – presumably the figure heading there now is the man himself.

Kees has Van der Pol on speed-dial. He'd been given a phone along with the car.

Van der Pol answers before the first ring's even completed.

'Got him,' Kees says.

'OK,' replies Van der Pol. 'Here's what you're going to do.'

He listens, then hangs up.

Kees reckons he should be feeling sick. But, as he pops the glove compartment and finds the gun he'd not known was there, he realizes he's not feeling anything at all.

The figure with the cap moves away from the tenth garage door, and quickly to the end of the row. Kees loses sight of him for a second, before he sees him reappear on the flat roof, walking back towards the tenth door. Kees slips down his seat.

The man pulls out a gun, lies down on the roof and reaches over the edge to hit the door a couple of times with the butt of the gun.

After a few seconds the garage door starts to open, revealing shoes, legs, then a torso.

Once it's fully up Kees recognizes the man.

It's his target, Alex Haanstra.

Further back in the garage there's a large screen, a movie playing on it. And in front of it, someone – a woman – is tied to a chair, kneeling with her head to the ground like a religious penitent. On the screen a man is doing something Kees can't quite work out, too far away to properly see the detail.

Haanstra stands there for a second, scanning the surroundings. Kees slips even lower. Haanstra steps forward, and at the same moment the man on the roof reaches down with his gun and shoots him in the head.

Haanstra stands for a moment, swaying like a drunk, the bullet having ripped most of his lower jaw off, then his whole body collapses.

The man with the gun stands up, pulls out a phone and makes a call.

There's something *really* familiar about him.

But he can't see his face.

Sirens split the air. The man lowers his phone, moves to the next garage along, and lowers himself back down to the ground.

The sirens are getting closer. The man moves towards Haanstra's body, weapon out, even though there's no way he's getting up again.

The man kicks him. Haanstra doesn't move. The man shoots him in the back of the head a second time. Then he turns towards the garage. Kees sees him start, as if he's just had a shock. It's almost like he hadn't expected there to be anyone in the garage, far less someone tied up. He stands there for a moment as if making a decision, before heading into the garage towards the woman, glancing round just before he does.

Kees gets a glimpse of the man's face.

And that's when he decides to get the hell out of there.

78

The woman's thrashing about, but he's heavier and stronger.

He has her pinned, knees on forearms. She's not going anywhere.

She stops thrashing, he watches as the fear in her eyes turns to resignation.

The last rays of sun are hitting the very top of the quarry's edge, the limestone painted pretty pink. The drone's in close, but hasn't moved. It's all Jaap can do to stop himself from reaching out and grabbing it. Smashing it into a million pieces.

And he hates to admit it, but the anger is helping what he's doing, as if his mind's transferring it from Haanstra to the woman in front of him.

Is this how they felt? he thinks. Kamp, Groot and Wilders?

He leans forward, whispers right in the woman's ear, and starts wrapping her head. The layers accumulate, the soft swish of the cling film unravelling barely audible under the drone's rotors.

On the ground his phone starts buzzing, the screen lighting up.

He carries on wrapping, lifting her head up and back as the roll passes under and dropping it down again.

The sun falls away, the quarry darkens.

He notices the glow from his phone. He stops for a second, glances at it.

The drone starts to move slowly, sideways and away from him.

Beneath him the addict has stopped fighting, her body perfectly still.

The drone's still drifting, as if it's a drunk asked to walk on a straight line.

The name on the screen is Tanya.

79

Tanya hangs up, the swirl of emotions too much.

Smit takes the phone, and after a moment of hesitation, puts his arm round her. She leans in, exhausted, still not quite able to believe it's over.

She catches a glimpse of the body lying just outside the garage. Even from here she can see there's not much left of his head.

'Stupid question,' Smit says, 'but are you OK?'

In the last forty-eight hours she'd had a suspect fall on her, break her ribs, then blow his brains out in front of her. She'd had emergency surgery, been kidnapped, forced to watch as Jaap was being coerced into killing someone, only to be saved at the last moment by Smit.

And she has a baby growing inside her with a hole in its heart.

She doesn't know what to say.

'C'mon,' Smit says, guiding her out of the garage, past Haanstra's body and towards a patrol car which has just skidded up. 'Let's get you checked over.'

She's light-headed.

Time no longer seems linear.

But still she has to ask. 'How did you know?'

'I didn't,' Smit says as they reach the car, a uniform opening a door for her like she's a celebrity. 'Roemers got lucky, managed to trace him here. But we had no idea what was going on. We didn't know you'd been kidnapped, didn't know what he was doing to Jaap. If we'd been a few seconds later then . . .'

He looks away, the thought too painful to acknowledge.

Another two cars pull up. Officers get busy taping off the scene.

'Thank you,' she says. 'Thank you.'

He squeezes her arm, but seems unable to say anything further.

It's only once the car has pulled out that she throws up all over the back seat.

80

It's hours later and the adrenaline which has been propping Jaap's system up suddenly runs out.

The tunnel vision he's been existing in broadens.

He becomes aware of where he is, what's around him.

He's in an interview room in the basement of his own station, the overhead lights too bright, too clinical. He can see minute detail, the little bumps of paint which had run down and dried, scuffs on the concrete floor, the loose line of dust where the wall meets the ground.

'. . . and then what?' asks the man opposite him. Jaap turns his focus back to him, he has a strange face, like his nose is the centre of gravity, all his features being pulled towards it. But his eyes are intelligent. And right now they're showing doubt.

'Like I told the previous guy—'

The door opens, pushing a wave of air towards Jaap's face, and Smit walks in.

'OK, that's enough,' he says.

The interviewer turns and eyes him up. When he speaks his voice is calm and level. 'I'm trying to ascertain exactly what happened. In every case where a police officer is injured—'

'Get out.'

The man eyes Smit some more. Then he pulls his files

together and leaves the room, Smit holding the door for him. He stops in the doorway, turns and looks at Jaap.

'We're not finished,' he says.

Once it's closed Smit leans back against the wall.

'You OK?' he finally asks.

Jaap doesn't know what to say. He feels like putting his head down on the table.

'C'mon,' Smit says after a while. 'I'll take you home. Tanya should be there soon, she's been given the all-clear.'

'What about Arno?' Jaap asks as they leave the room.

'Arno's . . . well, he's pretty badly concussed, but he'll pull through. I've got someone with him, just as a precaution.'

They make it out into the night and Smit opens the door of an unmarked, parked in a cone of light by the canal's edge.

'I should call him,' Jaap says once they're moving.

'Really, he's fine. Speak to him tomorrow.'

The neon of Amsterdam moves by. Jaap stares out at it, not really taking it in.

A few minutes later Smit pulls up outside Jaap's house-boat. He turns the motor off and they sit there in the sudden silence.

'Listen,' Smit says, 'I'll need to go through the full debrief tomorrow morning with you, but after that I suggest you take some time off.'

'Sure, but I'll need to do the full report as well.'

'No need, I'll get it all in the debrief and do it for you. Once it's done you can OK it, but there's no need for you to slave away on that right now.'

Headlights appear ahead, nosing forward slowly along the canal side.

'Thanks,' Jaap says. 'And for getting there in time.'

'No worries,' Smit says. He pauses for a moment as if unsure, then says, 'I know things haven't been great between us, but I think we should put that behind us, if you agree?'

He holds his hand out.

Jaap looks at it for a moment.

He just saved Tanya's life, he thinks. And mine.

No one's all good or all bad.

Jaap reaches out and claps it. They shake.

The headlights are getting closer, then the car stops and the lights flick off.

'I think that's her,' Smit says. 'Time for you to go.'

Jaap gets out just as Tanya emerges from the car ahead. He's not aware of running across the space separating them, but suddenly she's in his arms.

The two cars pull away, reversing in unison, leaving them alone.

Later, sleep eluding them both, they sit on the sofa, staring out at the streak of moonlight smeared across the canal.

'So she's all right?'

They've tried to avoid talking about it, all that matters to Jaap is that Tanya is unharmed, but their conversation had gradually gravitated towards it, as if they couldn't resist its creeping pull.

'Yeah, I mean, she's not got much of a life waiting for her. But I didn't kill her.'

'Why her?'

'You mean why did Haanstra pick her?'

She nods.

'I don't know. I still don't get why he chose the victims. The women, I mean. Or if he told Kamp, Groot and Wilders to find their own victims. And he played us, he knew we were after him and moved first. How is that even possible?'

He watches a ripple pass through the moonlight.

'This case is just so screwed up,' he went on. 'You've got a guy who goes to all this trouble to get video of someone killing someone else. Haase said it's linked to some childhood trauma. But I'm not feeling it. When Haanstra called me he seemed too cold, too in control, y'know? It's not like he was emotional about it. He was businesslike.'

'He was. I hardly got to see him, but he didn't strike me as crazy. Everything he did was deliberate.'

Jaap shakes his head. Beside him Tanya nuzzles closer. In the end he wonders if it matters. He's got Tanya back, that's the important point.

That's rational, how it should be, logic triumphing.

'Yeah, maybe. Anyway, Smit's offered to write the report up for me, once he's debriefed me tomorrow.'

But even as he says it he knows logic can't trump the feeling in his stomach, that simultaneous contraction and expansion which tells him something's not right.

'Sure he'd love to take the credit.'

'He saved you. He saved me, for that matter. Right now I don't really care if he gets a good news story out of it.'

He kisses her.

'Let's go to bed,' she says.

The thought comes to him just as he's drifting off, jolting him awake. It was something Haanstra had said.

We'll be watching you.

Emphasis on the 'we'.

Did he mean him and Tanya, or did he mean someone else?

Day Six

81

Smit's not in when Jaap makes it to the station. Which is hardly surprising; he'd left his houseboat well before the sky had even thought about getting light, never mind actually doing something about it. He'd woken at the point in his dream where he'd been wrapping the cling film round and round. His heart had been thudding, and he'd needed to get up, get out, anything to try and bring things back to normal.

Whatever that is, he thinks.

He caffeinates himself well beyond standard levels and starts work, his mind humming like a loose electrical connection. As he goes through the process of compiling everything Smit's going to need to write up the final report, the feeling which had woken him so early, the feeling which he has been trying to ignore since last night, just gets stronger.

He tries telling himself it's nothing, just the stress, something which will die down of its own accord. But that does nothing to dampen it.

Because the more he sits there going through the details, the more he feels there *is* something wrong with this case, something which doesn't fit. He's been an inspector long enough to know that his instincts are usually right, that he should trust them. But maybe, counters another part of his brain, it's just an after-effect of yesterday, the adrenaline still wreaking havoc in his body, his mind.

By the time Smit makes it in, the sky finally brightening and the caffeine wearing off, Jaap's still no closer to shaking the feeling that something's wrong.

He walks into Smit's office with a pile of notes, sees that Smit's already set a recorder up next to a large cafetière of coffee and a plate of pastries.

Jaap wonders if Smit's the one with something wrong in his head. Maybe he's had a mini-stroke which no one has noticed, but which has altered his personality. Because in all the years Jaap has worked for him, all the times he's been in his office, he's never once been offered so much as a glass of water, let alone coffee and pastries.

'Thought we might need this,' Smit says as he invites Jaap to sit and pours him a cup. Jaap thinks this will go down in station legend.

They take a moment – a few bites and sips, the cup almost scalding against Jaap's hand – before getting down to it. Jaap takes Smit through what he's got, unfolding the investigation like a complex piece of origami returning to a flat sheet of paper. Smit listens closely, asks for the odd bit of clarification. Once Jaap's finished, Smit then takes him through the bits Jaap doesn't know: how Roemers suspected Haanstra had rigged the drone so it could be operated remotely, then found where the signal was coming from, which led Smit right to the garage, and the confrontation which ended in Haanstra's death and Tanya's rescue.

No one in the police, far less Smit, had any idea what was going on, just how time-critical it had all been. They'd had no idea that Haanstra was holding Tanya, using her as a bargaining chip to get Jaap to kill.

'We got lucky,' Smit concludes. 'A few minutes later and things would've been different.'

Jaap shakes his head. All this effort, all this energy being used for something so destructive.

'Also we found this at the scene.' Smit hauls out an evidence bag with a small plastic spray bottle, half-full of clear liquid.

Jaap takes it. 'What's this?'

'Had the lab test it, just got the result back in. It contains scopolamine dissolved in DMSO.'

'DMSO?'

'Dimethyl something-or-other.' Smit checks a bit of paper. 'Here we go, dimethyl sulfoxide. According to the lab it's an incredibly potent solvent; if you dissolve something in it and then put a drop on your skin the DMSO takes it right into your body. From what I've read, a few seconds after it hits their skin people get a garlic taste in their mouth, so this stuff works really fast. Haanstra could have got close enough to the women, sprayed a bit on their hand or neck or whatever, and within a matter of seconds the scopolamine's taken effect. Then all he'd have to do is suggest they go somewhere, and the victim would just do it.'

They carry on, Smit confirming that the addict is now in hospital. Jaap had wrapped the cling film loose enough that she'd still been able to breathe, hoping that the drone wouldn't be able to transmit that detail back to Haanstra.

Once they've been through everything, the sleep Jaap missed overnight starts creeping up on him, trying to embrace him tight. Clearly it shows, as Smit looks at him, concerned.

'So, time off. I think you and Tanya should take a bit. Go away somewhere maybe.'

'That an order?'

Smit looks at him, breaks into a smile. 'If that's what it takes, then yeah, it is.'

'OK,' Jaap says, getting up, everything a struggle, his limbs heavy. 'And, uh . . .'

Smit puts his hand up as if to say it was nothing. 'You'd've done the same. Really, there's no need. I'm just glad as fuck I got there in time to save her.'

The air outside is on the way to steam; Jaap feels smothered by it as soon as he steps out of the station. He takes a few moments, feels how the moist air defines the boundary between him and the world. Then he starts walking back to his houseboat, thinking about what Smit had said, about taking a break, just him and Tanya.

She's up, at least judging by the mess the kitchen table's in when he makes it back. But he can't see her. He calls out, a stab of sharp panic jolting through him.

Her voice answers from the bathroom, telling him she's just got out of the shower.

He breathes and starts clearing up, allowing his heart to work back down to more healthy levels, and is nearly finished by the time she comes out.

'How'd it go?' she asks, clothed but still towelling her hair. He takes her in for a moment, trying to work out if she's showing yet, if there's any change in her shape. But he can't make up his mind.

'Smit was like a child gloating over a favourite toy,' Jaap says. 'I almost felt like saying I'd write it up after all, just to spoil his fun.'

'I guess we both owe him on this one,' she says, her head held sideways as she works her hair.

Jaap watches, entranced suddenly by the movement of her hands, her fingers sliding through her red hair, darkened by water, her bruised cheek like an overripe fruit.

'You're right,' he finally says. 'That's kind of why I'm letting him run with it. And he's the one who actually shot and killed Haanstra.'

'So,' she says, finishing her hair, 'everything tie up?'

Jaap shrugs, moves to the kitchen area. He's suddenly thirsty, desperately so. He pours himself a glass of OJ, knocks it back in one.

'It all makes sense,' he says, putting the glass down and wiping his mouth. 'Sure.'

'You sound doubtful.'

'There's something . . . not right.'

'Hey,' she says, stepping towards him, draping the towel on the sofa, her hair still a touch damp, hanging loose. 'You need to let it go. Let's go out somewhere. Somewhere we've never been before.'

The machete swings through the air, glinting like a flash of teeth, and takes the top off the green coconut. The man deftly inserts a straw into the hole and hands it to Tanya, repeating the performance for Jaap's. They pay and carry on walking down Lindengracht, dodging groups of tourists wielding selfie sticks.

'Isn't it a bit weird?' Jaap asks, having taken a few sips.

'What, the coconuts?'

'This filming obsession. I don't get it. It's like everyone is trying to prove to everyone else how much fun they're always having by filming it and posting it somewhere. And this thing tastes rancid,' he says, holding the coconut up, checking that it's not rotten.

'This is supposed to be fun,' she says, elbowing him. 'Remember?'

They carry on heading east towards the pop-up art fair they'd come to see which had a space at the end of the market. As they pass a bin, Tanya drops her coconut into it. Jaap looks at her.

'You're right, it didn't taste that great.'

They amble through the stalls, stopping at some to admire the artwork, and walking quickly past the more desperate-looking artists with imploring eyes. Once they've seen enough they end up in a café on Brouwersgracht, a few round tables clustered on the canal's edge.

'OK, what's up?' Tanya asks once the waiter has taken their order.

Jaap shakes his head and picks up a paper tube of sugar from a glass in the middle of the table.

'There's something not right with the case. I just can't see what it is.'

He's pushing the sugar from end to end, feeling the small grains through the paper. Tanya reaches out and stops him.

'You need to let it go,' she says. 'Because, really? I don't want to be reminded of it constantly. The whole time he had me it felt like I wasn't scared for myself, but I was for the baby. Like I was somehow failing. I don't want to keep reliving that, OK?'

Jaap starts to feel guilty. He realizes he's too wrapped up in the case instead of seeing what's right in front of him, taking care of Tanya. Because that's all that matters now, he thinks.

And yet part of him feels a tinge of resentment, as if he's being thwarted somehow.

He reaches across the table with both hands, clasps her cheeks and leans forward to kiss her. 'Sorry,' he says. 'I'm all yours now.'

Their drinks arrive and they try their best to just enjoy the moment, but Jaap feels the mood has changed. They finish up and carry on walking, Jaap trying to be present, attentive, but Tanya's gone quiet, any joy they may have felt gone from the day.

As they're heading back to the houseboat, crossing the bridge at Egelantiersgracht, it hits Jaap, what's been bothering him.

'Listen, I know we said we wouldn't talk about this but—'

'Jaap—'

'Please, this is the last time, I promise. Then it's done.'

She gives him a fed-up look, but then nods.

'When you were there, in the garage, did he call anyone, anyone other than me?'

'For fuck's—'

'This is important.'

'No, he didn't, all right?'

A passing couple turn their heads, secretly enjoying the fact that another couple are on the edge of a full-blown domestic in public.

'He had all this computer equipment set up, but the only person I heard him talking to was you. Happy?'

She starts walking away from him, and he has to race to catch up.

'At one point he said, "We'll be watching you,"' Jaap says as he reaches her side. 'Do you remember that?'

She doesn't say anything, keeps on walking as if he's a minor annoyance, some insect buzzing round her head.

'Tanya, please, this could be really important.'

She stops dead and turns to face him. The anger's gone. Now she just looks exhausted. 'Kinda. Not really,' she frowns. 'You think there was someone else involved?'

'Haase said Haanstra was filming the killings as a trophy, a way to get him through some past trauma. But that doesn't make sense to me, he was too controlled. Too in control. Was he making you watch me?'

'No. But you're right.' She looks out across the waters leading to Prinsengracht, as if searching for something. He watches her, and in the moment feels a kind of fear, an inevitability about what she's going to say. 'He called someone. He went outside so I couldn't hear it. But he definitely spoke to someone.'

82

'. . . Yeah, missed opportunity, if you hadn't been so fucking . . . Yeah, all right. What's done is done. Just means you're going to have to sort it out yourself. He's getting too close, it has to be done today.'

Van der Pol, phone clamped between shoulder and ear, motions Kees into the back of the car he's sitting in.

'Yeah, today.' He listens for a few seconds. 'I know he's a cop, you fucktard. What difference does that make? We've killed cops before. Just get it done. And you do remember that if I go down you do as well? I'll make sure it all comes out at trial, how do you think your cop buddies will react when they find out about you?'

He shuts down the call, takes the SIM card out of the phone and puts it in a pocket. Then he removes the battery and puts the phone in another pocket. 'Let's move,' Van der Pol says to Lumberjack as soon as Kees closes the door.

Lumberjack gets them going and Van der Pol starts talking.

'I got your message,' he says to Kees without looking at him. 'You sure he's dead? I mean I'm not seeing any proof here.'

Kees finds his heart's pounding. It's happening so often these days that he's starting to be able to ignore it. He's so close to being able to walk away, he just needs to control things a bit longer. And from what he's just heard, he needs to find out who Van der Pol was talking to, because it sounded an awful lot like Van der Pol was not only talking to a bent cop, he was ordering the death of a straight one.

For a moment part of him awakens, tells him he can't allow that. Another tells him he's done, out, he deserves this. It's not his problem any more. He's no longer a cop – Smit had told him he's been kept off the books. And having seen the way he killed Haanstra – 'executed' was a word which kept floating round his head in the hours afterwards – Kees believes him.

What he doesn't get is what Smit really wants. Kees has given him more than enough to take Van der Pol down, but he keeps him on, keeps Kees going even though with each day, each passing minute, the chances of him being found out increase. Smit's argument has been that he needs to make the case watertight, make sure Van der Pol not only goes away, but never comes back.

But, Kees realizes, he doesn't care about that any more. The only thing which matters is getting the money for his ID and disappearing. And key to that is getting Van der Pol to pay out.

'He's dead. Absolutely,' Kees replies, trying to keep everything loose, natural.

'I asked for a photo, didn't I?'

The car takes a long, slow corner. Kees feels the Gs. The windows are tinted, but in any case he's not looking out of them. Or if he is he's not seeing what's outside.

'Yeah, you did,' Kees says. 'But as soon as I shot him I

382

could hear the police coming. I had to get out of there. Like fast.'

Van der Pol mulls it over, all the while his eyes locked on Kees' face.

'I've been in this business a long time, y'know?' Van der Pol says finally. 'And I've done that because one—' He raises a hand and holds up his first finger '—I'm careful. And two—' He lifts his middle finger '—the police aren't fucking omnipotent beings who just happen to turn up right at the precise moment when someone has to be dealt with.'

Kees shrugs. The movement dislodges a globule of sweat which has been forming in his armpit. It runs down his side with agonizing slowness.

'I don't get it either. I think they may have been onto him already. I was lucky and just got there first.'

Van der Pol shakes his head. 'You sure he's dead?'

'He's dead,' Kees says. 'So I'd like to get paid.'

The car slows down, and stops. Silence seeps into the interior as the engine dies. Kees looks out the window, sees they're in the middle of nowhere. No one around.

'All right,' Van der Pol finally says, 'I'll get you your money.' He gets out of the car and motions to Kees to follow him. As Kees steps out of the car Van der Pol's already opening up the boot. Kees walks round, expecting to see it filled with a plastic sheet, like something from an old mob movie. But there's a row of sports-kit bags, four at least. Van der Pol's unzipping one of them, it's black with the Nike logo picked out in reflective silver. Inside are bundles of notes. Van der Pol reaches for one, his fingers clasping it the exact same moment Kees realizes three things.

The first is that Lumberjack is behind him.

The second is that something hard is just about to obliterate the back of his head.

And the third, as the blow hits and his mind spirals down into darkness, is that he's totally, royally fucked.

83

Roemers is at his desk, earphones in, moving to an unseen beat, his hands drumming, head nodding rhythmically. Occasionally he reaches out, smashes an imaginary hi-hat.

As he approaches, Jaap thinks of the quote on Sander's door. He stands for a moment, trying to remember the exact wording, but it doesn't come.

Roemers sees him, but doesn't stop, he just swings round in his chair and continues his drumming as if Jaap's not a human being, but a living drum kit.

'Don't want to interrupt anything,' Jaap says loudly. 'You're obviously doing important work.'

Roemers reluctantly does a final flourish, then slips his headphones off, stowing them carefully back in their retail packaging. He's obviously treated himself to a new pair.

'You're like the angel of death,' Roemers says.

Jaap looks at him as if to say *What?*

'Here, take a look at this.' Roemers swings round in his chair, works the keyboard and mouse. A window opens on screen. Jaap can see sky. The camera dips and he gets a bird's-eye view of the quarry as it scans around, hunting its prey. Then it's moving fast, homing in on the back of a figure he knows to be himself. He sees himself turning.

'No,' he says, reaching out and closing the window before the camera catches his face.

'Seriously, it's a great watch. Probably one of the scariest things I've seen. When you start wrapping that woman's head up in cling film? I got the shivers. So the question is, would you have gone through with it?'

Jaap had kept the cling film loose so that she'd been able to breathe. He'd whispered his plan in her ear, told her to fight then eventually play dead. But during the night part of his mind had questioned that, questioned if it wasn't just an excuse he'd made to make it easier for himself.

He knows it's going to be one of those things which is always attached to him. He could be ninety and people will still whisper as he goes past, eyes ballooning in shock. So he's not going to dignify it ever, starting now.

'You've been going through his computer, right?' Jaap says.

Roemers points to a laptop, hooked up to his desktop with a single short lead. It looks like two computers mating, rise of the machines.

'I'm pulling apart his hard drive now and . . .' He moves the cursor around and opens up a different window with a solid string of numbers and letters. He scrolls down, the symbols blurred.

'Seeing as you won't know what this is, I'll tell you,' he says after Jaap fails to say anything. 'This here is a key for secure communication. It's called PGP and it allows whoever has this sequence to encrypt a message, and only someone else who's been given the linked key can decrypt it.'

'Can you break it?'

'No. The key itself is 4,096 characters long. Even if I

hooked up pretty much all the computers in the world and ran them constantly, we're talking thousands of years to break this code. And I'm not exaggerating.'

Which as far as Jaap's concerned means Haanstra *was* communicating with someone else, and it was something he wanted hidden. Otherwise, why go to all the trouble?

'And there's more, though again possibly not that helpful. He uploaded several large files over the last few days, big enough to be videos like yours.'

'Where did he upload them to?'

'Yeah, that's the thing. On the darknet somewhere. Gonna be hard to trace. And when I say hard, I really mean next-to-impossible. Also, to make it worse, he deleted the files after uploading. Like proper deleted, not just whacked them in the trash can, y'know?'

'When were the uploads?'

Roemers taps a few keys, clicks a few more windows into existence and points at a list of times.

Jaap leans in to get a better look.

He doesn't like what he sees.

There are seven in total. But it's the last four which draw Jaap's attention.

Because each one was uploaded only hours after the deaths of Dafne, Nadine, Heleen and Kaaren.

84

'You still here?' Smit asks as he opens his office door to find Jaap running down the corridor towards him.

Jaap's breathing hard, having raced up the stairs from the DCU's basement home.

'There's something I think you should know.'

Station Chief Henk Smit's a busy man, he has important things to do, important people to meet, and he lets Jaap know all this by the way he checks his watch.

'All right,' he says, standing aside, allowing Jaap to step through. 'Two minutes.'

Inside, Jaap takes him through Roemers' discoveries.

'I'm sure he was working with at least one other person,' Jaap finishes up. 'Maybe more.'

Smit taps a finger on his desk, a frown curling his mouth down. 'Could be,' he eventually concedes.

'It makes sense, the killings had two main variables, the victim and the man chosen to kill them. Would make it so much easier to cover them both if there were two of you.'

Smit nods, he can see the logic. 'But two of them, both into killing the same way? That's just . . . I just can't see that. Serial killers generally work alone.'

'C'mon, you know there are some.'

'Fine, agreed. I'll look into this,' Smit says, standing, glancing at his watch again. 'But I have a press conference called for midday, and I'm going to need a pretty compelling reason to *not* go out there and announce we've managed to neutralize the threat. Now, if you'll excuse me.'

'The thing is, I think I know who it might be.'

Smit freezes.

Yeah, got your interest now, Jaap thinks.

'Who?' Smit asks.

'Bernard Kooy. He's a possible for the supply of scopolamine. We were looking for him as a likely route to Haanstra just when everything kicked off, so no one's spoken to him yet. If I can get him—'

'Whoa, let me stop you there.' Smit holds his hand out like the traffic cop he presumably once was. 'I appreciate your drive for this, I really do. But given what you and Tanya have been through I can*not* allow you to look into it. I'll get someone else on the case.'

'Really, it'll be quicker if I do it, you'll have to get someone up to speed and they're just not going to have the full background quick enough.'

The stare Smit gives him is potent stuff.

But the fact he hasn't yet spoken makes Jaap think he's winning the argument. So he pushes his luck.

'There's one thing, though. I'd really like to put a guard on Tanya. Haanstra knew where we live, there's a good chance whoever he's working with will also.'

'OK, here's what we're going to do,' Smit says, all action suddenly. 'You're going to give me your badge and step off the case—'

'But—'

'And that way you can stay at home, make sure Tanya's not in danger. It'll be a weight off your mind,' Smit says as he ushers Jaap to the door. 'If we get anything significant I'll let you know. You can hand your weapon in on the way out.'

The door swings shut behind him.

A few minutes later he's leaving the station when he hears his name being called.

He turns to see Roemers.

'You need to see this,' Roemers says.

Jaap's about to tell him he's off the case, but when he finds himself, two minutes later, down in the DCU staring at a screen, the only conclusion he can draw is that he didn't. Or Roemers didn't hear him.

Or whatever.

'So what am I looking at?'

'These numbers here are bitcoins,' Roemers says. 'Which aren't in themselves interesting. But the fact that I can see them is, because Haanstra really screwed up here. A phone of his was recovered from the garage he was operating from, and I could see there was a bitcoin wallet on it. The thing with these is, they're as secure as the PGP encryption I was telling you about earlier, but I—'

'Short version,' Jaap says, knowing Roemers can get very technical.

'Yeah, OK. Short version, he screwed up. I found his wallet key and was able to get in. See here? These are all deposits, and what's interesting is the dates. Check them out.'

It doesn't take Jaap long to see they come and go in waves. There are periods of virtually no deposits at all, then they start coming in with increasing frequency, growing towards specific dates where they reach a peak, then drop off a cliff.

Jaap's stomach lurches as he sees the dates themselves correspond with each killing.

He focuses on the current total, Ƀ347.87

'What's that worth?'

'If I were to cash that in right now—' He opens up a browser window, finds a conversion site, punches in the numbers '—just over two hundred thousand euros.'

'Whoa,' Jaap says. 'How'd he get them?'

'That's the thing, bitcoins are actually traceable to some extent; each transaction is logged and verified by multiple computers on this open ledger called the block-chain, so in theory, by studying it, you can work out where they came from. In practice, though, people who're not down with anyone knowing what they're up to "tumble" the coins first, the digital equivalent of money laundering. You send your coins to a tumbler and they send back other coins, for a fee.'

'Can you check the coins he's got?'

'Takes time, but I could get someone to have a look.' He clicks back to the wallet. 'Fuck.'

Jaap's seen it too. A moment ago the balance had been showing Ƀ347.87. Now it's zero.

'Someone's just emptied it,' Roemers says. 'Looks like you were right, he *was* working with someone.'

85

It's not the pain that's bothering him. Kees is used to pain – he's almost become a connoisseur, able to distinguish between the different types. The type he has now is the crushing, pressure type, like if he moves too quickly his head will explode.

Like Bart's did.

But it's kind of irrelevant, the movement thing, because right now he's trapped in a tight space, limbs up near his chest, arms hooked round them. So that's OK, he can check movement-induced head explosion off his list of worries.

The thing which *is* bothering him is that he's finding it hard to breathe, like the air's running out. He tries to shift his head, finds that there's tape across his mouth, the edge riding up to his nostrils, closing them off. There's clearly a tiny gap, because he's getting just enough air to keep him alive, but he's not sure how much longer he's going to last.

He tries to focus on his breath, slow it down, his mind spinning through his options.

Which right now seem somewhat limited.

He's in the car boot – even in the darkness he can work that out – but the car's not moving. He doesn't know if that's good or not. He tries to move a leg into position, kick the boot open, but he's too crammed in, can't get a proper angle to do anything more than just tickle the thing. Next he works on the tape, but finds his wrists are bound – cable ties, he's sure from the thinness of them – and he can't move both arms up to his face. There's also, he decides after a bit of exploration, a bag between them and his face; one of the sports-kit ones which had been filled with money is now making it impossible for him to reach his face.

He gives up and lies there, focusing on taking small sips of air, just enough to keep him going, even though his head is swirling. When he was younger he'd not really thought about death. Even in the years he'd been working as a homicide investigator, constantly exposed to it, he'd somehow managed to keep thoughts about it at bay. Sure, the victims were dead, but his focus had been on finding out the person responsible, and he had managed to avoid ruminating on death itself. It was something which happened to other people, and it almost felt like as long as he was the one doing the investigations he could keep himself removed from its sting, like being around it constantly exempted him, made him immune.

But all that had changed with his diagnosis, and yet even though he knew it was going to kill him, that wasn't the thing he feared. What he feared most of all was being alive.

Being alive whilst his body gradually broke down, the long slide into frailty and disability and reliance on others. The long, slow slide into a nightmare future of pain, regret and the tyranny of the everyday.

Now, trapped in the boot of the car – knowing that soon they'll come for him, that they'll kill him in an orgy of gore and hate, that it will at least, no matter how pain-ful, be relatively quick – he finds an odd sense of peace.

Whoever kills him is actually doing him a favour.

Later – how long he's not sure, time an irrelevance in the dark – he hears footsteps crunching dry grass, two people at least heading towards him, and finds his breath-ing is slow and calm.

86

There *is* someone else.

Jaap needed to get out of the station, so now he's on a bridge spanning Prinsengracht, overlooking the canal itself. Clouds curdle in the water below. Behind him, further down the canal, a floating digger works on the daily task of removing tons of silt from the canal bottom, along with assorted bike frames, some twisted, others missing wheels.

He'd left Roemers trying to track the bitcoins, the bitcoins that prove Haanstra wasn't working alone. Only someone he was working with would have access to his wallet, and it looks like they were emptying it and getting out.

But that's not the worst thing about what he's just seen.

The payments leading up to the deaths themselves mean that he's been wrong about this case, even though he's known all along there was something off with it.

TV and films perpetuate the myth that there's always a bad guy, someone external, a lone sicko, the fairy-tale villain killing for reasons buried deep in their screwed-up psychology, the killer who is nothing more than the personification of evil. And it seems to be what people would like to believe.

There's safety in the extra-ordinary, Jaap thinks.

But here the crime – or at least the motive – is so

everyday, so ordinary, that he suspects no one will want to believe it.

Because Haanstra, and whoever he was working with, were doing it for good old-fashioned money. They'd found a product people would pay for and then, like any good businessmen, worked out how to supply it.

For a profit.

Which in Jaap's mind is even worse than a lone psychopath or two.

He dials Tanya, noticing his hand is clammy on the phone. She answers and he tells her what he's discovered.

In the sky a plane ducks behind a cloud.

'I . . . There's something you should know,' she says when he's finished taking her through it. 'When I was on the case with Borst there were some rumours floating around that Van der Pol was involved in snuff movies, an urban legend kind of thing. But if what you're saying . . .'

'Looks like Haanstra could have been working with Van der Pol. He could be the missing man.'

'Van der Pol could be behind it, but I doubt he'd be getting his hands dirty. So most likely it was Haanstra and someone else working for him.'

Below Jaap the tip of a barge emerges from under the bridge, the deck piled high with green-grey silt.

'Could you do a couple of things for me?'

'Sure, but I thought you didn't want me involved.'

'I don't, but if you could call Borst, tell him what we've got, see what he thinks.'

'I can probably manage that. What's the other thing?'

'Check into a hotel, and pay with cash. And get a pre-pay phone on the way, leave yours at the houseboat.'

The barge is still moving below. Suddenly he feels unsteady on his feet.

'Tanya?'

'Yeah, I'm here. You think it's really necessary?'

Jaap thinks of his promise, that he's never going to put her in danger again. He thinks of people who force others into killing for them, so they can make money by selling the videos. He thinks of Van der Pol, head of the largest criminal organization in the country.

'Yeah,' he says, the barge finally breaking free from the bridge. The captain's at the wheel, already starting to spin it in preparation for the tight turn up onto Leidsegracht. 'Yeah, I do.'

A slit of light appears in the darkness.

Then it widens, Kees' eyes complaining at the onslaught.

But he fights, just keeps them open, enough to see two figures standing against the clouded sky in the ever-widening gap. One of them reaches down and grabs him.

As they bundle him out, something on the lip of the boot catching his hip on the way, he can see it's Lumberjack and Van der Pol himself.

They're at the edge of a field, the grass brown and broken, a thin wire fence marking out the perimeter just a few feet away. Clouds press down on them, and the humidity feels like it's going for some kind of record.

'I know it was you,' Van der Pol says. 'I know you're working for the cops.'

Kees is standing, Lumberjack to his left, using his physical presence to intimidate, an alpha dog claiming his space in the pack. But really the alpha here is Van der Pol, that's where all the bad energy is coming from.

They stand as if they're waiting for Kees to say something.

But really, what is there to say?

'I know Smit sent you to spy on me,' Van der Pol says after some more grass has died. 'And the punishment for that is . . . Well, put it this way. It's not pain-free, or quick.'

For some reason, the only thing which matters to Kees now is not saying anything. If he's going to die, fine, but he's not saying another goddamned word in this fucked-up excuse for a world. No matter what they do, no matter how hard they push, he's going quietly. Stoically.

Beside him Lumberjack pulls out a knife.

Jaap pulls up on a street in Amsterdam-Zuid, scraping the front tyre hard against the kerb.

The house itself is easy to spot, festooned with red and white police tape. It's the one Haanstra rented. Smit had told him in the debrief earlier that nothing of interest had been found there, but Jaap wants to see for himself.

One uniform stands guard. He's overly tall with a narrow face, and challenges Jaap when he approaches.

'I've orders not to let anyone in,' he says, eyeing Jaap.

'This is my case,' Jaap says. 'Who gave those orders?'

'Station Chief Smit,' the uniform replies, as if by saying those words he gets to bask in the exalted one's glory. 'He was *very* specific.'

'Well, I'll be even more specific,' Jaap says as he steps past him, ducks under the tape and pushes open the front door. He's always been a believer that actions speak louder than words.

The house is small, some prefab eighties job, and smells damp. There's nothing of interest on the ground floor, Jaap concludes, after a search of a messy kitchen and forlorn living room looking out over a tiny concrete area filled with junk.

Upstairs are two bedrooms and a tiny bathroom, the latter so small that the door hits the toilet bowl. The main bedroom doesn't yield much, but a yellowed pine wardrobe in the second bedroom is full of boxes. Jaap goes through them all, even though someone should have been through them already.

He's on box four when he gets a call from a number he doesn't recognize.

'So I spoke to Harry,' Tanya says when he answers.

'And?'

She breathes out. He can hear reluctance in it, and something else he can't quite place.

'He confirmed what I'd heard, that there'd been rumours Van der Pol had been making snuff films. This was years ago though, and Harry says they never found any evidence of it. His view was that it was simply a story, probably put about by Van der Pol himself.'

'Bigging himself up? Part of the image?'

'That's what Harry thinks,' Tanya says. 'You're some small-time dealer and someone approaches you to take over your patch. If you've heard the man at the top is a total psycho who makes films of people being killed it's probably gonna help sway your decision.'

Jaap's still working through box four when he spots, at the bottom, the corner of a passport.

'I don't think it was an image thing,' Jaap says, pulling it out. 'After each killing Haanstra uploaded a large file to the internet. That's not a coincidence.'

'No.'

'Is Harry still around or did he go back to Rotterdam?'

'He was driving down when I got hold of him. He turned round once we'd talked, though, says he's going to be in Amsterdam pretty soon. He's gonna call you when he's close. He *really* wants to get Van der Pol.'

'We might just be able to help,' Jaap says. 'You're some-where safe?'

'Yeah, I checked into the—' She stops herself. 'Well, somewhere.'

'Promise me you're not going anywhere.'

When they'd rung off, Jaap goes through the passport. Inside there's a photo of a young man, staring angrily at the viewer.

A motorbike rips down the street, slowing down until its deep rumble shakes the world apart.

There's something familiar about the face.

But it's the name which grabs him: Bernard Kooy.

89

So much for going quietly, Kees thinks.

Resolutions are all very well, but at some level the animal-self kicks in. We haven't evolved, had our genes carried through unthinkable numbers of repetitions from the first single-cell organisms to the fully functioning modern humans we are today, just so that in the face of death we give up. That's not how it works.

In Kees' case, the desire to survive flares into life when the blade starts towards his abdomen. And he's grateful for it sharpening his focus, making things slow down enough so he can react properly.

He ducks sideways, grabs Lumberjack's arm with both hands, sticks his foot out, and then yanks Lumberjack across it. Lumberjack goes down hard – Kees can't help but think of falling timber – and his grip loosens on the knife's handle just enough for Kees to prise it free, grab it in his own hand, sweat making it slippery. He flips it over and slices the cable tie, catching his left wrist at the same time.

Van der Pol's already moving forward, Kees knows he's got a matter of seconds before impact. He stamps down on the back of Lumberjack's neck and the man goes limp.

Van der Pol notices that it's down to just him and Kees, the protection he's always relied on suddenly unavailable.

His eyes flick between Kees and the man lying on the ground.

For a moment, standing less then ten feet apart, Kees thinks Van der Pol might give in and run.

Van der Pol weighs up his options. Then a huge smile cracks open his face as he rushes towards Kees, bundling him backwards into the wire fence.

Which turns out to be electrified.

The shock pulsing through his body gives Kees extra impetus to fight back, like it's the burst of energy his body needs. He leans back into the wire, using the next pulse of stinging electrical energy to explode forward, pushing Van der Pol off him and onto the ground.

Kees lands his full weight on him and hears the deep grunt of Van der Pol losing air. He flips him over, grabs a wrist, and shoves it right up between the man's shoulder blades. For good measure he kneels in the small of his back.

Van der Pol tries to squirm. Kees takes a holistic approach, shoves the arm higher, puts even more weight on his knee. It seems to work. There's less resistance now.

He leans forward until his mouth is right by Van der Pol's ear.

'Who were you talking to?' he says. 'Who did you give orders to kill?'

90

'I think you might be on to something,' Harry says as he slides into the seat opposite Jaap.

They're in a café on Waalstraat, one of the old-style ones which still holds the stink of smoke and doesn't purvey thirty different artisan-roasted coffees from remote villages in faraway places. You want a chai latte with whipped soy cream, sweetened with stevia syrup and sprinkled with raw cacao powder? You'd better go elsewhere, because when you order coffee here you get a chipped mug of hot brown stuff, sugar and cream already added.

Despite this, perhaps because of, it's always busy.

They're at a table towards the back, tucked away in a curved half-booth, the seat fabric worn, the wood shiny with age and use.

'Have you got any evidence that Van der Pol deals in that kind of thing?'

'No,' Harry says, looking around to check that no one's in earshot. 'But really? He does everything else. I know that snuff movies are supposed to be an urban myth, but if anyone is doing it then he's gotta be a pretty strong candidate. In my view anyway. So Haanstra's dead?'

Jaap nods. A waiter hustles over. He looks like he's only waitering to prop up his career as a drag queen, eyebrows plucked thin and exaggerated hips swinging like Marilyn

Monroe. Harry waves him off. The waiter pouts, spins round and flounces away.

'Looks like Haanstra was working with Bernard Kooy – he's a possible scopolamine supplier. And I've got someone trying to track the bitcoins.'

Harry nods, like, *computers*. 'Well, I've done a little digging and come up with something which might be of interest to you. Less digital, more real world.'

'What is it?'

'Actually it's more of a him.'

'Right, where is he?'

'Luckily for us, he's in prison.'

Harry gives him the background as Jaap drives them to the Bijlmerbajes prison complex in De Omval. The prison itself consists of six towers, each joined by underground tunnels. The only thing which makes it look different to social housing are the bars on the windows. And, Jaap knows, those were only retrofitted years after the original construction. The plan had been that no one would want to jump out of the window of their prison cell if they were on the fourth floor or above.

But it turned out they did.

After the fifth inmate ignored the fact that none of the previous four had managed to escape – one killing themselves outright, the other three snapping various limbs – the council had had to stump up the cash for putting the bars on. And now, in a cruel twist of monetary fate, the council's stumping up again, this time to remove the bars, as the whole prison complex is being turned into a holding area for asylum seekers. The Netherlands' propensity to rehabilitate not incarcerate, combined with the crisis in Syria, means that there are more refugees in the country than convicted criminals. So turning prisons into housing seems pragmatic.

They park and get out, Jaap looking up at the towers against the sky. Wisps of cloud streak behind them. He tries to work out how many men he's put in this very prison over the years but finds the thought too depressing.

Inside, they sign in and Jaap asks to speak to the duty officer. Who, it turns out, likes beer and fried food. At least that's what the enlarged stomach which precedes him into the room seems to be saying. He listens to Jaap, makes a few calls, and minutes later Jaap and Harry find themselves in an outside area overshadowed by towers on all sides.

The square space is filled with metal cages. Jaap knows this is where inmates deemed either too dangerous to mix with others or potentially at high risk of violence to themselves are given their hour-long chance to commune with nature.

Each cage is no more than two metres by two metres, with a smooth concrete floor and chain-link sides.

The guard giving them the guided tour stops at the third one and runs his baton back and forth along the chain-link. The man inside, standing with his back to them, doesn't move.

His head is shaved, tattoos running right up his neck to his scalp. They're intricate, works of art compared to the usual dull, blurred images most people choose to mark themselves with. Jaap's reminded of a painting he'd once seen by Bosch, a writhing mass of bodies having sex and shoving a wide range of hideous torture implements into various body cavities. No auto-fellating aliens, he notes.

'Hey, fuckhead, you've got visitors,' says the guard.

The man turns, takes them in.

Jaap notices his eyes seem oddly dark.

'We'll take it from here,' Harry says to the guard, who nods, hitches his belt, and saunters off.

'Well,' says the man once the guard's out of earshot. 'This is exciting.'

His voice is soft, self-assured. He has an unhurried aura. Jaap sees why his eyes look so dark: the man hardly has any whites. He's wearing the standard jumpsuit, his hands and feet chained together with prison bling.

On the drive over Harry had given Jaap the run down: Koen Kramer's an ex-associate of Van der Pol's, caught twelve years previously torturing a young woman. The arresting officers had written in their report that they'd been called to a small wood just outside Gouda where a couple of teenagers had sneaked off to drop some acid surrounded by nature, but had, in the come-up, heard some pretty terrifying screams. By the time the two officers made the woods a full forty minutes later they could still hear the screaming, and followed the noise through the trees.

The scene they'd come upon had clearly shocked them. A woman lay on the ground trussed up, while a man was bent over her, gradually working a knife across her flesh in long lines. He'd done the legs, arms, neck, and was now working on her torso, working slowly and meticulously.

The officers had rushed in and managed to take the man, but in the struggle one of them noticed a second figure disappearing into the trees. The officer who gave chase didn't catch them, but did note in the report that he thought the man had been carrying a video camera. However, he'd not got a look at his face, and because they caught the man doing the torture, and he denied all knowledge of any one else being there, it was never fully pursued.

The woman, despite the best efforts of the medics, died on the way to hospital.

So Koen Kramer had been convicted of murder, and had never spoken of his reasons for committing the crime, nor about the other man, refusing to answer all questions put to him.

Even in the liberal-minded Netherlands, he'd got life. This was one case where rehabilitation was taken right off the table. Because anyone who's capable of what he did just has to be beyond any kind of talking cure.

'We could use your help.'

Koen turns his dark eyes towards Jaap. 'I'm doing something serious here, I'm outside trying to get my vitamin D. It's for my health. So maybe you can come back later.'

Which is funny. Because once Harry'd given Jaap the background he'd handed him a two-page medical report. Jaap had glanced at it, noted the words 'pancreatic cancer', and read the summary, which, although dressed up in medical language, basically stated that the patient was pretty much fucked.

'That's good,' Jaap says. 'Thinking of your health. I like that, shows a certain responsibility.'

Koen shrugs. 'Gotta do what ya gotta do,' he says. 'But I'm sure you're not here out of concern.'

Jaap tells him they're not, and lays out what they want.

'Weird that the initial investigation didn't really *delve* into that side of things, don't you think?' Koen says when Jaap mentions the report of a second man.

'We're here now.'

In a cage two down a man starts howling like a B-movie werewolf. Koen appears for the first time unsure, an internal battle going on.

'Fuck it, why not?' he says after a few moments. 'I wasn't the only one there that night, obviously. There *was* someone else, and he was there to film it.'

'Film you torturing the woman?'

For the first time Jaap sees Koen's eyes blink. He's reminded of Sanders' ghost dragon.

'Yeah,' Koen says, slowly running a tongue over his lips. 'That's right.'

'Why?'

'Because that was his job. That's what he'd been paid to do.'

'By him?' Harry holds a photo of Van der Pol up against the cage.

Koen flicks his eyes towards it and then back to Jaap. He nods. He nods again when Harry pulls out a photo of Haanstra and asks if he was the other man there that night.

'Had you done the same before?'

'Yeah, sure. A couple of times at least. Van der Pol paid big for video. He didn't like to go without, so after I ended up in here I heard someone else took my place.'

Jaap holds up a photo of Kooy. 'Recognize him?'

Koen mulls it over then shakes his head. 'Nah, but I

was inside. I did hear the guy that took over was called Kooy. That him?'

'Yeah,' Jaap says. 'Yeah, that's him. So tell me, what did Van der Pol do with the videos once he had them?'

'Fuck knows. Maybe he jerked off to them.' Koen steps closer. He fumbles his dick out of his jumpsuit. It's limp, pathetic. He grabs it and starts trying to coax it into life.

'You think I'm bad?' he says, giving up, tucking himself away. 'Haanstra and Van der Pol are worse. *Waaay* worse.'

91

Knowledge is not enough.

To actually convict, evidence is required, enough facts to prove beyond any kind of doubt that to do otherwise would itself be criminal.

But can I get enough evidence? Jaap thinks as he accelerates hard away from the kerb where Harry is just getting into his own car. Can I get the proof?

Because finally things are starting to connect.

Harry's fired up too; he missed what he thought was his best chance to bring Van der Pol down when the raid Tanya'd worked on turned out to be a set-up. But the news Jaap's brought him is resurrecting his chances. Jaap gets the feeling he's not going to let another opportunity slip by.

He checks the time. Smit's press conference is due to start in less than half an hour, and Jaap reckons he should have the most up-to-date information beforehand. After all, this could be a much bigger coup for Smit to pull off. Linking these killings and the distribution of the films to Van der Pol would be enough to bring down a massive criminal enterprise.

Somehow Jaap believes Smit will be up for that.

He dials Roemers on the hands-free.

'Anything?'

'Give me time. And Jaap?'

'Yeah?'

'Don't call me, I'll call you.'

Smartass, Jaap thinks as he hangs up.

Despite knowing the broad outline, there are still details which he can't work out, small things about the case flapping round his head like loose ropes in the wind.

Not that that's unusual; if you went into the police hoping that you'd know everything about every crime you investigated, you were going to be *very* disappointed indeed. There are some things, Jaap's learnt the hard way, you're just never going to know. But that doesn't stop his mind from probing.

And one of the things it keeps coming back to is, he still doesn't get how Haanstra knew Pieter Groot had been transferred to the hospital. Sure, he may have been watching the station and got lucky. But really, why would he? Same goes for Kooy.

Just by the Concertgebouw a lorry starts a three-pointer, blocking traffic in both directions. Only it turns into a nine-pointer before the driver actually makes it round, allowing the sluice gates of traffic to flow again.

Two minutes later Jaap's at the station. He rushes towards the press room, just catching Smit before he goes in. When Jaap's finished updating him, Smit says, 'You've got the say-so of a dying man in prison? He'll be dead by the time it goes to trial so his testimony will have to be recorded. It will get ripped to shit by the defence. You know that.'

They're standing just outside the room where the biggest and most important conferences are held. Smit's team has done a good job of rousing pretty much any journalist within driving distance. He's sold this one big.

And he's not happy to have anyone, least of all Jaap, make him step out there and cancel it. Cancel his big moment in front of the cameras.

'I'm just asking for more time, I think there's a bigger prize here.'

'Van der Pol?'

'Yeah.'

'Have you got anything other than the testimony of a convicted felon?'

'Not yet, but—'

'Listen—' Smit looks around, before continuing '—Van der Pol is basically untouchable. People have been trying for years to get him and no one has. And I'll tell you why that is, he's smart, and he doesn't make mistakes. I've been closer to the current investigation to bring him down than you think, and sometimes I get so fucking *frustrated* that we can't get him on anything. So unless you've got something concrete, I'm going out there to announce we got the killer and you are going to take that leave.'

A press officer steps out of the room and gestures to Smit.

'OK?' Smit says after a few moments' silence.

'Yeah, OK,' Jaap replies.

Smit gives him one last look before turning round and pushing through the door, walking up to the lectern like a returning hero. As Jaap walks away he hears Smit opening up, welcoming the press, warming them up for something big.

Something stings his mind. He stops dead in the corridor. Then he walks back to the door and looks through the glass pane.

At Smit holding the stage like an orator. His suit crisp, the scrape on his shoes still there, but hidden from the press by the lectern, his gestures and speech designed to give the impression of a strong hero, fighting the good fight. And winning it too.

The sting in his mind intensifies, and starts off a cascade of thoughts.

Suddenly he starts to run.

92

Harry Borst's just stepping up to his car when he feels a squirt of something on his neck. He's just been calling in a favour, and has a possible lead on Kooy's current location. Instinctively he puts his hand up and can feel a liquid, stinging slightly. He turns round, ready to lay into whoever or whatever has just sprayed something on him. But things are slowing down, and the turn seems to take for ever, his reflection in the shop window becoming increasingly distorted.

He has the strangest sensation that he's just eaten some raw garlic, his mouth almost puckering from the pungency.

The whole world's suddenly heavy, the dimensions all wrong. He can feel the miles of air above gradually crushing him down towards the ground, even though he's still standing, His feet feel weird, like they're not there but there at the same time. And now there's a face, a face which seems familiar, but he can't quite place it.

'Let's go,' says the face, the words slow and underwater. The figure turns, and Borst finds himself following, each step on a world which is no longer stable. Some footfalls are hard and jarring, others sinking voluptuously into the spongy earth.

As they reach the figure's car and he opens a door, a name comes to him, deep in the confused ballooning thoughts he's having. He knew he was supposed to be doing something, for the inspector he'd just been talking to. But he can't remember what. Or the man's name.

He gets in, sits, does as he's told, a sense of strange unease lurking under a sort of apathy.

Bernard Kooy slides in behind the wheel, turns the key in the ignition.

Borst thinks he should call someone.

But he can't think who.

Half a second later he can't even remember his own name.

Despite himself, he grins. More and more until there's nothing left.

93

Kees has a choice.

Up ahead is a fork in the road, left leading to Schiphol airport, right leading to Amsterdam.

He's used some of the money from the bags in Van der Pol's boot to get his new passport, his new identity, and as a bonus – to pay for the sheer shitness of his life these past four years – there's enough cash to last him pretty much whatever time he has left.

That should be enough; he should, by rights, be celebrating. He has the opportunity to get out. For good.

He could be comfortable – hell, he could even start to enjoy himself a little, leave this whole nightmare way behind. All the things he'd wanted to do in life but had somehow never had the time were now a possibility, and the feeling that he owes himself, that now is the time to Just Fucking Do It, is filling him with a kind of nervous joy.

But he also knows that Van der Pol and someone he's conspiring with in the police are trying to kill Jaap Rykel. And he knows where it's due to happen.

Hence the left or right decision.

A new life vs his old one.

He's getting closer and he slows down, both sides of the argument waging ferocious war in his head. An ambulance screams past, going the opposite way.

Van der Pol's trussed up in the boot. Kees had planned to drop him off at a police station on the way to the airport with all the evidence he's collected during his time working for him, all the evidence he's passed on to Smit and Smit never acted on.

As the fork comes closer Kees suddenly realizes the war in his head has been won.

Or lost.

Depending on your outlook.

He takes a slow breath in, calmly checks the rear-view, and indicates left.

Then, with seconds to go, he finds himself spinning the wheel hard, skidding the car across the small triangle of tarmac slashed with diagonal white lines.

94

Koen had insinuated that the investigation into the killing he and Haanstra had done wasn't as rigorous as it might have been. Jaap's starting to think he was right.

The file is pre-digital, so he has to go down to the archives, hoping that they have a paper copy. The old files are in the process of being scanned into the new database, but it's slow work and not top of anyone's priorities, so the current estimate for a completion date is sometime mid-century, by which time it'll probably be useless.

Jaap sees an officer slowly sifting through a file and scanning it in, and wonders what he's done to get such a bad posting. It soon becomes apparent that it's his dynamic attitude and verve. 'Sure, knock yourself out,' he says when Jaap expresses an interest in finding an old file.

Jaap steps into the room, row upon row of shelving crammed with cardboard-backed folders. At the end of each row there's a date range, and each row holds six months of police work. He locates the correct row based on the dates of the original arrest in Koen's file.

It takes a while, Jaap suddenly appreciating just how quick searching on a computer really is, but finally he's standing with the correct file in his hand. Diving in, he reads the whole thing quickly, closes it and puts the file back on the shelf.

'Yeah, should have,' admits the sergeant in charge of

the station's interview rooms when Jaap turns up a few minutes later and requests some footage from one of the cells.

He turns to his computer, clicks through a few files, and finds the one Jaap's looking for.

'Tell you what, I need a break. You want to watch this here whilst I go and get a coffee?'

'Suits me,' Jaap says.

The sergeant disappears on his noble hunt for caffeine and Jaap sits, clicks on the file.

It's the interview he conducted with Pieter Groot and he hits play, fast-forwarding till he sees himself leaving the room. It occurred to him earlier he's not actually reviewed the tape, and an idea had popped into his head which he couldn't shake.

He slows it back down just as the door closes and the uniform's got Groot under control, finally leaving him on his own in the cell. He fast-forwards again and suddenly the screen goes black for just a second. Again he slows the footage down to normal speed. He goes back to before the blackout, notes the time-stamp in the right-hand corner, then notes it again when the picture returns. There's a full minute and a half missing. Just as the picture comes back he sees that someone was leaving the room, the only thing visible a section of leg and a shoe.

A shoe Jaap's seen before.

His phone buzzes. He checks, seeing a text message from Borst. It says he's got a lead on Bernard Kooy, and gives him an address to meet. Jaap pockets his phone, going back to the computer footage.

As soon as the door closes, Groot rips off his T-shirt,

twists it up and starts shoving the tangled snake down his throat.

It's one thing to be told about someone trying to kill themselves, Jaap thinks. Quite another to actually *see* it.

He watches right up until a uniform steps in with a tray of food and looks up, dropping the tray and dashing forward to save him.

He rewinds to the shoe, gets a screen grab just as he hears someone coming, looks up to see Smit walking through the door followed by the sergeant who'd gone to get coffee. Only he hasn't found any, neither hand clutching a cup. He points to Jaap. Smit nods and strides over. Jaap quickly puts the screen grab into the trash can.

'Do we have a problem?' Smit asks. 'Given that you're no longer on the case and yet you're still here?'

'No,' Jaap says. 'I don't think we do.'

'In which case I need you to leave right now, before I have you arrested.'

Jaap puts his hands up, like, *you got me*. 'OK, I'm on my way out.'

Outside he gets into his car and pulls into the street.

His mind is brutally calm.

He doesn't notice the bike which pulls out after him.

It's making sense now. So much is making sense he's almost overwhelmed by it.

Ten minutes later, he still hasn't noticed the bike when he indicates and leaves the road for the car park where he's meeting Harry. The car park's a large square of concrete bordered by low prefabs on three sides. Clouds churn in the sky, the thin wisps he'd seen earlier at the prison meshing together into larger forms, heaving like a hungover stomach.

He spots Harry's car parked off towards the far left corner, parks nearby and walks up to it. He can see Harry sitting in the front seat.

He walks round the side.

And stops dead.

Harry is sitting at the wheel.

But his head's wrapped in cling film.

A whooshing, hissing noise starts up. He's aware of his brain trying to work out what it is.

But before it can, the side of his face detonates with pain.

He's spun round like a scarecrow in the wind, then he's falling.

As he goes down he sees the face of the man who hit him.

Bernard Kooy.

95

Kees pulls up just as everything kicks off.

He sees Jaap spiralling down, and, as he starts running, the guy who hit him – classic long biker beard and leathers – raises the baseball bat for a second hit.

The other man, Bernard Kooy, is standing slightly back. He hears something and turns just as Kees reaches him.

'What—'

Even under normal circumstances Kees is not a great conversationalist, and right now he's *really* not in the mood for wasted words. He launches forward, knocking Kooy down and lunging for the man with the bat, going in low, his shoulder ramming into the man's waist. The man stumbles, lets go of the bat so his arms are free to break his fall. Kees is on it, has the bat in his hand. He swings hard, and gets the job done in one hit.

Bart would be proud, he thinks as he turns back to Kooy, who has managed to get up and is now grappling with Jaap, getting him into a headlock and forcing him to the tarmac, one knee bent like he's proposing.

Kees steps up.

At the same moment Jaap gives way, dropping to the ground fast, surprising the man and managing to break from his arm. Jaap twists round, swings his hand up and onto the back of the man's head, and slams it into the car's bonnet. Kooy's top teeth catch the edge.

Kees hears them break.

All of them.

Inside the car a man's head wobbles, and falls out of sight.

Kees catches a glimpse of his head as it goes down. He can't be sure, but it looks like it's cling-filmed.

What the fuck?

Jaap's still got hold of Kooy, blood all over his face.

Kees moves in and they have him cuffed in seconds.

They're both breathing hard, and it takes a few moments before either can speak. Jaap's face is already swelling up – by tomorrow he's going to be unrecognizable.

'I don't even know where to begin,' Jaap says, looking at his old colleague.

96

'Long story,' Kees says.

Jaap's reeling, from Harry's death, from the blow to his head, and now this.

'Short version,' Jaap says. They're standing near Harry's car, waiting for backup.

'I've been working undercover in Van der Pol's gang for just over a year now. Today was the day I was getting out. But I heard Van der Pol talking to someone on his phone, saying he needed to get rid of a cop. He even said they'd done it before. He sounded angry, but also maybe a bit scared, like it was a big deal to get whoever it was.'

'Who was he talking to?'

'Yeah, I'll get on to that. But first you've got to under-stand that—'

The sound of a gunshot, dry in the air.

Kees bucks, slumps against the car, and starts a lazy slide off the bonnet towards the ground. Once there he grunts and bends forward.

Jaap has his own gun in his hand. The action's smooth, practised, all on autopilot. He can see the man who's just shot Kees, running, head low. Jaap catches glimpses of him between cars. Another biker who must've kept back.

He's heading for the road.

It takes one shot and the man's down. Jaap swings back to Kees.

'Kees, you OK?'

Kees grunts again. He's slumped down, body folded, a hand clasped to his stomach. Jaap watches as blood seeps through Kees' fingers.

'Officer down!' he yells into his phone once he's managed to dial, fine motor skills obliterated by the adrenaline rushing through his system. 'Gunshot. I need a medichopper here immediately.'

He leaves his phone on so they can trace his location and moves to help Kees. The blood flow's bad. Really bad. Kees is breathing hard, in shock, his whole body convulsing.

Jaap presses his hand against the wound, trying to slow the blood down.

It's not working. Blood seeps through his fingers. He presses harder.

Kees tries to speak. 'In my pocket,' he whispers, his hand fumbling for something. Jaap helps him, pulling out a passport. Jaap can feel something between its pages; he opens it up to find a SIM card.

'It's on there,' Kees whispers. 'What you need.'

Jaap clasps it, carries on trying to stop the bleeding. He feels the moment Kees passes out, his muscle tone changing, like an electrical charge has just been extinguished.

He's still trying when he hears the whirr of the helicopter, still trying as he feels the strong downdraft, and still trying, through tears which are blurring his world, when the paramedics shove him aside and get to work.

97

Three years ago Jaap had been kneeling on a container ship's deck, moored in Amsterdam's docks. He'd been blindfolded, the freezing kisses of snowflakes on his face and neck. Beside him Tanya was slumped, bleeding from a shot she'd already taken to her leg.

Ahead, Jaap knew there was a man, standing with a gun, just about to pull the trigger, end it for ever. He tried in those moments to find some kind of peace, prepare himself for what was to come.

A gunshot rang out, muffled slightly by the falling snow.

Then he heard a noise ahead of him, like a body slumping onto a snow-covered deck.

Kees had worked out where they had to be, and had arrived just in time to save them both from the bullet.

Now, standing in the heat, his pulse racing, Jaap realizes that Kees just saved him for the second time.

Clouds weigh down the sky. The helicopter carrying Kees and two paramedics lifts off, as if struggling against their weight. They've done what they can, but Kees needs to be at a hospital.

Jaap watches the chopper as it shrinks away, in his hand the passport and SIM card Kees had given him.

The car park's full, police everywhere, and the ranking officer is trying to grill Jaap whilst Borst's body is being taken out of the car by his men.

'So I'm still not getting it,' says the man. 'You say that—'

Jaap's not in the mood. He walks away, towards the back of the ambulance where they're just now loading Borst's body.

He stands as first one door is slammed shut then the other, a familiar creeping loss taking hold of him. He wants to scream. But all he can think about is what Kees had told him, about the SIM he's still got clasped in his fist. He opens it up and stares at it. Then he opens his wallet and puts it inside.

Everything is starting to merge together, to fit into one whole.

He can see clearly now.

This case has already claimed too many lives.

And he's going to put a stop to it.

98

Amsterdam must be the only city in the world, which, when it needed a new town hall and a new opera house, decided to combine the two into one purpose-built building. They called it the Stopera.

The building was controversial, had been through many designs and setbacks, and finally came in several million guilders over budget. But since no one remembers what the guilder-to-euro rate was pegged at when the change happened it's a non-issue.

Jaap had requested an urgent meeting with Commissioner Bergsma, and had been told he's at the Stopera for a meeting, but Jaap can see him as soon as it finishes.

The building itself nestles in a kink in the Amstel. Tourists amble, bureaucrats hustle, and musicians from the orchestra, on a break from rehearsal, cluster into small factions and bemoan their lives.

The rail is hard against his forearms. He's leaning on it, peering down at the Amstel's water rippling below. But he's not really seeing it.

He's spent the last few hours going over everything, checking out all aspects of his theory. He wasn't surprised when it all came together.

His face throbs. Earlier he'd caught a glimpse of it in a car window. He'd barely recognized himself.

The commissioner's made time in his schedule to see

Jaap, but when he'd arrived ten minutes ago a secretary had told him they're running late and that she'd come out to get him when he was ready. Jaap's using the time to work out exactly what he's going to say, get it all straight in his own head, prepare for the scene.

Because what he has to say will be received like a hand grenade tossed into a pre-school nursery.

Much of it's still unknown, and probably won't ever be verified, but the gist of it is clear. Haanstra had worked for Van der Pol as an enforcer, just as Harry had said. Jaap doesn't know if the original impetus to film the beatings was Haanstra's idea, to prove to his boss he'd actually done what he'd been tasked with, or Van der Pol's for the same reason. But at some stage one of them had hit on the concept of selling the videos, and had built up a business doing just that, finding a willing clientele on the darknet, people willing to pay real money to watch others die.

More recently, though, Haanstra had decided to go self-employed, a decision that Van der Pol, when he'd discovered it, had not taken well and which had prompted Van der Pol to go after him.

To add to the insult, Haanstra had set up on his own with the help of some of Van der Pol's crew, Kooy in particular for the supply of scopolamine and help with logistics, and the odd bit of freelance work when he needed some intimidation. Kees had talked about him and another gang-member going to visit Francesco Kamp the day before the botched arrest. It's clear to Jaap that Haanstra kept the threat alive in the minds of the men he'd picked out to be killers, stopped them going to the police.

So far it all made sense, but Jaap knew there was more, something else which had been pulling at him like an underwater current, something underneath which wouldn't let him go.

The dying prisoner, Koen, had hinted at it, asking why the investigation which had put him away hadn't delved deeper, why the officer in charge hadn't followed up on the man who'd been videoing the killing and had run away.

Jaap, wondering about police collusion, had checked the names of the officers in charge, neither of which he knew, and neither of which had turned up in connection with any other crime committed by Haanstra.

But it had made sense when he'd gone higher up the chain.

Made sense and not made sense at the same time.

Because it looked like Van der Pol wasn't acting alone. Van der Pol, and by extension Haanstra, had had help.

'Heard you had a bit of trouble,' Smit says, leaning on the rail next to him. Jaap can smell his aftershave. 'Whoa, that's nasty. You need some ice. Or a new face.'

'I'm meeting with the commissioner,' Jaap says, watching a waterbird swoop in to land on the water in front of him. Ripples spread out, an ever-widening triangle as it moves forward on the water.

'I can see that,' Smit says. 'But I've got something to show you first.'

He holds out a file. Jaap continues to watch the bird, bobbing its head into the water, over and over, like it couldn't believe what it could see under the surface, a whole new world it'd not known existed.

'So how far back were you working with Van der Pol? I heard you got some good clearance rates early on in your career. Must have been useful. But I think it was more than that. I *know* it was much more than that. You've been colluding with Van der Pol for years.'

'I have no idea what you're talking about.'

'I think that you were still involved, but you didn't trust Van der Pol fully so you embedded Kees to keep an eye on him for you. That's why you've not arrested him with any of the info Kees got you, it wasn't an official under-cover operation.'

Smit puts a hand in his pocket, the other still holding out the file.

'I also think,' Jaap continues when it's clear Smit's not going to say anything, 'that both you and Van der Pol saw the danger Haanstra posed, he was going off the rails and he was going to get caught. When he did he might well have talked. Which wouldn't be good for you. So you killed him. Bad timing on your part, if you'd left it just a few minutes later then who knows what might have happened.'

Smit's watching him now, very still, hardly breathing, a predator waiting for the right moment.

'And it was you who killed Kamp, afraid he might talk. You gave me your cuffs, remember? Maybe you even took mine off me on the drive there. Then all you had to do was unlock them, claim I didn't do them up. From there it would have been easy to shoot him, then fire a second gun, and claim Kamp had it on him, making it all look like my mistake.'

Smit looks out across the water. There's a small orange

powerboat, the outside formed to look like a Dutch clog, the man at the wheel's hair wind-buffeted.

'And then there's Pieter Groot. I checked the security tape in his cell. Someone went in to talk to him, someone who knew how to later delete a part of the footage, or had enough clout to get the officer in charge to do it. My guess is whoever went in there told Groot to keep his mouth shut, and when Groot realized that Haanstra had people inside the police he'd've taken the only way out he could think of. Make sense so far?'

On the surface Smit's impassive, unemotional. But Jaap senses he's struggling hard to keep it together.

'So, that's all good. Someone who could potentially point the finger at Haanstra, which might end in other people higher up being exposed, had been neutralized. All that needed to be done was to get rid of any evidence, but the person deleting the footage screwed up. There's a shot of someone leaving the cell just before Groot tries to kill himself. I've got an image of that person's shoe. And guess what? It's got a scratch, just like yours.'

Jaap points. Smit looks at his shoes.

They're the same, patent leather, expensive. Only, Jaap can now see, without the scratch.

'All just spinning stories,' Smit says, still calm. 'And seeing as there's no proof for any of your totally outlandish claims, the only conclusion we can draw is the pressure of the job has got to you, maybe forced you into some psychotic breakdown. It's been hard on you, I get that, what with Tanya being kidnapped and all, so we can probably work out some kind of medical leave.'

'I'm not taking medical leave, I'm going to—'

'The offer is on the table once, and once only. Think about that before you say anything else.'

'There's more, you and Van der Pol have been trying to get Haanstra as well, only when you found out that Borst and I were close to exposing this thing, the decision was made to kill both Borst and me. Were you part of that, or are you going to claim that was Van der Pol acting alone?'

'I have no connection with Van der Pol, all this conspiracy you're coming out with is just in your head. And really I don't have to listen to any more of this—'

'I know you're connected to Van der Pol, but that you didn't fully trust him either, that's why you embedded Kees into his organization, so that you could keep an eye on him at all times.'

'Crazy ramblings of an insane cop. Keep it coming, the more you talk the crazier it gets. And the easier it becomes to ignore.'

'I spoke to Kees. He told me he'd given you enough information to put Van der Pol away many times over, but you never did. Why is that? Is it because you knew that if Van der Pol got caught he wouldn't think twice about shopping you? Yeah, ring any bells? Or how about this: you've been working with him since you were in Rotterdam, you struck a deal where he was left alone to quietly take over the drug trade in your precinct, as long as he kept the violence out of sight. He got to expand his empire, you got great crime stats and a boost up the ladder.'

'Seeing as you obviously talked to Kees, I'm guessing he told you why he went to prison in the first place?'

'It was an undercover operation backstory. He was working for you, so he didn't really go to prison.'

'He did actually, but did he tell you what crime was used as his cover?'

'No, but I don't care. Fact is, Harry Borst's dead, all very convenient for you. I guess you gave the order to Van der Pol to have him, and me, eliminated.'

Smit heaves himself off the rail and turns to Jaap. He holds a file out. 'Trust me, you're going to want to see what's inside.'

'I don't.'

'You do. Because this is the investigation into the murder of Ruud Staal. Heard of him?'

'No,' Jaap says, even though he thinks he may have. He tries to remember, but nothing comes.

'You might want to ask Tanya about it then. Why don't you call her now?'

'What the fuck are you talking about?' Jaap says, taking an angry step towards Smit.

Smit holds his ground and continues to offer the file.

'What I'm talking about is that she is guilty of the murder of Ruud Staal. He was her foster father, and he abused her sexually for years, before she escaped. Very sad story. Especially as it all became too much and she killed him for it.'

Jaap finds the ground tilting away from him with a sickening slowness. Soon he's going to slip and fall off the world. He does remember the name, he heard Tanya say it in her sleep two days ago.

'It's all in here,' Smit says. 'I think you should read it. And once you have, think about this – do you want your child to be born to a murderer in prison?'

Smit drops the file into Jaap's hand and walks away,

pulling out his phone and holding it to his ear. He listens, walks back to Jaap and hangs up.

'That was the hospital. Kees Truter's dead.' He leans close, whispers in Jaap's ear. 'So you see, right now I'm fucking *un*touchable.'

He walks away, Jaap staring at his back.

Five minutes later the commissioner's secretary comes out of the Stopera to tell Jaap the commissioner is ready to see him.

But she can't find him anywhere.

99

Tanya's lying on the hotel bed when she gets the email.

She's been staring at the ceiling, thinking, against the express wishes of the specialist, about the baby. She was sure she'd felt it kick whilst lying there. She tried to take that as a sign that it was OK, that it would make it, that the hole in its tiny heart would heal over well before it was born. Right now she feels like she'd do anything, absolutely anything, to make sure it's OK.

She finds herself online – Jaap had told her not to bring her phone, but she's sure her laptop's fine – researching everything about the heart, when the email comes in. She can hear a chambermaid chatting on the phone just outside her room.

The email is from someone at the Schiphol morgue. They'd tried to get her on her phone but had no luck. They ask to be called as soon as possible.

She grabs her pre-pay phone and dials the number, fear clasping her throat.

She listens to the woman's voice on the other end of the line, and then, once she's finished, asks her to repeat herself.

Then she thanks her and hangs up.

She calls a cab which arrives just as she's ready. On the drive she wonders about calling Jaap, but thinks this is the last thing he needs right now.

She's been to the city morgue out near Schiphol airport many times, but only in an official capacity. She's never been called there because someone she knew needed to be ID'd.

She's met by a detective she's never worked with but seen around a few times. She signs in, and he takes her through to where the official identifications are made. It's like a dream; she doesn't see how this is real.

When the sheet is whipped back it turns from dream to nightmare.

The woman she'd spoken to earlier said she'd been named next-of-kin. Apparently he'd actually had a document drawn up by a lawyer which also gave her control of his estate, such as it was, and requested that she identify him.

She steps forward, the slab Kees is laid out on seeming to move away from her in space-time as she does.

She looks at the face.

It *was* him she'd seen four days ago.

Then, as the tears dribble down her cheeks and create a sour tickle under her chin, she nods.

'Yes,' she says. 'It's him.'

Jaap sits in the night, wondering if it's going to work.

He's at Grote Vijver, a lake buried deep in Amsterdamse Bos, a place he and Tanya sometimes visit.

They'd stroll along the reed beds, marvelling at how far removed from the city it all felt, even though the centre of town was less then twenty minutes away. The last time they'd come, a few months ago, they'd been walking back along the path hugging the northern shore when Tanya had stopped abruptly and grabbed his arm, using the other to point across the water.

It took Jaap a few moments to focus in, find what she was pointing at. Then it moved and he saw it, a heron, fish in its beak. The heron was disturbed by something, maybe sensing their presence, looking around for signs of danger. They watched as it finished its scan of the surroundings, satisfied itself that there was nothing amiss, and tipped its arching neck back, the slip of silver disappearing down its throat.

But there wasn't going to be any romantic stroll tonight. Jaap checks the phone he'd bought at a second-hand stall at Waterlooplein, an old model capable of taking the relatively ancient SIM. He'd sent the message, and had received a one-word reply less than ten minutes later.

He breathes in deeply, suddenly aware that he can smell something sweet, almost sickly. It's dark, the clouds overhead obscuring any moon, and the air feels totally still. After a few more sniffs he recognizes that scent – honeysuckle.

Over to his left there's a rustle, ending in a soft splash, as something slips into the dark water stretching away from him. He envies it, whatever it is. Right now he'd like to slip into that same water and disappear.

Because ever since he'd opened the file Smit had handed him a kind of raw chasm had opened up in his stomach.

He'd read through the investigation, the details of how Tanya had been abused by her foster father for years before she'd finally escaped. And then she'd gone back, finally plucked up the courage to confront him, and he'd wound up dead.

He can't believe she never told him. But he can see why. He feels like he should have known somehow.

A voice says to him, *You failed her again.*

He tries to block it out just as he hears the noise of an engine.

His heartbeat doubles up.

He can see the lights now, coming closer, and he instinctively shrinks back into the rushes to watch the car pull up. The lights go out, the car ticks, nothing else happens.

Then the door opens.

'Where the fuck are you?' Smit says.

Jaap steps out from the rushes, Smit turns, shines a torch right in his face. Jaap had used the SIM to send a message to Smit, hoping that Smit would think it was Van der Pol. Looks like it'd worked.

Or, Jaap thinks suddenly, seeing the gun in Smit's hand, maybe not.

'Yeah, you think I'm stupid?' Smit says. 'Sorry to disappoint.'

He flicks the torch off. Jaap can still see the trace of it wherever his eyeballs move.

Smit holds up a photo.

Jaap can see a man, curled up like a foetus in the boot of a car. A third eye in his forehead turns out to be bullet wound.

'Van der Pol,' Jaap says.

'Looks like Kees killed him.'

'Convenient for you, blame it on a dead man. I'm disappointed.'

Smit laughs. 'Really?' he says. 'Boo-fucking-hoo. Piece-of-shit inspector is judging me.'

'How much did you make?'

Smit stares at him, eyes shining in the dark.

A flash in the sky behind him could be a plane coming in to land at Schiphol, or it could be lightning.

'A lot. More than you can imagine. And you'll never find it. It's all well hidden.'

'Did you watch the films, or did you just sell them to others?'

'Oh I watched them,' Smit says. 'I definitely watched them. Someone like you will never understand I'm sure, all your righteousness gets in the way. But there's an immense freedom in watching someone else die, this feeling of lightness. And let's be honest here, all the victims were scum. People we'd only have to lock up anyway. It was unfortunate that Haanstra went rogue, started killing innocent people, but we got that under control. He's paid for that.'

'So what, you'll just find someone else to carry on doing this?'

Smit shrugs. 'Don't see why not. You're not going to say anything.'

He holsters the gun and steps back to his car, pulls the door open and gets in. The window slides down. Jaap suddenly notices the car's a top-of-the-range Maserati, well beyond what Smit's salary alone would buy.

'Think about this,' Smit says. 'You don't want to do this to Tanya. She's been through a lot, what with being fucked stupid by her foster father and all, it just wouldn't seem fair.'

He laughs.

Rage explodes inside Jaap. Everything, the whole universe narrows in on Smit's mouth and the laughter coming from it.

Before he knows what he's doing he has his gun right in Smit's face.

Smit's no longer laughing. The barrel pushes his lip up, revealing teeth on one side of his face. It looks like he's sneering. There's a thin band of yellow plaque on one of his canines where he's not brushed properly.

Jaap sees his Adam's apple bob.

He can feel the clouds pressing down on him, the soft breeze which has sprung up caressing his right cheek, cooling it slightly. The ground's there under him, it's stable for now. The air is breathable, his lungs working perfectly, blood rushing round his body.

He remembers the feeling he'd had, wrapping cling film round the woman's head.

The breeze offers up honeysuckle, the scent thick and cloying.

His hand's trembling, he can see the movement transferring to Smit's cheek. It almost looks comical.

He thinks of Tanya, feeling a rush of love which almost stops him.

But maybe it's love which pushes him on.

He doesn't know.

The feeling that he's not in control washes over him.

Some physicists believe that there are multiple universes, where each and every variable can be played out; each time you make a decision another universe springs into being with the alternative action taken.

For a second he knows he's been here before, he can see many versions of himself, multiple copies of the whole scene. Repeated again and again and again.

They speed up into a blur.

Then they stop dead.

Everything is clear.

He takes a breath in, readying his finger on the trigger.

Then he pulls it.

101

'This is the one?'

The uniform's voice jolts Tanya out of her head.

She looks around, sees that he has brought her right back to the houseboat. She doesn't recall seeing anything on the drive back from Schiphol. She should have gone back to the hotel, but the thought of sitting there thinking about Kees' death had filled her with some emotion she wasn't ready to go through. So as the car had hit Amsterdam proper, she'd told the driver to change destination.

She thanks him and gets out, closes the car door gently, and walks across the swaying metal gangplank which leads onto the deck.

The car pulls away as she inserts the key into the lock.

She stands there for a moment, waiting for something, though she doesn't know what.

Eventually she turns the key and steps inside.

The houseboat's empty.

She's half been expecting to find Jaap back, had yearned for it on the journey, but it's clear he's not.

Ever since the moment she'd been guided into the room to ID Kees' body and she'd seen his face as the sheet was lifted back, everything had been numb, like she was no longer part of the world. The numbness had persisted right up until now.

Because now it's turning into something sharper, sweeter almost.

It's rising, filling her up and she finds herself heading for the bedroom.

By the time she flops down on the bed she's crying hard.

For Kees, for what he'd done for her.

For herself, her past.

For the baby growing inside her with a hole in its heart.

And for Jaap, who doesn't yet know.

102

Jaap's feet are heavy, each step hitting the ground with too much force. He feels like there are many of him now, all the versions of himself he'd glimpsed earlier.

Only this time all have made the same decision and are walking with him in solidarity.

He's walked this route so many times and yet it feels different, like it's another world, a mock-up which has been put in place of the original just to fool him. Everything is familiar, the same houses huddling together on the canal side, the same trees with branches waving over the water.

Everything the same, but also different.

Up ahead is his houseboat, their houseboat, and the lights are on. The street lighting isn't uniform, and he finds a patch of darkness where he can stand and look down on the boat. He stares into the living room for a few minutes, not seeing her. Thunder rumbles and the first delicate drops of rain quickly turn into something heavier. He's soaked through in half a minute. He doesn't feel it.

Then she appears, walking from the bedroom towards the kitchen area. Rain cries down the glass, rippling his view of her.

Rain hisses on the street, hisses round his feet.

Or maybe the hissing's in his ears.

He's not sure.

He can't tell any more.

103

Once she's cried it out she lies there for a long time.

She feels calmer, cleaner somehow.

Suddenly, out of nowhere, she knows she's forgiven herself. All the fear and anger and guilt she's carried for years has gone.

She was put in a bad situation, and she'd done what she had to do.

She's done blaming herself. That's past. All that matters now is the future. All that matters is the baby, and her and Jaap and the future they're going to build together.

She feels a blossoming of expansive hope.

Rain hammers on the houseboat's roof, and she's suddenly struck by how beautiful it all sounds, like some kind of natural symphony full of contrapuntal lines and percussive riffs. She listens to it, lying there, breathing quietly, losing track of time.

By the time she gets up she's just starting to wonder where Jaap is.

In the kitchen she finds a clean glass and pours herself an orange juice. There's hardly any left so she'll need to pop out and get some later. Or Jaap can get it on his way back.

Thinking of which, where is he?

The rain's harder now, if that's possible, streaming down the windows in thick, ever-shifting rivulets. As she heads back to the bedroom to get her phone to call Jaap, find out when he's going to be back, she glances out of one of the landward portholes.

For a moment she thinks she sees someone, a figure keeping to the shadows.

By the time she gets her phone the rain has intensified, hiding the figure from view.

If they were even there at all.

104

He's standing there like there's no rain.

In his pocket he has the passport Kees had given him. Kees had planned on a different life, a better one, only it hadn't worked out.

Jaap knows he could use it, get away with it, his face so swollen that no one's going to question the similarity or otherwise of the photo.

Because although he's done all he can to make sure Smit's death isn't traced back to him, he's been an inspector long enough to know that there's always something the killer overlooks. Someone will eventually work it out, and then they'll come for him.

It might be the day their child is born, it might be a year from now, two. It might take five or more, but some day there's going to be a knock on the door, and he'll have to answer for what he's done.

And he doesn't know if he can put Tanya through that. Not on top of what she's been through already.

Better to make a break now.

He spots her again, walking past the window, carrying something he can't make out towards the kitchen, her movements fluid, familiar.

The pain's sharp.

If he goes he's not sure it'll ever leave him.

But what choice does he have?

He had to do it to protect her. At the same time knowing that he'd end up hurting her as well.

The rain's hiss intensifies, dulling his view of the houseboat, of Tanya. Of his life.

He knows this is it, the moment when everything changes, two futures spiralling out in front of him.

His phone starts to ring. When he gets it out he can see it's Tanya calling, rain spattering the screen.

He's still for a few more moments, before he wills himself to move.

Acknowledgements

My thanks go to Simon Trewin at WME, and at Penguin Emad Akhtar, Rowland White and Sophie Elletson. Thanks are also due to Eugenie Todd, copyeditor extraordinaire. In Amsterdam I'd like to thank G.H. for exposure to the rouge horticultural arts, and T.P. for technical insight into the workings of the DarkNet.

The Animal for keeping my feet warm during many long hours of writing.

And most importantly Zara, for the continuing journey.

WELCOME TO

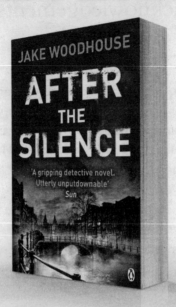

'A gripping detective novel ... Utterly unputdownable' *The Sun*

'Does for Amsterdam what Ian Ranking did for Edinburgh'
Crime Thriller Hound

Someone is left hanging on a hook above the canals of Amsterdam's old town, a mobile phone forced into the victim's mouth.

Inspector Jaap Rykel knows that he's hunting a clever and brutal murderer. Still grieving from the violent death of his last partner, Rykel must work alongside a junior out-of-town detective with her own demons to face, if he has any hope of stopping the killer from striking again.

Their investigation reveals two dark truths: everybody in this city harbours secrets – and hearing those secrets comes at a terrible price ...

AMSTERDAM.

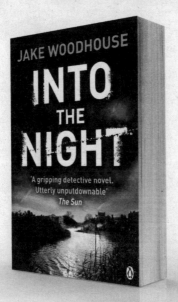

'Utterly enthralling ... Looks set to be one of the key sequences in modern crime fiction' *Crimetime*

'A strong sense of place is matched by a capacity for storytelling that keeps the plot accelerating' *Daily Mail*

A body is found on a rooftop, the dead man's hands blowtorched, his head removed.

The man tasked with tracking down the killer is Inspector Jaap Rykel. But as he searches the headless body for clues, Rykel finds something which makes his blood run cold – a picture of himself on the victim's phone.

And then a message from the killer reveals the location of a second mutilated corpse. It's another day in Western Europe's murder capital ...